SHADOWS OF INNOCENCE

Shadows of Innocence

of
Innocence

A Story of Selfless Love

MALIKA D.

First paperback edition: 2025

Paperback ISBN: 978-1-968389-01-7
Hardcover ISBN: 978-1-968389-02-4
Ebook ISBN: 978-1-968389-00-0

Edited by Sam Willow at Scrollwork Edits.
Proofread and edited by Sejal Shah Srinivasan
Cover art and design and page formatting by Ciara Hartford
Promotions by Epica Book PR

For all who wander, longing to be found…
May you discover that sometimes, the truest home is not a place,
but a heart that welcomes you in.

Content Warnings

Thank you for taking a chance on this book. As an Indie Author, every reader is appreciated and cherished. But this book is not for everyone. It is intended for adults and while there isn't anything explicit, the themes in it may not be suitable for those under the age of eighteen. I like to think that if it were a movie, it'd be rated somewhere between PG-13 and R. Everyone is different in what they enjoy and what they find triggering. Above all else, please protect yourself.

Mature content includes:

- Alcoholism
- Post-traumatic stress disorder
- Profanity
- Reference to pregnancy loss (in the past)
- Reference to rape (in the past, no actual depictions of)
- Mild violence including:
  - Gun violence
  - Blood
  - Domestic violence
  - Use of drugs to incapacitate a character

Welcome to Shadows of Innocence.

Glossary

Abu: Father

Ami: Mother

Api and Baji: Elder sisters (Api is said with more reverence)

Bahu: Daughter-in-law

Beta: Son

Bhai: Brother

Bua: Old nanny/maid

Chachoo: Paternal Uncle (father's brother)

Dada: Paternal grandfather

Dado: Paternal grandmother

InshaAllah: God willing

Jagirdar: Feudal lord

Khala: Maternal aunt

Khaloo: Khala's husband

Kismet: Destiny

Mamoo: Maternal uncle

Nana: Paternal grandfather

Nikah: Islamic marriage

Nikahnama: The marriage agreement

Phuppa: Phuppo's husband

Phuppo: Paternal aunt

The Night It All Began

One cold January night was all it took to destroy the lives of four children, two of whom were yet to be born.

On that night, the adults of the Tariq family gathered around their patriarch, Masood Tariq, in their family mansion, located in Karachi's poshest area, just off Sunset Boulevard. The fireplace was lit—its warmth enough to turn pale complexions ruddy—but it was no match for the cold hearts in that room.

"I don't bloody care what those half-witted, money-sucking *female* doctors say! There will finally be a grandson in this family. How dare they recommend an abortion?"

His son, Mustafa, looked at his wife, Naeema. Her down-cast eyes were a silent acceptance of her life. No matter how good of a wife she was, or a *bahu*, and despite having given her father-in-law three healthy granddaughters, she would always be deficient in his eyes because she could not give him a grandson. Until now, that is.

Mustafa shook his head and pleaded with his father. "No, Abu. The doctors said it is not safe for her to have this baby. She is forty-five years old; the placenta is attached to her uterus in the wrong place. She could die in the process of giving birth."

"And you, a mere mortal, will interfere in *God's* work?" Masood Tariq's voice boomed across the room. "Besides, only a grandson can take this family's name forward."

"That's not true. Kiran will take the Tariq name forward," Mustafa argued. His seventeen-year-old daughter, the oldest of three, had always been a brilliant student, showing not just interest but also an aptitude for the family's real estate business.

"Get that girl married off before her smart mouth brings more shame to this family." The patriarch refused to budge.

In the tense silence that followed, a meek voice spoke up.

"Abu, I am also pregnant," said Zarine, the daughter of Masood Tariq and wife of Asif Ghazanfar. "Soon I too will find out if I will have a son or not. Please, don't play with Naeema's life."

She had recently found out that after trying for years to have a child of her own she had finally succeeded. Though, the joy that typically accompanies such news had been experienced by her before. Four times before, to be exact. Yet each time, tears and heartache had followed soon after.

"All you do is have miscarriages. How will you ever give me a grandson?" Masood taunted his daughter.

The disdain and accusations burned her heart—one that had already repented many times. Asif glared at his father-in-law, but that didn't stop him from continuing his tirade against his own daughter.

"You'll never be able to pay the price for your sins in this life," Masood said to her as her eyes filled with moisture.

Naeema couldn't take the patriarch's heartlessness anymore. She leaned towards Zarine and squeezed her hand. "InshaAllah, things will go well this time."

There was a good reason behind her optimism. Zarine finally had a diagnosis that explained her previous miscarriages, and her physicians had a treatment plan to help her. Yet, none of that mattered to the man who ruled this family with an iron fist.

He only desired a grandson he could raise in his own image. Not one like his own son, who was soft-hearted and honest to a fault. Nor like his daughter, whose public elopement with Asif, a former employee of the Tariq Enterprise, had caused him humiliation in society.

Naeema recognized that stubborn look on her father-in-law's face; he was never going to yield. She had, after all, been a *bahu* of this family for nearly two decades. Truth be told, her maternal instincts were reluctant to heed the advice of her doctors too, especially after witnessing the joy in her daughters' eyes when she and her husband shared the news of a new baby with them. She couldn't bear to disappoint them or bring further shame to her sister-in-law, who had earnestly tried to atone for the mistake she had made years ago.

Neither could she force her beloved husband to choose between his wife and his father. She sucked in her breath, said a prayer, and made the choice for him. If *kismet* was in her favor, she would be the mother of a son, as well as three beautiful daughters.

Zarine left her father's home that night, her heart heavy with sorrow. Her only consolation was her sister-in-law's kind words—from one pregnant woman to another.

Seething with anger, Asif drove her home—an unassuming two-story structure in a middle-class neighborhood—but left her at the doorstep. "I have some important work to do," he told her, and buried in her own regrets, she didn't question him.

Asif Ghazanfar did not return home until well past midnight.

At the other end of town, Shabnam Murad, a young mother, only twenty years of age, gazed at her baby daughter with a love she hadn't known she possessed until she laid eyes on the delicate human handed to her after a grueling twenty-hour labor.

Now, at the age of two months, this little girl, with her caramel brown eyes and a smile that could brighten even her mother's worst days, was inseparable from her. In some ways, this infant had become her only companion.

Ever since the birth of their daughter, her husband, Zakariya Uzair, had begun staying out late at night. His breath always carried a pungent smell she recognized too well, and when he spoke to her, it was either incoherent or loud and abusive. Though, having married into a political family, her husband's indiscretions were almost anticipated in this segment of society.

All of that, she told herself, she could put up with. For, at the end of the day, she had something he could never take away from her: her acting prowess, God's gift to her. By all accounts, she had the talent and the looks to become the next big thing in the Pakistani entertainment industry. All she had to do was work hard on her next project, a drama about young love at the wrong time. With a stellar cast and a budget that rivaled that of blockbuster movies, that drama was sure to propel her to the heights she yearned to reach.

She kissed her sleeping daughter and laid her down gently in her crib. When her phone rang, she leaped across her bed to grab it. The call was one that she had been waiting for all day.

"Yes, Mr. Akbar, when do we start shooting the first episode?" she asked excitedly, getting straight to the point.

There was silence for a long moment before the man on the other end cleared his throat.

"Shabnam, you're still young. There will be many more opportunities that are suitable for you. This is the way the industry is. They need someone who can travel on short notice and work long hours. Women with young children are just not able to do it," he explained, his voice mellow, as if that would soften the blow of his words.

She hung up, numb to the core. Her gaze settled on the mirror in her room and on the reflection that looked back at her. Her eyes were still the same caramel brown color that had enticed many men. Her complexion was still fair, her cheeks still a light shade of rose, and her hair fell in soft waves across her shoulders. Even her lithe figure had returned to its pre-pregnancy state.

But there was one key difference.

She looked towards her sleeping daughter. She was a mother now. A status that should have been revered now weighed heavily on her.

"You are the worst thing that has ever happened to me," she heard herself murmur. Instant remorse inundated her subconscious, but the seed of regret over her daughter's birth had already been sown. From there on, its roots would only grow deeper.

Shabnam tried to call Zakariya, not wanting to be alone with a broken heart and awful thoughts, but he gave her a curt reply about meeting some business associates and hung up. She then called someone else from her past. That was a mistake. But a lot of mistakes had been made that night.

Zakariya Uzair did not return home until well past midnight.

Several months later, Osman Tariq came into the world, but his mother's ill-fated *kismet* prevented him from reveling in her love. His eldest teen-age sister, Kiran Tariq, found herself thrust into a role where she not only upheld the Tariq name, but did so with utmost grace and dignity as she navigated her family through a tempestuous storm.

A month after Osman and Kiran lost their mother, their cousin Zain Ghazanfar was born, much to the joy of his mother. Meanwhile, the little girl, Sanam Uzair, was growing up into the very reason her Dado prayed daily, asking God to grant her a long life, enough for her granddaughter to become self-sufficient. Dado was aware that if He were to call her back to Him sooner, the beautiful little girl would have no one to care for her.

As these children grew older, their lives stood in stark contrast to each other. Yet, unknown to them, there was a common thread from their past forcing their destinies to collide: a cold January night in Karachi, when choices made by adults would fracture their peace for decades to come.

In the shadow of their innocence lurked greed, lust, and despair. Yet, in those very shadows, they would discover love, friendship, and hope. For life, in all of its imperfectly glorious beauty, is worthy of living—and no matter the depths of darkness, if light is in your *kismet*, light shall shine one day.

Shadows of Innocence

PART ONE

When we were young and innocent.

CHAPTER 1

Romeo and Juliet

OSMAN

Sanam Uzair gave me a lollipop in eighth grade, and my life was never the same again.

We both attended Kingston Academy, one of those private colonial-era Karachi schools where your family name and home address mattered as much as your grades and ability to pay the fees. Though, that was the extent of what we had in common between us.

She belonged to a family of politicians, socialites, and well-known media personalities.

I was an orphan from a middle-class family.

My mother died while giving birth to me. My father died three years later in a car accident, though some say it was from a broken heart. That same year, my paternal grandfather had a heart attack, which left him incapacitated, and us at the mercy of our only other family: Zarine Phuppo, Asif Phuppa, and their son, my cousin Zain.

If it wasn't for Kiran Api, who took me and my two older sisters in when I was only four, the three of us would have been left without a home.

Although it shattered her marriage and left her to single-handedly raise her infant twins, together we forged a family of our own.

Throughout my upbringing, all I could recall was that my sister somehow managed to provide me with everything I needed in life, including an education at Karachi's most prestigious school, where she had bargained for a reduced fee for me in lieu of her teaching high school math.

I was blissfully unaware of that arrangement until eighth grade when my cousin stood in front of our entire English language class and was asked to use the word *impecunious* in a sentence.

"Impecunious means having little or no money," Zain started off like the rest of us had when called to the front of the class, but then, he looked at me and smirked. "Osman is so impecunious, he can't even afford to pay the full school fee."

Laughter filled the classroom, drowning out the teacher's irritated voice. Every face turned towards me, mocking and jeering, while I attempted to retreat deeper into my seat.

Every face, except for one.

The new girl with caramel brown eyes, seated across the room, initially seemed shocked and angry at Zain. Then, her gaze softened as she looked at me, shaking her head slowly. That day, during lunch break, I was sitting alone in my usual corner behind the school building, buried in a book, when that girl suddenly appeared next to me.

"Here," she said, handing me a lollipop. "This helps me when I feel sad."

Before I could say anything, or even find my voice to thank her, she got up to leave. "I am Sanam, by the way. I am new here." She smiled.

I nodded. Yet, we never exchanged another word until eleventh grade, when we were both in a modern-day reenactment of *Romeo and Juliet*, a play put on by our high school's theater club.

She played the role of Juliet, the beautiful young woman who falls in love with a man she is supposed to hate. Her fate was locked with his, yet their destiny was as tragic as their love was pure and eternal.

I was the cameraman and the lighting operator, on loan to the drama club from the technology club. I had no role in the actual play itself. Those positions were only for the popular, extroverted kids like my cousin, who played the role of Lord Capulet, Juliet's father. My only jobs were to capture the play on video and manage the stage lighting—shining the spotlight where it was needed and dimming the lights when the scene required it.

In retrospect, that might have been the day I realized that Sanam Uzair wasn't who everyone perceived her to be. There was much more to the popular, articulate, and attractive girl whom everyone sought as a friend.

We were at the balcony scene in Act 2, Scene 2. Romeo, played by Farhan, also one of the popular kids, stood on stage. Only a dim light fell on him, the backdrop dark except for a shining moon and accompanying stars. He paced the stage, grumbling to himself about the words of his close friend, Mercutio.

"Mercutio has never felt the pain of love. How else would he be able to talk about it in jest?" the actor said in a hushed tone.

He looked up at the makeshift balcony of Juliet's room, supported by the rolling stairs, masterfully hidden away from the public eye. I shone a spotlight onto the balcony.

"Is it her?" Romeo spoke out in a slightly louder voice. "Is she the sun that spreads her warmth across the earth, more beautiful than the moon ever will be?"

He stopped pacing and clasped his hands to his face dramatically. "It is her . . . oh my love, it is you."

I couldn't help rolling my eyes or laughing internally. *What kind of a stupid play was this?*

For sixteen-year-old me, whose only loves were books and computers, romance, courtship, and that intense longing for someone were not just foreign concepts—they were ridiculous emotions I was convinced were confined to novels and century-old plays with no relevance to modern life.

They certainly wouldn't ever affect me, I had told myself.

Yet, when Juliet did come out onto that balcony in her white nightgown, her wavy hair in a loose braid, her cheeks brushed with pink rouge, and her eyes distant but glistening under my spotlight, I was the one trying to deal with a tightness in my chest, one that I had never felt before.

Back then, all I knew was that I wanted to pause that moment. For a second, I wondered what it would feel like to be Romeo, to be so close to my Juliet and to be able to peer into those glistening eyes and unravel the secrets they held.

Except that time cannot be stopped, and I was not Romeo. I was the lighting operator, who was still shining a bright light onto a girl whom I had wordlessly gone to class with for almost three years. Meanwhile, her Romeo was standing on the stage in complete darkness, hesitantly reciting his lines, even though no one could see him.

The frantic footsteps of our drama teacher headed towards me. "Osman, *what* are you doing? Dim the light on Sanam and increase the light on Farhan *now*," she whispered harshly.

"Yes, Mrs. Mehmood. I am sorry," I mumbled to the teacher towering over me, keeping my eyes on the camera in front of me rather than the stage where Juliet's soft voice rose again.

"What's in a name?" she said, and her voice hitched a bit. "That which we call a rose by any other name would smell just as sweet; hence, if Romeo is called anything but Romeo, he would still be the perfection that he is now."

For the remainder of the play, I avoided that voice and face. Once it concluded, I headed straight to my family, who had all gathered to support me.

As the youngest brother with three older sisters, now with their own little ones, I carried my personal cheering squad wherever I went.

"Mamooo!" cried out one little girl as she rushed towards me, followed by her mother, Kauser Baji, my second oldest sister.

Behind them were Kiran Api's twin boys, only four years younger than me. Technically, I was Daniyal and Danish's mamoo as well, but we had decided a long time ago that our small age diff erence made it very awkward to use the name given to our official family tie. So, for them, I was simply *Mani*.

"I'm impressed, Osman," said newly married Kaukab Baji, my third oldest sister. "That was some professional lighting, except for that one snafu in the balcony scene. Did you fall asleep or something?"

Her husband, Hussain, nodded but never looked away from his smiling wife. The man was utterly smitten by my sister.

"Uh, no . . . I, uh . . . was managing the camera as well and got confused for a second," I stumbled through my excuse, hoping that no one would notice my burning cheeks.

Kauser Baji's husband, Dr. Iftikhar, remarked, "Well, if you decide not to go into medicine, I hear people make a lot of money with professional lighting companies as well."

Kiran Api shot him the warning look I was very familiar with. "Iftikhar, please don't go around putting ideas in his head. He is going to go into medicine, and he had better work hard for it."

The renowned surgeon immediately faded behind his wife, making her laugh—a sound I had rarely heard from her while growing up.

The twins had been quiet the whole time, observing the fancy high school they had never been to before, even though their mother taught there.

"Mani, I want to see more of this place. *Please.*" Daniyal clasped his hands and pleaded, with his twin mimicking him.

"Fine, but help me put away the lighting equipment first," I told them. They grabbed what they safely could and followed me to the drama club's storage room.

"Leave those boxes at the entrance and get the rest of the stuff," I instructed. They raced out while I moved the boxes to the back of the room. That's when I heard the sound of someone quietly sobbing in the corner, startling me as much as my presence startled the girl still dressed in her Shakespearean garb.

"Sanam?"

I glanced at her but promptly shifted my gaze away before her teary eyes stirred that unfamiliar feeling in my chest once again.

"I'm sorry. I thought I was alone," I quickly apologized, moving away.

"It's okay, Osman. I don't mind you being here," I heard her say.

Pausing to find my voice, I asked, "Are . . . are you sad about something?" I mentally slapped myself the next moment for asking such a stupid question. Of course, she was sad. Why else would she be crying?

"Yes. I am," she whispered with so much sorrow that my resolve not to look at her instantly crumbled away.

If I had been a mature sixteen-year-old, I would have asked her what had made her so unhappy or offered a shoulder to cry on, or even lent her a sympathetic ear. Yet, whether it was my immaturity or the fact that the pretty girl standing in front of me—dabbing her eyes with her delicate fingers—was short-circuiting my neurons, I did nothing of the sort.

Instead, I rushed out of there, checking to see if I had enough cash to buy her something from the cafeteria.

Ten minutes later, I was back in the drama club's storage room. So were a dozen other students and their parents. Among them were Zain and my Phuppo, who were standing next to Sanam, laughing. Any trace of that sorrowful girl I had left alone had disappeared, as had any ideas I might have had of her needing me or my bag of *stupid* lollipops.

I finished what I had gone there to do in the first place and left with Daniyal and Danish, without greeting my Phuppo or glancing at the girl she was talking to. My Phuppo wouldn't have cared anyway. She and her family represented everything that my sisters and I were not.

Rich. Powerful. Influential. They were our polar opposites.

So was Sanam, for that matter. Yet somehow, she was different. To me, she seemed as much a stranger in that world as I was. I didn't even know how I knew that, but I did.

That was a belief I held on to for a long time—till the day she called and left a wretched message on my phone while I lay in the hospital recovering from bullet wounds.

SANAM

What's in a name?

That was a line I could never forget. Nor the way that I almost broke down in the middle of my eleventh-grade play when I realized that, like Juliet, my name may have given me much worldly benefit. Yet, it also kept me away from so much.

I was the granddaughter of Abdullah Uzair, a shrewd man whose life started in showbiz and ended in politics. He quickly ascended the ladder to become the Chairman of the Awami Workers Party (AWP), a political party that had been started by his father soon after Pakistan and India became independent countries. That was a position he held for almost three decades before his demise. His younger son, my Chachoo Zaviyar Uzair, had since taken over the helm of that party while also serving as a member of Pakistan's National Assembly.

My father, Zakariya Uzair, was the older son of Abdullah Uzair, but the least interested in politics. It was no secret that his youth was spent as a playboy and resulted in a marriage that should never have occurred. When he was thirty years old, he married my mother, Shabnam Murad, who was only eighteen at the time. Beautiful and witty, she had stolen his heart at an awards ceremony after being nominated as Best Actress for her debut drama on the silver screen.

When I was ten, their marriage ended in a contentious divorce, but the life of glamor and wealth I was born into did not diminish. On the face of it, I had it all: a huge house in the city's poshest locale, a slew of staff waiting on me, the funds to go anywhere and buy anything I wanted. What I couldn't find, though, was a cure for my loneliness, a family that wanted me, or true friends I could confide in.

The day I played the role of Juliet was the perfect example of why I felt so alone in the sea of people around me. My mother was on her honeymoon with her new husband. My father hadn't been back in the country for almost six years, which left Dado as the only one who could have attended my play.

Then I got a call from her nurse.

"Sanam, your dado is insisting on going to your play. But every time she gets off the bed, she feels dizzy. Could you please tell her she needs to stay home?"

The nurse handed my dado the phone, who immediately denied everything I had just heard. "Don't listen to this woman. She wants to make money by pretending I am sick. I am just dehydrated. Let me drink some water, and I'll be on my way."

I could imagine Dado pouting like a little child while her nurse rolled her eyes. It took me a while, but eventually, she conceded.

"No one will be there for you," she said sorrowfully.

"That's not true, Dado. I have all my friends here." I put on my stage voice and insisted. Like my mother, I was an excellent actress. No one ever knew what went on inside me.

That day ended with me standing alone on the stage, while everyone else stood surrounded by their families. Even the quiet boy who had been sitting at the side of the auditorium, illuminating the stage and its actors, had people who loved him.

That boy never spoke to me, but I wasn't oblivious to him. I saw the way he sat in class, lost in his thoughts, always in the furthest corner of the classroom, and the way others jeered at him sometimes. Or called him a teacher's pet whenever he did what the rich, entitled kids in our class never would.

Perhaps that was why I had noticed him more and more as each year had gone by. He was my daily reminder that there were people in this world who were altruistic and kind without expecting anything in return.

Before my loneliness could consume me on center stage, I headed back to the drama club's storage room to get away from a simple pleasure in life that was so alien to me, and called my mother.

"Hello, Mama. How is your vacation going?" I asked nonchalantly when she picked up, pretending that I hadn't desperately needed her.

"Oh, Mauritius is absolutely fabulous, Sanam. I'll send you pictures soon. And Malik is the best husband anyone could ask for. He'll have a day in Karachi when we get back next week before he must return to Islamabad. Maybe we can all go out for a nice dinner then."

I nodded to myself. Mr. Malik was a member of AWP as well, and like many politicians, he lived in Islamabad, the capital of Pakistan.

"Okay, Mama. And today my . . ." I started to tell her about my play, but she interrupted me.

"Sweetie, I have to go. We chartered a private boat tour, and it just got here."

The call ended. My mother had forgotten that I was the lead character in a play, just as she had been before her on-screen debut. My attempt to make her care about me had failed once more, even as I tried to emulate her very own career. I couldn't contain the tears streaming down my cheeks or stifle my sobs when the quiet boy stepped inside the room.

"I'm sorry. I thought I was alone," he said, looking embarrassed.

"It's okay, Osman. I don't mind you being here," I replied quickly, hoping that he would stay.

Yet, he rushed out of there, leaving me to bring out my inner actress as soon as the first of my fellow students arrived. The girl who effortlessly laughed and mingled with everyone was back. Still, I couldn't stop myself from glancing around that crowded room every now and then, wishing to catch a glimpse of the only student who never paid attention to me.

Instead, I saw his cousin, Zain.

"Ah, Sanam, meet my mother." He gave me a smile that showed off his perfectly aligned teeth and pointed to the impeccably dressed lady standing next to him.

Her hazel brown eyes with flecks of green had a striking resemblance to a boy in my class who was not her son. A boy who was relentlessly bullied by her own son. Though, who was I to question relationships when my own were so messed up? As always, I hid my true self and put on my dazzling smile.

"Hello, Aunty. Hope you liked the show."

"Yes, I did," she exclaimed. "Your performance as Juliet was exquisite. You'll make a beautiful bride one day."

In the background, Zain glared at his mother. He was never subtle about having an interest in me beyond simple friendship, even if I had never acknowledged his advances and he had never said anything out loud.

"Thank you. Though, I don't ever intend on getting married," I told her with a straight face and walked past her, ignoring her appalled expression and her son's fl ushed cheeks.

There were plenty of people to mingle with, plenty of fake praise to drown in, and just enough commotion in that small room for me to tempo-rarily forget about my lonely life—and the boy who had caught a glimpse of the real me, only to turn on his heels and fl ee.

It wasn't until I was ready to leave almost an hour later that I noticed the bag of lollipops on top of my backpack, and memories from eighth grade came rushing back.

"Osman," I muttered his name, clutching the bag close to my chest, as that innocent girl within me, whose sadness dissipated with each suck on the candy, came out again.

The wide smile on my face while I sat in the back of my car on the way to Dado's home wasn't only because of the strawberry flavor bursting in my mouth or the bag laying on my lap. It was because that night, after a long time, it felt like someone had remembered me for me, and not for my name.

I made a decision then.

I had never been interested in science subjects, but a boy I had a sudden urge to be close to, and explore more, had declared to our class that he wanted to become a doctor. Surely, he would be on the pre-med track in A-Level (Grades 12 and 13). Physics and chemistry gave me the shivers, but biology was a subject I could put up with.

That is how I, the exact opposite of a science nerd, ended up choosing biology in my senior years—in the hope that I would land in the same class as *him*, the one who had wordlessly lit up my world.

In my teenage naivety, I tried to control my fate. Little did I know my destiny was already written in the stars, just like his was.

Our story wasn't a typical teenage love story, but it was a story about love nevertheless—the kind that I would go to any lengths for, even if it meant letting destiny change me at the very core of my being.

CHAPTER 2

Sunset Boulevard

ZAIN

From the scrumptious spread of granola with Greek yogurt, croissants, omelet, and a selection of fresh juices laid out by our butler, to the expansive, lush gardens and blooming shrubs of fuchsia and red roses visible from our breakfast room, the mansion I had grown up in was no different from the handful of other ultra-luxury homes in Karachi's most exclusive gated community—just off Sunset Boulevard.

What was different were the people who lived within its walls. We pretended to be a family, going through the motions and keeping up appearances. Yet, beneath the facade, there was no warmth or sense of connection. Fancy cars, expensive jewelry, and vacations to exotic places were what held us together.

It was the only life I had known. And at seventeen, on the first day of my A-Levels, the glitz more than made up for the darkness that lurked in the shadows.

Ami spoke in a quiet voice as we sat at our breakfast table that morning. "It is a make-or-break time, Zain. You cannot afford to get distracted in your senior years of school."

My father's gruff voice interrupted her. "Leave the boy alone. He does not need advice from a stupid woman."

She flinched, but not a word was said in reply. Instead, with her gaze lowered and lips pursed, she poured him more tea till he raised a hand without looking up from his morning newspaper.

Demure. Obedient. Spineless. Just as she had always been.

In the heavy silence, we went on with our meal, each lost in our own thoughts. Mine focused on the words my mother had said. Words that I knew to be true after barely getting high enough grades to keep my seat at Kingston Academy.

Not that I needed to be a straight-A student to get ahead in life. My future had already been mapped out by my father.

"I met with a college counselor recommended by my friend Moeez Khaver. He's asking for a small fortune but guarantees admission into any of the top universities in California, Stanford included."

Stanford. I smiled. Life was that easy for a wealthy C-grade student.

Abu gripped my shoulder as he got up from the table, putting an end to my premature celebration. "That doesn't mean you can slack off. A hefty donation to an Ivy League school and a path to becoming the future CEO of GT Enterprise comes at a cost." His dark eyes bored into mine. "Show me you want it badly enough."

"I do, Abu. I won't disappoint you." The words quickly tumbled out.

Decisive. Confident. Assertive. My father's story spanned from being the middle child in a lower middle-income family to a real estate tycoon and one of the richest men in South Asia. A self-made billionaire who bought and sold property as easily as he did men.

In my teenage naïveté, I understood the cost of becoming like him to be a few years of hard work and decent grades. Never did it occur to me that it meant selling my soul to the devil.

That morning, I rode with my father to school, a place where I felt more at home than anywhere else, away from my parents' toxic relationship and the abyss of deadly silence that made up the Ghazanfar mansion.

Principal Hashim stood at the main entrance, greeting students as they returned for a new year. He spotted Abu and waved eagerly, and my father wasn't one to give up an opportunity to mingle with those who yielded power in any sphere of life.

The two were soon chatting like old friends while I slipped away and caught up with Farhan, my best friend and the son of a minister in the Sindh Provincial Assembly.

"Hey, man. How's it going?" he asked.

"Same ol', same ol'. Mom and Dad at it again."

Farhan sympathized; his own father had a secret mistress. A fact that had come out shortly before we left for summer break, leaving him embarrassed and disgusted. The two of us had hung out as much as we could in the summer before Abu took me on a trip across Europe.

"Where all did you go?" Farhan questioned.

"Britain, France, and Switzerland."

"Beautiful countries."

I smirked. "Beautiful women."

"You're never going to grow up, are you?"

"Eh, growing up is overrated."

We both laughed shamelessly, but my laughter died down quickly when Farhan reminded me of something I preferred to tuck away at the back of my mind.

"Wonder what Sanam would say about that."

Sanam, my classmate, was a pretty one, for sure. Perhaps that's why I should have been grateful that she was the one my father had suggested as a perfect romantic match for me. In reality, it was her family's connections that were perfect for him. She was merely the puppet that came with the package.

Did I have a crush on her at some point? Sure, but so did the rest of the boys in our school. I quickly got over it when she looked at me with nothing but utter disdain. Her attention was solely focused on a certain cousin of mine whom I had despised since I was in diapers. There was no way I would allow myself to have feelings for a girl too foolish to fall for his façade.

Surely, there were other girls in this city whose political connections could likewise entice my father.

"Who cares what Sanam thinks?" I frowned. "She is barely a friend."

Farhan started to say something, but I quickly moved on to another topic. "Seriously though, Abu bought this new apartment in London. It overlooks the Thames River and would be perfect for a getaway trip if you can ever convince your parents."

The distraction worked.

"I don't think they would really care. Dad is busy with his new woman, and Mom is too depressed to do anything." Farhan chuckled. "And I have their credit card, so I am in whenever you go next."

This was us. Always looking for the silver lining in our otherwise dark family lives, to drown our miseries in materialism and lust. Marriage and a special someone forever were the furthest things from our minds.

In the very next moment, though, my life flipped completely upside down. No amount of wealth and prestige could keep my heart protected from this cruel thing called *love*.

Farhan and I were chatting away with a handful of our friends, boasting about our summer travels, when I heard a voice call out to us.

"Umm . . . hello. Could you tell me where the administrator's office is?"

I looked up, and could only think of one word. *Wow!*

As a guy who was usually surrounded by good-looking girls, the one standing in front of me now wasn't the prettiest by most standards.

Yet, she was an enchantress, a goddess, a chaos that my soul could not have foreseen.

Dark brown curls framed an innocent-looking, heart-shaped face. Light brown eyes shone like drops of honey in the morning sun. Flawlessly tanned skin accentuated her perfect jawline and cheekbones.

And good Lord, those lips. Deep pink, they glistened as her mouth molded into words that I heard but could not process—like a sweet melody to my soul.

Sweet melody? What the fuck was wrong with me?

I shook my head and blinked away bizarre thoughts just as Farhan's elbow shoved into my side.

"I am sorry, the admin office is still closed," I replied, ignoring the several pairs of eyes that widened at my blatant lie. Instincts compelled me to discover more about this girl before I let her go.

"I can walk you there when it opens," I offered, making her smile more broadly, much to my delight.

"Oh, thanks so much. I just moved here from Boston, and they told me to check in with the office when I arrived."

I extended my hand. "I am Zain Ghazanfar. Welcome to Kingston Academy."

She took my hand, my rough skin meeting her soft, smooth one. Her grasp was firm, and her gaze so sharp it pierced right through me. With her spine straight as a steel rod, she stood undeterred by the sudden silence that engulfed us.

"I am Maham. Maham Qureshi."

The bell rang and the rest of the group dissipated. The new girl and I stood together as the schoolyard emptied.

"Could I help you carry your bag, Maham? We in Pakistan are obsessed with thick books and daily homework."

"We're not all that different in the US." She chuckled and opened her bag. "But maybe you could help me carry some of these? I don't know my schedule yet, so I brought all my textbooks."

She handed me a few books, and as she smiled again, I decided it was the most beautiful smile I'd ever seen.

KIRAN

"Why is everyone intent on getting themselves killed today?" I muttered as I swerved when yet another motorcyclist suddenly came in front of my car.

Karachi's traffic was always a nightmare, no matter the time of the day. Though nothing was worse than the morning rush as millions of children made their way to schools across the sprawling metropolis, where roads were littered with potholes and traffic signals were mere suggestions, not rules. In that amalgamation of humans, automobiles, and pollution, Osman and I were making our daily trek across the city. Our middle-class neighborhood and my twin sons' ordinary rated school were a good forty-five minutes away from Kingston Academy.

"Api, you know our lives would be so much easier if Daniyal and Danish were in the same school as us," Osman said, not for the first time, while holding onto his seat for dear life as I scowled at a driver who honked at us.

Usually, I would avoid such talk, but he was old enough now to understand our reality. "I can't afford to send all three of you to this school, even with the discounted fee."

Guilt overshadowed his innocence in an instant, and I remembered why I had never mentioned this before.

"That's not fair to Daniyal and Danish. They are your sons. They should be in this school, not me," he said quietly.

"Osman, I've always treated the three of you the same. It's not a matter of my sons vs. my brother. You are older. You can finish high school before they are at an age where a top-tier school will be helpful for their future."

It was the pragmatic approach for a family with limited resources, nothing more. Another tight bend I had to navigate through. Just like

I always had since the day my three siblings showed up at my doorstep, drenched in rain, carrying nothing but a small bag of clothes.

At the time I was twenty-two and had been married to my high school sweetheart for almost two years. Kauser was seventeen, Kaukab was fifteen, and Osman only four years of age.

Thirteen years later, that boy's forlorn expression tugged at my heart. When we finally reached the school's parking lot, I turned towards him. "I wouldn't change a thing, kiddo. But I do need you to promise me that you'll make this worth it. It's your last two years of school. I need you to study as hard as you can so you can get a scholarship for medical college."

Osman immediately nodded—exactly what I expected from my brilliant brother. A straight-A student, a member of the debate and technology club, humble and polite, he was the kind of student teachers loved having in their classrooms.

He was still naïve, though.

"Why not ask Phuppo and Phuppa for money? We can pay them back later when I become a doctor."

My body stiffened, and memories I had long suppressed threatened to emerge. I frowned, quickly putting an end to it. "Do not ever mention their names again."

Usually, that was enough to quell my brother's questions. But today, he seemed intent on making his point.

"But why? Zarine Phuppo is Abu's sister. She is supposed to take care of us," he argued.

"You're a child, Osman. Not everything has to be explained to you. I've gotten our family this far without anyone's help. I can keep doing it. All I am asking you to do is study hard and not get distracted by useless people and unnecessary things."

Shoulders slumped, he nodded once again and got out of the car. There were less than five minutes left until the school bell rang. I took a minute to take deep breaths and calm my nerves.

Osman was the challenge thrust upon me when I was only a year older than he was now. I questioned myself every day if I could have done something differently when he was born.

No alternate path ever came to my mind.

"Abu, please get up. We must go see the baby."

At eighteen, I found myself pleading with my father who had been sitting on the hospital floor, his back up against the wall, and his head tucked between his knees after getting the worst news of his life.

He didn't respond, so I tried again. "Abu, Kauser and Kaukab are hungry. We can't stay here forever."

His eyes shifted towards me, but there was barely any sign of life in them. The woman who was dearer to him than anything in this world had returned to her Maker while giving birth to his son. And it seemed she had taken his will to live with her as well.

My own vision kept blurring with unshed tears, but my mind was too occupied to fully comprehend the tragedy.

"Okay, it's fine, Abu. I'll take care of the baby and my sisters," I said to him.

Over the next hour, I comforted Kauser and Kaukab, filled out the paperwork for my newborn brother and deceased mother, and checked in on my father.

Finally, after Phuppo and Phuppa reached the hospital, I headed to the neonatal ICU to do something that no one from my family had done yet—hold the slightly premature baby whose arrival everyone had been waiting for, but who had brought with him unanticipated sorrow that would change the course of our lives forever.

"Assalamu Alaikum, little one." I teared up again as I held him gently in my arms and the nurse adjusted the oxygen tubing around his face. He opened his eyes and silently looked at me, as if he was memorizing my face because he knew that he and I would be facing this world alone, but together.

In the midst of my world crashing around me, that tiny boy in my arms gave me a strength I didn't know existed.

I kissed his forehead and whispered, "I love you so much, and I promise to take care of you even if no one else can."

Perhaps I should have left my brother in the nursery and prevented Asif Phuppa and Zarine Phuppo from taking my sisters back home with them. But no one told me that you were not supposed to trust family at a time of urgent need. So I chose to stay with my baby brother.

I was so naïve back then.

You can do this—one step at a time, I told myself for the umpteenth time and got out of my car, ready to make a dash to the administrative offices to clock in for the day.

Instead, I came face-to-face with the devil himself.

"Good to see you, dear niece," Asif said, his hushed voice sending a shiver through me.

"What the hell are you doing here?" I frowned.

He scoffed. "Is that how your parents taught you to talk to elders?"

"You lost the right to be called our elder the moment you went into Kauser's room," I shot back.

The school bell rang. I would be marked late for the day. Three lates, and I'd be penalized with a pay cut. Yet, I stood my ground as the rest of the schoolyard emptied. I'd be damned if I yielded even an inch to this man.

He slowly shook his head, his dark eyes never leaving mine. "Keep telling yourself lies."

"My sister doesn't lie."

He moved closer, the sharp scent of his cologne filling the air. "Then go ahead and tell the world your story." He paused, letting out a deep chuckle. "You've been trying ever since your father died, haven't you? No one believes you. Ever wonder why?"

The answer was as old as humanity itself. He was rich and powerful—we were not.

Without blinking, he stared at me until his gaze suddenly shifted over my shoulder, and his frown deepened. I turned to see his son, Zain, with a new student. The two were smiling and walking towards the administrative offices.

Just as quickly, Asif's attention snapped back to me.

"To answer your earlier question, my dear Kiran, I was here to meet Principal Hashim. He is a good friend, and you should know that he owes me plenty of favors."

"Why should I care?"

Dark eyes bored into mine. "Try to malign me again, and you will lose your job as easily as you got it."

"I got this job because I was qualified for it."

My fists clenched as he leaned in further and said, "You got this job because I like to keep my friends close, but my enemies closer. And you, dear Kiran, are intent on making yourself my enemy."

Without waiting for a response, he walked away, leaving me speechless and seething. The man had laid a web around my family, and once again, I was powerless to free them from it. Taking a deep breath, I retreated behind my façade of grit and gumption.

Today, Asif Ghazanfar may have rattled me, just like he had for many years before. But the need for revenge was etched into my bones. I wasn't a naïve young woman anymore, and I refused to rest till I got justice for my family. Until that day, I had to keep us afloat, even if it meant playing by the rules dictated by Satan himself.

When I reached the inner corridor, a student hurried past, nearly knocking my purse from my shoulder. She stopped briefly, apologizing, "Sorry, Ms. Kiran."

I was about to chide her for running in the corridors when she asked, "Did Osman come to school today?"

"It's the first day of school. Of course, he came."

Her smile broadened, and I noticed the subtle mascara and blush that accentuated her cheekbones. "Good. I'm in the same bio class as him," she said before skipping away, leaving me perplexed.

Now, why would Sanam Uzair, the most popular girl in school, be interested in my brother? I didn't like it at all.

CHAPTER 3

Partners

OSMAN

What about a certain Juliet? I wanted to ask my sister when she warned me about getting distracted by useless people.

If the few months before summer were any indication, Sanam Uzair was definitely a distraction. But her being useless was an absolute no. There was something about that girl, an undeniable grace in the way she spoke and carried herself, that made her stand out like a beautiful swan among a flock of vultures.

Alas, she'd never shown any interest in the sciences, so I was certain her being a distraction would never be an issue.

Oh, how wrong I was.

My gaze landed on her as soon as I walked into biology class. She stood at a lab bench lined with the usual science paraphernalia—some beakers, racks of test tubes, a Bunsen burner—talking to a smaller cohort of her vulture friends.

Stunned by her unexpected presence as much as her summer glow, I came to an abrupt halt in the doorway.

I am so failing this class, was the first thought that came to my mind.

Farhan, the former Romeo, bumped into me from behind and yelped. "Watch it, loser."

Sanam glanced my way. I quickly looked away and headed to the corner table where I could fade into oblivion as always and sulk. *Good job, idiot.*

But that was only the beginning of my rapid descent into becoming the class fool that day.

Mrs. Nazim, our formidable biology teacher, tapped her pen against the desk. Peering over her glasses, she announced, "This year, I'm pairing you up in alphabetical order for all lab work. So, for the next two years, forget you have any friends when you enter this room."

Despite the murmurs of disapproval, she began calling out names.

"Samreen Ali and Faryal Ashraf."

"Akram Basit and Faisal Choudhary."

"Nida Daud and Farhan Kamal."

On and on it went, down the list, name after name. Normally, I wouldn't have cared who I was paired with. If they ignored me, I would ignore them. If they were friendly, I could be friendly too.

My eyes began to wander around the room, scanning the people who were still unpaired, while I calculated who would be matched with whom. That's when my heartbeat quickened, and it dawned on me that T comes right before U.

"Osman Tariq and Sanam Uzair," a voice echoed through the room. It wasn't Mrs. Nazim's. To my horror, it was mine.

Deafening silence followed as twenty-four pairs of eyes stared at me.

Mrs. Nazim was first to speak. "Thank you, Mr. Osman. Would you like to come up here and take over the rest of my job too?"

"No, ma'am," I muttered.

Someone laughed and called me a weirdo. Another scoffed and called me dumb. Mrs. Nazim ignored them all and went back to the list in front of her.

My new lab partner picked up her bag and took a seat next to me.

"Hi, Osman." Her soft voice made my already embarrassed face flush even more.

"H-hi," I stuttered, without daring to meet her gaze.

No further words were exchanged between us till the teacher distributed the lab safety instructions. The stack of papers made its way through twenty-two other students before Farhan handed the last two sheets to Sanam. He whispered something to her, but she shook her head and swatted his arm. For once, I admitted to myself, I wished she would talk to me with the same ease she had with her friends.

Unfortunately, my wish came true.

Sanam held out a sheet for me. A normal person would have simply taken it. Instead, my arms forgot how to work, and my foot got caught on the base of my stool. As I tried to stand, my stool tipped backwards. Reflexively, I reached out to grab the table and steady myself. Instead, I found glass beakers and a rack of test tubes.

Before I could stop myself, I was tumbling to the ground with glass crashing onto the floor all around me. Twenty-four pairs of eyes homed in on me again... less than two minutes after I had last drawn attention to myself.

"Oh God!" a voice exclaimed.

Caramel brown eyes filled with concern gazed at me. Laughter echoed in the background. Farhan called me a klutz. None of it mattered when a gentle hand rested on my arm.

"Osman, are you okay?" she asked.

There were drops of crimson on the crisp white of my uniform. Small cuts littered my palms and wrists, some with tiny shards of glass embedded in them. It should have hurt, but somehow it didn't.

Perhaps it had something to do with the beautiful Juliet who wrapped her arm around mine, coaxing me off the floor.

"I'm taking Osman to the nurse," she declared to the rowdy class and a grumbling Mrs. Nazim.

Out in the hallway, her hand still rested on my arm. Her rose-tinted lips curved into a smile as she said, "I'd give you a lollipop if I had one, but for now, you'll have to do with my company."

I couldn't muster the words or the courage to tell her that I had a feeling if she was by my side, I would never need anything else.

Kiran Api's caution was relegated to the back of my mind, with scholarships and medical school easily forgotten. They would always be the reality I couldn't escape, but for that moment, life became a fantasy. And I followed my thudding heart to discover how it felt to be so close to Juliet and gaze into her warm eyes.

It was exhilarating enough to believe in the kind of love written about in novels and centuries-old plays.

ZAIN

The school dismissal bell rang, marking the end of a day like none I had ever had before.

"You're still holding that American girl's books?" Farhan gaped at me. "What magic did she do on you?"

"Not magic. Just being polite," I replied, picking up the pile of Maham's books that she didn't need that day. High schools in Pakistan didn't have the kind of lockers common in American schools. She was already rubbing her shoulders by the time we walked to our first class of the day. How could I not offer to carry her books after that?

"Zain Ghazanfar *and* polite. Never thought I'd see the day," Farhan said, following me out of the class.

In all honesty, I couldn't refute him. Being anyone's personal assistant, let alone that of a girl I had just met, wasn't like me at all. Yet, she had called me "sweet" and "kind," and I wasn't that either. It didn't stop me from grinning like a fool, as if she'd handed me my favorite toy.

It was odd, unexpected, and absolutely addictive.

"Doesn't hurt to try something different," I told my friend.

Farhan smirked. "A different kind of girl. Yeah, I get it."

Except, he hadn't gotten it at all. I had meant being a different kind of boy.

As we neared the main gate, two students stood chatting like they'd been friends for a while. One was a popular student in our school. The other —an enigma I was still trying to unravel.

"Looks like Maham met Sanam," Farhan remarked, not that it was unexpected. Sanam had always been the kind of girl everyone gravitated towards. Right now, though, I needed her to disappear.

"Tell Sanam a teacher is calling her. I want to talk to Maham alone," I told Farhan, unable to avert my gaze from the new girl with dark curls that bounced over her shoulders, catching the sunlight every time she laughed.

Farhan raised a brow. "Which teacher is calling her?"

"Make some shit up, man. Just get her away from Maham." I scowled at him.

He raised his hands and walked away, muttering, "Okay, weirdo."

Whatever he whispered to Sanam had her hurrying back into the school building. Meanwhile, Maham's gaze wandered around the schoolyard until it settled on me, her lips molding into a smile once again. That meant my transgressions had not been the topic of conversation between the two girls.

"Is your car here yet?" I asked when I walked closer to her.

"Not yet. Dad insisted on driving himself to pick me up today, and he's not really used to driving in a place where no one follows the rules."

"You have to be a special kind of brave to drive in this city."

"That's the thing." She chuckled. "He is a Professor of Mathematics. Bravery isn't usually his defining characteristic."

Professor of Mathematics? Not someone who would make it to my father's carefully curated list of powerful individuals he chose to interact with. That thought shouldn't have bothered me. But it did, and I wasn't sure why.

She asked what my father did but had never heard of GT Enterprise. "What kind of business is it?"

"They build houses," I told her, leaving out the part where those houses were exorbitantly expensive high-rise apartments in residential enclaves across the country.

"Cute."

Her perky voice was a sharp contrast to how "un-cute" my father's business really was. Cutthroat and relentless, it was a world where money spoke louder than actions, and decisions were made with cold precision. I wondered if this innocent girl could even fathom such a world.

As the two of us waited, chatting about everything from popular hangout spots to extracurricular activities the school offered, my black Mercedes SUV arrived. The chauffeur parked it a short distance away. Its tinted windows were a cover from the sun as much as a symbol of its luxury. Ordinarily, I would have sought refuge from Karachi's August heat in its air-conditioned interior, but Maham was talking about her life in Boston and how she was looking forward to living with her grandparents once her parents returned to the US. Her excitement was far more fascinating than my car.

"Most people I know can't wait to get out of this country. What made you come back?" I asked out of genuine curiosity.

"The culture, the language, the laidback lifestyle, my grandparents—I just wanted to know my roots, I suppose. Mom suggested I spend some time in high school here, and I didn't see a downside."

If she had inquired, I could have provided a long list of downsides, but who was I to question her Pakistani pride, or discourage her from spending the full two years of A-Levels in this school?

A nearby car honked at us. "My dad's here. Come . . ." She gestured. "I'll introduce you to him."

With her books still in my arms, I followed her to an older white sedan. "Dad, this is my very helpful friend, Zain," she said.

Very helpful. I'd never been called that before.

The bespectacled middle-aged man with a wide smile got out of the car to shake my hand. "Thank you, Zain beta, for helping Maham. I'm so glad she has already made a friend. Her mother and I have been so worried about leaving her in a new school and a new city."

"There is nothing to worry about, sir. I'll be here if she ever needs me." That was an offer I had never made to anyone else.

Maham was about to sit in the car when she glanced my way again. "Since you're offering, could I have your economics notes from last year? I was a little lost in class today."

"I'll bring them tomorrow. Maybe we can revise them together."

I smiled when she nodded, which was a significant problem. I had no notes for any of my classes. What C-grade student ever does?

Shit. I needed notes from someone, and I needed them now. Back in the schoolyard, I could only spot one person who would have kept meticulously catalogued notes, because that's how irritatingly obsessive she was.

"Hey, Sanam," I called out to her as she exited the school building. She scowled at me; that was nothing new.

"Where is your stupid friend?" she asked immediately.

"Farhan? No idea. Why?"

"He told me Osman was in a fight with someone, but I can't find him anywhere."

Farhan's ingenious solution had to be lauded. There was no better way to get her to respond quickly than to mention her beloved wimp.

"There was no fight. Farhan was playing with you," I admitted. "You're just dumb enough to fall for it."

Hands on her hips, she glared at me as I asked for her notes.

"What makes you think I will ever share anything of mine with you?"

A smile spread on my face; I had her exactly where I wanted her.

"I think that you'd do anything for my cousin, wouldn't you?"

Her eyes widened as I stepped closer. "Give me the notes, don't ask questions, and I will never bully that loser again."

She didn't budge. "Why should I trust you?"

"You shouldn't. But this is your only opportunity to save Osman from me. Be a good girl and take it."

Slowly the arrogance in her eyes melted away, even if the scowl remained. "Fine."

"Good choice, Juliet. I'll have them picked up tonight." I laughed, patted her head, and walked away, much to her annoyance.

"I fucking hate you," she called out.

Without looking back, I let my middle finger do the talking. I couldn't stand her or that boy she'd do anything for. Two pathetic losers, perfect for each other.

My car was parked where I had last seen it, but its engine was still purring, and the chauffeur was standing outside.

"Why is the car still running?" I asked him.

"Your father is sitting inside, sir."

The revelation sent a chill through me. I wasn't sure why until I sat in the car and his first question was, "Who was that girl you were talking to?"

"Sanam? She is Shabnam—"

He cut me off angrily. "I know who Sanam is. The *other* girl."

"That is Sanam's friend. Sanam asked me to help her. I was doing Sanam a favor." Lies tumbled out faster than I could process.

Abu's eyes narrowed. "Next time, do favors with less enthusiasm."

"Yes, Abu."

A brief, tense silence followed before he asked, "How is Sanam doing?"

"Very well. I was going to hang out at her house tonight, if that's okay with you." Another lie, but it was worth it to see the frown ease from his forehead.

He nodded, pulling out a wad of rupees and tossing it towards me. "Take the girl out for a nice dinner or something."

That night, my chauffeur picked up the economics notes from Sanam's house while I got high on weed at Farhan's. A month later, I partially made good on my father's wishes and took a girl out for a fancy dinner.

She told me I was smart and had a good heart. I didn't tell her she was starting to feel like an addiction.

CHAPTER 4

A Confession

SANAM

One day, we were fresh-faced juniors in A-Level, determined to make the most of our last two years of school. The next, we were stumbling out of classrooms at the end of a grueling week of midterms, ready to give up on life as a student altogether.

Amidst all that, neither of us was prepared to navigate the complexities of the heart.

"I am so ready for the winter break," Maham said to me as the two of us walked out of English literature class.

"Are you going back to the US?" I asked.

"Actually no. My mom is visiting Karachi, so I get to spend the next two weeks here. Besides, I will take Karachi's winter over Boston snow any day," she replied, her eyes wandering over the crowd of students gathered in the school's inner courtyard.

In full confession, I had been skeptical about the new American girl when she arrived four months ago. Yet, her cheerful compassion had won me over quickly. Quite the opposite of the boy she was now searching for.

With a knowing smile, I couldn't resist asking, "Is Boston snow the only reason you're excited to stay in Karachi?"

Her cheeks turned a crimson hue, and it wasn't because of the cold, dry winter wind.

"I know what you guys think of Zain," she said. "But he isn't like that with me. He's so caring and sweet. He even FaceTimes with my parents."

As unbelievable as it was, I had to agree with her. Zain, the biggest jerk in our class, had been a changed boy ever since she had entered his life. Personally, I was convinced his reformed ways were only to impress her.

Then again, who was I to judge? It's not like I hadn't changed my behavior for a lanky boy with tousled hair. Heck, a bag of lollipops was enough to convince me to become a biologist.

"Hey, you know what? Forget about what other people think. I believe people can change, and if he's willing to change himself for you, isn't that the whole point of being in love? To bring out the best in each other?" I told her, and meant every word.

She turned the tables on me pretty quickly.

"Speaking of love, I've been hearing murmurs about you and Osman during debate practice," she teased. Both were members of the debate club.

Yet, the crimson hues that blushed her cheeks never made an appearance on mine. Instead, it brought on a deep sigh.

"I don't know what you heard, but he barely even looks at me." Four months of twice-weekly biology lab classes, and all I had gotten out of him were quiet explanations about the experiments we conducted and an occasional smile when I cracked a lame joke.

"He's just shy," Maham said.

"He's not like that with flirty Faryal," I pointed out. Had I resorted to giving my classmates nicknames? Yes. Did it placate my jealous heart? A tiny bit.

Maham laughed, her gaze shifting behind me. "Is that your romantic rival?"

I turned to watch as a girl with neatly braided hair approached Osman at the far end of the school courtyard. He was crouched on the ground next to Snarls—our school's resident stray cat, who snarled at everyone except Osman, it seemed. His nimble fingers caressed its milky-white fur as it rubbed against his leg, and a smile spread across his handsome face.

Faryal tried to pet the cat too but jumped back when Snarls hissed at her, making Maham and me chuckle.

"Make your move, Sanam. Snarls isn't always going to keep your boy safe from flirty Faryal," Maham said.

That was the thing, though. It wasn't my move to make. If Zain could ask Maham out, why couldn't Osman ask me? Hadn't I smiled, joked, and talked enough to make my intentions clear?

Only one answer kept coming to my mind: he wasn't interested.

Almost as if she had read my mind, Maham pressed a reassuring hand on my shoulder. "Hey, don't appear so dejected. I've seen the way he looks at you."

"What are you talking about? He doesn't even look at me when I am standing right next to him."

"But he does when you're not next to him, Sanam," she insisted. "When you walk into a room, he looks at you like you're the reason he believes in fairytales."

"Fairytales are not real."

"The magic of falling in love is."

Maham clearly had it bad for her boyfriend, but my gaze drifted to the boy who stood alone in the corner of the courtyard.

"Why hasn't he ever said anything to me?"

"Maybe he would if he wasn't always digging through his stash of lollipops when he saw you." She seemed amused at that oddity; I wasn't.

Lollipops? Eyes wide, I swung to face him again. For a second, his gaze met mine before he looked away and pulled out a familiar candy from his pocket. A candy that was meant for moments when there was no other way to melt away our sadness.

Did I make him sad? I couldn't fathom a reason why—until Maham urged me again.

"Make your move, Sanam. You know he has too much baggage to ever feel comfortable approaching you."

He was an orphan raised by his sisters, which explained his soft-spoken personality and, perhaps, the baggage Maham mentioned. It occurred to me that perhaps following his heart was a fantasy he thought he couldn't afford in reality.

If only he knew how much I craved the normalcy of his reality.

"There you are," I heard Zain's voice.

Maham's face lit up when he gave her a quick hug. The two were cute together, I had to admit, but I had my own romantic story to write.

"Osman Tariq," I called out cheerfully as I neared the boy leaning against the wall with his backpack slung over one shoulder. "How dare you have a lollipop all by yourself?"

He smiled and reached into his backpack. "Here," he said, holding out a strawberry-flavored lollipop.

"Strawberry is my favorite," I exclaimed.

"I know," he whispered.

He knew. I smiled.

Truths straight from my heart should have been enunciated after that. Instead, I leaned against the wall next to him, a sweet, tangy flavor bursting in my mouth, and let his quiet serenity wash over me. I wondered if Zain's hugs ever gave Maham the same warm comfort that now surrounded me.

"How do you get that snarly cat to like you?" I eventually asked.

"Patience. I wait for it to come to me."

"Is that what you do with people too?" I turned towards him. "Wait for them to come to you?"

He stood up straighter. "People have better things to do than bother with me."

"People might. I don't," I whispered.

For a fleeting moment, unrecognizable emotions flickered in his hazel eyes—deep, raw, and captivating. I held my breath, my heart pounding as his gaze lingered, searing me despite the chill of that December afternoon.

That moment was quickly over. If he understood what I meant, it was lost to the arrival of his eldest sister.

"We're getting late, Osman," she said, without acknowledging me. I hoped the edge in her voice was a figment of my imagination.

"Yes, Api," he replied.

"Have a good winter break," he said to me and rushed to catch up with Ms. Kiran.

I watched as he reached out to take the canvas bags bursting with books and papers that she was holding. Midterm exams of her students now became part of the baggage Osman carried. How much more was still hidden from me remained a mystery.

Walking back to where my friends stood, I saw Snarls a couple of feet away. Her green feline eyes watched closely as I crouched on the ground and held out my hand. Five seconds passed, then ten, fifteen, and twenty. I had almost given up when the white cat took her first step towards me. Slowly, cautiously, she approached me, until she was so close she could rub against my leg.

"Well, look at that. Patience really does work." I smiled and stroked her fur.

The cat was still purring when Maham called out, "Hey, Sanam, party tonight at Zain's. Will you be able to make it?"

"I already had something planned with my family," I replied without a second thought.

She never asked me for more details. It's not like I would have had an answer for her anyway.

My mother and stepfather were in Islamabad. Dado and Zaviyar Chachoo were attending a political rally somewhere in Karachi in preparation for the upcoming elections. Last I knew of my father, he was in Texas, USA, living with his second wife, who was more than two decades younger than him.

Then there was me: a forgotten part of everyone's life.

Pretending that I had a family who cared had become such a norm, I didn't even have to think about the lies I spouted. Usually, they worked, becoming a convenient excuse when I didn't have it in me to socialize. Today, an unexpected voice challenged them.

"Stop making excuses, Sanam. There won't be anyone at your place tonight," I heard Zain say, as I walked alone towards my car.

"And how do you know that?"

"Abu told me about the political rally your grandmother and uncle will be attending alone today, since the rest of your family is not in the city."

Why would Asif Ghazanfar be keeping such a close eye on my family? It was creepy, to say the least, but Zain had other things on his mind.

He raked his fingers through his hair as he spoke again, softly—so unlike him. "Could you please just come to the party? I need to tell Abu about Maham, and if things don't go the way I hope, she'll need a friend."

I gaped at him. "You haven't told your father you're dating Maham?"

"He is very rigid about who I should and shouldn't socialize with."

That's all he said, but I understood his predicament. I wasn't sure what was worse: being ignored by your family or being suffocated by them. Either way, Maham was a friend, and what kind of a friend would I be if I didn't support her relationship with a guy who was trying his best?

"Can you call Osman too?"

"He's not allowed in my house," he replied dryly.

"Why?"

"I don't know, Sanam," he grunted a reply. "Maybe because his family hates mine. I don't give a shit. Call him if you want. But it's not on me if he gets thrown out."

The stark contrast between Zain and Osman baffled me. How was one cousin able to buy his way through life, coasting on family wealth and connections, while the other barely scraped by, shouldering burdens far beyond his years?

At seventeen, I was old enough to ask that question, but not wise enough to answer it. Perhaps that's what made me an easy target to be used as a pawn.

ZAIN

That wasn't the first time I had thrown a party for my classmates, leaving out only those who would snitch on the rest of us and our not-so-legal beverages. And then there was the one whose name was never mentioned in our house. The 'why' of it had never interested me. I simply hated weak people, and with his sob stories of poverty and misfortune, Osman was the epitome of weakness.

It also wasn't the first time that Maham would be in this house. Though it was the first time that Abu would find out about us being in a committed relationship.

Maham's magnanimous heart and optimism made me want to be different. She didn't see the insensitive jerk I could sometimes be. Her focus was always on the good, making me want to permanently bury the ugliness that would occasionally creep to the surface.

Hiding our relationship was a matter of pragmatism. Nothing else. I needed time to come up with a plan so that Maham saw the best of my father, and in turn, he saw that I had no choice but to go against his wishes.

"Loosen up, man. You look constipated," Farhan said, offering me a beer. I refused it. Maham did not drink alcohol, so now neither did I.

Ignoring my friend's questioning glance, I asked him if he remembered the plan.

"Make an excuse to stick to Sanam."

"Exactly."

"What if she kicks me? I am not her favorite, you know."

"Well, then don't be an asshole," I snapped at him. "If nothing else works, say something nice about Osman."

"I hate that Goody Two-Shoes." Farhan made a face and disappeared into the smoky haze hanging over the crowded dance floor set up in our front yard.

We had told all the parents that this was an adult-chaperoned event, but Ami was nowhere to be found. A bit later, I noticed Abu standing next to Sanam near the table laid out with snacks and desserts, a glass of scotch in one hand and a half-empty bottle in the other. Farhan found them at about the same time. He offered Sanam a beer, which she refused, but thankfully her face didn't contort with disgust.

If it had, it would have been hard to sell that the two of them were dating.

"Sorry I am late." I finally heard the voice I had been longing to hear the whole evening.

"Maham." I turned around to face her, my jaw nearly dropping to the floor.

Dressed in a cream-colored maxi dress with a form-fitting bodice adorned with delicate sequined embroidery, she looked like an angel on earth. *I am going to marry her one day* was the only thought that came to mind as I stood there, drinking in her perfection.

"Do I look okay?" she asked innocently.

"Gosh, Maham, I can barely breathe. You don't just look *okay*—you look *gorgeous*."

She blushed and batted her long, dense eyelashes and now I couldn't breathe, *and* my heart nearly stopped.

"Thank you, and you look really nice too." She smiled before averting her gaze to the rest of the place.

"I didn't realize there was going to be alcohol here." Her eyes narrowed. "Do you drink alcohol too?"

"I used to," I replied truthfully. "Not anymore, though."

"How come?"

"You don't like boys who drink," I told her. For her, I would do anything—become anything—as long as I could be the boy worthy of her.

"Okay." There was that smile again, making my heart flutter with the trust she placed in me. Nothing in this world could ever give me the high that one look of approval from her could.

It gave me courage as well—to go against the man who had meticulously planned every detail of my life. I took her hand in mine and said, "Let's go meet my father."

She gave me a worried look. "What if he doesn't approve of us?"

"Don't worry. It will all be fine."

Farhan noticed us coming and moved closer to Sanam. Sanam saw her friend approach and her smile widened. My father saw the two of them and frowned. Then he turned towards us, and his frown deepened.

It will all be fine, I repeated to myself. No one could take Maham away from me, not even my father.

"Hi, Abu. Please meet Maham, my girlfriend."

His grip tightened around the glass of scotch, his jaw ticked, but not a word came from his mouth. Maham greeted him politely. He swung his gaze towards me. If there was anger in his eyes, he didn't make it obvious. No man of his stature would lose control of his emotions in front of a crowd of teenagers.

"You look so beautiful," Sanam told Maham and gave her a tight hug.

"I was telling Sanam what a great party this is. Thanks for inviting us," Farhan said to me, his hand hovering behind Sanam's waist. To the casual eye it appeared to rest on her waist, like he was a boyfriend exploring the liberties given by his girlfriend.

"I am so glad you two could make it," I replied, making sure to look at both Sanam and Farhan while the former was still talking to my girlfriend.

A seamless conversation, perfect timing, unsuspecting actors, and exquisite acting. For now, those were enough to make my father raise his glass to me and say, "Well played, son."

"Just following my heart, Abu," I replied.

It was all fine indeed.

That night, as the clock struck twelve, Maham and I stood alone on the patio of my house. The swimming pool shimmered with silver hues from the stars above and golden shadows cast by the fairy lights around us. Wearing my jacket, she huddled close. With my heart pounding against my chest, I pulled her even closer.

It was magical. She was magical.

Though I was young, I knew what I wanted. She was my destiny, one that my father would have no control over.

"I am so in love with you," I whispered.

She glanced at me, surprised, but didn't pull away. There was so much more I needed to say.

"I know that I may not be who you thought you would end up with, but I have never met anyone like you, and I don't think I ever will. So Maham Qureshi, I promise you—I will spend the rest of my life loving you."

Time had no meaning then. We stood still, our hands clasped, our gazes locked. In that moment, we existed only for each other. Until finally, her arms wrapped around my neck and mine around her waist, and she whispered back, "I love you too, Zain Ghazanfar. And I am going to hold you to that promise for the rest of my life."

I wish I had held on to her for longer, or stopped time then, or even just made her mine and hidden her from the world.

But how was I supposed to know what the future held for me? Or that a pair of hooded eyes was watching us from the upstairs bedroom?

Turned out, at seventeen, I was old enough to dupe my father but not wise enough to grasp the repercussions of my actions. He was the grandmaster of chess, and I was barely a novice, fumbling in the dark, unaware of the traps he'd set.

CHAPTER 5

Patience

SANAM

"Hi, Osman," I said, taking a seat next to him in biology class.

That scene had replayed itself countless times over the past year and a half or so. As always, his hand stilled over his workbook, and he turned towards me just enough that I could see his lips mold into a half-smile.

"Hi, Sanam," he replied softly.

Phir se pukaro mera naam. (Say my name again.)

My heart ached with desire, fully aware that I could never say those words aloud. And still, every time he said my name, something inside me gave way. It wasn't spoken; it was breathed out, so serenely, like the whisper of a breeze across a field of daffodils.

Lame. My brain groaned at my heart's lunacy.

We were now in our second term of the final year of A-Levels, and time was passing by like sand between my fingers. The sun would rise, the sun would set, and another day was gone, thrusting us all into the inevitable—when we would no longer be kids or high school students.

Yet the time between each biology class moved agonizingly slow, squeezing out every drop of my patience. Those classes were the only moments in my life when I felt some sense of serenity, surrounded by a comfortable silence and the few wise words of a cute, quiet boy as he listened to me talk about my family's political ambitions, Mama's absence, and my uncertain educational future.

Like all days prior, Mrs. Nazim walked in, and the class fell quiet under her looming presence. We huddled around her large desk in front of the room. Over the next half hour, the rest of the class observed how she carefully sectioned the stem of a eucalyptus plant and mounted it onto a slide.

I, on the other hand, took that opportunity to intermittently observe someone's perfectly structured jawline, the thick eyebrows that furrowed when he scribbled something in his notebook, and those full lips that sucked on the end of a ballpoint pen. And how I wished I could run my fingers through the locks of dark hair that fell over his forehead. Or feel his forearm encasing me as his muscles tightened and stretched.

So delightfully nerdy and handsome.

He started twirling the pen in his fingers, and I couldn't stop watching his sensual, well-proportioned fingers and neatly cut nails. Round and round the plastic pen went, between his fingers and over his thumb, mesmerizing me. All while his eyes and mind were singularly trained on Mrs. Nazim.

"Miss Sanam . . ."

"Yes. Yes, Mrs. Nazim." I swung my gaze towards our teacher, whose wrinkled skin made her steely gray eyes bulge out of their sockets.

"Eyes. On. Me," she growled.

The class giggled, heat rose in my cheeks, and I was ready to dig a hole for myself. Luckily, she told us to head back to our benches and start the experiment ourselves, so my classmates immediately dispersed. Unluckily, I felt an arm around my waist and an irritating voice speak in my ear as his hot breath hit my neck.

"You can stare at me all you want. I won't tell Mrs. Nazim."

It was only then that I realized that, between Osman and me, stood an immature buffoon who had once had the audacity to tell everyone that he and I were dating.

"Leave me alone, Farhan," I hissed under my breath.

"Oh, but sweetheart . . ." He started to smirk when a hand yanked him away from me.

"*Listen* to her," Osman's throaty voice threatened, surprising me as much as it did Farhan, who stepped away when Osman positioned himself in front of me.

"She said leave her alone."

"The boy speaks," Farhan sniggered, but my view of him was blocked by Osman's tall body, which I suddenly realized wasn't as lanky as it used to be.

"I may be quiet, but I am not weak," Osman replied, with such firmness that the room fell silent.

"Stop it, you two!" Mrs. Nazim's voice boomed, forcing the boys to step apart.

"I am sorry, we were just leaving," Osman mumbled, his eyes still glaring at Farhan. But consciously or not, he placed his arm around my shoulder and guided me to our bench. Even when we reached it and he turned to face me, his hand didn't leave my shoulder. Under the fabric of my uniform, my skin tingled with a mix of warmth and nerves at the weight of his touch.

"Are you okay?" he asked.

Concern clouded his countenance, but his tender gaze and gentle voice did nada to slow down my racing heart. I almost feigned an injury so he wouldn't withdraw into his shell again, and I could continue to bask in the security of his presence. But that would have turned me into flirty Faryal.

"Yes," I answered him honestly, even if reluctantly.

He let go and straightened up, but his hardened gaze shifted back to Farhan.

"Has he harassed you before?"

"No," I replied, which wasn't exactly the truth, but something told me that in the interest of peace, it was the right thing to say.

Nodding, he sucked in his lower lip before slowly releasing it, making my insides quiver. And I wondered how I had never seen this side of him before. He had always seemed so aloof and withdrawn, but now I could almost feel the heat radiating from his body as he stood close, unmoving and unwavering, a passionate rage swirling in his eyes that never left the boy who had made the mistake of thinking I was alone.

"Tell me if he ever touches you again," Osman whispered intensely, his gaze finally landing back on me.

A faint "thank you" was all I could muster as I let myself drown in the emotional storm he had conjured in my soul. My imagination yielded to the unspoken sentiments of the past few minutes. For the first time in months, there was a glimmer of hope for me, for us.

I expected him to step back after that and dive straight into the assignment. He didn't. His gaze lingered on me, lips parting slightly, as if he wanted to say something more but couldn't bring himself to form the words.

"*Ahem.*" Someone cleared their throat loudly right next to us, making us jump apart.

"Are you two going to keep standing here staring at each other, or are you planning to get some work done too?" Mrs. Nazim barked.

"Sorry," we both muttered and hurried to our bench.

Osman immediately started the experiment, meticulously following each step: section the eucalyptus plant, stain it, destain it, put the cover slip on it, mount it on the microscope.

"You can take a look at my slide. We're running out of time," he said when he was done.

I placed a hand on his arm and dared to say, "Osman, *we* are running out of time."

The bell rang, but his silence prevailed. Frustrated, I focused on filling out my worksheet, cursing my heart and the illusions it had created.

I didn't see him again until after school, as I waited for my car. Footsteps crunched on the gravel behind me as the wind carried my name.

"Sanam . . ."

There he stood, hair tousled, tie loosened, lips slightly parted, with that intense, searing gaze that held me captive once again.

This time, he formed the words.

"Some things are meant to last beyond time itself."

He retreated as quickly as he had appeared, leaving behind only the echoes of his words, each one so open to interpretation that they were at once comforting and unsettling.

"Oh, Osman, how long are you going to make me wait?" I whispered to myself.

A white cat with glassy green eyes meowed nearby.

Patience. Yeah, I got it, I sighed to the universe at large.

KIRAN

As soon as we got home, Osman went into his room and slammed the door, its rusted hinges creaking in protest.

Kaukab, my youngest sister, looked up from the dining table where she was sitting with my twins, helping them with their homework. Her husband was visiting Dubai in hopes of expanding their textile business overseas, which meant she was often found in this cramped apartment more than in her own house.

"Is Mani okay?" Daniyal asked.

"Why is he so angry?" Danish inquired.

"Must have gotten into a fight again," Kaukab guessed.

She was partially right.

"He fought with me," I admitted.

Surprise flashed across all three faces because Osman and I did not fight. The lines between motherhood and sisterhood often blurred for me when it came to raising Osman, but the boy knew well not to cross certain boundaries. He respected me, and I, in turn, protected him fiercely. That had always been our strength, until today.

"What happened?" A worried Kaukab followed me into the kitchen.

"His biology teacher complained about him trying to instigate a fight in class—over a girl. She didn't report him, as a courtesy to me, but warned she wouldn't hold back next time."

Kaukab found it amusing. "Aww. Our baby brother has a crush. Who is the girl?"

She wasn't smiling after I pulled out my phone and opened a video from a recent Awami Workers Party rally.

On stage, surrounded by party supporters and the usual political fanfare, stood the leading figures of a party that had recently risen to prominence on the national stage. Beside them stood an older woman, a well-known actress, and the pretty girl who seemed to have captured my brother's heart.

"Zaviyar Uzair, the party leader, is her paternal uncle. Malik Awan, the party treasurer, is her stepfather. Both men are members of the National Assembly. The actress Shabnam Murad is her mother."

My sister's eyes rounded. "That's not good."

Standing in my small apartment above a grocery store in a neighborhood where the AWP leadership would never set foot, it was clear why Osman's willingness to get reported to the principal's office for the pretty girl was *not good at all.*

"I told him he needs to forget about her, and now he thinks I am the villain holding him back."

Kaukab placed a gentle hand on my arm. "Kiran, maybe it's time to tell him why he lives in this old place and not the mansion on Sunset Boulevard."

Revealing the truth to him would mean reliving a day when I was utterly powerless, armed only with my words to shield my family against the forces of evil. My words had been no match for loaded guns.

With newly born Danish and Daniyal finally asleep in their cribs, I walked over to the spare bedroom that had been my siblings' room for the past week. Kauser and Kaukab lay on either side of the queen bed, and in between them, curled up into a ball, was Osman. I bent over and kissed his forehead, and pulled the covers over all of them.

"I am going out and will be late. Don't bother calling me," came my husband's curt voice from the living room.

I hurried out. "It's midnight, Shafiq. Where are you going?"

He scowled. "Away from this freaking hotel you've opened for the homeless."

"They are not homeless," I shot back, but he had already walked out of our front door.

Struggling from dealing with infant twins, Shafiq had not taken it well when my siblings arrived at our doorstep. Yet I had never expected him to be so cruel towards them.

Heaving a breath, determined not to shed tears over a situation I had no control over, I returned to my bedroom when I heard the front door open again.

"Shafiq . . ." I stepped out to meet my husband.

Instead, I came face-to-face with masked men. Three carried guns; one carried a folder filled with papers.

I tried to run towards my phone, but the men were faster and stronger. "Just sign these papers and no one will get hurt," one of them said.

"I won't sign . . ." A sharp pain in my temple cut me off, and the warm trickle of blood confirmed these men meant business.

The unarmed man shoved me onto the sofa and growled, "Sign here."

A quick glance revealed what they wanted: the transfer of ownership of Tariq Enterprise, the company my grandfather had built from scratch, along with all its subsidiaries, assets, and properties.

"I can't. It was left in Osman's name, and he's still a minor," I protested, but the man didn't budge.

He tightened his grip on my hair, yanking my head back, forcing me to look into his soulless eyes. "Don't lie. You have legal guardianship of the boy. You know exactly what that means."

"Kiran . . ." Kauser's trembling voice made me look towards their bedroom. She and Kaukab cowered in the doorway, but that's not what made my heart nearly stop.

Behind them, Osman still lay curled up in a ball, peacefully asleep, unaware of the gun's barrel pressed against his temple.

"Sign the company over or watch us kill the future CEO of Tariq Enterprise."

I signed every page in that file and saved my brother's life.

So deep was my grandfather's conviction that only the grandson raised in his own image could carry forward his name, that he ensured Osman would be the sole heir of his company. He never expected to die so soon after my father met with a fatal accident.

So corrupt was the justice system we encountered that every safeguard placed by law to protect the properties of minors was bribed into submission by Asif Ghazanfar.

With all the assets transferred to him, we lost the house I grew up in. Tariq Enterprise became Ghazanfar-Tariq Enterprise, or GT Enterprise for short. To the world, Asif Ghazanfar had graciously stepped in to help his young niece manage a multi-million-dollar company in exchange for a small share. Yet, his nieces and nephew never saw a paisa after that day.

All we had left was the meager inheritance we received from our own parents, just enough to put Kauser and Kaukab through college and buy the apartment we lived in.

To answer Kaukab's question, I shook my head. "There is no point in telling him. That boy already carries so much guilt for being the reason our mother passed away. If I tell him about that night, he'll blame himself for our riches-to-rags story too."

People talk about the eldest daughter being a third parent, but no one talks about her being the sole parent. All I had ever wanted was for my siblings to be safe in a world where we only had each other. Instead, I had been naïve with Kauser and powerless with Osman. That was the guilt I silently carried.

Kaukab had always seen through my silence. Today was no different.

"You're wrong about one thing, though. Our story didn't end with us in rags. Shafiq may have walked out on you, and we may have lost our wealth, but we are together. And minus that boy's current predicament, or whatever it is, we've been happy too."

"Kauser—" I started to remind her.

She didn't let me finish. "Has been to therapy, is married to a man who understands her completely, and is a mother to an adorable daughter. There is nothing more she could have asked for."

I bowed my head, not in shame, but in sheer exhaustion. My sister lifted my chin. "Kiran, you've always taught us that we may be voiceless, but we are not weak. You have to believe in that yourself too."

Forcing a smile, I nodded at her. She wasn't wrong. Strength wasn't always loud and obnoxious. It could be quietly perseverant and patient as well.

I knew, too, that Osman's outburst was a teenage heart struggling between patience and impulse. Perhaps the only way to help him was to forget Asif Ghazanfar's threats and show him that even in a jungle of thorns, patience can still bear fruit.

CHAPTER 6

Late Nights

SANAM

After enduring a grueling college application season, where I lost count of the personal statements I wrote, I now found myself in the midst of a national election season fraught with scandals, mudslinging, and power plays.

"Sanam, when did you sleep last night?" Dado asked as I dragged my sorry self down the stairs for breakfast.

"No idea . . . three . . . four . . . whenever I finished my homework." My drowsy head hit the table as soon as I sat down.

I refrained from divulging more secrets lest I disturb the tense peace between her and her ex-daughter-in-law who had essentially turned her Karachi house into campaign headquarters for her politician husband. Mr. Malik was running for the National Assembly on AWP's ticket from a constituency in Karachi but had been struggling recently due to rumors of a drunken altercation with a taxi driver.

Desperately needing an image makeover, his campaign team had devised a strategy to rebrand him as a family man, and I unwittingly became a part of that strategy. The press saw Mama and me with him, and suddenly, he was a loving husband and a doting father who believed in second chances.

Dado had returned to reading her newspaper after advising me to manage my time better, when I remembered what day of the week it was. Eyes wide opened, my late nights were quickly forgotten. The thrill of knowing who I would see in biology's theory class was enough to dispel any annoyance with my mother. It wasn't the same as lab day, but it came close. Especially now that I was convinced I wasn't as invisible to him as I had been for nearly a year and a half.

A cup of milk and buttered toast later, I was splashing water on my face and applying a very light layer of foundation with au natural lip gloss.

"Going to school?" a warm male voice asked when I reached the main door, making me smile immediately.

"Zavi Chachoo!" I skipped over and hugged him tightly.

As the chairman of AWP, he was here to bolster Mr. Malik's campaign. But in his heart, I knew he welcomed the trip so he could meet his beloved mother and niece, i.e. me. It was no secret that, like Dado, he had been more of a parent to me than his older brother, my own father, had ever been.

"I'll be back in the afternoon. Do you want to hang out then?" I asked him excitedly.

His eyes crinkled with humor. "Sometimes I forget you're a teenager like your cousins. They would rather be dead than hang out with their old man."

My cousins had a father who loved them; I didn't. Of course, they would take his love and affection for granted. Not like me, who hung to any morsel of attention my family gave me, much as I tried to hide it.

"They have no idea how much fun it is to beat you at UNO," I replied cheerfully.

"You're on, young lady." He grinned before his demeanor became more serious.

"Listen, Sanam," Chachoo said in a hushed tone. "Is Malik treating you okay? If not, you know you can always come to me. I don't like to interfere too much in my party members' campaigns, but I will if you want me to."

I reassured him that he had been pleasant overall, and the only reason I was going back home to my mother's place these days was because she had insisted that I be there.

"Well, be careful. Politics and the public eye are no place for a young girl. Your mother should know that better than anyone else."

He didn't have to warn me. Sitting on the stage under public scrutiny had been one of the most uncomfortable things I had ever done. Yet, these past few days were the only times it seemed that my mother was eager to see me. Why wouldn't I chase that fleeting feeling of being wanted?

Though something about the allegations against Mr. Malik hadn't added up. "Do you really think Mr. Malik got drunk and assaulted a taxi driver simply because he asked Mama for an autograph? I mean, she's an actress, after all. People ask her for autographs all the time. Besides, I've never seen him drink alcohol."

Zavi Chachoo's face contorted with dismay. "The allegations are absolutely false. He wasn't even in Karachi when this event supposedly happened. He was in Lahore with me. Someone paid off the taxi driver, and the man in the grainy video that was shot at night could be anyone."

He sighed. "But you know how it is these days. Falsehood travels faster than truth, especially when someone has deep enough pockets to pay the right people."

Before I could question the intention behind those false rumors, Chachoo asked, "Is there a Zain Ghazanfar in your class?"

"Yes, why?"

"Steer clear of him," he warned while walking me to the car.

"Why? He's a decent guy, even volunteers at a school for homeless children."

"It's not him I am worried about. It's his father. The man considers himself a kingmaker, and while I want AWP to ascend to power, I refuse to take the help of men like Asif Ghazanfar who will demand our souls in return for any favors."

"So then don't take any favors." Seemed like a simple solution to me.

Chachoo's hand rested on my shoulder. "We're not going to. But Asif preys on the weakest link in a party, and I know that our anti-corruption agenda is starting to bother him."

Dado called out from inside the house. I was getting late for school, and she wasn't happy her youngest son was the reason for that. Zavi Chachoo patted me on the cheek quickly.

"Go now, before Ami grounds me," he chuckled.

He never mentioned who he thought the weakest link in AWP was. I never bothered asking. Why should I have? I was just a teenager who loved going to school.

OSMAN

She entered the classroom for the last class of the day, and the rest of the room faded away. I watched as she put down her bag and her gaze locked onto mine from across the room. Unlike before, I didn't look away. I took in those caramel-brown eyes and her luscious pink lips, which curled up into a slight smile.

And I smiled back, despite Kiran Api's voice in my head.

What is wrong with you, Osman? I taught you better than this.

Yet somehow, *this* did not feel wrong, because Api *had* taught me better. How, then, could my pure intentions be wrong?

My nerves frayed at the mere glimpse of her, but for the first time, I felt at ease. She was still forbidden fruit. Untouchable and unattainable. I was unworthy of her; I knew that. Yet, there was something about the small smile that played on her lips and the glint of joy in her eyes amidst our stolen glances that gave me the courage to foolishly dream of a future with her.

The beauty who stole an orphan's heart. I imagined that could be the title of our story.

"Settle down, class," Mrs. Nazim's voice boomed across the room before I could say anything to Sanam, who took a seat diagonally across from me.

The rest of that hour was spent learning about the anatomy of the heart: the atria, the ventricles, and the valves that connected them, all labelled on a schematic diagram drawn on the whiteboard. Mrs. Nazim pointed out the sinoatrial node, the bundle of nerves responsible for making the heart beat with a regular rhythm.

"Can anyone tell me what can affect the electrical activity of the heart? In other words, make the heart skip a beat?"

I glanced at the girl with wavy brown hair as she chewed on the end of a pen and raised my hand.

"Osman?"

"A breathtaking view."

Murmurs broke out across the classroom. Mrs. Nazim said something, but I ignored it. The school dismissal bell rang. I couldn't have cared less. All I saw was the girl who sat diagonally across the room, and her radiant smile when she turned to look at me.

My sinoatrial node misfired. My heart skipped a beat.

"The answer is potassium—that's what can affect the heart's activity," I blurted out when I saw Sanam walking towards me in the hallway outside the classroom.

She paused and blinked. "Oh . . . okay."

I nearly slapped myself. Who talks to a girl about *potassium*?

"I saw you on TV last night," I added quickly, hoping she'd forget how awkward nerds could be.

It worked. She took a few steps closer.

That's when I noticed the puffiness around her eyes and heard the exhaustion in her voice when she said, "You must have thought I looked like such a mess. It's been really busy at home with all the crap my family puts me through. Between the political rallies, donor dinners, and homework, I barely get time to sleep."

I had never been interested in politics, but last night, I watched the whole AWP rally, just to catch a glimpse of her standing next to her mother and stepfather, looking like a true political heiress in the way she waved and smiled at the masses. Yet, I should have known that her perfection was a farce, only on display for others.

For me, she kept lowering her façade, letting me see a side of her she kept hidden from everyone else. And that realization was maddening to my teenage self.

Maddening, yet respectfully emboldening.

"You are not a mess, Sanam. You are real. But if you want, maybe I can help you with your homework after school."

Her eyes brightened. "I'd love that very much."

The hallway had emptied; the schoolyard was full. A cacophony of sounds floated in the air. Someone was laughing, another was yelling, and a scurry of footsteps followed. Somewhere, a fight had broken out.

Away from it all, the two of us lingered in silence, and I was struck by two undeniable realizations. One, that we were no longer friends.

Dostoun aur ashiqoun mein zameen asmaan ka farq hota hai.

Dosti ho tou baar baar milne ka dil karta hai.

Ishq ho tou kabhi na bicharne ka dil karta hai.

And two, nerds become poets when their sinoatrial node misfires.

(There is a vast difference between friends and lovers. With friendship, the heart wants to meet again and again. With love, the heart never wants to leave.)

ZAIN

"Who the fuck does he think he is?" Farhan's angry voice echoed in the near-empty hallway, subduing Maham's softer tone as she and I walked out of the school building at the end of the day.

"What's wrong with him?" she asked.

I paused where I was, debating whether I should go and join him and a couple of my other friends, who were spitting out plans to take revenge on a junior.

"Farhan said something to a girl. She complained to her boyfriend, and her boyfriend got all in his face," I told a frowning Maham.

"And you're thinking about taking part in whatever those idiots are about to do?"

"Farhan is my friend—" I started to reply when she cut me off sternly.

"Who is always getting you into trouble." She let go of my hand and waved towards him. "But if you want to be like him, go ahead. Just don't expect me to be okay with it."

Without another word, she turned and headed in the direction opposite my friends. Following her was a no-brainer. The panic filling my heart at the silent void she left behind was nothing new.

I wasn't good enough for her. I knew that. Everyone around us knew that. Yet somehow, she was still with me.

Not for long, my father's voice mocked me.

"Are you going to leave me?" I asked when I finally caught up with her.

She stopped and faced me, her gaze softening. "No, I won't. I love you, Zain. But you have to stop hanging out with those boys. You're so much better than them, and I hate to see you waste yourself the way they do."

"I promise. I won't hang out with them." I nodded fervently, but that didn't quell my desperate need for reassurance. "Why do you love me?"

"Because I see you. The real you." She brought her hand up to place it over my chest. "You have an amazing heart. Don't try to hide it because of what you've been taught."

This wasn't the first time she had said that to me. I wanted to believe her, to trust that her love for me was genuine. But every time, a nagging voice returned.

She only loves you for your money. Why else would anyone love a loser like you?

Pushing my father's words aside, I slipped my hand into hers as we headed towards our cars. "We're kind of like the Beauty and the Beast. Aren't we?"

"Who told you that?" she asked, giving me a sideways glance.

"Abu did. He said I'm ugly inside and out, and that you could do so much better." I cringed, remembering the sardonic look on his face when he said those words in front of his business associates.

"Zain, you're not a beast. Everyone thinks you're one of the most handsome guys in school, including me. Plus, you're kind and honest, and I like you the way you are. We don't always have to listen to our parents, okay?"

I shrugged. How could I not? He was my father. Unlike my mother, who was either a doormat or a zombie drugged up on anti-depressants on any given day, my father was the epitome of power and success. He wasn't a fatherly figure, but he was the only parent who was consistently around.

"Hey, Abu is throwing a dinner party for all his business associates this weekend. Can you come? Please say yes." I clasped my hands in front of me, hoping my puppy eyes would sway her. Then I could show my father that, even a year later, the beautiful girl he taunted me about still thought I was worthy of her.

The spark in her eyes faded. "I made plans with my cousins. Maybe next time."

"Alright," I replied.

Since she lived with her grandparents and had several uncles and aunts in Karachi, it wasn't unusual for her to have plans with her cousins. But this was the fourth time in a row she'd turned down an invitation to my place.

I watched her walk to her car, keeping a close eye on the classmates she passed along the way. She was stunning, and the testosterone-fueled guys at our school were always tempted to steal a glance.

But by now, I'd quietly threatened enough of them that everyone knew she was off-limits. I felt a wave of satisfaction as no one bothered her.

Before she sat in her car, she waved and called out, "See you at the street school?"

Set in a slum area, the street school was a project supported by Kingston Academy. A way to give back to the community. She had signed up for it a few months after being in Karachi. I signed up for it because she did, and I couldn't bear to leave her alone in a place where poverty justified stealing from the rich.

"I'll be there." I waved back, mustering a small smile.

My father was wrong, I reassured myself as I watched her drive off. Maham could never leave me. How could she, when I was always by her side?

CHAPTER 7

Birthday

KIRAN

"We can meet outside your school when it's over," said the man on the phone, raising alarms within me.

"No. Not outside my school. There's a coffee shop around the corner from Kingston Academy," I replied, leaving out Asif's threat to have me fired from my job if I tried to go to the press again.

"Perfect. See you in the afternoon."

That was Sikander Ahmed—an award-winning investigative journalist whose sole passion in life was to bring down corrupt politicians and businessmen. His latest target, much to my relief, was Asif Ghazanfar. The best part was that he had reached out to me, which meant that, for once, my truths wouldn't be ignored.

"What are you smiling about, Api?" Osman asked as he walked into the kitchen in his school uniform.

He and I had quickly gotten back to our usual selves after his little outburst: a boy with an innocently warm heart and a sister who would do anything to keep him that way. Yet, at eighteen, having just celebrated his birthday yesterday, I knew the ugliness of this world couldn't be kept hidden from him forever.

"Sikander Ahmed is doing a piece on businessmen with illicit money that funds politics in Pakistan. And he wants to interview me about Asif Ghazanfar."

"Cool," he replied in the midst of a yawn and went about making a breakfast sandwich for himself. I had to remind myself that his lack of enthusiasm was simply a function of his lack of knowledge.

"Anyway, have you decided how you're going to spend your birthday money?"

"Not really." He stifled another yawn, making me raise a brow as I guessed why he was so tired.

"How long were you up talking to Sanam?"

He stilled for a second before his flustered reply came. "I wasn't talking to her. She is just my lab partner. You told me not to talk to her, so I don't talk to her." Sandwich in hand, he hurried out of the kitchen, leaving me to shake my head at how dumb kids could be.

Did he really think I hadn't noticed his flaming cheeks? Or that I didn't receive reports from Mrs. Nazim, who watched the two of them like a hawk? If it hadn't been for Kauser and Kaukab convincing me to ignore his teenage crush on a pretty girl, I would have done something about it too.

For this morning, though, there were more pressing matters, like an important phone call I couldn't make in front of Osman while we drove to school.

"Assalamu Alaikum, Kiran. Everything okay?" Kauser answered when I called her from the privacy of my room.

I told her about my upcoming meeting and asked the question I knew she would hate answering.

"Would you like to talk to the journalist about what Asif did to you?"

"No."

Quick and curt. A single-word reply that betrayed the years of disappointment she had faced at the hands of similar journalists, none of whom had been willing to go against an influential billionaire.

"He seems like a genuine person—"

"I don't care. I've moved on. You need to forget about that night too."

She hung up before I could say anything more. Perhaps it wasn't even my place to convince her to keep revisiting her nightmares. After all, how many women had gone up against powerful men and won?

I wondered how many others like Kauser had asked themselves that same question before sitting back down quietly, forcing themselves to go on with life in the shadow of their past.

"Osman, Daniyal, Danish, hurry up. We're getting late for school," I called out to the boys.

Work for unending hours. Take care of the boys. Collapse in exhaustion. Repeat the next day.

Like Kauser, my life had to go on. But today, I saw a glimmer of hope.

SANAM

For the life of me, I couldn't remember the structure of a heart. Had Mrs. Nazim given us a lecture on matters of the heart, I might have done much better. Disappointment, betrayal, agony, abandonment, and now elation and fluttering—my heart had gone through it all in my lifetime.

None of that mattered when Osman entered the lab that morning.

"Hey, Sanam," he called out and quickly came to sit next to me, a far cry from the way he used to avoid me just a few weeks ago.

Though when I looked more closely at his drooping eyes, I had to ask, "Did you not sleep last night?"

His lips parted for a yawn before he gave me a heartwarming smile. "I'll be fine—I managed to get an hour's worth of sleep. But I have something for you."

He opened his backpack and carefully took out an object the size of a fist, covered in Bubble Wrap, and handed it to me.

"Open it." His excitement erased any signs of fatigue.

Slowly, I unwrapped the hard object and gasped when I saw what it was. "Did you make this?"

His cheeks became an obvious shade of pink, and he shrugged, looking away from me. "It's not a big deal."

How could it not be? Within my palms, I held a lifelike model of an actual heart. Made of white painted clay, the model had all the veins and arteries marked on it, as well as the major blood vessels protruding from it.

I was still shocked at the intricacies of this handmade model when he reached out and gently parted my hands, leaving me speechless at what I saw within.

"See, the heart opens up too. And you can see exactly where all the four chambers are and how the valves and blood vessels connect to them."

"You stayed up the whole night to make this?" I finally glanced up at him.

He shrugged again, and I noticed the faint red and blue paint marks on his fingers. "I thought it might help you remember the anatomy better," he said quietly.

The painfully shy Osman was back in front of me, but I didn't bother to avert my eyes from this handsome boy who never ceased to surprise me. No one had ever put in so much effort for me, let alone spent an entire night creating something to help me succeed in my upcoming exams.

This wasn't a romantic gesture—it was something much deeper, making me want to trust him with everything I had.

A humorous thought crossed my mind, and even I blushed at the idea.

"Osman, did you just give me your heart?"

Eyes rounding with confusion, he shook his head. "Umm, no. I didn't make this for myself. This is for you. To help you study."

"Okay." I bit my lip, trying not to chuckle at how cluelessly cute he was.

Warmth filled my chest as another thought occurred. Had I been wooed in the purest way possible?

I only wished I could hear him say those words to me too. Without them, all we had between us was a tacit friendship which could be interpreted in a thousand different ways.

OSMAN

We were dissecting an actual goat's heart when Mrs. Nazim snuck up behind me, startling me.

"*Mister Osman Tariq.* Why are your eyes so red? Were you out celebrating your birthday late last night? How many times have I told your sister to make sure you get a full night's rest before my class?"

Sanam raised her eyebrows. Her gaze on me sent heat creeping into my face.

"Uh, no, Mrs. Nazim, I was at home. But I promise to get enough sleep from now on," I told her, trying to ignore my lab partner.

"Boy, make sure you do. I won't have you failing my class because you're distracted," Mrs. Nazim huffed and walked away.

"I am not failing at all," I mumbled after her, making sure she couldn't hear me.

"But you are distracted?" Sanam whispered.

"Nopes," I lied.

We went back to dissecting the goat's heart in front of us. She used the scalpel to slice the organ across the horizontal plane while I helped keep the muscular tissue in place. Silence surrounded us as usual, but this time it wasn't comfortable, like something needed to be said, but the words had willingly been imprisoned.

For me, that was our preferred status. Words, once released into the universe, can never be retracted. Emotions, once enunciated, are no longer dreams—they become a reality. And the reality that I lived in was very different from that of the girl who stood next to me.

It was so different that I could tell she was desperate to release those words, whereas I was building a more fortified cage around them.

"Osman." She put down the scalpel and turned towards me.

"What?"

"Look at me."

"Yes, Mrs. Nazim?" I met her gaze and saw her frown turn into a smile.

"Oh, you've got jokes now, huh?" She laughed softly, and for a moment, I forgot the panic inside me as I found myself lost in that glorious sound. But then she took a deep breath, and the panic settled in again. I knew what her next question would be.

"Why did you spend your birthday making this model for me?"

"I just wanted to."

"Why?"

"Because . . ."

I searched for words I could say instead of telling her the truth. I wished I could have spent my eighteenth birthday with her, instead of staying in, watching yet another Netflix movie, and eating more pizza with a family that pretended my birth hadn't deprived them of a loving mother.

My mind went blank, lips frozen, nothing coming to mind except the words *I crave you when I am not with you*. Words that I could never say to her, because despite what I wanted, people like me did not end up with people like her.

Like water and oil, cats and birds, pineapples on a pizza, we made no sense together.

I stayed quiet. She gave up, her shoulders slumped, and I looked away before the disappointment in her eyes could rip through my resolve.

I am doing the right thing for her, she can do so much better than me, I placated my heart.

"Here." She slipped an object in my hand. "Consider this a birthday present."

The object was a pen with sleek, dark gray metal casing and an elaborate motif engraved on it. I held it in both my hands, turning it around, admiring the craftsmanship of this weighty and very expensive-looking pen when I noticed something.

"It has your name on it."

"I know. Dado had it specially made for my eighteenth birthday a few months ago."

"I can't take your Dado's present to you." I tried to hand it back, but she refused.

"I want to give it to you."

"Why?" I was genuinely confused.

She paused, a small smile played on her lips. "Because . . ."

That's when I realized I had lost this battle of wits to a girl as refined and complex as the pen I held in my hand.

And like a pen built to last, beneath her captivating beauty lay a quiet strength even she was unaware of, one that would hold her together when no one else could.

Not even me.

At the end of class, I opened my bag to carefully place the pen in the inner pocket and noticed the notification light blinking on my phone. Kauser Baji had forwarded a news alert to our family group chat, along with a message that said, "This is why I said no."

No to what? I had no idea. Ordinarily, I wouldn't have bothered reading the news alert in the middle of school, but the name it mentioned caught my attention.

"Sikander Ahmed, Renowned Journalist, Fighting for His Life in ICU After Hit-and-Run Incident This Morning"

Coincidence? I wondered, but quickly put that thought away. A lot of bad things happened in this world; none affected me right now.

Why would they? I was just a teenager falling in love.

CHAPTER 8

Family History

ZAIN

"Abu, did you know the Jeep has dried blood on its bumper?" I asked my father when I found him sitting in his home office on his plush leather chair behind an expansive mahogany desk.

The Jeep wasn't the car I typically used, but on that Saturday morning, Maham had asked me not to pick her up in my SUV on our way to the slum school. It made the difference between us and the local population too jarring, and she wasn't comfortable with that. The Jeep was the only car we possessed that could pass off as an older, ordinary vehicle. It would have been perfect, had it not been for the streak of blood on its bumper.

Instead of responding, my father's face twisted with anger as he bellowed for Azhar Saqlain, one of his most trusted associates. The intimidating man appeared in the office in under thirty seconds.

"Who cleaned the Jeep?" Abu scowled at the man.

"I don't know, sir. But I can find out."

"Do that. Then make sure he never walks again," my father replied, the words said with such heartless finality that I found myself silently gasping as his ruthlessness sank in.

"Whose blood was it?" I dared to ask.

Abu leaned back in his seat, his dark eyes carefully studying me before he replied, "A rabid dog's. The kind that will kill you if you don't kill them first."

"Oh yeah. I mean, no one can fault you for killing an animal in self-defense."

He smiled slowly. "Exactly my point."

Azhar appeared again, this time with news that broadened Abu's smile. "Mr. Malik from AWP is here," he announced.

Getting up from his chair, my father gestured to me. "Come on, Zain, you should get to know the man too."

"Sanam's father, Mr. Malik? Why is he here?"

He smirked. "To play a game of chess."

I knew my father well enough to realize that the chess he was referring to wasn't to be played on a checkerboard. Whatever it was though, I was in no mood to be roped into my father's plans when I had a beautiful girl waiting for me—a girl whom I had chosen myself.

"Maybe next time, Abu. I am busy today," I told him and started to back out of the room.

"You're busy?" he scoffed. "What could possibly be more important than meeting someone who is crucial to GT Enterprise's future?"

I should have asked him why he was so focused on AWP when there were plenty of other politicians willing to be bought, but under his glare, I could only whisper, "I am meeting Maham."

The disapproval on his face was instant and surprising because he had never stopped me from meeting her before. "Be a man, Zain, and stop living in some fantasy world with a girl who amounts to nothing," he said through gritted teeth.

Feeling a rare flicker of courage break through in his presence, I replied, "But, Abu, there's no one else in this world for me."

He shook his head, taking two steps forward, as his jaw ticked with restrained anger.

"You disappoint me, Zain. You have given her so much power over you that I don't even recognize you as my son anymore. You're withdrawing from classmates that will rule this country one day and hanging out with losers instead. And now, you're refusing to meet a Member of the National Assembly for that measly girl."

"She is not . . ."

"*Shut up*." My father's voice reverberated in that room, freezing me in my spot.

He stepped closer, his eyes narrowed. I felt his breath on my face as he shoved my shoulder. "That girl is making you weak. She's ruining your future. The future that"—his voice rose—"I have worked so hard to give you."

Maham was my weakness, but I didn't think she made me weak. She tamed me and showed me a future in stark contrast to my parents'. I wished I could have explained that to my father.

"I thought you were a man. But I see now that you are nothing but your mama's boy. So weak and pathetic like her."

He walked out of the room and left me reeling from his words. Had I been older or wiser, perhaps his statement would not have stung. But at eighteen, all I wanted to do was find a way to not be weak and pathetic. I had a cousin that fit that definition, and I would be damned if I let myself become him.

I called Maham and told her the slum school's principal had called about cancelling classes for the day.

"Really? How come?" she asked.

"There is a rabid dog in the area, and the kids have been told to stay at home until it's hunted and killed," I replied.

Then I went to the living room and sat quietly in the corner, listening to the adults argue about some bill drafted in the National Assembly. It was boring as hell, enough that a few minutes later, I was scrolling through the list of colleges Maham had sent me.

Thoughts of spending four years with her as a college student in the US, away from my father, became my escape in that increasingly heated room.

SANAM

What's gotten into everyone today? I wondered while walking to my first class after lunch break on that Monday morning. I was used to students looking at me, the guys even ogling me, but something seemed off today. No one said a word. There were just whispers everywhere I went.

"Sanam," a voice called out to me as I climbed the stairs. The whispers and weird looks were quickly forgotten as I turned around and saw the boy I couldn't get enough of.

"Hey, you." I smiled and stopped on the stairs to let him catch up. "I didn't see you at lunch today. I thought you were absent."

"Oh, I was here, but had extra debate practice for the tournament this evening."

"That's tonight? I can't come tonight. Dado is in the hospital." I pouted.

"Yes, Maham told me. How is she feeling now?" he asked me with so much concern that you would have thought she was his own dado.

"She's better, but still having some trouble breathing, and the doctors are not sure why."

He started to say something, but I had a better idea. Standing on the stairs outside class with the bell ringing was hardly the kind of setting in which you could have a real conversation with a boy whose words anchored your life. Besides, I was kind of getting addicted to his gentle voice that tended to get lost in the noisy hallways.

"Osman, is it okay if we continue this after school? I have to get to my class now."

"Sure. I'll be around." He gave me a smile and jogged off. But the warmth he had elicited in my heart lingered throughout that class and the next, and didn't fade away until our school's principal called me in the middle of my last class of the day.

"What's the matter, Mr. Hashim? Did I do something wrong?" I asked him nervously as soon as we were alone in his office.

"No, Sanam. You didn't. But unfortunately, I have some news for you."

My heart almost stopped. "Dado?" I whispered.

"No, no. I understand that your Dado is sick in the hospital. And I am sorry to hear that. But this is not about her."

Thank God. I breathed out in relief. Yet, the uncomfortable look that Mr. Hashim gave me as he adjusted his glasses left me confused.

"There is some press gathered outside the school today. We've cleared them away, but I suggest that you stay within the school building until the other students leave. Then we can let your car come into the school grounds, and you can head home without risk."

The press?

"Why is the press here? Did something happen?"

He stared at me for a second, as if I should have known what he was talking about.

"I guess kids don't read the news these days," he started hesitantly. "A private video of your mother and stepfather was released yesterday."

"So, what's the big deal? They're married."

I was well aware of how politics was played. A compromising video—whether real or fabricated—would be leaked to the media for leverage. While this would certainly cause another PR disaster for Mr. Malik, it had no connection to me.

But oh, how wrong I was.

"It was from eight years ago," Mr. Hashim said softly.

I blinked, my mind going numb, unable to do simple math.

"I just turned eighteen . . . Eight years ago would have been when I was . . ." I glanced at my principal, willing him to finish my sentence.

"Ten," he answered sympathetically.

I was ten? The age my father left us. Long before my mother married Mr. Malik.

"What was in the video?" I dared to ask.

"I don't know, Sanam. I purposely don't read this kind of news. They're fake half the time anyway."

His desk phone rang, and he picked it up immediately. "Yes, Mrs. Malik. She's in my office . . . yes, you can speak to her."

Mr. Hashim handed me the phone and whispered, "I'll step outside."

For a moment, I simply sat clutching on to the handset. My mother's faint voice came through the phone several times before I mustered the courage to put the handset to my ear and ask her the only question that mattered.

"Did you have an affair with Malik?"

"No," she said emphatically. "Sweetie, I did not have any affair. The press is completely misleading the public. All they have is a video of me talking with Malik in a car. That is all there is to it. It's political blackmail. Nothing else. I am sorry that you are getting dragged into it."

Remorse tinged her voice but did nothing to quell the anger that was starting to boil within me. "Why the hell were you in a car with him?"

"I had something important to tell him, and he was a friend. No different than your male friends—"

"Don't you dare bring my friends into this. I do not have the press following me, or a husband and daughter at home."

"Watch your language, young lady!" she yelled through the phone. "You have no idea what I was going through with your father back then, how hard I tried to keep that marriage alive and keep my own sanity, only for your sake."

"Let me guess. You decided to sneak around with your married male friend to vent about your husband, only to be caught by someone with a camera." I paused, waiting for her to say something.

When she didn't, I had to confirm my suspicions. "Abu saw that video, didn't he? That's why he left so abruptly."

Her remorse turned into icy bitterness. "He would have left anyway," she replied.

Betrayal. Anger. Disappointment. I wasn't sure which emotion I was supposed to feel. Perhaps numbness was the only appropriate emotion at that time.

Mama's voice broke the heavy silence. "Well, as you can imagine, this is a PR nightmare for Malik, and staying in Karachi is not the best option. So, we're leaving for Islamabad in a couple of hours. I suggest you stay at Dado's house tonight. Zaviyar will be there sometime later in the evening."

She hung up soon after, while I sat there wishing I hadn't been born.

Mr. Hashim was kind enough to let me stay in his office, but the claustrophobia was so severe that I left soon after the school dismissal bell rang. There were still plenty of students around, and their whispers and side glances were only worse now that my puffy eyes and frazzled hair made it obvious that I had been crying for the last half hour.

Before I knew it, my legs had already carried me to a place at the back of the building where I had once given an eighth grader a lollipop. Away from prying eyes, I hunkered down in a spot I had always wished I could come to.

Osman wasn't there, but his warmth still coursed through me, saving my soul from despair. His purity, the essence of my utopia, became the hope I desperately needed in my reality.

His parents had tragically died, yet I was the one who felt completely alone in the world—finding solace only in thoughts of him.

CHAPTER 9

Coffee (not) Date

OSMAN

"Maham, have you seen Sanam anywhere?"

Our mutual friend glanced around the inner courtyard. "No, but if you find her, tell her to call me. I can't imagine what she's going through, first with her grandmother and now the mess her mother has created."

Nodding, I rushed off to look for her outside again, but she wasn't anywhere to be found. The crowd of students was thinning at the end of the day, and I had almost given up when I decided to check one last place.

I never expected to find her sitting on the ground, knees pulled to her chest, leaning against the wall just as I used to. But instead of holding a book, her arms were wrapped tightly around herself, her head buried in them, and her hair falling over the sides like a curtain.

"Sanam?" I called out, but there was no response.

Crouching near her, I pulled back her wavy tresses and called her name again. This time, she woke up with a start, and I stepped back quickly.

"Don't go, please," she whispered with so much pain I couldn't have left her even if wanted to.

"I am right here, Sanam."

"You know?" she asked hesitantly.

"The stuff about your mom? Yes. I do."

"I'm not like my mother. I promise," she blurted out.

Curled up along the wall, she looked so innocent in that moment that I literally sat on my hands to prevent myself from pulling her into my arms. That was a boundary she was too vulnerable for right now, and one I wasn't sure I could stop at. I chose to comfort her in the only other way I knew of.

"You're not like your mother or anyone else I know. You're strong, courageous, honest, and trustworthy. And despite everything your family puts you through, your brilliance never dims," I uttered in one breath and meant every word of it.

She sat up straighter, and some of that ethereal light was back in her eyes. But her wet cheeks remained damp, capturing strands of the soft brown waves that framed her beautiful face, as much as they captured my heart.

In the thick silence surrounding us—watching her watch me, feeling the sorrow and grief she felt because of a life she never asked for but lived every day—something came over me, and I gave in to her. Gave in to that moment when she needed me, and I wasn't strong enough to hold back.

I wiped off her tears with my thumb, caressed the softness of her wet cheeks with my fingers, and tucked her hair behind her ear. All while I drowned in the sentiments swirling in her caramel brown eyes. "You are proof that one can be surrounded by hell and still emerge an angel, so don't ever doubt yourself."

Her lips slowly curled up, and she let out a small laugh. "Did you read that somewhere or make it up?"

"The first part was all me, the second inspired by a quote I read online. But it made me think of you when I first read it, if that counts," I admitted.

Her smile disappeared in the next moment, and she closed her eyes, cutting me off from her world temporarily until she opened them again and sighed.

"Why do you do this, Osman?"

"Do what?"

"Say things and do things that make me want you so much, then pretend like there is nothing between us?"

I froze.

I shouldn't have because God knows I wanted her with every breath I took, but she wasn't supposed to have said those words aloud. Out in the universe, they cornered me into a reckoning. They laid bare our tortured reality, forcing me to answer a question I had long avoided.

With a mere four months left till graduation, what the heck was I trying to achieve with her? Any path I took would be lined with agony, just of a different flavor.

The gentle rustle of leaves and the chirping of birds were the only sounds that filled the void between us, left gaping by a question I had no answer for. The longer I waited, the deeper the chasm became, and so I tried to speak.

"Sanam, I . . ."

She got up, avoiding my gaze as she said, "It's okay. I didn't expect an answer."

It was cowardly of me not to address the nebulous cloud of unsaid words and unfulfilled desires we had found ourselves in the last few weeks. Yet, what she and I had, as undefined as it was, was too precious for me to get it wrong. I needed time to get it right, and at that moment she gave me an out that I quickly took.

"Where are you going?" I asked, getting up as well.

"To Dado's home."

Her voice trailed as she almost sprinted away from me, into the inner courtyard of the school and then out into the front field where a Range Rover with black tinted windows and burly men with curled mustaches and AR-15s slung on their shoulders waited for her.

"Who are these people?" I inquired.

"Extra security that my mother thought I would need since there won't be anyone at Dado's house this evening."

Grabbing her arm, I stopped her from walking any further. "Are you going to be alone at Dado's home?"

Clearly, this was not her first time, because she casually shrugged her shoulders. "My chauffeur's wife is at home, and I think Zavi Chachoo arrives around nine this evening."

She thinks? The lack of a secure plan made me nervous, even though I had no control over it. Perhaps I would have been able to ignore my angst if I hadn't noticed the way one of the younger guards was assessing her with narrowed eyes, following her every move, creeping me out.

Nopes, she is not staying alone, I decided.

"Hey, why don't we go somewhere and have coffee? I think we need to talk."

"Don't you have a debate tournament?"

Oops. I had forgotten that minor detail.

"It's okay. Maham can take my place. If not her, we have two other extra students on the team as well."

Reluctant at first, she finally gestured for me to follow her into the car. I took a quick survey of the grounds, making sure my sister wasn't anywhere to be seen.

"Do you want to let Ms. Kiran know?" Sanam asked as we left the school premises.

"No. I'll tell her later."

She'd skin me alive either way. Might as well delay the torture.

SANAM

It's only coffee, I told myself repeatedly.

Though, how could I not be nervous? The last hour had been the clearest indication yet that I meant something to the boy sitting next to me.

We drove in silence to a coffee shop ten minutes from school. In that time, I couldn't stop replaying his words and reminiscing about that tingling sensation when his warm fingers met my heated cheeks.

We ordered coffees, like I would have with any other friend, except he paid for them even though I offered. Then we sat in comfortable chairs in the corner, like I had so many times before. But nothing was the same. Not the way we explored each other's pasts and discussed our academic futures, or the awkward pauses in between when we realized just how different our paths would be in the next few months.

"I would stay in Pakistan for my undergrad if I could. But when Abu agreed to pay for my college, he insisted it had to be in the US. I think he assumes Mama will siphon off any money that he sends here."

That agreement between my parents included Mama suing Abu in a US court for child support, a case that had dragged on for years and only concluded recently, in time for college applications. As the owner of an indie movie production house in Houston, Texas, money had never been the problem for my father. I suspected that I was—the same way I had always been a problem for my mother.

"At least he agreed," Osman said, voicing what was on my mind. Without Abu's money, Mama would have made me go to a local art school and then into showbiz like her. A path I had no intention of pursuing.

"I don't have to declare a major yet, but I have always been fascinated by psychology. Maybe that will help me understand why my family is so crazy." I tried to laugh it off, but the solemn expression on Osman's face didn't change.

"I've always wanted to do medicine, but I can't afford to go to the US to do that," he admitted.

Therein lay our problem. In four short months, we would likely be on opposite ends of the world pursuing dreams we had dreamt before we became lab partners. Dreams that hadn't included each other.

He looked at me, his hazel eyes filled with despair. "Sanam, I didn't mean to ignore the question you asked me earlier. I just don't know what to do."

The dilemma was obvious, but I wasn't ready to give up. "Maybe we make the most of the time we do have left together."

He gazed off into the distance for the next few moments before quietly destroying any hope that I had let seep into my heart.

"What's the point of starting something we can't finish?" he said slowly, like he was trying to soften the blow of what he was about to say. "Our paths are so different, as are the things we want to achieve. I think we owe it to ourselves to tread our paths alone—to grow and become the people we have always wanted to become before we get together."

He glanced at me, and even as he doused my fire with ice-cold words, I recognized the sincerity in his voice.

"In the meantime, I promise I will always be here for you. Even if we stay just friends."

OSMAN

I didn't even have to look at her to sense the disappointment she was feeling, but what was I supposed to do? Date her for four months and then say goodbye?

Besides, who knew what the future held for us? Out in the world, she could certainly find someone better than me. Did it really make sense, then, for a couple of eighteen-year-olds to decide their fate sitting in a coffee shop?

"Osman, what are you doing here? We were so worried about you." A familiar voice interrupted the tense silence, making me realize how late into the evening it was.

"Oh, hey, Maham. Sorry, I should have let you guys know. How was the debate?" I glanced at our friend, who was staring at us, wide-eyed and confused.

"We won. But forget about that." She broke out into a grin. "Please tell me you two are finally going out."

"No. We're *just* friends," Sanam answered bluntly, rising from her seat. For the second time, she hurried away from me.

"Sanam, wait." She didn't stop.

I caught up to her as she stepped outside the glass door of the coffee shop. She spun around to face me, her eyes brimming with anger and unshed tears. My heart ached for her, but I had no words to offer comfort, and she did not mince hers.

"I am not going to beg you for affection or a relationship, Osman. You know what we have is enough to last us a lifetime. But if you're too much of a coward to fight for it, then so be it. I've been on my own for years—I don't need you now."

"I'm so sorry." My voice caught.

"So am I," she said as she wiped her eyes, backing away from me.

And I let her, without a word or an attempt to stop her. I ruminated on her words as I stood watching the girl who meant everything to me sit in a car and drive away. She was right. I was a coward for putting the promise I had made to my sister, my studies, my career, my future—all above her.

"Where did she go?" Maham came to stand next to me. This time, Zain was with her, much to my chagrin.

"I don't know. Could you call her? She's going to be alone at home this evening, and I don't want her to be."

"We can go be with her if she wants, but what the hell did you do now?" Zain answered for Maham.

Yet today, I deserved it—her anger and that of her friends. I deserved to be called a wimp or sissy or useless or any other name Zain could come up with.

I swallowed the bile rising to the back of my throat. "I think I broke her heart."

KIRAN

My frantic search for Osman led me to the coffee shop where his debate coach said he had just seen him. He had skipped the debate tournament after prepping for it for weeks, and then disappeared without calling me or picking up the phone when I left dozens of messages.

With Sikander Ahmed's near-fatal incident still fresh in my mind, the worst-case scenarios had seemed almost certain as I called his friends and our family. Even Kaukab and Kauser were out looking for him. So, imagine how my blood boiled when I saw him standing outside the coffee shop, talking to the one girl I had warned him to stay away from.

But the closer I got, the heavier my steps became. Their voices didn't reach me, yet I could see the agony on their young faces. It was the unmistakable pain of letting go of someone against your will. All I could do was stand still as my baby brother watched her drive away, and my heart shattered for him and the choice he had been forced to make.

I let him finish talking to Maham and Zain, a couple whose relationship stood in stark contrast to his, before I walked closer, and he noticed me.

"Api, I know I messed up. But please don't be angry at me right now."

"I am not angry." I hugged him tightly, my anger completely melting away. "I am proud of you, Osman. You did the right thing—for her and for yourself."

"Then why does it hurt so much?" His voice croaked.

"Because what you have is real."

It was real for both of them. I had no doubt about that now. These two teenagers had found something that even adults have difficulty finding: a soulmate. My own life's history was a testament to that.

He slumped onto the dusty steps in front of the coffee shop, and muttered, "She hates me."

I sat down next to him. "I don't think she could ever hate you, Osman. But if something is meant to happen between you two, it will, however long it takes or wherever in the world you are."

"I hope so, Api, because . . ." His eyes dampened. "I think I am in love with her."

With my arms around him, he let out soft sobs against my shoulder. Nothing in the world could have prepared me for this moment. Not the baby books I had read when he was born, nor the online parenting groups I had joined as he grew older.

There was no manual with instructions on how to fix a young man's heart when he himself had been forced to break it.

SANAM

Zavi Chachoo had managed to catch an earlier flight, so I went to pick him up from the airport straight from the coffee shop, and then we went to see Dado at the hospital. Which was just as well, because I desperately needed a distraction, and Chachoo's dad jokes were perfect for that.

But it didn't last long. I broke down while we were sitting in front of the TV. When he asked if I was excited about moving abroad for college, I couldn't hold back the tears. He listened quietly, as always, letting me sob on his shoulder and release all my painful emotions about Mama and Abu, but mostly about Osman.

"Do you want me to go beat him up?" Zavi Chachoo asked, only half-jokingly.

"No. I have a feeling he is already beating himself up right now."

The emotional teenager in me hated him. After opening my heart to someone for the first time since Abu left, his rejection burned my soul. Yet, I had to admit, he had never given me a reason to doubt his intentions.

"I wish someone would choose me first, you know," I confessed to Chachoo the real reason why it hurt so much. Right or wrong, I had lost to his career, just like I always lost to my mother's career, her husband, or my father's new family.

No one ever chose me.

"You know, kiddo, sometimes one has to choose themselves first before someone else can. You are a smart and independent young woman. You don't need a boy to shine in this world. You, by yourself, will always be enough." He smiled and patted my cheek.

Those words, and reruns of the latest cricket match while we ate bowls of ice cream slathered with chocolate sauce, were enough of a bandage to make me feel a little less broken and a little more self-confident. Perhaps Osman had been speaking the truth, as bitter as it had been. I was responsible for forging my own path and shaping my own destiny, just as he was.

Maybe the best way to convince him that we belonged together was to first be the best version of myself that I could become.

The late-night news came on TV, and Mama's name was mentioned almost immediately.

"MNA Malik Imtiaz and his wife, the prominent actress Shabnam Murad, are embroiled in yet another scandal. We bring you the latest update on this and other news from around the country after the break."

Chachoo was frowning and frantically dialing a number on his phone when I asked the obvious. "How did this make the headlines? I thought Mr. Malik's PR team was handling it."

Whoever he was calling seemed to have picked up, and the two had a tense discussion before he hung up and replied to me.

"I don't know. But first, it was the fake news about him beating up a taxi driver, and now the leaking of this tape that I was sure we had destroyed when he married your mother. Someone is out to get Malik."

Chachoo didn't elaborate further. I usually kept out of politics and certainly out of my mother's personal life, but something seemed amiss to me now.

"Why would someone have a problem with him? Your party is not even the ruling party right now."

"That is true, but AWP has a strong backing among the public these days, and our popularity is only growing. If the projected numbers are correct, the next government will be a coalition, and we'll be able to negotiate placing our people in several ministries. Malik is popular because he has always been a man of principle in the political arena, as messed up as his personal life is right now."

Things were starting to make sense to me. I remembered him and my mother talking about how he had single-handedly led the land reform bill a couple of years ago and managed to get it passed in the National Assembly with a slim majority. He was now set to work on the tax reform bill.

"Has he ruffled the feathers of someone important in the business world, or maybe some feudal lord who is uber rich?"

"That is my guess. There are very few people in this country who have pockets deep enough to wield this kind of influence over the news channels, despite all our efforts to the contrary."

His phone rang, and he put it on speaker. Mr. Malik was on the line.

"I am telling you, Asif Ghazanfar is behind this. I went to meet him this weekend—"

Chachoo slapped his forehead. "Now why the heck would you do that?"

"Because we cannot show these people that we are afraid of them."

"Well, congrats. I guess you showed him, and now your scandal is on national TV."

Chachoo's sarcasm, and the political drama unfolding in front of me, was entertaining enough to temporarily forget about the boy who had broken my heart in a coffee shop.

"Don't worry—it'll blow over. Otherwise, we can always tell the press why Shabnam and I were meeting that day."

Suddenly, Chachoo took Mr. Malik off speakerphone and walked out of the room, but not before I caught part of his conversation.

"You think this is funny? If Zak's history comes out . . ."

That was all I heard before Chachoo was out of earshot, leaving me to wonder if they were talking about Zak, as in Zakariya, my biological father.

What exactly had he done?

CHAPTER 10

Goodbye

ZAIN

Today was officially the last day of high school. It should have been a day of triumph and jubilation. After thirteen long years of schooling, we were finally graduating. Yet, I hadn't been able to sleep last night, just like I hadn't for most other nights this month.

To everyone else, the dullness in my eyes was due to a newfound aptitude for studying. In reality, I lay awake at night, replaying the argument I had had with my father a month ago.

"Have you figured out housing on campus?" I asked Maham over the phone while sitting in our TV lounge at home.

"Why? Are you planning to stay in the same dorm as me?" She giggled, and I wished I could see the crimson color creeping into her cheeks.

"Uh, where else would I live? Someone has to protect you from all those college men," I teased.

"You don't have to worry . . ." she was saying when I felt a hand snatch my phone. Before I could react, it went flying across the room.

"*Are you out of your fucking mind?*" my father yelled. "*You're going to some third-rate community college because of that low-life, useless girl?*"

"*Abu!*" I raised my voice, afraid Maham would hear him.

"*Speak respectfully.*" He gritted his teeth.

"*You need to speak respectfully about Maham. She . . .*"

Suddenly, his hand struck my face, and darkness swallowed me whole. Words faltered as my mouth hung open while I struggled to process what had happened.

Abu had slapped me—for the first time in my life. Though the man I saw standing in front of me was not my father. Neither were his words, nor was the hatred pouring from his dark eyes.

"*I love her, Abu.*" *It was meant to be forceful; it came out as a whimper.*

"*UMass is not a community college. It's a really good public university. Her father teaches there too,*" *I tried to argue.*

His anger only swelled at that, and he grabbed my collar, shoving me against the wall. I was a few inches taller than him, but the rage in his eyes paralyzed me.

"*I don't care what kind of a university it is. You are not going to be anywhere near that gold-digging girl and her family.*"

He let go of my collar and stepped back, but his glaring eyes never left mine. "*I should have known that is why you insisted on applying to universities in Boston. Not anymore, though. You're going to California. End of discussion.*"

He stormed out of the room, with me on his heels. "*California? Abu, that is the opposite end of the country.*"

"*So?*" *He suddenly stopped and swung around to face me.* "*I have put up with this nonsense of yours long enough. I will not have my son be with the daughter of some beggar professor.*"

"*We are in love,*" *I repeated.*

He walked closer to me, poking me in the shoulder, his dark eyes searing into mine. Slowly, menacingly, he spoke, making my heart sink with every word. "She is not in love with you. No one could love a failing asshole like you. Maham is only in love with your inheritance. She will leave you as soon as she gets her hands on it."

"That's not true," I whispered. "She said she loves me."

He grabbed me by the collar and dragged me to the mirror above the side table in our hallway. "Look at yourself. Who in their right mind would love a coward like you? She is a beautiful girl, and men will be lining up to get a piece of her. Why would she stay with you then?"

His voice, a harsh whisper in my ear, was enough to sow the seeds of doubt.

He was right about one thing. She could do so much better than me. Despite trying, I sucked at my studies, and I wasn't articulate or sophisticated like her. And when I did look in the mirror, I saw a scared little boy pretending to be a man, with unkempt hair and unruly stubble. A boy who was not worthy of a beautiful girl's love.

Yet, I couldn't bear to be without her. I needed her like she was the life jacket keeping me afloat, an oxygen mask helping me breathe, the very essence of my beating heart. Without her, I would wither and die.

Abu let go of me, but the cadence of his threatening voice did not change as he sealed my fate. "You will go to the University of Los Angeles because that is the only university I will pay for. And if you dare to defy my orders, you yourself will pay in ways you can't even imagine."

That evening, my father handed me beer, told me to man up, and shoved a file in front of me. "Sign these," he said. "If you can defy me like an adult, you can take care of your own property and pay for college like an adult too."

At eighteen, nursing a despondent heart and a numb mind, I never asked which property he was talking about. Neither did I read those papers before signing them.

Rookie mistake, one might say. But under the weight of my cowardice, nothing else had mattered. I had failed Maham, and I could never forgive myself for that.

Neither could I tell her the truth. Instead, I made up an excuse about wanting to change my courses and ULA being the best school for them.

But dozens of sleepless nights later, I gathered the courage to make things right with her.

My father may hold all the cards when it came to my life, but this was *our* life—mine and Maham's. And I wasn't about to give up on us that easily. I was going to make sure we would be together, even if we were apart.

The small box with a glistening piece of jewelry would seal my relationship with her. It wasn't made of diamonds, but for now, it would have to do.

Tonight is going to be the night, I told myself one last time.

At the seniors' graduation party, I was determined to follow through with my plan. Though, I would need a friend, and despite our differences, I knew who to call.

"Hey, Sanam, I need your help."

SANAM

"Maham, you look stunning!"

She had stepped out of my dressing room, wearing a midnight-blue chiffon lehenga adorned with light sequins and sterling-colored embroidery—perfect for one of the biggest nights of her life. A surprise, one that only I and her boyfriend knew about.

That was one call I had never expected. Zain, the literal definition of a playboy until two years ago, was ready to settle down with a girl just because she was going to spend the next four years on the other side of the country from him. That, too, at the age of eighteen, no less.

Had I tried to talk him out of it? Of course, but the guy was adamant, and so clearly in love with Maham, that I reluctantly gave up.

So, now I stood in my room, helping my friend get ready for the senior's graduation party with an 80s theme, while trying to ignore my own heartache.

"Do you think I should straighten my hair or leave the curls?" Maham asked, thankfully, before my mind could get diverted by the boy whose call I was desperate for but never received.

"Leave the curls. I think Zain likes them."

She smiled. "You're right. He does really like them."

Silence descended on the room as I applied my own makeup, something subtle to match the light pink lehenga I was wearing. But the void that came with it was enough to bring back the crushing feeling in my chest, like I was losing something tonight, even though it might never have been mine to begin with.

Yet, at least I still saw him in lab and heard his friendly voice, even exchanged a tortured glance.

After tonight, Dado was moving to Islamabad to live with Zavi Chachoo. As expected, AWP had done exceptionally well in the elections, and Chachoo was now the finance minister of the new coalition government. Given her health issues and Chachoo's busy schedule, he had argued that leaving Dado alone in Karachi was a terrible idea. Mama had already moved back to Islamabad after Mr. Malik was re-elected as well. Thus, I was left with no choice but to follow the rest of my family.

It's not like I have anything keeping me in Karachi, or in Pakistan for that matter, I thought bitterly.

Maham's hand squeezed mine. "You know, he loves you too."

"Who?"

"The boy you're thinking about."

No, he doesn't. I shook my head. "I wasn't thinking about anyone."

"Yes, you were." She smiled. "You wear your heart on your sleeve just like Osman does. I am sorry it didn't work out now, but that doesn't mean it won't in the future."

Maham pulled me in for a hug. And once again, I was fighting back tears, hoping for the impossible.

"Come on, let's forget about those damn boys and finish getting ready. Tonight is about *us*," she said warmly.

For her sake, I nodded, telling myself that her night would only get better, and I had no right to bring my misery into it.

"Exactly. After midnight, we are no longer high school students. That's something we did all by ourselves, and it's worth celebrating!"

"That's my girl." Maham laughed.

For the remainder of that evening, those were the words I kept repeating to myself.

I was worth celebrating, with or without the handsome boy I deliberately avoided, because even a glimpse of his tall self in an off-white shalwar kurta made my heart race. Besides, there was plenty to keep me occupied between marveling at how the juniors had transformed the school's drab courtyard into a tastefully decorated party venue and keeping Zain from losing his cool as we waited for the main events of the night to die down.

"What if she says no?" he asked in a low, shaky voice when Maham went to use the restroom after dinner was over and the closing remarks of the evening were being made by our principal.

I tried to reassure him. "She loves you. If she says no, it's only because of our age. Don't take it to heart, okay?"

"Okay. I know this is crazy, but I can't let her be away from me without doing this first." The poor guy breathed heavily, and I actually felt sorry for him.

By now, the music was blaring. Some people were dancing off in the corner, while others had started to head out.

In the thinned crowd, I saw Maham walking back towards us as we stood at the exact spot she and Zain had first met, almost two years ago.

"Now is your chance. Take a breath and say what you have to."

He nodded. I whispered, "Good luck," and moved away from them with my phone camera ready to capture their moment.

Zain took her hand as she approached him. People began to notice them as he started speaking. Murmurs and gasps filled the air around me. Despite feeling awkward, I stood still, determined to support my friend regardless of her decision.

"Maham, the second I saw you, I knew you were special. And every minute I have spent with you since then has only made me realize how much I love you and need you in my life. I know we're young, and I am skipping a whole bunch of steps here, but before we go our separate ways to college, I need to ask you something."

He got down on one knee. Maham's hand flew to her mouth. He held out a silver ring with a string of zircons embedded into it. Her glistening eyes widened. Speechless and frozen in place, she looked like a princess in a fairytale.

"Will you marry me?" he whispered, choking back his emotions.

Her eyes darted to me, then to him, then back to me again. I gave her a reluctant smile, not knowing what else to do. Perhaps that was enough to convince her, or she had already made up her mind, because in the next moment, tears streamed down her face, and she nodded.

Cheers erupted around us, mostly from the students.

The teachers were stunned. The school's strict no-PDA rule had never accounted for a proposal, leaving them awkwardly exchanging glances, unsure whether to intervene, end the celebration, or counsel their barely-graduated students.

I paid no attention to them. My concern tonight wasn't Zain and Maham's future. My task was to capture their present moment. Panning across the courtyard, I recorded the excited squeals of our classmates, the nervous whispers of the adults, and finally, the shocked face of a boy in an off-white shalwar kurta, who stood alone.

His gaze locked onto me as I lowered my phone. My breath hitched at the sight of him. He ran his fingers through his hair, his lips parting as if to speak before he hesitated. Yet, it was his eyes that captivated me the most.

Guilt. Regret. Or a desire unknown. I had no clue which emotions they held. Perhaps they simply questioned the unfolding events. Whatever it was, I knew I would drown in them again, even from a distance.

Save yourself, my conscience whispered.

Maham was busy showing her ring to a couple of smiling teachers, while a horde of boys gathered around Zain. Neither seemed like they needed me. So, I walked away—from the courtyard, from the celebration, from the boy who had turned his back on me.

Yet, it seemed like I had refused to learn my lesson, because I found myself in the same spot as I had the day he had taken me to the coffee shop. That corner's solitude spoke to me again. My body went limp as soon as my back hit the wall of the building, and I slid down to sit on the floor, gathering my light pink lehenga, now covered in dust.

Be strong, Sanam.

Put yourself first, like he did.

You don't need him.

My brain reminded itself of the vow I had made, while my heart put up barriers around itself. With arms wrapped around my body, I willed my eyes to not show any weakness. I would have succeeded, too, in my brazen attempt to forget him, had it not been for the soft sound of approaching footsteps and the rustle of cotton clothes, or the boy who sat down next to me, his body's heat pulsing between us, even from a foot away.

Why must he torture me? Agony tensed every muscle in my body.

"Sorry, I am in your spot. I'll leave." I started to get up.

He grabbed my wrist, pulling me down again. "Stay, please. It's not just my spot," he said, his voice thick with mysterious emotions.

A feeble protest left my lips. "I can't be near you."

Despite my every attempt, the barriers around my heart were disintegrating with each passing second his fingers claimed my skin, leaving me deathly afraid of my own vulnerability in front of him.

A vulnerability he was wholly unaware of when he whispered again—so quietly, I was convinced what I heard was my imagination or the wind rustling the leaves.

"I will marry you one day."

My head jerked towards him. *What?*

He let go of me, and his gaze went off into the distance. A tormented sigh escaped his lips, mirroring my own shuddering breaths.

"What?" I asked aloud, hesitantly.

He took a sharp breath and raised his voice ever so slightly.

"As soon as I make something of myself, I'll ask you to marry me, and I'll send my family to yours." His hand gestured towards the courtyard. "I'll even go down on my knee at a fancy place, if you want . . ."

Finally, he faced me, and I recognized the emotions swirling in his eyes. A desire, a passion, a fire so intense it burned for the both of us.

"But right now, in case my intentions weren't clear, I am telling you that one day, I *will* marry you."

Stray strands were tucked behind my ear. His fingers withdrew quickly, but his tender gaze lingered on me.

"If you agree to marry me, that is," he said with a small smile.

"Of course, I agree."

The words slipped out before I could control my frenzied brain or even release the breath still caged in my chest.

Then, there was silence. Achingly beautiful silence engulfed us in that dim corner of the school. We sat apart, hands to ourselves, eyes modestly averted, breathing in tandem. But distance meant nothing when our souls were enraptured with each other, our destinies already entangled.

We sat there, sinking into the depths of our unspoken emotions. We weren't just two lab partners, or friends and acquaintances anymore. We were a promise to each other, our present a commitment to our future.

I stole a glance at him, fighting the urge to reach out and trace the profile of his handsome face and run my fingers through his mop of dark hair. I wished I could move a bit closer and feel his warmth encase me, his scent enthrall me, his fingers lock into mine.

But I didn't. For our time hadn't yet come.

One day, it will, I told myself. I could believe that with all my heart now. *One day, I'll be his wife, and he my husband. And we will build a life together.*

That realization was maddening, enlightening, and unimaginable all at the same time.

"Osman, to be clear, did we just agree to marry each other?" I had to ask once my thudding heart slowed down, wondering if all this was a dream, or if I was misreading him again.

"Yes, I think we just did." He chuckled. "Or at least, you agreed to wait for me to become less of a coward."

"Sorry about that," I replied sheepishly.

It had been said in anger, but reality had sunk in pretty quickly too. We both needed to grow up and experience life before we committed to a relationship. Zain and Maham may have spurred Osman to say what he did, and while we both wished the best for them, it was clear—we were not them.

"To each their own, I guess," Osman shrugged as we walked back to the courtyard.

Maham was still busy talking to some of her girlfriends, but Zain walked up to us as soon as he saw me.

"Thanks, Sanam. I really owe you one," he told me, ignoring Osman.

I was going to mention that, when I heard Osman say, "Congrats, Zain."

Equally unexpectedly, Zain replied, "Thanks, man."

He even extended his hand and added, "Also—I am sorry for being such a jerk all these years. I hope we can start over one day."

Osman didn't hesitate to reciprocate that gesture. Maham walked over, and we exchanged a look of relief. As friends, nothing could be worse than the boys in our lives being mortal enemies.

That night, the four of us stood under the starry sky, naïvely assuming that life could only get better as we stepped into adulthood. We were with the people we cared most about, ready to embark on life's great adventures.

Little did we know that our lives were nothing but a facade, lulling us into a false sense of security. Like the artificial lights illuminating the darkness of the night sky, the joyous moments we had forged for ourselves were temporary, only serving to provoke the evil that lurked in our shadows.

Zain and Maham knew they had an uphill battle convincing their parents of their decision. With a final goodbye to us, they headed out, leaving me standing alone with Osman.

"I hate goodbyes," I admitted out loud.

"Me too," Osman replied solemnly at first, before warmth permeated his hazel eyes. "That's why we'll say 'Allah Hafiz.' May Allah always protect you—that's a prayer, not a goodbye."

This was why I was willing to give my life to him. There wasn't a moment when he wasn't there to comfort me—with his words, his actions, his mere presence.

"Allah Hafiz, Sanam," he said softly.

"Allah Hafiz, Osman," I replied with a smile and turned to walk away when I heard him call out again.

"Hey, I still have your pen, the one Dado gave you. Do you want it back?"

"No, it was my gift to you. Keep it," I told him. I had plenty of other gifts from her and wanted him to have something of mine, as a keepsake, if nothing else.

I, too, had something from him that was securely packed in my bag, but the cheeky romantic in me wondered if he would answer my question differently now than the first time he had given it to me.

"I still have your heart that you gave to me in bio. Do you want that back?"

"No." He slowly shook his head, his gaze never leaving mine, inducing those all too familiar butterflies. This time, he had taken the bait.

"My heart is yours to keep, forever."

And mine is yours, forever.

New Beginnings

OSMAN

The red brick buildings of Karachi Medical Center's college campus loomed in front of me as I walked towards them with a mix of excitement and apprehension. My brand-new clothes and the backpack slung over my shoulder were an attempt to make me look the part of a student who could afford to be at this private medical school. Yet, I only had to glance at the vehicles my classmates were arriving in as I stepped off the public bus at the gate to know that I was never going to fit in with this crowd either. No different than high school.

"Osman Tariq," I replied to a woman who handed me a name tag.

"Please put your phone on silent," she said, ushering me in.

If I had felt small and insignificant before, the large auditorium, with its high ceiling, recessed lighting, dark wood-paneled walls, and maroon carpet, was utterly overwhelming. I found my seat according to my student number, and soon, Dr Ali Nadir, the dean of the medical college, appeared on stage and began his welcoming address.

"You are the cream of the cream," his voice echoed through the auditorium as wide-eyed medical students listened. "You are the future of this country. We expect you to lead in biomedical excellence . . ."

The intensity of his speech was interrupted by someone giggling next to me. A woman with gray eyes whispered to her friend, "I got lost on my way to the bathroom. Not sure I'm fit to lead anyone."

At least people here had a sense of humor.

During introductions, we were asked to say our name, the city we grew up in, and a fun fact about ourselves. A young man stood up in the front row, his back stiff like a rod, and said, "I am Faisal Bangash, son of Adil Bangash, jagirdar from Khyber Pakhtunkhwa. I am an expert marksman and horseback rider."

The woman beside me continued her whispered commentary. "Oh, just shoot me dead. Do we really have to spend the next five years with Genghis Khan?" she said to her friend, who burst out laughing.

Dean Nadir frowned in our direction. I leaned away from her. She sank into her seat.

Finally, it was my turn. "I am Osman Tariq. I grew up in Karachi and was part of my school's debate team, which won the Sindh debate tournament this year."

Next spoke the girl beside me. "Ameerah Sheikh, also from Karachi. And my recent fun activity was learning how to drive. So, watch out, oh people of this city."

Laughter rang through the auditorium, and the woman settled into her seat, a smug smile on her face. As the rest of the students in our row introduced themselves, she leaned towards me and whispered, "Hey, you know when they said 'something fun,' they didn't mean things like debates. There must be something else you did recently."

"I promised someone I would make something of myself," I replied, hoping she'd keep quiet after that.

She shook her head. "Jeez, so boring."

Her gaze fell on my hand. "Nice pen."

"It is." I smiled. *Given to me by a beautiful girl with a breathtaking soul.*

SANAM

Texas University, Houston campus.

I read the brass letters etched into the brick wall as we drove onto the bustling campus grounds.

"This is Smith Hall," the cab driver announced, pulling up in front of the three-story building where I'd be spending my freshman year. The area was teeming with students and their parents. Everywhere I looked, people were hauling boxes, luggage, and bags, the excitement and chaos of move-in day buzzing despite the hot and humid weather.

Must be nice to have parents, I thought bitterly.

"Tussi fikr na karo. Main isanu upar lai javanga," the Indian cab driver said to me in Punjabi and took my luggage out of the trunk. (You don't worry. I'll take this upstairs.)

I had landed in Houston, the city where Abu lived, but there was no one to pick me up from the airport. Naïvely, I had expected him to be there when I sent him my itinerary. Yet, I should have known better when he never even bothered replying.

"Bohat shukriya," I told him. (Thank you very much.)

"No worries. You're like my daughter." He smiled graciously before insisting on giving me a discount.

How lucky his child must be, I couldn't help thinking.

A voice called out when I reached my floor. "Hey, are you my new roommate, San—something?"

I glanced around to see a girl with forest-green eyes and auburn hair standing in the doorway of a dorm room.

"It's Sun-um," I vocalized my name. "Are you Alice?"

"I sure am." She gave me a wide smile and introduced her friend. "This is Yasmin—she goes by Yas. Her family is originally from Pakistan too."

Both girls were native Houstonians with plenty of advice about campus and the surrounding areas. As they helped me settle in, I intermittently checked my phone, hoping to see a reply from the three people I had texted when I had reached my dorm.

Only one had replied so far.

Zavi Chachoo: Good to know, beta. Dado sends her love. Did you get in touch with your father?

I didn't reply to him. How does one tell their uncle that his brother hates his own child? It would require letting yourself feel the pain of being unloved by a man responsible for your birth.

No, I told myself, *I will not wallow in pain. I am here to study and make something of myself, and that is all I am going to do.*

That night, I glanced again at my phone for the last time before closing my eyes.

There was still no reply from my mother. Perhaps that should not have surprised me. She often didn't reply to my texts even when we were in the same time zone.

What truly hurt was the last text I had sent that was still unread on WhatsApp.

Me: I miss you.

Silence—once intriguing, then comfortable, almost reverent in Osman's presence, now felt like an abyss. A vacant darkness within my soul.

I will marry you one day. My mind reminded the despondent soul of his words. Six words, one heartfelt promise. Whispered to me, to himself, and to the silence that surrounded us that night. Words I needed to trust as I lay in bed while he was probably rushing about his day.

He needed space to grow. I needed him to survive.

I made a choice and clicked on my message to him—chose "delete for everyone"—and typed another message.

Me: Settled in dorm room. My class schedule is horrifying. Hope your first day is going well.

ZAIN

I was walking towards baggage claim at Los Angeles International Airport (LAX) when my phone rang. It was Maham, with whom I had flown to Boston a week prior.

She asked about my flight, and I filled her in on the mess caused by ULA's admissions office. "They somehow enrolled me in twice as many courses as I was supposed to take, and I had to request withdrawals from the extra ones."

"How did that happen?" she asked, as confused as I had been.

"No idea. Abu had even paid for all of them. But thankfully, he will get refunded."

Our pleasant conversation took a darker turn when her voice filled with trepidation and she asked, "Did you let Uncle and Aunty know you've landed?"

She had good reason to be anxious about my father. The chill of his eerie silence at our engagement's announcement, his deadpan eyes, the calm detachment from me in the days before the two of us moved to the US, unnerved me too.

On the face of it, the outcome of my proposal to Maham should have been a simple one.

He had lost. I had won.

Yet, that's not what it felt like in the brief amount of time I had spent in his presence since the night of our school's farewell party. He had given in too easily, when he was never one to give in without a fight. That night, there had been no loud curses, no threats to pull my college funds—simply a cold acceptance of Maham standing next to me.

"You will not go to the same college as her," was all he had said, much to my reluctant relief, before turning around and leaving us standing alone in the massive foyer of my house.

My mother simply nodded, submitting as usual to her husband's whims.

"No, I haven't called Ami or Abu yet. But I will as soon as I reach my dorm," I replied, while wheeling my bags towards the taxi stand at LAX.

"Okay. I hope he comes around," Maham sighed, and I wished I could soothe her nerves, or just be with her at that moment, but words of reassurance were my only option.

"Don't worry about my father. You have me. You'll never need anyone else."

I alone will always be enough for her, I told myself.

Her father's voice sounded in the background. "Is that Zain?" he asked, and Maham handed him the phone.

"Assalamu Alaikum, Uncle."

"Walaikum Assalam, beta Zain. How was the flight? Hope the immigration officers didn't bother you."

His cheery voice was in sharp contrast to my father's. No different than it had been on the day Maham and I had called her parents. Not only were they supportive, they were ecstatic. Instead of icy indifference, there was talk of the timing of a wedding.

Before we moved to the US, they came to Karachi and arranged a grand engagement party—fit for the son of a billionaire.

Ami came with me. Abu refused. Or, as Ami and I told the Qureshis, he was on an international business trip.

"Did you thank your mother for the gifts? She didn't have to send them at all."

She hadn't sent them. I had—a Rolex for Uncle and a bracelet made of rubies for Aunty. For now, it had been enough to convince them that at least my mother had accepted our relationship.

"I did. She sent her salaam," I lied.

When Maham came back on the line, she had something to thank me for too. "You really didn't have to get me a new phone."

"A new life calls for a new phone, sweetheart."

I heard her soft chuckle, and my chest tightened, wishing I wasn't so far away from her.

"What are your plans for the evening?" I asked.

"I am going out with a couple of my old friends for ice cream."

"Will there be any guys?" I frowned.

"No. Why?"

"What time will you go and where?" I asked her, noting down her response.

"Probably, around 9-9:30. And we're going to Molly's Cold Treats. Why all the questions, Zain?"

"I want you to be safe."

That's exactly what I told myself again when I pulled up an app on my phone at 6 p.m.—9 p.m. in Boston. She didn't leave her parent's house till an hour later, though she did head straight to Molly's. I kept checking my phone until the little red dot on my app hovered over her parent's place once again, at close to 11 p.m. EST.

Some might call me an obsessed lover, but I was just an ordinary man, ruined by her love. A love that I did not deserve but was prepared to protect with my life, even if it meant walking through hell.

See, Abu, you did lose. And I won.

PART TWO

Three summers and we all grew up.

CHAPTER 12

Dado

SANAM

It was the beginning of my fourth year of college when I got a call from Zavi Chachoo one evening while I was in the library, buried in my senior-year studies.

"Sanam, I don't want to alarm you, but Ami isn't feeling well," he said.

He insisted there was nothing to worry about, but with the sound of machines beeping in the background and overhead announcements calling for doctors, his location was obvious. Though it was the finality, a quiet acceptance in his voice, that unnerved me more than anything else.

"I am coming home," I told him, already on my laptop, emailing my professors.

Twelve hours later, with my bare essentials in a carry-on, I was sitting at the gate, waiting to board the plane and trying to ignore the sinking feeling in my stomach.

Dado was my mother, my father, my sister, my friend, and my confidante, all rolled into one woman with a gentle face and a fiercely protective tongue. Losing her would mean losing myself.

As I sat alone, fearing the worst, I needed a distraction.

I took my phone out.

Osman: Have fun on your trip to the beach. Beware of the riptides. I read Texas beaches are known for them.

That was his last message. Nothing special on the face of it, just a friend-ly note from a high school classmate. Until you realize that I had mentioned that beach trip two months ago, in passing, and never expected him to remember it. Or take the time to read up on Texas beaches and riptides.

That was Osman. Never present, yet always there in his own way. Never romantic, yet always making my heart flut ter.

Two years left, I told myself, counting down to the moment when he would graduate from his five-year medical program, and he and I would no longer have to rely on text messages. When I could be in his arms and he in mine, as we discussed our days and complained about our colleagues. Others might dream of Birkin bags and Louis Vuitton shoes—I dreamt of the warmth in his eyes and the comfort of his silent presence.

"Zavi had to book you on this flight too, didn't he?" An irritated voice pulled me out of my reverie.

I glanced up at Abu's scowling face. Next to him, her hands intertwined with his, was a strikingly attractive younger woman—probably in her early thirties. She looked at me with an amused smile and extended her hand.

"You must be Sanam. I am Myla. I keep telling Zak to introduce me to his daughter, but he never listens."

Before I could say anything, though, Abu pulled her away and scoffed. "I don't even know if she is my daughter."

"But she looks . . ." the woman started to say, but stopped when Abu glared at her and told her to keep walking. She gave me a sympathetic smile before disappearing around the corner with her husband.

Once again, I was left alone to fight back tears because of my father and mother, and an emotional infidelity that I'd had nothing to do with.

Abu knew I was his daughter. I'd had to take a paternity test to prove it in court, which brought me back to a question I had tried not to ask since I was ten: *Am I really that unworthy of being loved?*

My gaze wandered to my phone again, the messaging app still open to the string of texts that usually held me together. This time, they fell short.

I gave in and dialed his number.

"Sanam?" a sleepy voice answered almost immediately.

"Sorry I woke you up." I had forgotten it was well past midnight in Pakistan.

"No worries. I had to get up to study anyway. Is everything okay?" he asked, clearing his throat.

"No," I whispered, as a lone tear found its way down my cheek.

Agonizing words about my Dado, Abu, and his young wife, and the way he made me feel tumbled out. The more I unloaded, the better I felt, until finally, the tears had dried and his words of support started to sink in.

"Do you want me to come to Islamabad?" he asked.

Yes, please, yes, my heart begged.

Yet my mind remembered its resolution and said otherwise. "No, you need to focus on your studies. I'll be fine."

Soon, it was time to board the plane. I slipped into my window seat and looked out onto the tarmac.

The overcast sky and the summer rainstorm had given the black asphalt a shimmering sheen, on which the plane's lights seemed to dance to their own sweet song. Their rhythmic pattern, a mystery to most, probably held a message for the aviators they were intended for.

Breathe in. Breathe out, I repeated to myself in tandem with the flickering lights.

Dado will be fine. Abu will love me one day. And Osman, well, he . . .

My phone's buzzing interrupted my thoughts.

Osman: You may not be able to control the events in your life. But you can choose not to let them bring you down.

Osman: Besides, even if your father doesn't love you—

His typing paused. I held my breath for some unknown reason.

Osman: You are loved by someone.

I breathed out, staring at the message in front of me. Another one came quickly after that.

Osman: I meant like Dado and Chachoo. And your friends.

The middle-aged woman who sat in the seat next to me remarked, "Are you okay, honey? You look flushed."

"I am fine, thank you." I smiled at her politely before returning to my phone's screen, repeating his words in my head till they, too, sounded like a sweet song. A song that might be a mystery to others, but held a message for me.

For the first time in months, and despite my circumstances, there was a serenity within me. I was telling the truth. I was more than fine.

I was worthy of being loved—by *him*.

OSMAN

What the hell is wrong with me?

I sat up in bed, wide awake after almost confessing to her in a dreamy moment of poorly-timed courage. It's not that I was lying. I had been certain about my feelings since we left high school, and they had only intensified despite the distance. But over text, after she had poured her heart out to me about her ailing Dado and a man who didn't deserve to be her father, was not the time to be playing Romeo.

I peeked at my phone again.

Sanam: Thanks so much. You always know how to cheer me up!

Whew! She didn't know. I dragged my tired self out of bed and got back to studying for my upcoming rotation. It wasn't until about twenty-four hours later, while Sanam was still en route, that I was woken up to the Fajr adhan (call to prayer) blaring through the early morning silence.

Though that wasn't the only sound that woke me.

"Osman?" Kiran Api was calling out from the hallway.

"Have you spoken to Sanam recently?" she asked as soon as I opened my door.

"Yes, before she got on the plane to Islamabad. Her Dado isn't well. Why?"

She handed me her phone, the solemn look in her eyes making my stomach churn even before I saw the Breaking News Alert she was pointing to:

"Founding Lady of Awami Workers Party Passes Away After Cardiac Arrest."

Panic replaced anxiety. Visions of Sanam's beautiful face drowning in tears replaced the smiling one I usually dreamt of.

"She won't know till she lands. It'll be devastating for her," I stated the obvious as Kiran Api nodded.

"I know. I hope she gets the support she needs."

"Api, her Dado was her biggest supporter."

I swallowed the lump in my throat and prepared for my sister to vehemently refuse my request.

"I want to go to Islamabad. I need to be there for her. Please, Api. I have never taken a day off in college. One day won't hurt. I can catch the morning flight and come back tonight on the last flight out of Islamabad," I pleaded. "I've already studied for this rotation, and I'll study more all the way there and back. I have enough money saved for a ticket. I'll even give extra tuitions when I come back."

Something worked on her. She pursed her lips in disapproval and muttered, "Fine. You're an adult. I can't stop you anyway."

Grateful to her—and to my lucky stars when I was able to find a seat on the flights to and from Islamabad—I rushed through my morning, somehow managing to make it to the airport on time, and as I had promised Kiran Api, I brushed up on the next exam's syllabus throughout the flight.

At no point during that time could I have realized that I would be setting myself up for a trap. Or that, unknowingly, I was putting a target on an innocent girl's back. But that day, opportunistic moves were made in a game that I didn't even know I was playing.

The residence of Pakistan's finance minister wasn't hard to find. AWP and its leaders were clearly popular among the locals, and the taxi driver dropped me off among the throes of mourners that had gathered outside their house.

"Osman Tariq?" the guard asked as soon as I neared the main gate.

I nodded, and he gestured for me to follow him.

"Sir Zaviyar wants to meet you," he said as we walked through an empty hallway lined with tasteful artwork, the only sound that of our footsteps on the marble floor echoing off the walls.

"He is in a meeting. Wait here," the man instructed when we stopped outside a heavily carved teak door, before turning around and leaving himself.

Muffled noises and footsteps came down the same hallway soon after. Men were arguing, loudly and ferociously. Words such as *corruption, murder,* and *extortion* were being thrown around. I reminded myself I was in a politician's home and ignored the voices, instead focusing on sending a text to Sanam to let her know I was waiting for her.

The voices came closer and became louder as I continued to type, until a name I recognized forced me to stop and listen.

"Asif, you dug your grave with your illegal practices and now you are going to be buried in it. Not by me, but by the law," a gruff voice said.

There was silence, except for the approaching footsteps. Three men came into view and stood still a few feet away from me, none of them noticing my presence.

Phuppa, Sanam's Zavi Chachoo, and her stepfather, Mr. Malik, were locked in a battle of death stares.

"Name your price, Zaviyar." Phuppa scowled.

"I told you already, I have no price. I only follow the rule of the land," Zavi Uncle scoffed.

Phuppa's eyes seemed ablaze with fury, but if he was unnerved by the other two men glaring at him, he didn't show it one bit. Instead, he leaned closer to them and hissed, "The rule that you and your bastard party members are using for political gains?"

The condescending sneer on his face did not diminish when he turned towards Mr. Malik. "I was almost successful in making you lose the last election. I can do it again. You may not have a price, but every politician has something to hide. And mark my words, I will find and expose your secrets—or your videos."

"Asif, the mother of this house just passed away. If you had an ounce of humanity in you, you would not be threatening us right now," Mr. Malik replied.

Zavi Uncle looked away from Phuppa, and I could've sworn I saw a sheen in his eyes.

Phuppa's voice softened a smidge when he replied, "I have humanity, which is why I'm warning you, otherwise . . ."

He stopped, as did my heart, when his steely gaze locked onto me.

"What are you doing here?" he bellowed.

The other men turned to look at me too, startled, until I introduced myself, and Zavi Uncle immediately walked towards me and shook my hand.

"Oh, thank God you're here, son. Poor Sanam has been crying non-stop. She keeps asking for you. Go into my study, and I'll call for her." He motioned towards the teak door. I started to move, but a hand on my shoulder held me back.

"Good to see you, *son*." Phuppa's cheerful voice surprised me as much as his tender touch on my cheek.

"You two know each other?" Mr. Malik asked, his eyebrows furrowed into a slight frown.

"Of course. Osman is my nephew. I've raised him since he was in diapers."

"That's not . . ." I started to protest his lies, when a flurry of footsteps distracted me.

In the next moment, I forgot about him, his wife, his son, and how they had treated me and my sisters. My focus was entirely on the sorrowful angel who wrapped her arms around me, her tears soaking through my shirt. I held her shuddering shoulders because she needed me to, despite the awkwardness of standing like that with our uncles and stepfather nearby.

Some unit of time passed—seconds or minutes, I had no idea—before she pulled back to look up at me, her caramel-brown eyes searching for something in mine.

"Why don't you talk more in the study," Zavi Uncle told us, this time with an edge in his voice. If I had to guess, that had less to do with me hugging his niece and everything to do with the corrupt man who had just threatened him also claiming to be my relative.

"Sanam, I am so sorry to hear about your grandmother," Phuppa said to Sanam, and swiftly moved towards her to place a hand on her cheek.

It was such a sudden move that Sanam jumped back towards me, mumbling a thank you. But before I could retaliate, Phuppa had been yanked back and shoved against the wall by a furious Zavi Uncle. If eyes themselves could kill, his victim would surely have been a goner.

"How dare you touch her," he growled at the man whom he had in a chokehold.

Yet that man seemed to be made of titanium. There was not a sliver of fear in his eyes as they met Zavi Uncle's glare with equal intensity. Instead of a whimper, his voice was calm and even, each word spoken with an unflinching defiance.

"So much anger for a niece?"

"Niece or daughter, she is family. Dare to touch her again, and I'll cut your hands off." Zavi Uncle nearly spit in his face.

"I'll remember that for next time," Phuppa sneered.

"Come on inside, Osman. Forget about them," Sanam whispered and tugged at my arm. As much as I wanted to stay and see what would happen next between the two men, the clock was ticking, and I reminded myself that I was not here to witness political drama.

"You need to leave. I am calling security," I heard Mr. Malik say as Sanam led me into the study.

"Gladly. I got what I needed," Phuppa replied, his icy tone sending a shiver through me, despite the warm hand clasping mine.

"Thank you for coming." A soft voice forced me to look at the girl in front of me. Once again, everyone else and their issues faded into oblivion.

"No force on this earth could have kept me away," I told her. My thumb grazed her wet cheeks, turning them into a ruddy shade that I couldn't help smiling at.

I wrapped my arms around her again when she sighed against my chest. Silence, worth a thousand words, engulfed us, as it always did. As the moment unfolded, her breathing slowed down. Her grip on me relaxed.

When she finally let go of me, I pulled out a small bag from my backpack. "I got you something."

Her eyes widened, and I couldn't help laughing when she almost lunged at the lollipops in my hand. "Oh my God—thank you, thank you, thank you." She tore the wrapper off and popped one into her mouth. "After you, I was craving this the most."

She craves me? My heart flipped.

Fix your smile, idiot. I reminded myself why I was here in the first place.

Her shoulders drooped again when we sat on the sofa. "I can't believe she's gone," she said in a small, broken voice.

"She'll always live through you, Sanam," I consoled her.

For the next hour, she relived all the moments her Dado had been her stalwart. From birthdays where Dado was the only one who had remembered her special day, to the school events she never missed, the woman had been the only constant in her life.

Her eyes brimmed with tears. "If it wasn't for her, I'd probably be drunk and depressed, maybe even dead in a ditch somewhere."

"I bet she was so proud of the woman you've become."

She gave me a weary smile. "I wish she'd met you."

If she had, perhaps she would have been wise enough to see how doomed my relationship with her granddaughter was. Or she might have taught the two of us how to play the game of life itself.

Soon, it was time for me to leave for the airport.

The ride there was a quick one. Too quick for two souls meant only for each other, the agonizing distance between us made worse by the pace with which our time apart was passing.

"I hate this part." Sanam sighed when the car stopped outside the domestic departure terminal.

"One day we won't have to do this anymore."

"Till then, we say a prayer and not a goodbye?"

My heart swelled when I realized she remembered my words from three years ago. I nodded and repeated what I had said back then.

"Allah Hafiz, Sanam."

"Allah Hafiz, Osman."

She promptly lowered the window of her SUV when I got off and gazed down at me with eyes that shone bright despite the dark night, almost convincing me to ditch my clinical rotation and stay in Islamabad for a few days longer. Or perhaps it was her words which followed that were more convincing.

"Osman," she called out.

"Yes?"

Her pink lips curved into a slight smile.

"You are loved by someone too," she whispered.

She knows. My breath caught.

If only our story could have stopped right then, suspended in time for us to revere.

If only she had known how many times I would replay that moment in my head in the years to come.

If only my family and I hadn't been so naïve.

CHAPTER 13

Mansion

KIRAN

In Karachi's sweltering September heat, I stood in front of the massive wooden gates supported by thick pillars of steel and concrete, took a deep breath, and rang the bell. These were the gates that had once opened for me the moment I approached them, leading me to a home whose sights and smells I dreamt of even to this day.

This was the house built by my grandfather, off Sunset Boulevard in the heart of Karachi's poshest area, where I had been born and lived for the first two decades of my life.

"Who are you?" a man with a thick mustache and an AR-15 slung over his shoulder asked me through a crack in the gate.

"My name is Kiran. I wanted to meet Ms. Zarine. I am her niece," I told the guard, but he refused to let me in, saying that Zarine Phuppo didn't have a niece. Not that I could fault him; it had been years since I had last visited.

The only reason I now stood here was pure desperation. All I wanted was a fraction of what was rightfully mine, but had been ruthlessly snatched away.

"Kiran?" a voice croaked behind me.

An old woman was gingerly getting out of a rickshaw. Bent over and frail, she carried with her several bags of vegetables in one hand and a walking stick in the other. I instantly recognized her.

"Bua? You still work here?" She had been hired as our nanny when I was born.

"Yes, what can I do? Us poor have no choice but to keep working for whoever the master of the house is," she lamented. "But what are you doing here?"

I told her that I was hoping to meet Zarine Phuppo, but the guard wouldn't let me in. That was enough to light a fire in her. She almost completely straightened up and marched to the gate as fast as her cane would let her, banging on it until the same guard as before faced her.

Standing at a distance, I couldn't make out their hushed conversation. Instead, I watched Bua's animated expressions go from irritation to fury. Whatever she said worked, and soon I was following Bua inside.

Thanking her profusely, I took some of her bags as the two of us slowly made our way down the winding driveway, still surrounded by lush gardens, but now with thorny rose bushes and pebbled pathways. Though, I wasn't here to judge my aunt's horticultural taste.

I needed a chance to talk to her—niece to aunt, mother to mother, woman to woman—and appeal to the love she'd once had for me and my siblings, even if that love had suddenly disappeared one night when she had turned them out onto the street.

Bua led me through the dark, polished wooden doors. The carved wooden flowers that used to welcome me had been completely obliterated. The house itself was still huge, with the same wide staircase leading up to the hallway that connected the east and west wings of the mansion. The whitewashed walls and marble flooring, with their intricate patterns, remained. The same expensive, even if slightly worn, wall decor now inter-mingled with contemporary art and furnishings.

Yet something was missing—a soul. The sights, sounds, and smells that had made it into a home had been replaced by a sterile silence. It felt as if the house was mourning the days it had once seen, and the life it had once held within its walls.

"Come and sit here. I'll go find Madam Zarine." Bua motioned for me to follow her into the living room, where I had once sat in my father's lap as he read book after book to me, while my mother knitted next to us.

My eyes moistened at those memories, but I wiped them away instantly and squared my shoulders, determined to go through with what I had come here to do.

After working day and night to keep my family afloat, I was tired and exhausted. I, too, wanted to sit on my sofa and knit in peace like my mother used to. But now, with two sons in an elite private school, when it used to be just my brother, and that same brother now in medical college, all I could do was dream.

Osman hardly ever asked me for anything. With the tuitions he taught in the evenings and his scholarship, he was funding his own education. But he still had about two years left of his five-year-long medical college. It wasn't hard to notice the toll all the extra work was taking on his mental and physical health.

After Bua left, I sat still, bracing for what was to come. When twenty minutes passed and there was no sign of a living soul, I got up to look around. In this wing of the house, the kitchen was on the left side of the living room and the study, dining room, and smaller lounge were on the right.

The kitchen was empty, so I hesitantly walked towards the other end of the floor.

I passed the opulent formal dining room and a recreation room where the TV screen was bigger than any of the walls in my current apartment. Yet, there was nothing other than eerie quietness in that space, sending a shiver down my spine.

The further I pushed into the bowels of that house, the more courage I lost. Almost ready to give up, I decided to check one last room. It used to be Abu's study at one time. Now, I could hear muffled voices through the closed door as I neared it.

Curiosity got the better of me, and I took up position next to the upholstered chair beside a side table with an old-fashioned landline phone and several pieces of crystal.

Phuppo seemed to be pleading. "For God's sake. He is your son. You know how sensitive he is when it comes to Maham. Don't ruin his life by continuously taunting him."

The venom-filled reply of her husband followed. "He betrayed me, and now he is failing a semester because of this wretched girl. If he has turned into a psychopath as well, it is not my fault."

He scoffed. "But you are right. Zain is my blood. Not Maham. And it is quite easy to get rid of girls like her."

There was a gasp and a pause, and then my Phuppo's distressed voice again.

"No, please, forgive that girl. She is from a respectable family . . ."

Phuppo's whimper was drowned out by the shattering of glass and the thud of something hitting the floor. Startled, I moved back, but in doing so, I tripped against the table, sending some of the crystal pieces flying to the ground.

There was silence in the room, and then quick, heavy footsteps headed towards the door, the only thing separating me from doom. I attempted to run back into the hallway, but an iron grip on my arm stalled my escaping feet.

"What do you think you are doing here?" Asif hissed in my ear.

I gulped but straightened my back. Pulling my arm out of his grip, I held his vexed gaze with every bit of restraint and calm I could gather to conceal my fearful, racing heart.

"I wanted to meet Zarine Phuppo."

He sneered, his hand gripping my arm tightly again, pulling me into the room behind him. My attempts to free myself made no difference as I barely managed to keep my balance.

"Here. Meet her."

His taunting gaze landed on the floor beside me. Mine followed, and I gasped. There, on the floor, was my Phuppo. A shell of her former self, she was slowly getting up from the floor, with one hand to her head, and blood trickling down the side of her face.

"You hit her?" I bent down to help her sit up. She was dazed and confused, but her hazel eyes silently cried for help. Despite everything, I couldn't leave her or let her husband get away with hurting her.

"She needs to get to the hospital. Her head is bleeding."

I reached for my phone, but Asif's iron grip was back, pulling me up from the floor and towards himself until his face was mere inches from mine. His rancid breath fanned against my cheek, and his dark, piercing eyes wandered over my face.

"Do you remember what happened the last time you tried to call for help?" he whispered harshly in my ear; the rough hair of his graying beard scratched the exposed skin of my neck.

"You are still gorgeous, even if a tad bit old for my taste."

Memories of the day he was referring to froze me in place.

The masked men in my house, a gun held over my sleeping baby brother, my torn dupatta (veil) and the ripped buttons of my shirt, all harboring a threat of what was to come if I didn't sign the papers presented to me.

"Checkmate, dear niece. You seem to have forgotten that I always win." Asif let go of me, and I stumbled back.

He picked up the phone on his desk and ordered, "Send that old woman in," before growling at me. "Leave before I call the men in this house to deal with you."

I didn't hesitate. Wrapping my dupatta tightly around myself, I ran. And I kept running until I was through the gates and back into my car. That's when I broke down—mourning my past, my present, and my future.

I mourned for the young, unsuspecting girl who had been caught in a web so deadly even her fiancé wouldn't be able to get her out of it.

My hardened heart even sobbed for an aunt who used to play with me in the very room in which she now lay battered and bruised.

The deep-seated resentment against the Ghazanfars reared its head. But this time, I wasn't going to wallow in misery or let my past petrify me. This time, I was going to act to save another girl from the same future as my sister.

"Osman, are you still in touch with Maham?" I asked as soon as he answered my call.

CHAPTER 14

Two Loves

SANAM

It was 10 p.m. on a Saturday night when I lay on my bed with a book in hand, buried under a duvet while the air conditioner blasted air on its highest setting, keeping the room cool despite an unusually warm October in Houston.

That was, in summary, how I had spent almost every weekend in college, and I had no intention of changing anything as a senior. Stripped away from the expectations of high society, this was me—at peace with myself—enjoying the solitude of my empty dorm building while everyone else lived the social life one expects of a college kid on the weekend.

A name flashed on my phone, as if the universe had decided to reward my patience. With a wide smile, I accepted the call.

"Hey, you."

"Hey, Sanam. Is this a bad time?"

"For you, never."

As always, we chatted about nothing in particular, until inevitable words were said. With tongues tied and voices lowered, we were reminded of the bond our hearts shared but deliberately avoided—lest the pain of being apart became unbearable.

"So, how is that girlfriend of yours doing?" I teased when he complained about his classmates.

"I have a girlfriend?" His confusion made me chuckle.

"You know, the one who talks a lot? Ameerah Sheikh."

"Oh God," he groaned. "Please don't call her that. I am stuck with her because her last name starts with an S, and for some reason, she is obsessed with bikes."

He had told me about this Ameerah girl who was always talking about riding bikes, *his* bike in particular, after he had bought it a year ago. I called her *Amorous Ameerah*.

Of course, this adorably clueless boy of mine had no idea about her intentions. "She is not obsessed with bikes, silly. She is obsessed with you."

"No way."

"Yes, way. Girls flirt with you all the time, and you never notice. I should know; I was one of them for over two years."

He paused, and I flushed. I had never admitted to him that I'd had a crush on him for that long. Yet, I wasn't the only one to divulge secrets that night, or intensify the silent passion of that moment.

"Well, Ms. Sanam Uzair." His voice deepened. "You weren't exactly a genius when it came to picking up on nonverbal clues—for over two years."

Silence followed. Realization sunk in. We had wasted so much time being next to each other, pining for each other, but all in secrecy. Time we could never turn the clock back on.

He tried to change the subject. "Anyway, I don't give rides to girls on my bike. So, I don't care what Ameerah is obsessed with."

Of course, he wouldn't care. He was nothing if not loyal. I had trusted him with my heart and knew that *Amorous Ameerah* or anyone like her could never be a threat.

Yet, my mind sought reassurance. "What about me? Would you give me a ride?" I heard myself ask.

I was special, right? was the real question.

"No."

He said it so quickly that I couldn't hide the hurt when I whispered, "Oh, okay."

Though, I should have known, he hadn't finished his reply yet.

"You deserve so much more than a poor man's dusty bike."

It hit me then. His promises of moving forward after he made something of himself weren't just because he wanted to pursue a career in medicine. It was for me too. He was trying to give me the life he thought I came from. Even if I adored him because he was the exact opposite of the people in that life.

"Those fancy cars and SUVs you see on the road come with a price, Osman. And I am sick and tired of paying that price. I would gladly sit on a dusty bike or a rickshaw, or even walk on my own two feet, with you."

I tried to hide my angst but failed. "I have lost so many people and relationships to glamor and wealth; I can't lose you too."

Silence, a constant between us, followed again. When he spoke, it was in a hushed tone, slow and deliberate, as if he had mulled over every single word, each carrying the weight of his affection and undying commitment.

"I am yours, Sanam. My heart, my thoughts, my prayers—they are all yours. How could you lose me when I've already lost myself in you?"

His words. I stilled, barely managing to breathe.

They may be mere vibrations of air molecules spoken by him in a moment of passion or simple kindness, but for me, his words would echo endlessly. They may have cost him nothing, but for me, they were worth my past, present, and future. For his words alone, I could move mountains or wait for eons. Even as I reeled from their impact, my soul submerged in the promises they held.

A boy's voice called out in the background, and he replied, "Go downstairs. I'm coming."

To me, he said, "Before I go, have you heard from Maham recently?"

How easy it was for him to capture my soul and move on.

"No," I told him through parched lips. "I haven't heard from her for a while."

"Weird. She hasn't replied to my texts either. I'll try to email her."

That last part of our conversation was quickly forgotten when I fell back into bed. Maham had, after all, found her happily-ever-after a long time ago. I couldn't fault her for being too busy to keep up with friendships.

Ordinarily, I, too, would have sought refuge in the perfect world of the romance novel I was reading. But today, I realized that no fiction could be better than my reality.

That night, I dreamt of standing in front of him, my fingers raking through his hair, our gazes locked, his arm around my waist as he drew me in. And I admitted my truth to him as well. *I am yours too, Osman. Don't ever let go of me.*

The irony was, he was not the one who let go.

ZAIN

"Maham, we just started talking. Why are you leaving again?" I rubbed a hand over my face.

"I have to go to dinner with Dad and some of his colleagues. I told you that this morning when we spoke," she replied curtly.

"Are you trying to say that I call you too much?" My voice rose, anger that I was failing to rein in threatened to disrupt yet another conversation.

Foreboding silence followed, making my heart sink. How could I not call her? I missed her terribly the whole day. There were days I could barely focus on my classes because of her, or rather the absence of her. And yet she had the heart to complain that I called her too much.

"You are *mine*, Maham. I can't stand anyone else being near you or with you."

She pushed back. "I have a life as well, Zain. I am at a conference with my father in New York. I cannot spend hours on the phone with you."

Her objections might have carried a truth, but the more she rejected me, the more rapidly my fear of losing her turned into rage. The voices in my head spoke a truth I had always known but had ignored.

"He is at a math conference; you are a journalism major. Why are you even there with him?"

Conspiracies swirled in my brain, trapping me in a whirlpool of doubt and dread. "This is an excuse for you not to meet me in Boston this weekend, right?" My voice cracked.

Her tone softened. "Zain, I've met you almost every weekend for more than three years now. Between living in a dorm and my studies, I barely get to spend time with my parents, even though I live in the same city as them. Please, let me do this. I promise to meet you next weekend. I'll even spend tomorrow morning with you on the phone if you want. Just let me have one uninterrupted dinner with my father."

I could go on trying to persuade her, but something in her voice made me stop. A desperate plea, an angst I couldn't comprehend. She had never bargained with me like that before.

Was she afraid of me?

No, Ami is afraid of Abu; Maham can never be afraid of me. I am not like my father.

"I am sorry, Maham. I didn't mean to keep you from your parents. You have every right to go to this conference," I told her.

See, unlike my father, I can say sorry. Even when it's not my fault.

"That's okay, Zain. Bye."

"I love you," I said quickly, but she hung up without replying to that three-letter sentence that anchored me in moments like this.

She hates you. She will never be yours.

The voices were back, the self-doubt, the self-hatred, propagated endlessly within me. And the one woman whose tender gaze and soft voice was the balm to all my sores was busy on the other side of the country. I had no choice but to grab my wallet and head out to a place she would never condone.

It is her fault I am doing this, I told myself. Other than her, there was only one other way to quieten the dissenting voices in my head.

"Zain, my man. The usual?" the bartender asked when I reached the bar around the corner from my apartment.

After downing my third glass of whiskey, I took out my phone and logged into an email account that wasn't mine.

The first email was a homework assignment from her professor. The next came from a name I recognized. Despite the boozy haze, I sat up immediately and called a number from back home.

"Why the fuck are you emailing Maham?" I asked as soon as he answered.

A confused voice replied, "Zain?"

"Yes. Zain, her fiancé. Answer my question, idiot." My speech slurred, but determination and jealousy had taken over.

"Kiran Api wanted to talk to her." Osman's voice hardened. "I have no idea why. But I am pretty sure that Maham wouldn't appreciate her fiancé being drunk."

I let his words sink in slowly, calming my nerves and the dread within. My cousin may have been a better man than me—the type of quiet nerd Maham probably deserved—but that idiot only had eyes for one girl, and she for him. Even I knew that.

He is not a threat, my slumbering brain concluded.

"Mind your own business, fucker."

I hung up before he could reply.

What the hell does Ms. Kiran want with her? That was a question I had no interest in answering. Instead, I did what I had done countless times before with emails I considered a threat—I deleted it from her inbox.

What she didn't know couldn't hurt her, or me.

Once I was done going through the rest of her emails and socials—a harmless pastime—I put my phone away. Soon, it buzzed again. The flutter in my heart quickly died down when I realized it was a news alert and not a text from her. But unlike other news, which I typically ignored, this one caught my attention.

"Azhar Saqlain from GT Enterprise Arrested on Suspicion of Murder."

The man practically lived at our house and was my father's closest associate. He had now been accused of killing an elderly woman.

My phone rang, but it still wasn't Maham. Invisible threads forced me to pick it up anyway.

"Yes, Abu?"

"I need you to do something," came his gruff reply.

"Do what?"

There was a long pause before he spoke again.

"Marry Sanam Uzair."

CHAPTER 15

Pawns

ZAIN

Marry Sanam?

Half drunk, I could barely hear myself in the noisy bar, let alone my father. That had to be the explanation for what I thought I had heard. Stepping out onto the dimly lit street, fl anked by towering palm trees swaying in the cool October evening breeze of L.A., I asked him to repeat himself.

But I hadn't heard him wrong the firs t time.

"Marry Sanam Uzair. She was your friend, wasn't she?" he repeated harshly.

"Why?" I demanded to know. My slumbered senses had been shaken to life.

"I need to get these bastard AWP politicians off my back before the next elections. And that Zaviyar Uzair, their leader, loves his niece. Marry her now, and that whole party will be under our control for good."

Anger and resentment soared within me. Rage erupted as a thunderous objection. "Are you out of your fucking mind? I will only marry Maham. I love—"

"*Behave yourself.*" My father's voice, low and threatening, cut me off .

I could hear his jarring breath through the phone—could almost feel its heat on my face when I closed my eyes. He was a man who got what he wanted, *always*. It was terrifying that he wanted me to marry a girl I had no interest in.

That feeling of dread only deepened when he said, "Maham will refuse to marry you. And you will marry Sanam. I can guarantee you that."

He hung up without waiting for a reply. I simply stood there.

With my fingers curling into a fist, nails digging into my flesh, my mind tried to wrap itself around what had happened. The dark night without a star in the sky, and the thunder off in the distance seemed to send an ominous signal. A premonition of the unseen future. A destiny out of my hands and under the ruthless grasp of my father.

I knew what he was capable of. You don't live for eighteen years with a man and not overhear the whispered secrets or ignore the shifty gazes among his associates. None of that had mattered to me then. That was not a world I was a part of, even if I reaped the benefits of it.

But this was different.

This was a declaration of war against my life. Against Maham, who *was* my life.

Nocturnal creatures rummaging through the trash were the only ones who heard me grit my teeth and proclaim, "I will destroy anyone who dares to take my Maham away from me."

OSMAN

The TV was blaring in the student lounge, tuned to some sports channel that was showing reruns of a T20 Cricket World Cup final. In the middle of the room sat some seniors poring over open textbooks. Off to the side was a small kitchenette where a couple of students were making tea for themselves.

"Osman, do you want chai?" one of them called out.

I desperately needed some caffeine as our small study group crammed for the upcoming exams, but not from the woman who was calling out.

"Thanks, Ameerah. Not at the moment."

She shrugged, walked back to our table, and started switching channels on the TV.

"Ameerah, focus, please. We have work to do," a classmate chided, but something on the news channel had her frowning.

It was a still photo of Asif Phuppa, in a black tuxedo, and Zarine Phuppo, looking stylish as usual in a black saree. Both stood together, glasses of some drink in hand, carefree laughter on their faces as they mingled with Pakistan's elite at a private event.

"Mr. Ghazanfar, along with his wife, was seen in Islamabad at the annual charity gala to raise funds for Save the Children. The real estate tycoon showed no signs of concern about the multiple ongoing investigations into his company and those of his closest associates. Our reporter caught up with him, and here is what he said," the newscaster announced.

A video of my Phuppa, surrounded by dozens of reporters, played on the screen.

"These are all lies, all allegations, that are being used to malign a company that brings thousands of jobs to this country every year and generates billions of rupees in revenue," Asif Ghazanfar said in a calm voice against the backdrop of a Save the Children banner.

"But how much of that revenue do you pay tax on?" someone off the screen asked him.

He looked straight at the camera, his eyes devoid of any emotions. "On every single penny of it."

Asif Ghazanfar's impromptu interview concluded, and a video of his associate, Azhar Saqlain, aired on TV instead. The man, his eyes filled with triumphant glee rather than remorse, stood next to his lawyer outside a police station.

"GT Enterprise regrets the death of Mrs. Suraiya. But as we have told the press again and again, my client is innocent. He was neither present nor aware that she was inside her residence when that house was being razed to the ground to make way for a new housing society. And I will point out again that the land and all the houses on it were purchased *legally* by GT Enterprise."

The smugness on the lawyer's face rivaled that of his client when he dramatically paused before adding, "Yet Mr. Ghazanfar's and Mr. Saqlain's generosity knows no bounds, and they have agreed to compensate Mrs. Suraiya's family regardless of the fact that she died due to her own negligence."

"Can you believe this man?" Ameerah exclaimed. "Isn't it their responsibility to ensure a property is empty before running a bulldozer over it?"

The newscaster came back on the screen. This time, she had a guest with her. "Mr. Sikander Ahmed, a renowned investigative journalist, joins me now to give his expert opinion. What do you think about these allegations against Mr. Saqlain? Do you think they'll stick in court?"

"First, these allegations have been lodged against the CEO of GT Enterprise too, not just a low-level associate. Second, I wouldn't be surprised if the case gets thrown out for lack of evidence. Though, we have to remember that while Mr. Saqlain's counsel has provided several documents showing that Mrs. Suraiya had sold her house to GT Enterprise, her family insists that she had refused to do so again and again."

There was an animated discussion both on TV and in the study room about how the rich get away with everything—even murder. I was immediately on my phone, texting Kiran Api.

Me: Remember that journalist who was badly injured in a hit-and-run? He is alive.

Api: I saw. Asif Ghazanfar's end is near!

It was clear many people would feel relieved by that. What I couldn't understand was why Kiran Api would.

Me: What has Phuppa done to us personally? Phuppo was the one who kicked us out of her house.

There was a pause in her replies, then a question.

Api: Have you heard from Maham?

Me: No. I've emailed twice already.

Api never gave me an answer about Phuppa. I soon found out anyway.

We were almost at the end of our study session when the dean's secretary peeked into the student lounge and asked me to step outside.

"Are you free on Tuesday in the second week of November for a fund-raising event sponsored by the dean's office?"

"I should be. But are you sure you want me and not one of the more senior students?" I glanced back into the student lounge where there were at least a dozen fifth-year students.

She shook her head. "Students are generally not invited, but the chief guest specifically requested your presence."

Weird. "Who is the chief guest?" I inquired.

"Asif Ghazanfar."

CHAPTER 16

Bait and Trap

ZAIN

Maham will refuse to marry you. And you will marry Sanam. I can guarantee you that.

It had been almost a month since Abu's threat. After his call, there had been absolute silence, and that scared me. I had grown up in silence between my parents. Under the same roof, in the same room, their silence was always the calm before the storm. And I couldn't shake the feeling that the past month had been just that.

His words had to be a premonition.

My guard had to stay up. I had no choice.

Though Maham had had enough of my paranoia—especially after my latest outburst.

"Zain, you cannot go around beating people up because they're talking to me." She tugged at her dark brown curls that gleamed in the setting sun as we sat on a bench outside her dorm.

Last year, around this time, we had huddled together under my coat to keep out the November cold in Boston. This year, it was still cold, but so was the distance between us.

"He had his hand on your arm." I blinked, trying to get rid of the image of a young man with glasses and blond hair sitting next to my fiancée as I watched them in the cafeteria.

"He was only trying to get my attention for an urgent matter. Our exam results—"

"I don't care. No one touches you, except for me." My voice cracked, the terror inside threatening to expose itself.

She paused. I knew she had a lot to say, but for a moment, her gaze softened, and her hand came up to touch my cheek. "I know you're worried about what your father said. But the way you've been acting is making me go insane," she said slowly, like she was talking to a child.

"If I lose you, *I* will go insane, Maham."

She sighed and sat back on the bench. "What more do you want me to do, Zain? No matter what I say to you, it's never enough."

"Marry me," I replied, like I had a dozen times since my conversation with Abu. Every time, she had refused, saying that her parents didn't approve because we were too young.

"We're seniors now, Maham. We'll be graduating in less than a year—"

"My parents are not the only ones who want us to wait until after graduation," she interrupted. "Your father doesn't approve of us either."

I reached out to hold her hand, making her look at me. "You're not marrying my father. You're marrying me. His approval shouldn't matter."

"Zain . . ." She closed her eyes, dismay flitting across her face.

"Do you still love me?" I asked for the thousandth time.

"Yes," she whispered. But instead of a spark in her eyes, her shoulders slumped. I loosened my grip on her hand, and it slipped away. Much like she herself seemed to be slipping away from me.

I was tempted to ask her if she was happy and excited for a future with me, or if she thought we were a mistake. Instead, I turned my gaze off into the distance, like she had. Her answer wouldn't have mattered. I was too far gone to let go of her easily—or at all.

"You made a promise to me, Maham. I won't survive if you go back on it. You don't want to be responsible for something bad happening to me, do you?"

The silence surrounding us was deafening, but it didn't last long. Qureshi Uncle was here to pick up his daughter for the weekend, and he wasn't alone.

"Oh, Zain, good, you're here too. Meet Saeed, my *baby* brother. He is a pediatrician and moved here from San Francisco this week."

With a wide smile on his face, Dr. Saeed extended his hand. "So good to finally meet you. I have heard great things from my *elderly* brother."

In the good-natured leg-pulling that ensued between siblings, two things were very clear: first, Saeed Qureshi was a world-renowned pediatric cardiologist, and second, Maham's father loved me.

"You must join us for dinner," he said to me.

"Absolutely," I replied gleefully.

Not a word left Maham's lips. Not during the car ride, nor when we reached her home and her parents gushed over the gifts I had brought for them, just like I had almost every time I visited: a Giorgio Armani perfume for Uncle and a CHANEL handbag for Aunty.

"Maham's a lucky girl," said her smiling mother.

"That's what I keep telling her," added her smiling father.

Maham never smiled.

Back in L.A. the following Monday, in the second week of November, I sat in an afternoon class listening to a lecture on microeconomics when my phone buzzed with a message from my father.

Abu: Call me, son. I have some good news for you.

Son? I couldn't remember the last time he had referred to me as that. Though, curiosity about the "good news" had me calling him at the end of class. He didn't waste any time.

"Do you still want to marry Maham?" he asked, as if he didn't already know the answer.

"Yes, of course. I told you—"

"Good. Because I just spoke to her parents, and they have agreed to a *nikah* between you two next month."

"Yeah, right," I scoffed and was about to disconnect the call when his voice came through again.

"Wait, son."

"Stop calling me 'son.' You've made it quite clear that you don't care about me at all."

He took a heavy breath and answered, "If I didn't care, why would I be footing the bill for your extravagant lifestyle in L.A., or paying for your weekly trips to Boston?"

There was no malice in his voice. No undertone of disgust. It was enough for me to ask, "What made you call Maham's parents?"

His tone softened further. "The love for my only son forced me to, Zain. You are more important to me than any business could ever be. Maham may not be my first choice, but if you're happy with her, then so am I."

Those were the words I had been dying to hear for years. However, as his sudden change of heart sank in, the alarm bells started ringing.

"I don't believe you. A month ago, you were adamant about me marrying Sanam to save the company. What could have possibly made you change your mind?"

A long pause later, the truth came out.

"Maham is a US citizen, isn't she?"

"Yes. She was born here. So?"

"So, once you marry her, you will become a US citizen too. And I realized that one way to save GT Enterprise from these corrupt politicians on a witch hunt is to move the company out of Pakistan."

He had long dreamt of opening offices in the US, but opportunities for non-US citizens to establish companies in the country were limited. Maham would be his way into the US market, he insisted.

I wasn't convinced.

"You still won't have US citizenship. Who will run the company here?"

My father chuckled. "You, of course, with my help. I may have been tough on you, Zain, but that was only to teach you the difficult choices you have to make as a leader. Think about it—who else could inherit this company that I've literally built from scratch, if not my own son?"

When I stayed quiet, more truths spilled out. "I would expect you to eventually sponsor my US citizenship too. Can I get your word on that?"

"Sure," I replied, too quickly.

Perhaps if I had slept well the night before instead of being on a red-eye flight from Boston to L.A., or hadn't had the glass of scotch before class, I might have been able to see through the web of lies my father was weaving. But the words he said were so sweet, the picture he painted so perfect: *Zain Ghazanfar, Maham's husband and the head of GT Enterprise.* I never saw the web at all.

Instead, I asked, "How did you manage to convince her parents?"

There were his mellow words again, explaining things with such clarity, it was enough to veil my senses. "Everyone has a price, Zain. It's either something they want, or a weakness you can exploit. You simply have to find out which of those will work in your favor. Maham's parents wanted their daughter to have in-laws who would accept her. So, I called and apologized. Besides, nothing says we accept Maham as our daughter-in-law quite like donating a million dollars in both of your names to a hospital in Karachi, and giving you money to buy an apartment for yourself and Maham in Boston."

The money had been pledged for a new surgical ward at Karachi Medical Center. He had a long history of sponsoring charitable institutions; this wasn't an anomaly. The apartment in Boston was so Maham and I would have a place to stay when we met on the weekends.

"How soon did they say we could get married?"

"Next month, December. As soon as this semester is over for both of you."

"Okay then. Qabool hai." (I accept.)

My father laughed, the sound resonating with warmth. "See you soon, son. I'll start preparing for the wedding tomorrow."

Son. I smiled to myself and turned off the alarm bells. My selfish father was doing this for himself. How could this possibly be a trap?

In the future, as I would sit in a room with bare essentials, I would laugh at the excitement I felt in this moment. And then I would punch the walls, appalled at my naïvete.

My father kept his promise, though. He started preparing for my wedding the next day—by moving his first pawn at the fundraising gala at Karachi Medical Center.

CHAPTER 17

Secrets

OSMAN

The day of the fundraising gala was here. I was conveniently on my surgical rotation, which meant erratic timings and late nights, ensuring that Kiran Api would not be suspicious of my absence at home that evening, giving me an opportunity to quell my own suspicions about our family's past.

Several hours remained until the evening, and before I became a special invitee to a star-studded gala, I still had to go through life as a regular fourth-year medical student.

A senior resident called out, running past me. "Come on, Osman. We have a trauma case in OR 3."

I started following him, adrenaline pumping through my veins. The resident and I reached the OR as our young patient, already on a ventilator, was being wheeled in. He seemed no older than Daniyal and Danish.

"Assalamu Alaikum, Dr. Iftikhar," I greeted the senior trauma surgeon, who also happened to be my brother-in-law, as he rushed in.

"Walaikum Assalam, Osman." He gave me a quick pat on the back and asked the resident for more details on the patient.

"Sir, he is a seventeen-year-old male, Nael Razzak, who sustained multiple gunshot wounds to the abdomen. Blood pressure is tenuous, at about 90/50, despite multiple fluid boluses and pressors. We had to intubate him in the ER."

Iftikhar Bhai, the senior resident, and I quickly scrubbed in and gowned up. Standing silently towards the side of the OR table, my heart thumped, and fingers itched to contribute somehow to save this boy's life as he literally bled out in front of us.

"The liver and spleen are both damaged. Blood is pooling in the abdominal cavity," the resident reported as soon as the first incision was made.

As his blood pressure dropped further, it was clear that the boy was losing blood faster than we could replace it.

"Osman, get into the surgical field. We're going to pack his abdomen with as many sponges as we can," Iftikhar Bhai called out to me, his eyes laser-focused on the patient in front of us. I didn't waste a second.

Over the next several hours, we would desperately try to control the bleeding, remove intact bullets where we could and leave behind bullet fragments where it was too dangerous. The innocent child had been shot at least three times, whereas his father, who had been with him, had been miraculously unscathed.

"Let's go update the family," Iftikhar Bhai said when the teenager was in a semi-stable condition. If he survived the night in the ICU, we would need to take him to the OR again to repair his large intestine, which had only been temporarily repaired.

Breaking news to families was never easy, no matter how many times you'd done it before. At least this time, we could tell the father who stood there in his police uniform, covered in blood, none of which was his own, that his son was still alive. We had heard that this was a revenge attack on the father by some criminals he had tried to put away.

"Thank you, doctor. Thank you so much." The officer, whose badge read "Junaid Razzak," clasped Iftikhar Bhai's hand, struggling to maintain his composure as his gaze darted between me and his son's surgeon.

"Trust in God, Inspector Junaid." Iftikhar Bhai put his hand on the policeman's shoulder. "We are doing everything we can for him."

As we walked back to the ICU, I realized how late it was.

"Everything okay, Osman?" my brother-in-law asked.

"Uh, yes. I was actually supposed to be at this gala."

His brows furrowed. "The fundraising gala? Students are not typically invited."

"The chief guest invited me."

Furrowed brows turned into a deeper frown. I instantly regretted saying anything. Iftikhar Bhai was a senior, well-known surgeon. Of course, he would have been invited to the same fundraising gala.

"Why would Asif Ghazanfar ask for you?"

"I don't know. But please don't tell my sisters. They never tell me anything, and I really want to find out what Phuppa is cooking up now."

"Whatever it is, it has got to be evil."

"Which is why I should go and find out, right?"

I had to argue some more, but he finally ceded—with a condition. "I wasn't going to attend the gala, but I will now. If anything out of the ordinary happens, you come straight to me. Understood?"

I understood. Didn't mean I had to follow his instructions though. I wasn't a child anymore.

The gala itself took place in the grand ballroom of a hotel not too far from the hospital. On Iftikhar Bhai's insistence, I rode there with him.

Dressed in my ill-fitting suit and unpolished shoes, I felt like a fish out of water in a room that exuded sheer elegance. From the crystal chandeliers that cast a warm glow over the polished wooden floors to the designer gowns and exquisite jewelry, this was a world I had never experienced before.

The hospital and medical college's top leadership—CEO, deans, and department heads, were all in attendance. That wasn't surprising; over a million dollars had been collected to fund a new hospital wing, with the largest donation coming from a single donor.

"Ghazanfar Pavilion will be the largest surgical center in the country, providing state-of-the-art equipment and facilities to our patients." Dean Nadir beamed at the man who stood next to him on stage. "And it's all due to the leadership of Mr. Asif Ghazanfar, who has tirelessly led this fundraising effort."

When the man of the hour came to the podium, his steely gaze landed on me immediately.

"No need to thank me, Nadir," he said. "While this pavilion is dedicated to my son and his fiancée, you can thank my nephew, Osman Tariq, for giving me the idea."

A hundred pairs of eyes turned to me all at once as Phuppa continued his speech. "Ever since he joined this medical college, I've had a front-row seat to the exceptional standard of teaching here and the dedicated care you provide to the people of this country. This center is a small token of my appreciation."

Thunderous applause erupted, echoing through the room. Strangers I had never met came forward to greet me, while others offered warm smiles from afar. In an instant, I went from being just another student to *the* student—and I had no idea why.

Iftikhar Bhai, standing nearby, looked equally baffled, his gaze darting between me and the man at the podium. Both began moving towards me at the same time, but in the silent race between a trauma surgeon and a billionaire uncle, there could only be one winner. The other was intercepted by an exuberant Dean Nadir.

"So glad to see you, dear nephew," said Asif Ghazanfar, as I stood alone, captured by his dark, unblinking gaze.

"I am not sure I can say the same, dear Phuppa."

He moved closer. "You've got quite the tongue on you, boy."

I didn't move an inch. "Perhaps because I am a man now. Not the four-year-old who was kicked out of your house."

His arm snaked around my shoulders. "Let's have a real chat then, man to man. What do you say?"

It wasn't like I had any say at all. Gut instincts screamed, Api's words of caution yelled, but the promise I had made to Iftikhar Bhai couldn't be kept. What kind of a man would I be if I let fear consume me?

Out of the hotel ballroom, another man appeared. I recognized him from the TV. He was Azhar Saqlain, recently acquitted of the murder of Mrs. Suraiya, whose house had been razed to the ground.

"The car is ready, boss."

"Car?" I frowned.

Phuppa smirked. "Don't be afraid, little one. We're only going out for some chai. This fancy food upsets my stomach."

I was certain this wasn't about chai. Still, I kept walking, driven by curiosity and determined not to show fear.

"Why did you call me to this event?" I asked, climbing into a Porsche that had pulled up in front of the hotel.

"To give you this." He handed me a cream envelope as the chauffeur pulled out of the hotel driveway.

In it was a wedding invitation—to Zain and Maham's wedding.

"They're getting married?" I questioned. After my last conversation with Zain, I was sure Maham would have dumped him.

"Yes, next month . . ." He paused. "Though if I had it my way, I would have brought that girl home a long time ago."

His voice lowered. "For myself."

"Excuse me?" I was sure I had heard him wrong.

"Maham is gorgeous and a little naïve. Girls like her are easy." He looked at me again, his eyes hooded as he leaned in and whispered, "You studied with her. You know what I am talking about."

"I don't."

I honestly had no clue.

"Oh, come on. You said you're a man." He continued in a low, breathy voice, like he was sharing a secret with me. "Haven't you ever wanted to suck on her lips, or feel every curve of her bare body flush against your own?"

I heard him. But I couldn't believe him. Revulsion at the man in front of me, and dismay for a classmate I respected, overtook the words that I should have said. Yet, my facial expression must have been a dead giveaway.

"What happened, dear *boy*? Did your sisters cut your balls off? Guess you're not much of a man then." He smirked and signaled to the driver.

The car stopped on the side of the road. He reached across to open the door on my side. "Good talk, son, but I should get back to the gala now. Ab tou Maham ki mehndi walay haathon se hi chai piyein gay." (We'll just drink chai from Maham's henna-painted hands now.)

Nauseated and at loss for words, I got out of the car. The Porsche sped off, yet the disgusting look of lust and greed in those dark eyes stayed with me as I walked to the hospital, then rode my bike home.

Zain had always been a dubious character, and now he was a drunkard reading his fiancée's emails. Whether or not he knew about his father's intentions for his future wife didn't matter.

All that mattered was that Maham needed to know—*right away*.

KIRAN

"Go to your room and do your homework, *now*," I told Daniyal and Danish in my mom voice for the third time in the last ten minutes.

One of the twins groaned. "But it's chai time."

The other pouted. "I want a samosa."

Both scrambled into their room when I glared at them, while Kaukab and Kauser threw each other a look that was just shy of them rolling their eyes at me.

"Good thing Iftikhar isn't here," Kauser chuckled.

Kaukab laughed. "He is so scared of her. Poor guy would have been scrambling into the room after the twins."

"Hey, at least my husband dares to show his face in front of her. Hussain hides out in Dubai."

There was a running joke between these two: I intimidated their husbands. I prayed they never found out why.

It's impossible to recover from a failed marriage in our society. I may have found the strength to move on from my own, but the world only saw me as a poor, broken woman, raising her sons all by herself. How many times was I to repeat that my husband asked me to choose between him and my siblings? Or that once he found out I'd lost control of Tariq Enterprise, he packed his bags and left overnight, never to be seen again?

So yes, I let my brothers-in-law know that my sisters were not toys to be played with. Luckily, both Iftikhar and Hussain were absolute gentlemen.

Ignoring my sisters' jokes, I sat back and smiled as I took in the scene in front of me. A pot of steaming chai, a plate of potato samosas and chicken patties, and another of homemade brownies and almond cookies. Laughter and hilarious jabs filled the air in my small living room.

Life was good. With grim memories forgotten, we were making wonderful new ones.

For a few minutes, I forgot that we still lived in the shadows of our past. The moment was quickly over.

Kauser's phone rang. A smile curved her lips. That's how I knew her husband was calling.

Then her eyes widened, and her smile disappeared. "What do you mean Osman is missing?"

That's how I knew Asif Ghazanfar was involved.

With Kauser's phone in one hand and my car keys in the other, I was almost out of the door when Osman appeared in the stairwell outside my apartment. My thumping heart and panicking brain had so many questions, but they had to wait when he immediately asked, "Why were you trying to get in touch with Maham?"

Kauser and Kaukab rushed past me, fretting over our brother. He seemed distraught to one, and unwell to the other. We all came back into the apartment, but his questioning gaze never left me.

"What are you not telling me, Api?" he asked again, his voice firmer. "I am not a child. Tell me, why were you so concerned about Maham?"

I glanced at Kauser. She sucked in a breath and sat on the nearest chair. "Tell him," she whispered.

"I overheard Asif Ghazanfar say that girls like Maham were easy to get rid of," I told my brother. But that sentence alone wasn't why Kaukab's hand gripped Kauser's shoulder.

It was because Kauser had once been a girl much younger than Maham and had stayed in the same house as Asif Ghazanfar. She hadn't wanted to tell Osman anything before because he was a child. Now, he crouched in front of her, his hand resting on her knee, a grown-up brother who understood his sisters much more than we gave him credit for.

"What did he do to you, Kauser Baji?" he asked gently.

Her voice shook, but the words flowed.

"The night Ami died, Abu and Kiran stayed in the hospital. Phuppo and her husband took us to Dada's home and stayed the night with us. We all had dinner and then went to our rooms. I had almost cried myself to sleep when my door opened, and that man walked in. He told me to stay quiet and said Phuppo had sent him to check up on me. Except he kept coming closer and closer, till I could smell his breath and feel his hands."

She didn't have to elaborate. Unlike the journalists and lawyers to whom she had told that sordid tale in detail before, her brother believed her, no questions asked. His arms wrapped around her; hers wrapped around him. They were each other's strength against a past that had become unbearably heavy.

"I am so sorry," he whispered as his jaw clenched and fists tightened. He was filled with rage but holding it in. Kauser saw it too.

"It was a long time ago, Osman," she said. It had been more than twenty-one years.

"I am going to *kill* that man," he replied anyway.

Kauser cupped his face in her palms. "No, Osman. That would make us no better than him. Besides, God has given us so much, and we have to trust Him to punish that man when his time comes."

It took us a few more minutes to calm Osman down. His anger was justified, his need for revenge not unfamiliar to us. Yet what kind of sisters would we be if we let his rage consume him?

"We may be voiceless, Osman. But we have never been weak." Kaukab reminded him.

He ran his fingers through his hair, his shoulders sagging—not in defeat or acceptance, but burdened by the weight of reality, just as ours had been for so many years.

Heaving a sigh, he pulled out an envelope from his bag and laid it on the table.

"What is this?" I asked.

"An invitation to Maham's wedding with Zain."

Kauser gaped at it. "Another girl will live in the same house as that man."

"And he has every intention of doing the same to her." Osman told us everything that had happened at the gala and during the car ride afterwards.

"Api, you have Sikander Ahmed's contact, right? Let's reach out to him."

That thought had occurred to me too, but Kauser shook her head. "Even if that journalist believes you, who else will? Osman has no proof of his conversation with Asif. Yet, Asif has not only video evidence, but also dozens of witnesses who will vouch for the generosity and love he showed towards his orphaned nephew."

As she spoke, I pictured Asif's lawyer addressing the press, weaving a story about greedy relatives who would never be satisfied, no matter what the benevolent Asif Ghazanfar did for them.

"We still have to warn Maham," Kaukab insisted.

"We don't even know where she is. I haven't heard from her, despite texting and emailing," Osman reminded us.

My gaze fell on the cream envelope and the wedding invitation it held.

"But we do know where she will be in a month from now," I told my family.

That day, sitting in my small living room, we planned to rescue a young woman from her treacherous father-in-law by following our moral compass.

We forgot that our moral compass was the fodder the devil fed upon.

CHAPTER 18

Wedding

OSMAN

Most Pakistani weddings are arranged by the girl's parents. But Maham's parents didn't have a house of their own in Karachi, making the fortified Ghazanfar mansion in front of us an understandable choice.

"This place is huge! How many rooms do you think it has?" I asked Api as I got out of her locally made Suzuki Cultus, parked among the throngs of German and Japanese luxury cars.

Api slipped her hand around my arm and muttered, "How am I supposed to know?"

"You've never been in there either?"

"No."

Her lips pursed. A signal I knew well—she wasn't in the mood to answer unnecessary questions.

Thus, in silent awe, I headed towards the massive iron gates decorated with an arch of white and red flowers. Burly guards with AR-15s guarded the entrance and lined the boundary wall at regular intervals. One of them asked us for the invitation and searched Api's bag before letting us in.

"Why is there so much security?" I whispered to Api.

"Illegal money can go as quickly as it comes. These people will protect it with everything they have," she answered pointedly.

"Oh, there you are. I was beginning to think you'd never show up," the voice I had grown to loathe called out as we walked on the cobblestoned path that cut across the main garden. Clad in a black sherwani, his peppered hair brushed back stylishly, Asif gazed at my sister so eerily I instinctively moved in front of her.

His coal-black eyes honed in on me. "Kauser and Kaukab didn't come?" he smirked.

"Do *not* take their names," I snapped.

"Aah." The man snickered and sidestepped me so he could face Api again. "I see you've filled his head with lies too."

"It is not a lie," my sister whispered harshly.

His hand reached for the dupatta on her shoulder. I shoved it away before he could touch her, nearly punching him in the face—held back only by my sister's strong grip on my arm.

"Don't you dare touch her. My sisters do not lie," I muttered through gritted teeth.

"Then why are you whispering?" His voice rose slightly, just enough that a handful of guests nearby glanced at us. "Tell everyone about it openly."

Bastard.

He knew we wouldn't do that. This was a matter of my sister's honor, and without her being present, or having a legal course of action, we couldn't ever openly talk about her abuse in public. Especially now, when he would just ridicule us in front of his guests.

I swallowed my anger and asked, "If you had to insult us, why have you called us?"

"I am not so crazy that I would call sick people like you to my house. Zain was the one who insisted on having his cousins at his wedding. The boy has gone soft living in America. Wants to mend relationships or some crap like that." The older man huffed and waved us away, telling us that he did not want to see our faces for the rest of the evening.

Zain wanted us here? I should have mulled over the legitimacy of that statement, but at that moment Zain's father had ignited the fire of revenge inside me.

"Who the hell does he think he is?"

Api pulled me into an empty nook of the garden, and her maternal voice came out. "Calm down, Osman. We are not here to create a scene. We are only here to meet Maham and her family. And that is it. After that, we go home."

"How am I supposed to calm down when he goes around spewing filth about every woman I know?"

"By focusing on the goal." I recognized the stern look in her eyes. She was in charge now.

We walked a few more steps towards the main event space. Ignoring the beautiful decorations, our gaze settled on the empty stage ahead. The nikah had not yet been performed.

"Come on. I see her parents." Api tugged at my arm.

"You know what to do," she whispered when we got closer to them.

"Ms. Kiran! Fancy seeing you here," a woman dressed in an elegant shalwar kameez called out to my sister.

"Assalamu Alaikum, Mrs. Qureshi, Mr. Qureshi." Api smiled and nodded politely at the couple. "We're actually related to Zain's family."

Mrs. Qureshi's hand flew up to her mouth. "Oh my, I didn't know that. I would not have complained so much about Maham's grades at her parent-teacher meeting had I known."

Api chuckled. "Don't worry—I didn't think you were complaining at all." She pushed me forward gently as she spoke. "This is my brother, Osman. He was also Maham's classmate."

With a warm smile, Mr. Qureshi extended his hand. "Oh yes, of course. You were on her debate team. I remember her mentioning you went to medical school."

I shook his hand and got straight to the point. "Uncle, where is Maham? One of her best friends from school, Sanam Uzair, wanted to speak to her before the nikah to wish her good luck."

Sanam, of course, knew nothing of our plan, but taking her name did the trick.

"Ah, Sanam, yes, I remember her too." We started walking towards the house where the bride was waiting for all the guests to arrive.

Maham's father talked excitedly about how grand her in-laws' house was—a castle fit for the daughter they had raised as a princess.

While he spoke, I wondered how her father-in-law could sleep at night knowing what he had done to a young girl, or how her mother-in-law could stay married to a pedophile.

We turned down a hallway and arrived at a dark wooden door. He opened it, revealing a woman pacing the room. She wore a crimson-colored dress lavishly adorned with gold embroidery, complemented by expensive-looking jewelry.

Kohl-lined eyes stared at me in surprise. "Osman?"

"Yes, sweetie. Why don't you two catch up? I am going to check when Asif Bhai wants to start the nikah ceremony," her father replied.

Maham waited for the door to close before saying, "I wasn't expecting you to be here."

"That would make two of us. But Zain invited us."

She looked away, her fingers twisting together as she sighed. "So, you're on his side now?"

"What? No, I am not on his side at all. Actually, I need to tell—"

She didn't wait for me to finish before her face contorted with agony. "I don't love Zain anymore," she blurted out and started pacing the room again. "I know he loves me. But love is supposed to be nurturing and kind, not suffocating and painful."

Her words caught me off guard, yet when I asked why she was dressed as a bride despite all that, her response wasn't surprising.

"My parents come from a humble background. Only they know how much they have struggled to get to their upper-middle-class status. They think Zain will be able to give me more than they ever can. And he has them wrapped under his charisma so tightly, they think his behavior is him simply courting me."

She sighed and sank into the sofa. "Zain won't let me breathe. My parents won't let me escape. That's why I am dressed as a bride—praying for divine intervention at the last minute."

Divine or not, the door slammed open, and the intervention arrived.

"You're not marrying that boy," Mr. Qureshi declared. His gruff voice startled both of us, and we turned to see the three older adults standing in the doorway.

He shook slightly, his own eyes matching the fury I had felt. His expression quickly softened as he walked up to his daughter, followed by Mrs. Qureshi. Api closed the door behind her, and the five of us huddled in that study.

"Maham, I know you love Zain, but his father is a disgusting . . ." he started to say when Maham interrupted him.

"But Dad, I don't love Zain. Not anymore. That's what I have been trying to tell you."

Api and I stood together, witnessing Maham's parents finally see through the façade of the Ghazanfars. With our message delivered, we thought our job was done, and Api gestured for me to leave, when Mr. Qureshi stopped us. This time, his face twisted with worry and fear more than fury.

"They are not going to let us just walk out of here and be okay with us making a fool of them in front of all their guests."

Api looked at me and gulped as the reality of our situation sank in. A reality that neither of us were prepared for.

"There are armed guards everywhere," I added, which only served to heighten the palpable panic in the room.

Tense silence replaced our outrage with helplessness, until Api spoke again.

"There's a gate along the back wall of this house, behind the kitchen. I remember it opening into a small alley between this house and the next. That alley is not visible from the main road, so it may have been left unguarded."

"We can use that to escape," Maham whispered, the hope of a way out immediately brightening her countenance.

Heads nodded; more hushed plans were made. The kitchen was only a short distance from the room we were in. Even if we met someone there, we could always pretend that we were looking for food or water.

"All of us can't go, though. Our own guests are arriving, and our hosts will get suspicious if the bride's parents are suddenly not there to welcome them," Mrs. Qureshi noted, and her husband nodded.

"But—" The panic in Maham's eyes returned immediately.

"We'll get you out of here, don't worry," Api reassured her.

We will? My eyes widened, but I kept quiet. The thumping of my heart at having to pull a James Bond move with a bride on her nikah day needed to be ignored for now.

The unplanned escapade began.

Mr. and Mrs. Qureshi exited the room to buy us time. With their poker faces on, their smiles hid the distress they must have been feeling.

Api insisted on driving the getaway car. The alley behind the house was apparently too hidden to be found by the untrained eye in the dark, and we could not afford any mistakes. She accompanied us to the kitchen first, walking hastily through the main corridor, across the foyer, and through a swinging door. There was no hesitation in her step, no double-guessing, almost like she knew this house like the back of her hand.

"How do you know this place so well?" I asked her. Hadn't she said she had never set foot here before?

Both women shushed me simultaneously.

"It's a long story. I'll tell you later," Api replied, much to my confusion, but I didn't pursue the matter. There were more pressing issues.

We peeked into the dark pathway behind the kitchen and the row of thick cedar trees that grew along the back wall. A few feet away, the back gate was clearly visible, and there was no sign of any human, guard or otherwise. With Api rushing back to the front door, Maham and I exited the kitchen from the back door. I ran down the path, my heart racing, sweat building up under the stupid tie I wore.

"Ouch." I heard a feminine voice behind me, making me pause.

Maham was several steps behind me. She bent down, her hand touching her left foot. "I can't run in these damn heels," she whispered frantically.

"Then take them off." I backtracked quickly to help her. Her heavy lehenga made it almost impossible for her to take them off herself. Not that it was easy for highly inexperienced me to unfasten the threads of gold wrapped around her ankle, but several curses later, I succeeded.

Grabbing the heels in one hand, her hand in the other, we rushed down the path again, reaching the metal gate a few seconds later. The gate only had a bolt on it, but no lock. Rust made it squeak, but luckily, there was still no movement in the darkness. I peered into the dimly lit narrow alleyway, almost expecting a gun to be pointed at my face. But again, there was no sign of any life other than the shadow of a car at one end of the alley.

As the car drew closer, Maham and I stepped out. I let go of her hand, and she turned towards me. Her eyes watered, but there was relief across her makeup-painted face. A moment later her arms were around my torso, and she was hugging me tightly, taking me by surprise.

"Thank you, Osman. Thank you so much. I don't know how I'll ever repay you," she said.

I gingerly patted her upper back. "You're very welcome."

She stepped back quickly.

The old Cultus was next to us now. "Get in," Api ordered.

"Mission accomplished!" I let out a whoop of relief as we drove out of the alley and away from the family that was steeped in a legacy of darkness. And it had all been accomplished seamlessly.

"What's the point of having so much security up front when the back gate is left unguarded?" I mused.

"When your entire life is a farce, you get stupider too." Api chuckled, as did Maham and I, because my elder sister was never wrong.

Yet this time, she was.

CHAPTER 19

Unrelenting Pain

ZAIN

Disbelief.

How could she not be in her room? She had been right there. I had seen her come in. I had met her in the foyer. I had walked her to the room she was to wait in. I told her to relax. I told her she looked beautiful. I told her she was going to be mine. I told her I loved her. I repeated those words until she repeated them after me.

"I love you. And you love me," she had said, clear as daylight.

Then where was she now?

I had been pulled into a meeting with Abu and his business associates despite my protests, when all I wanted was to hear her truth one more time and put my demons to rest. But by the time that damn meeting was over, she was gone. The diamond ring, two carats in a princess cut, sat on the table. Mocking me. Scorning my love. Tearing me apart.

Pain.

Abu's hand rested on my shoulder; his gaze was steadily on me.

"Mr. and Mrs. Qureshi said that Maham does not wish to proceed with this nikah," he said.

"No. No, Abu, forget about them. Ask Maham. She wants to marry me. Ask her. She said yes," I implored.

"She's long gone, son," Abu replied.

I dropped to the ground. The soft thud on the grass should not have hurt me. Yet every bone in my body broke, every muscle ripped, every vessel bled. Pain, unrelenting pain, seeped through my core, shattering my existence.

Anger.

Maham loves me.

Someone must have conspired against me; that was the only explanation I had.

I vowed to fin d out who it was, and then I vowed to rip their heart out and feed it to the dogs.

I vowed to make them feel so much pain, they would wish they were dead—just like I was.

I vowed to search for her in every corner of this earth until I found her. And if I didn't—

I would burn the world to ashes.

No Maham. No Zain. No humanity. Nada.

Disbelief.

Pain.

Anger.

Repeat cycle.

That was me. Two days, two nights. Locked in my room, I destroyed every tangible object within those four walls. It looked like a war zone, but nothing compared to the turmoil within me as I went over every excruciating detail of my relationship with her. From the moment I saw her, to the proposal in that very spot, to our move to the US.

Her words, both said and written, the look in her eyes, her expressions in my presence, all played in an endless loop in my head. A timeline of sorts developed. The initial chemistry between us had led to affection, which had led to trust. But distance and time had become our enemy.

The thoughts paused. A small voice inside me spoke: *Was it just that?*

I sat down on the edge of my bed, or what had been my bed. Broken springs from a slashed mattress now jutted out, catching the edge of my shirt, ripping it as I slid down the side of the bed onto the littered floor.

But I didn't notice any of that because the voice within me became louder.

Had time and distance been the only problems?

Or had she seen through the facade and caught a glimpse of the real me? The one Abu sees?

"Who in their right mind would love a coward like you? She is only after your inheritance," he had once said to me.

Was my inheritance not enough to keep her with me now? Or had she run away from my cowardice?

I had tried to be brave. I had tried to save her from this world, yet—

A knock on the door interrupted my self-loathing. I waited for the intruder to leave, but the knocking became incessant, the gruff voice calling out my name, unrelenting.

"Zain, you've done enough drama. Be a man and come out now."

I kept quiet. The last thing I needed was another lecture on how I wasn't man enough to even keep a woman under control. But then he said something that piqued my interest, making me approach my bedroom door.

"Our security team has something they want to show you.".

Opening the door, I saw him standing in his signature black suit, flanked by two men in uniform. "What is it?"

Abu shoved a laptop in my hands. "See for yourself."

He started the video, and grainy dark pixels blended to display images that might not have made sense to others, but were unmistakably familiar to me. The video rolled, and each image plunged a knife deeper into my hemorrhaging heart.

A woman in a lehenga, a path behind our house, a man stooping to help her take her heels off, him holding her hand as they rushed out the back gate.

Disbelief. Pain.

"Watch another video." Abu hit a key on the laptop.

The woman in a lehenga, her arms around the man, his around her, her smile, the shy look in her beautiful eyes, the laughter on his face, him holding the car's door for her, him helping her put her lehenga in the car, her showing him gratitude, them driving away.

Anger.

Every emotion in that video was supposed to be for me. Not *him*. Not my cousin. Not the fucking nerd who was supposed to be in love with someone else.

"I am going to fucking kill that asshole!" I yelled, and threw the laptop across the room, shattering it against the wall.

A rising tide of rage engulfed me. She had lit a fire, then she had extinguished the flames. But he—he had lit an inferno that could not be curtailed or contained; it could only feed on itself, scorching my mind, charring my soul.

Hell hath no fury like a lover scorned.

"Where are you going?" Wrinkled but surprisingly strong fingers wrapped around my bicep.

"To get Maham. He must have tricked her. There is no way she fell for him." I yanked my arm away. "And then I am going to kill that bastard."

Footsteps followed me, and a man—not my father—spoke hesitantly. "Uh . . . Mr. Zain, Ms. Maham has left the country. Her flight was last night. We confirmed it with the airport security."

What? I swung around. A new temporary target for my wrath had been acquired.

"You idiots. Why did you take so long to find this video?"

Fists pummeled the man who could easily have fought back, but I was his master, and he, my servant. I continued till my breathing evened out, blood that wasn't mine splattered across my shirt, and Abu's calm, cold voice broke through the thick smoke around me.

"Satisfied?"

The bloodied man lay on the floor, his colleague bent over helping him up. Anger turned to regret, which started to clear the way for guilt, but Abu spoke again.

"They were clever to have chosen that path to escape. Not many people know of that alley or that gate. In the dark, it took us a while to process the video footage from the security cameras and get some images off it."

I clutched the shirt of the bloodied man's colleague. "Where is Osman?"

He stuttered; words regurgitated out of him faster than blood would have had he not spoken. "In the hospital. He is doing his shift. He gets off at five."

Confusion briefly marred my mind. *If he ran away with Maham, why is she on a flight out of the country and he at the hospital, doing a shift as if nothing happened?*

Those thoughts became words, and the guards' heads lowered, while Abu's eyes narrowed. When he spoke, his face was inches from mine as he bared his teeth, and his hot breath forced me to blink. "You will never become a man. He came into your house, he took your fiancée, and all you're concerned about is that he is working at the hospital. Did you ever stop to think Osman is playing games with you?"

He spat in my face. "You're stupid *and* a coward. I am ashamed to even call you my son."

The smirk on his face as he stepped back plunged another dagger into my heart—already crumbling under the weight of betrayal. "No wonder Maham left you," he scoffed. "Your cousin has always been more intelligent than you. I am willing to bet he is also far braver than you."

Words. Spoken when your brain connects to the muscles of your lungs and vocal cords, forcing air through thin strings of cartilage, causing them to vibrate.

Words. Nothing but vibrations of air molecules around you.

Words. Vibrations that have the power to turn an innocent into a sinner, a lover into a hater, a coward into a hero.

The air around us stilled. All eyes honed in on me, while those words pounded my heart. Realization sank in—Maham was gone, and now I had nothing to lose. Nothing to tame the demon inside.

My jaw tightened, and my neck cracked as I tilted it left and then to the right, my mind focused on a singular target.

"Take the car out."

The bloodied guard started walking with me, speaking into his walkie-talkie. The other was held back by my father. They carried on a whispered conversation, which I foolishly ignored. In that moment, nothing else mattered.

Osman had taken everything from me. And now, he was going to pay.

KIRAN

I was sitting alone in my car in the school's parking lot when my boisterous sons climbed in.

"Come on, Mama, let's go home quickly; I have a football match in two hours," Daniyal said from the front passenger seat as he clicked the seatbelt in place.

Danish pushed his shoulder from the backseat. "Dude, you guys are playing your archrivals today. You better get revenge for the last time they thrashed you."

"Neither of you are going anywhere. I've already told you—no afterschool activities." I gritted my teeth, as much in nervousness as in anger, that my teenage sons seemed to have lost their ability to listen to anything I said.

I started driving, ignoring their cries and arguments.

"Why, Mama?"

"This is so unfair."

"What are you punishing us for?"

"What do you think is going to happen if we go out? The city's situation is fine these days."

But it wasn't the city's situation I was worried about. Neither was I interested in punishing my sons. In fact, truth be told, I wasn't sure what I was afraid of, other than the silence.

It had been two days since we had helped Maham escape her own nikah. And only a day since her parents had taken her out of the country, to an unknown location, with promises of never forgetting each other, but severing all contact for the purpose of safety.

Yet, there was silence.

It had been an easy getaway. Phuppa or Zain were nowhere to be seen as I hurriedly but discreetly walked towards the front gate. I had bumped into Phuppo, who had asked why I was leaving early. But a simple explanation of having an emergency with my sons had been enough to make her step back and not ask any more questions.

Or perhaps the way she averted her eyes was a reflection of her guilt, because of what she had done to us, or maybe it was shame because I knew her reality: a battered housewife, hiding behind a diamond necklace and designer saree.

Yet, the feeling of doom was persistent. Like the eye of the storm, things were too still. Too easy. It was odd enough that my maternal instincts had been firing nonstop and I had transformed into an unreasonable hag to my boys, who had no idea of what Osman and I had done.

Though, my brother hadn't been spared either.

"Call Mani," I instructed Daniyal.

"Why? Mani is at work. You won't reply to us, then why are you talking to him?" he shot back, rather insolently.

"Be quiet and call him," I snapped. He obliged.

"Mani? Talk to Mama."

"Osman, when are you coming home?" He knew me well enough to know why I was asking him that.

"It's 2 p.m., and I don't get off till five, Api. Don't worry, I am fine. There is no way anything will happen while I am at work. And after that, I will come straight home. I promise," he replied in that usual calm voice that was enough to put anyone's anxiety at ease.

Deep breaths, I tried to calm myself. He was right; the hospital was a secure place. He had repeatedly reassured me of that in the past as well.

"Api, go and take a nap. I'll be home soon," he reassured me again.

His pager rang and he had to hang up. Daniyal and Danish didn't ask any more questions. At home, they quietly had lunch and then did their homework, without a peep about their school's football match.

I, too, lay in bed, and despite my mind repeatedly going back to the events that occurred about two days ago, tiredness crept into my muscles and my heavy eyelids succumbed to the promise of peace. That nap was dreamless, and the peace fleeting. Before I knew it, my shoulder was being shaken and I opened my eyes to my twins' ashen faces.

"Mama, Iftikhar Uncle called. He said not to worry. He is with Mani," Danish said.

"Okay." I looked at my sons with confusion. "They work at the same hospital. Why do I need to worry?"

Daniyal handed me his phone and pointed to a Breaking News alert. "Because he is a trauma surgeon."

I read the news, and every nightmare I'd ever had turned true.

"Shooting at Karachi's Largest Hospital: At least one young doctor injured. Culprits fled the scene. This is a developing story. Stay tuned for more details."

CHAPTER 20

Smoke Screen

OSMAN

Getting shot hadn't been on my list of things to do that afternoon when I had stood under the clear blue sky, basking in the warm winter sun.

"Yo, Osman, you coming to the OR?"

Ameerah was calling out from across the courtyard. Her maroon hair shone in the bright sunlight, making her look like a lighthouse beacon. With her loud voice and incessant commenting on everything under the sun, it wasn't hard to be forewarned about her presence—giving me a chance to escape.

Right now, though, I had no choice but to nod to her in acknowledgement, and finish sending the message that I was typing out.

Me: A lot has been going on here. I'll call at some point. Have to run now. Case starting in the OR.

A reply came immediately.

Sanam: Okay. No rush. I know this is a busy time for you. Just wanted to see how you were doing.

The surgery rotation was one of the toughest in medical college. Add to that the drama of rescuing your friend and helping her family sneak out of the country, and a tough month becomes an insane one.

Me: Sorry it's been crazy, but I am fine. Surgery rotation finishes in a couple of weeks. Take care of yourself too!

How could I have known that would be my last message to Sanam for what felt like an eternity? Had I known, I would have told her that I wasn't afraid of dying for her.

But I was a student on my surgical rotation, following my classmate while pretending to scroll through my phone so I wouldn't have to converse with her. When we got off the elevator on the fifth floor, across from the locker rooms, Ameerah spoke anyway.

"Who are you always texting?" she asked.

"The girl I will marry one day."

Clear. Concise. True. I answered the question and walked past her to swipe my card and enter the men's locker room.

Why Ameerah cared about me texting was of no interest to me, but if Sanam was right about her trying to flirt, it was time I put an end to any fantasies she might be harboring. If Sanam was wrong, then her reaction wouldn't matter anyway.

The door shut behind me, and I thought I was safe—from Ameerah Sheikh and the world at large.

I couldn't have been more wrong.

ZAIN

We drove through the gates of the hospital but didn't turn towards the main entrance like we should have, surprising me.

"Where are you going?" I growled at the driver.

The guard next to me intervened. "We are going from the back, sir. There is a way to the operating rooms through the hospital wing being built in your name."

"Operating room?"

"Dean Nadir said that is where Osman will be."

How does he know the dean of this college? Before I could ask, the Jeep screeched to a halt outside a construction site on the side of the main hospital building. A makeshift board read "Site of Ghazanfar Surgical Pavilion."

"We don't have too much time," the guard said, jumping out and motioning for me to follow him through a half-constructed corridor.

Men in dusty uniforms and hard hats were working diligently around us, funded by Abu's donation, I presumed. But whether it was the guard in uniform next to me or the speed with which we were moving, no one questioned us.

"Come from here," he said.

I followed him through an open door at the side of the hospital building through which construction workers were hefting bags of cement. We got on an elevator, and the guard hit the button for the fifth floor.

"How do you know the way around the hospital?" I asked more out of curiosity than anything else.

Instead of answering, the man clicked his tongue and dared to shake his head at me. "Sir, you keep asking me questions, and the man who touched your woman, hugged the love of your life, is happily living his life. What does that say about you?"

Curiosity gave way to rage.

"*Shut up!*" I yelled at him.

He glared back. "Get as angry at me as you want. In fact, here. Take this." He slid out a concealed gun and put it in my hand, wrapping my fingers around it. "Kill me if you want to. But don't lose your focus from your enemy."

I had never held a gun before. The cold metal in my hand felt foreign. Yet, I would be lying if I said that the sight of my fingers curled around the grip, with one around the trigger, didn't send a thrill down my spine. So much power, concentrated in a piece of metal. It could end lives or save lives. You could be the hero behind it, or the coward in front of it.

The image of the bloodied guard on the floor outside my room flashed in front of me, and so did those interrupted feelings of guilt and regret. I looked up at the man, his dark eyes focused on me, unflinching and unafraid.

A hero can stand in front of a gun, and a coward behind it too, an inner voice reminded me, forcing me to blink.

I handed the gun back to him. "Stop being dramatic."

The man sneered. "People say true lovers are warriors. You're afraid of a measly gun. Are you sure you truly loved Maham?"

That was the straw that broke the camel's back. Before I could stop myself, I had pushed him against the wall of the elevator and had his head in a stranglehold. "Say her name again, and I will strangle you with my bare hands."

The elevator door opened, and the guard stumbled out. I followed.

"And what will you do to him?" he questioned, nodding towards two people in scrubs, one with red hair and the other who made me see red.

The man in scrubs had already disappeared into the room and the door shut by the time I reached there. But the redhead stood pale-faced and still, like a statue staring into space, until I tried to open the door my cousin had walked through.

"Hey!" she called out. "That's only for hospital staff. Who are you?"

"That man's worst nightmare." I gestured towards the keycard reader. "Open the damn door for me."

Stormy gray eyes glared back. "Why don't you go back to whatever hellhole you came from?"

"Open the door or else—"

"Or else what?" She clenched her fist.

Suddenly, her body lurched backwards, and a low, threatening voice said, "Open the door, girl, or your brain will be blown to pieces."

The guard had his gun at her temple and her arm pinned behind her. This time, those stormy gray eyes gave in.

"She is not who we want. Let her go," I whispered to the guard, who still had his gun pointed at the redhead as she swiped her badge. She was an innocent, even if feisty bystander. Shaking his head in defiance, the guard kept his grip tightly on the redhead and the gun where it was.

If I hadn't seen *him* the moment the door opened, I would have insisted again. But all I saw was the man who had destroyed everything I'd had.

The man who I had vowed to burn as intensely as I was burning.

"Ameerah, what the hell? Get out," he said.

"I . . . I can't," the girl whispered. "They threatened to kill me."

Fear. For most, it's an emotion as crippling as anger, but it is mastered by some. My once wimpy cousin, who now stood shirtless in front of me, his broad shoulders and toned abdomen on full display, should not have been one of those select few. But his narrowed eyes and wide stance said otherwise.

"Let go of her," he growled at the guard, repeating what I had just said to him. Thus, I should not have had a problem with the guard stepping back from the redhead.

But I couldn't let that happen. Could I?

My wimpy cousin couldn't be the hero who saved an innocent girl while I was yet again the villain who couldn't tame his demons, and lost another battle. If being a villain was my destiny, then it was time for me to fucking embrace it.

I grabbed the redhead and forced both her arms behind her as her body covered mine. "You want your little friend here? Tell me where my Maham is."

Wimpy Osman had the audacity to step towards me and say, "I have no idea what you're talking about."

My fingers yanked the redhead's hair, making her whimper, and he stopped in his tracks. "I know you came to our nikah to kidnap her—"

"I came because you invited us," he interrupted.

Lies, lies, and more lies.

"Why the fuck would I invite you?"

He tried to take another step towards me, his eyes focused on the redhead.

"Ask your—" he started to say.

Boom!

He didn't complete the sentence.

"Osman!" a voice shrieked from behind me.

Boom!

He fell. The redhead let out a bloodcurdling scream.

She shoved me aside and was on the floor next to him as he lay in a pool of blood. A hand grabbed my arm, pulling me out of the room, but my gaze stayed fixed on my cousin.

"Come on! We'll get caught," the guard said, dragging me behind him. My feet followed, but my mind stayed with the scene I had witnessed. None of it made sense.

"Hurry up, sir," he urged again as we ran down the stairs and through the construction site, ignoring the baffled looks of the men in hard hats.

A siren went off in the distance. We reached our Jeep, and the driver flung the doors open. He took off before we could even close them.

The sirens grew louder. Hospital security had gathered at the main gate. A wooden barrier descended quickly, but it was no match for our Jeep. The shouts of men and the sound of wood being ripped from its metal hinges filled the air around me. Air that I couldn't seem to breathe, the image of my cousin repeatedly playing in my head.

I turned to the man next to me. "Why the hell did you shoot him?"

He didn't meet my gaze, but the curl of his lips was hard to miss, as were his words when he quietly replied, "I didn't shoot him, sir. *You* did."

KIRAN

It was a family reunion of the worst kind, and it was because of Osman once again.

"Kauser, call Iftikhar, please," I begged my sister through tears that seemed unending.

"Kiran, he is trying to save Osman's life. Do you really want me to call and interrupt him?" She put her arms around me. "No news is good news."

It was so surreal—sitting here with my sons and my sisters at a hospital that I had sat in before, mourning my mother. In the years since, I had dared to dream of watching my baby brother at his graduation from the same hospital he had been born at.

Now, with dreams shattered and wounds reopened, I sat here again, desperately praying to God, alternating between bargaining with Him and complaining to Him.

How much tragedy could our family handle?

"Come on, boys, let's go get some food and water. It's been a long day," Hussain said to my sons. Their young faces were streaked with tears and their eyes still wet, but despite that, they both hugged and comforted me before leaving with Kaukab's husband.

"Mani will make it," Danish whispered.

"He has to," Daniyal replied.

"Pray for him," Hussain told them both.

This time was different too. We had family that we could trust to step up, rather than step on us.

With my sons gone, my attention drifted to another person sitting in the corner, hugging herself, her clothes still stained with my brother's blood. I had heard about the way she held pressure on his wounds and had fought to be in the OR with him, only for Iftikhar to push her back because she was too traumatized to be there. Since then, she had sat there, quietly sobbing.

"Ameerah, come sit with us," I told her.

"I am so sorry ... I couldn't ..." Her chest heaved when she walked over. I put my arms around her. "You were so brave today. You saved his life."

"I could have done more." Her shoulders shook in my arms. "He was trying to save me, and now . . ."

"Don't go there, Ameerah. None of this is your fault. There is only *one* criminal here."

Ameerah was wiping her tears when Kaukab called out for me. I gave the young woman a tight hug before walking to my sister, who stood next to a well-groomed policeman in uniform.

"This is Inspector Junaid Razzak. He will personally overlook Osman's case."

The man nodded respectfully. "Assalamu Alaikum. I am sorry to be here, but I want to assure you that I will leave no stone unturned to find this criminal and his accomplice."

"He is not just any criminal. He is the son of the richest man in Pakistan and can easily pay you off," I couldn't help saying. Bitterness seeped in as I asked, "Why should I expect any justice from you?"

He appeared surprised, but the emotion was fleeting, quickly masked by composure.

"Miss, I have never once taken a bribe in my career. But even if I did, no amount would be enough to cover the debt I owe your family. Osman and Dr. Iftikhar saved my son's life a few weeks ago. I owe them everything." His brown eyes softened with a paternal agony I recognized well.

He left as swiftly as he had appeared. A small part of me regretted snapping at the inspector, but a much louder voice reminded me of all the times I had sat in a police station, trying to report the man whose wealth and prestige overshadowed my family's harrowing experiences.

"Iftikhar?" Kauser's voice distracted me from the past.

My brother-in-law hugged his wife as he started to explain. "He's not out of danger yet. He lost a lot of blood, his right lung has collapsed, his liver is lacerated, and there is some damage to his diaphragm."

"Plain English, please" I blurted out impatiently. "Is Osman going to be okay?"

"Sorry, Kiran." He slowed down. "I don't know for sure. The next twenty-four hours will be critical. But don't worry, I'm not leaving his side until he is stable."

"Neither am I," Ameerah's resolute voice came from near us.

There is strength in numbers, they say. I realized how true that was, standing in the midst of a family that came together when everything seemed to be falling apart.

ZAIN

The midnight moon was the only light permeating the darkness surrounding me.

"The plane's here. Come on," Abu hissed from the corner of the hangar in a small private airport outside Karachi. I grabbed our two duffel bags, hurriedly packed with essential items, and followed him out.

"Isn't Ami coming?"

"That stupid woman is drugged up half the time. She'll just slow us down. Besides, they can arrest her and make her pay for your sins. I don't give a damn."

It was hard to argue against that. The last I had seen of her that night, she had downed some pills and was heading up to her room.

"Does she even know what happened?"

"You ask a lot of stupid questions for someone accused of attempted murder," he grumbled.

For the hundredth time, I found myself setting the record straight.

"I am *not* the one who pulled the trigger—the guard did. I shouldn't have to leave the country like a criminal at all."

"It doesn't matter who pulled the trigger. The fact is, your fingerprints are on that gun, and you are the only one who has motive to shoot Osman. The moment the police find the weapon at the construction site, they'll have hard evidence that you were involved. Even a half-witted judge wouldn't hesitate to put you in prison."

Touching that gun was a mistake, I agreed, but I had a witness. "That redheaded girl was there. She can tell everyone that I am innocent."

Abu swung around mid-stride, and his hand was on my collar before I could say anything else. "That girl's friend was shot in front of her. What the hell makes you think she will say anything in your favor? But if you are going to stay a stupid coward, then, fine—stay in Pakistan, go to jail, and die there. I couldn't care less."

He shoved me and resumed walking towards the small, chartered plane that stood ready for us on the tarmac.

How I had gone from a heartbroken lover to an alleged criminal in eight hours was a question I was still trying to answer. But one thing was certain: I was out of options.

Abu was right—Osman and that redhead saw me as the villain, and villains don't get to buy their way out of prison, especially not with our family and company under relentless scrutiny from the authorities.

I had no choice but to lie low for some time.

"Where are we going?" I called out, and picked up my pace. He didn't glance back at me, but I heard his reply, loud and clear.

"Houston, Texas."

CHAPTER 21

Guests

ZAIN

Karachi—Tashkent—Frankfurt—Houston.

After forty-eight hours of turbulent flights, cramped airport lounges, and economy-class seats, we finally found ourselves in the immigration line at George Bush Intercontinental Airport in Houston, Texas.

"Purpose of visit?" the immigration officer asked.

"Dropping my son off at college," my father replied, while I pulled out the student visa paperwork from ULA.

That's all Houston was supposed to be: a port of entry into the US before we caught a domestic flight to Los Angeles.

I never expected to exit the airport and see my father waving to a Mercedes that had pulled up outside the international terminal. When the car stopped, a man stepped out with a wide smile on his face.

"Asif Ghazanfar!" he exclaimed, embracing my father in a bear hug. "It's been a while."

"Far too long, my friend," Abu responded, before turning to me.

"This is my son, Zain."

Though surprised, I greeted the man and extended my hand. He shook it and grinned.

"Zakariya—call me Zak. I believe you know my daughter."

"I do?" My confused gaze darted between Abu and his friend.

"Yes, son. You remember Sanam, right? From school." My father smiled.

Sanam? The exhaustion of the past two days lifted in an instant. I stared at my father's back as he thanked his friend for letting us stay at his place.

How the fuck had I ended up at Sanam's father's doorstep?

"Abu, what is the meaning of this?" I asked my father as soon as we stepped into the guest suites at Zakariya Uzair's palatial home in the suburbs of Houston, Texas.

"Meaning of what, son?" he asked, without even a hint of the exasperation that I had witnessed in Karachi.

Emboldened by his subdued demeanor, I proceeded with the question that I had asked myself again and again the whole ride from the airport to this house.

"The meaning of the fact that we are staying at Sanam's dad's house. *Sanam*, the girl you asked me to marry, but whom I refused."

His voice stayed steady. "We are here because of Maham. Not Sanam. I don't have the same network here in the US that I do in Pakistan. Zak does."

"He'll help us find Maham?" Hope crept into my heart against my will.

Abu's gaze hardened. "Yes. And her bloody parents."

He pulled out a laptop and opened an Excel file. There were rows upon rows of purchased items with their prices, totaling well over a quarter of a million dollars.

"These were gifts I bought for them," I said aloud.

"Gifts that those con artists have run away with."

"Maham is *not* a con artist. Her love was real." My voice wavered. Even after everything she had done to me, how was I to forget those days when she'd held my hand and told me that she loved my heart?

The softness in her eyes, the warmth of her words—there was truth to it all. There had to be.

Tears blurred my vision, but no rebuke came from my father. Instead, he put a gentle hand on my shoulder and said, "Sometimes the people who claim to love us are the ones who hurt us the most."

My broken heart convinced itself that he was talking about Maham. But the thing about broken hearts is that they tend to be foolishly short-sighted.

OSMAN

Everything hurt.

The lights were too bright, my throat felt like I had swallowed needles, and when I tried to move my arms and legs, they could barely lift their own weight.

"You're awake," a familiar voice spoke from somewhere in the brightness around me.

"Turn the lights down, please," I whispered.

"Oh, sure." Footsteps rushed away.

With the lights dimmed, I blinked my eyes open a little wider. Tubes snaked out from the right side of my chest; wires connected to stickers clung to the left. White gauze wrapped tightly around my abdomen. The room was filled with all things familiar—beeping monitors, bags of clear fluid and one of blood, and a silent ventilator, its screen turned off, at the side of the bed.

A figure hanging back in the corner caught my attention.

"Ameerah?"

"Yes, it's me," she replied.

Her hoarse voice was different from the loud, shrill one I was accustomed to. She took a few hesitant steps closer, and I noticed her matted hair and drooping eyes.

"You look . . . horrible."

She rolled her eyes, but a brief smile appeared. "You look worse, idiot. And you got shot."

Memories came back—quick and painful: the locker room's door slamming open, the sight of a gun, my cousin taunting me, the look of terror in my classmate's eyes.

"He didn't hurt you, did he?" I asked her.

She shook her head slowly. "No. But he would have if it hadn't been for you."

The nurse walked in, and Ameerah stepped back while I answered all the medical questions I would have ordinarily been asking my patients. After another five minutes of interrogation, she smiled and nodded towards Ameerah. "You're lucky to have such a great friend. She hasn't left your side for more than two days."

Ameerah shrugged. "It's no big deal. Your sisters needed a break." She held up a pen and a writing pad. "Plus, I came up with some great ideas for our fifth-year research project."

"Thank you," I said, attempting a smile at my eccentric classmate, who I was certain had played a significant role in keeping me alive. But the pen she waved around triggered another memory, and I reflexively tried to sit up, prompting Ameerah to rush over.

"Hey, calm down. What are you trying to do?"

My gaze darted around the room for any sign of the object I had always carried in my pocket. "Where are my clothes? The ones I was wearing that day."

"Usually, any patient belongings are brought up to the room with them. There must a bag around here somewhere," the nurse replied.

"Find it, please. There was something in my pocket that I need," I pleaded.

The two of them nodded and looked around the ICU room, opening drawers and cupboards till Ameerah found a beige bag.

"Found it." She started digging through the bag and asked, "What am I looking for?"

"A dark gray metal pen with a design on it."

"Here." She handed it to me, and I lay my head down, relief washing over my aching muscles and torn skin. I closed my eyes and let my thumb trace the name engraved on it, just like I had so many times before when I had desperately needed her.

Visions of her beautiful face pushed out the horrid scene in the locker room. Caramel-brown eyes replaced the dark, beady ones that had threatened me, soft brown wavy hair replaced the sleek maroon one that was being pulled, pink lips replaced the snarling ones as they taunted me.

"Who is Sanam?" Ameerah's voice interrupted my peace.

"A girl," I whispered.

"The one you're going to marry?" she asked hesitantly.

"Yes."

I didn't bother opening my eyes to look at the classmate who cared more than she should. Instead, I told her, "Thank you for everything, Ameerah. But you should go home and rest now."

There was silence for a few minutes before the door opened and closed. I was hoping Ameerah would have left, but she spoke up again.

"My friends call me Aimy."

"What?" I opened my eyes to glance at her determined face.

"I think I've earned your friendship, haven't I?" She gave me a small smile.

God, what is this girl? I had to give her full marks for persistence, but she did have a point. We'd been through enough together to be friends by now.

"Yes, you have, Aimy." I smiled back at her.

KIRAN

I was dropping off Danish and Daniyal at home when Ameerah called to say Osman was awake. As I drove to the hospital, my mind raced—how much would he remember of the incident? What toll would it take on him?

I'd spent my life shielding him from the world and the pain inflicted by our relatives, yet, ironically, a relative had shot him anyway.

Was that his destiny—or my failure as a sister?

Rushing up the stairs to the ICU, I rummaged through my purse to call my sisters, but found Osman's phone instead. When I looked up again, my vision was suddenly blurred by someone in black and brown. Osman's phone slipped from my hand, bouncing off the concrete steps and landing at the base of the staircase.

"I'm so sorry," a deep voice apologized quickly.

Ignoring the offender, I quickly descended the stairs to retrieve the device, but he seemed to have recognized me.

"Ms. Kiran?" he said, following me downstairs. "Assalamu Alaikum. Are you alright?"

Ugh. Inspector Junaid.

This was the fourth time I had run into him over the last two days. Like always, the man stood there in his uniform, black shirt and khaki pants, his black peppered hair neatly gelled back, his beard trimmed to perfection. Years of standing at attention seemed to have made that posture second nature to him.

"No, I am not. You broke my brother's phone. Can't you look where you are going?" I snapped.

His gaze went down to my hand and the shattered screen. "I . . . umm . . . sorry about that. I'll get it fixed for him."

"No, thank you. I don't want our hard-earned belongings to be tainted with your bribery money."

His eyebrows furrowed. "As I have said before, I have never taken bribes in my life, Ms. Kiran. And I never will."

For a moment, we stared at each other suspiciously. I had no idea what was going through his mind, but I was sure his eyes would shift momentarily. Men who lied always had shifty eyes. They could never look at me when they spun tales about how we had no case and no evidence against the man who had taken away my sister's innocence, and whose men had held a gun over my brother. But Inspector Junaid's eyes never moved; they remained full of indignation.

He stepped back eventually, still holding my gaze. "I get that you may have had a bad experience with our police before, and no doubt there are many corrupt individuals. I am sorry for that. But there are plenty of others who will give up their lives before taking bribes."

His hand reached into his pocket, and he took out a folded piece of paper. "If you don't believe me, take this. It's a copy of the arrest warrant for Zain Ghazanfar. I personally filed it."

I blinked. "You did? Against Asif Ghazanfar's son, Zain?"

"Who else? We found the gun that was used to shoot your brother. The ballistics match the bullet recovered from him, and the gun had Zain's fingerprints on it."

"Then, what are you doing here? Go arrest him!" I exclaimed, my distrust in that man creeping back in.

His shoulders slumped for the first time since we had met. "Unfortunately, Asif Ghazanfar is far quicker than our justice system. He and Zain fled the country before we could get to him or put him on the exit control list. We have questioned Mrs. Ghazanfar, but she is either too good of an actress or she truly doesn't know anything about her husband and son's disappearance."

I suspected it was the latter, remembering the battered woman I had seen in their study. When the policeman's voice lowered, I couldn't deny the sincerity in his words either.

"I know what it feels like to have your family targeted, Ms. Kiran. I've lived through that fear and guilt. So please be assured that I will not rest till the man who shot your brother is brought to justice, even if he is in another country. Meanwhile, I have a police officer stationed outside your brother's room. So, you don't need to worry at all."

"Thank you," I muttered.

He nodded. "It's my duty as much as it is my honor."

Before I could walk away, he spoke again. "If you were heading to the ICU, may I come with you? I need to speak with Osman about what he remembers from that day."

"Sure."

This man's polite ways weren't anything I had experienced before from the mostly abrasive men I had dealt with in my life. Whether this was just a ruse, I couldn't tell. Yet, there was something about him that made me want to trust him. Enough to ask a question that had crossed my mind.

"Who shot your son?"

He didn't answer right away. But when he did, in the empty hallway outside the ICU, I understood why he hesitated.

"I am almost certain Asif Ghazanfar's men did."

CHAPTER 22

Panacea

SANAM

Four weeks had passed since Osman's last message to me. *Surgery rotation finishes in a couple of weeks.* There had been no word from him since then.

Me: Haven't heard from you in a while. Are you upset with me?

Me: Please call me.

He had warned me that he would be exceptionally busy during his surgery rotation, but so busy that he couldn't even send me a brief text telling me he was okay? I didn't know whether to be angry at him or worried, and therein lay the frustration of being apart from the boy I had fallen for more than three years ago.

At least I have his heart, I reminded myself, pulling out a small cardboard box from under my bed.

My room's door opened just as I took that handmade object in my palm, remembering the way a boy's hands had felt on mine when he gently pointed out all the structures of the heart.

Alice and Yasmin walked in, laughing loudly at something before they noticed me sitting alone on my bed.

"Uh oh, she's stroking that clay heart again," Alice said to her friend.

"Aww, sweetie, are you missing that boy of yours?" Yasmin sat down next to me and put an arm around my shoulders. Embarrassed, I quickly put away the clay model and came up with a feeble excuse.

"No, I was checking to see what the names of the coronary arteries were. I am reading a medical fiction novel these days."

Neither of them bought that excuse and literally hoisted me off the bed.

"Alright, enough. After years of you sulking away every weekend, we are staging an intervention. You're coming out with us tonight," Alice declared, while Yasmin went through my closet, looking for something for me to wear.

There was a time when I had a closet full of party wear, and I could be ready to go anywhere, anytime, with almost anyone. But that Sanam was long gone, replaced by a version that was finally comfortable in her own skin. And I had no intention of going back.

"Will there be alcohol? I don't drink."

Yasmin had given up on my closet and was looking through Alice's pile of clothes now. "It's a party to welcome the new students who joined our university this semester. So, yes, there will be booze. But babe, no one will force you to drink it. Just hang out with us, and we'll have a great time."

I vetoed every dress Alice and Yasmin showed me, and eventually, the two decided to drag me off to the mall.

"Why do I even have to go to the party?" I protested. "You two will get busy with your own friends, and I don't know anyone else here."

"Maybe if you weren't such a hermit, you would have made some friends of your own too," Alice quipped.

Yasmin's cheeks flushed when she turned to me. "I don't know if he'll come, but there is a really hot transfer student from California who is originally from Pakistan. Met him in my microeconomics class. I've already called dibs on him romantically, if he is available, but you're free to be friends with him."

Alice rolled her eyes. "You can't call dibs on people."

"Says who?" Yasmin replied.

The two friends bickered, like I had seen them do so many times before. I checked my phone again.

Still no reply from Osman.

ZAIN

Transferring from the University of Los Angeles to Texas University, Houston, as a senior wasn't something I had planned. It wouldn't even have been possible had my father not pulled strings the size of oil rigs. One hefty donation and the promise of a brand-new performing arts theatre—endorsed by local indie film mogul Zakariya Uzair—meant Texas University was not only processing my transfer but also waiving the usual residency requirements.

I didn't care much for the display of wealth and power, nor did I question it. What I did care about was that a private investigator hired by Zak Uncle had found no trace of Maham or her family in Boston.

Even her uncle, the pediatric cardiologist, seemed to have no contact with them. My heart refused to believe that Maham had tricked me in any way, but doubts about her parents had started to seep in.

My two sources of consolation were, first, that there had been no mention of Sanam at all. In fact, she was so estranged from her father that despite staying in his guest suite, I hadn't once seen her at his house. Neither had Abu mentioned her.

And second, my asshole of a cousin was still in the hospital. Something about post-surgical infections nearly killing him again.

Karma is a bitch, isn't it, Mr. Osman? I smirked at the thought of him stuck in the hospital and felt no guilt.

Still debating whether or not to attend the welcome party later that night, I walked into the living room, where the TV was blaring with a Pakistani news channel. I recognized the man on the screen as Zaviyar Uzair, Zak Uncle's younger brother. Over the raised voices of my father and his friend, I couldn't quite make out what the news was about. Though, that would soon become apparent to me when the men continued to argue, not realizing I was standing in the same room as them.

"How the hell did they get that bill passed through the National Assembly?" Abu gestured towards the TV but did not stop pacing the room.

Zak Uncle sat on the armchair, smoking a cigar. "I don't know, Asif. I haven't cared about Pakistani politics in more than a decade."

"Well, the new bill allows *your* brother, the finance minister, to set up the Financial Intelligence Unit. Do you know what his first order of business is going to be?" Abu snapped at his friend, who only shrugged.

"Prosecuting white-collar crime?"

"Prosecuting GT Enterprise, fool."

"So? What do I have to do with GT Enterprise?" The nonchalant reply angered my father so much that his forehead vein seemed ready to pop.

He stopped in front of the seated man, his frown deepening. "Really? Have you forgotten your past so easily? Because I haven't."

I had no idea what Abu meant, but whatever it was jolted Zak Uncle out of his slumber, and he nearly jumped off his chair. "There is no record of my past. I paid you a hefty sum to destroy it all."

Abu scoffed. "You really think a few lakh rupees would convince me to destroy the gold mine of evidence I possess?"

"If I go down, you go down," Zak Uncle spat. "Or have you forgotten who bought the vial of potassium you used to stop that old man's heart, so it looked like a heart attack?"

Potassium? To stop whose heart? I stood listening, thoroughly confused.

"So, you agree that our futures are tied?"

Their back-and-forth arguments got louder, forcing me to interject. "Abu, what's happening?"

Both men turned to look at me simultaneously before exchanging a glance. Abu was the first to step forward.

"With Zaviyar heading the FIU, he has more power than ever to fulfill his vendetta against us. And we have no way of stopping him." His voice was low and steady but full of concern, a tone I had never heard him take before. And that made me look at the other man in the room.

"Zak Uncle, Zaviyar is your brother. Can't you get him to back off?"

"I have no say in what he or the party does after—"

Abu didn't let him finish. "Zaviyar pushed Zak out of AWP. We have to figure something else out."

In front of these giants with a lifetime's worth of experience, I was no one to offer my opinion, but I did remember something Abu had once said to me. "Everyone has a price. It's either something they want or a weakness you can exploit," I repeated his words.

"Zavi has always had everything he's ever wanted. He has no reason to ever bow down to a bribe," Zak Uncle told us solemnly.

"Then he must have a weakness," I said.

Uncle's face lit up briefly. "His family. He would do anything for his wife and children."

Abu's dose of reality came swiftly. "There's nothing we can do about his family. They are protected by loyal government forces at all times."

"We're doomed," I said out loud. But that was before I looked up and noted that both older men were staring at each other. Their silence stretched into an abyss of unsaid words, which both confused and intrigued me.

Finally, Zak Uncle conceded and looked away, letting out a harsh breath. "He has another weakness. His niece," he said quietly.

"Who is his niece?" I asked.

This time, Abu answered.

"Sanam Uzair."

Of course, how could I forget?

"So, do we fake kidnap her or something?" I wracked my brain to come up with a way that she could be used as leverage against her uncle.

"Do you want to get thrown in jail in the US?" Abu glared at me, and I quickly shook my head.

He took a few more steps towards me, until his hand gripped my shoulder. His gaze bored into mine with an intensity reminiscent of the father I had grown up with. Suddenly, I knew what his next words were going to be.

"Then. Marry. Her."

I remembered the last time I had heard those words from my father, and the unbridled fury that had consumed me after that. The object of that fury now stood in front of me, but the beautiful reason behind it had disappeared.

Yet, there was hope. She had disappeared, but the man she had run away with was in the hospital, so he clearly could not have wed her. And that hope gave me the courage I needed.

"*No.*" I pushed my father's hand off me. "I am in love with Maham. Osman is still in the hospital, which means she is alone somewhere, and I will find her and convince her to come back to me."

Abu clicked his tongue with disapproval. "Love has turned you into a fool, Zain." He pulled his phone out of his pocket. "She is with someone. In fact, she has been playing you this whole time like I told you she would. She was nothing but a gold digger, and you fell for it."

"I don't believe you. Osman is—"

"Not with Osman, you idiot. He was a paid actor. A ruse to distract you while she went off and got married to a man she met two years ago. His name is Ahad Tanvir."

"No, no. That's not possible." I stumbled back as Abu thrust his phone in my face. But no matter how far I got, I couldn't look away from the pictures he was flipping through on his phone.

"The private investigator looked into your fiancée's activities for the last three years. He found these. They were taken from a hotel security camera at a math conference in New York."

My innocent Maham; the beautiful girl with flawless skin and curled hair, the girl who had promised to spend her life with me while we stood in front of our entire class under a starlit sky. That innocent girl's pictures were now tearing through every fiber in my body as I gaped at her, sitting with a man in glasses at a dinner table. She smiled at him while he gazed at her the way I used to. And then there were pictures with time stamps spanning the entire night while they sat in a hotel lobby, each on their own computer, laughing freely like they were meant only for each other.

The last picture was what broke down any defense I had against my father and his plans for me. It was one of their nikahnama. Maham Qureshi with Ahad Tanvir, bound to each other with an eternal bond that I had foolishly thought I was worthy of. Dated two weeks ago.

I could barely breathe; my vision blurred, my thoughts completely scrambled.

"Why didn't you tell me before?"

Abu cupped my face, his voice so soft it was barely a whisper. "Because, son, I knew this would destroy you."

He pulled me into his arms. Too numb from the pain of betrayal, I did nothing to protest. Though I was slowly realizing that I hadn't just been betrayed by Maham but also by my cousin, who had helped her. The man who had been emailing Maham, telling her to call him urgently. Surely, he must have found a way to contact her.

I knew exactly what he must have said to her.

This was the cruelty with which he was getting revenge for all those years in school. The game had flipped: he was the tormentor, and I the tormented.

I understood that now.

"Osman knew." I spat the obvious truth through clenched teeth.

Abu pulled back. "Yes, he must have known all along. Maham could not have done this alone. In fact, with the way Osman and his sisters hate us, I am sure they conspired with Maham's family to humiliate us in front of the whole country."

Every word of that sentence made sense.

"I should have killed him that day." The bitter words escaped me but didn't soothe my shattered heart.

"Killing will only end his misery. It is the living who truly suffer," Abu noted.

When he spoke again, it was slowly and deliberate. His words were the direction I needed to deal with the raging fire that threatened to consume me. They were the marching orders I sought to rein in my insanity.

"Maham is gone, Zain. Even if you find her now, she is already married. Besides, she was always a stranger. Take out your anger on the man who is your blood."

I nodded, looking at my savior for more guidance. "What should I do, Abu? How can I hurt him the way he hurt me?"

He stepped back from me, his lips curled up. "He is desperately in love with a girl. Snatch her away from him. Only then will he feel the pain you do."

They say love conquers all. They forget that anger and rage are just as powerful. Those were the emotions that earned Iblees, a devil, a place in eternal hell. Then what chance did I, a mere mortal, have in front of them?

Especially when love had burned my heart, leaving nothing but ashes. Now, I couldn't care less if I sold my soul to the devil or was forced to become a celibate saint.

With *her* gone for good, my demons won, and so had the devil.

"Yes, Abu. Whatever you say."

SANAM

The welcome party was held at a frat house on campus. Young men and women wandered across the grassy lawn in front of the massive two-story building, while even more packed into the house inside. They swayed to the pounding music, clutching beer bottles or red plastic cups filled with keg-poured alcohol. The scene was no different from secret parties back home—concealed from a judgmental society behind a façade of piety and family values.

What am I even doing here? I asked myself, not for the first time.

Yasmin and Alice had already walked ahead to meet their friends, leaving me alone at the door of the house whose sights and smells were making me dizzy. It didn't take me long to realize how out of place I was.

I might have gotten out of there too, had it not been for a voice from my past that stopped me dead in my tracks.

"Well, well, well . . . Sanam Uzair. Never thought I'd see you here."

Zain?

I swung around to see him standing mere inches away from me. His dark eyes looked sunken, but his characteristic charm with the side-swept hair, chiseled jawline, and perfect pearly white smile, was unchanged from when I had last met him, almost three and half years ago.

"Hey, Zain. I've been here all along. What are you doing here?"

He took a step closer. His musk scent wafted towards me. "California was too far away."

"From Maham?"

He paused; a frown appeared on his face but quickly dissipated. "Yes, from Maham. Now, I am only halfway across the country from her, rather than all the way at the other end."

"So, uh . . . how is she doing? I haven't heard from her in a long time." I couldn't come up with anything better to say.

Zain and I had been friends in high school, but our friendship had never been the kind where you could pick up and go from where you left off. Standing there with him in the darkness of the night, which did nothing to hide the way his gaze was wandering over my face, reminded me of how he had always made me uncomfortable. The red plastic cup with booze served as another reminder of how we had always been so different.

"Sanam, there you are!" a female voice called out before Zain could reply, much to my relief.

"Yasmin, you've met Zain already, right?" I asked my friend.

Zain shifted his gaze to her momentarily, but it was back on me as he moved even closer. The smell of alcohol mixed with the overpowering scent of his cologne forced me to step back from him.

"We have some classes together," she replied. "How do you know each other?"

He slipped an arm around my shoulders, pulling me closer to himself in a side hug. "We were classmates in high school. I used to have quite the crush on her back then," he told Yasmin, whose eyes widened.

"*Before* you fell in love with Maham and got engaged to her—and I found someone else," I reminded him.

He let go of me, turning his attention to Yasmin. "That's right. But Maham isn't here, and neither is my cousin dearest. So how about we all enjoy ourselves tonight, for old time's sake?"

"That's what I have been telling her." Yasmin smiled at Zain, her gaze holding his. Sweet but not subtle at all.

Suddenly, she hooked her arm through mine. "I say we all pretend to be unattached tonight and live our lives a little."

Despite my protests, the two of them half-dragged, half-pushed me into the house. Zain offered me a beer from a nearby table, which I refused.

"I don't drink," I told them both over the loud music.

"Don't worry, I saw some fruit punch in the kitchen as well," Yasmin replied.

"I'll get some for both of you. Need to get myself some water too," Zain offered, and disappeared before bringing both of us a couple of clear plastic glasses with orange liquid in it.

It tasted weird. "Mine has a bit of tangy taste," I whispered to Yasmin.

"It's a citrus drink, Sanam. It's supposed to be tangy. Don't worry—it doesn't have any alcohol," she replied, her body already swaying to the pumping music reverberating throughout the house.

Taking another sip, I licked my lips. The tangy taste had disappeared, so I took another, and another, until the whole glass emptied. Somewhere in between me drinking that fruit punch and listening to Yasmin flirting with Zain, the three of us had moved into the main living room.

The music was deafening. A mist of smoke and booze hung over the dozens of revelers. Where one body ended and another began was hard to tell.

You should leave, an inner voice urged.

Let her live, another countered.

I ignored them both. The music pulsing through my muscles had lit up my senses. Before I realized what I was doing, I was in the middle of a crowd of sweaty, dazed faces. Some I recognized, but many were a blur as I danced to the frenzied rhythm, trying to keep up with the beat of the music and the bodies pushing into me from all directions.

"Thirsty . . . I am thirsty," I whispered to Zain, whose arm had snaked around my waist, whether to prop me up as I felt my muscles give way or to hold me close, I couldn't tell.

He pulled me towards the edge of the crowd. "I feel dizzy," I told him as he made me sit on a nearby sofa.

"Here. You're dehydrated." He handed me another drink.

I gulped it down. My lips were parched, my mouth completely dry, like I had been lost in a desert for weeks. The cool wetness sliding down my throat was a welcome respite from the invisible fire which seemed to have set my skin ablaze.

"I need to go home."

"I'll take you," his deep voice whispered in my ear. He was so close, I could feel his warm breath on me, see the storm brewing in his eyes, threatening to destroy me.

Something is very wrong, my subconscious warned me.

Push him away, my heart pleaded with my brain.

But there was nothing I could do—my muscles refused to obey me.

An arm wrapped around my waist again, lifting me with ease. That familiar musky scent, tinged with alcohol, filled my lungs. And then there were his eyes, dark and unyielding, like black holes pulling me in. Or perhaps I wasn't being pulled at all—perhaps I was willingly letting myself fall.

"I got it all on video." That was the last thing I heard.

ZAIN

My father's instructions were clear.

Every woman has a weakness—her honor. Take it away, and she will succumb to any wish of yours.

Yet there was something my father had overlooked. His son had been born a bloody *coward*. I half undressed her, but that's all I could bring myself to do.

Hidden crevices on campus, a nearly empty dorm, an unconscious woman. So many opportunities, and you still couldn't fuck her? I imagined my father's vicious words if I told him the truth. Instead, I texted him a lie. What he didn't know wouldn't hurt him, or me.

Me: Her roommate walked in. But don't worry. I know of a better way to convince her.

Shutting her room's door, I cursed my cousin. *That bastard. This is all his fault.*

He would pay, one way or the other.

CHAPTER 23

Checkmate

KIRAN

It had been thirty-two days since the afternoon I had been woken up by my sons. Their ashen faces and unsteady voices as they had told me about their Mani's shooting were still etched in my mind. As were the moments when I had fled to the hospital, sat at his bedside, thanked God for his initial quick recovery, only to then bargain again with Him as Osman developed one complication after another.

A pneumonia, because of the bullet wound puncturing his lung, had landed him back on the ventilator just three days after he had first come off it. Bullet fragments left behind in his abdominal cavity punctured a part of his bowel, requiring an urgent trip to the OR again. The trip to the OR caused his blood pressure to drop precipitously, and he had to be placed on medications the doctors called "pressors."

Through all of this, I played the role I knew had become my destiny. I comforted my sisters and sons, as well as Ameerah—aka Aimy—who had become as much a part of our family as anyone else. I prayed and begged for my brother's life. I answered Inspector Junaid's relentless questions in the hope that my brother would get justice. I worked because someone had to pay the bills. I pretended that I was alright, because if I fell apart, there would be no one to hold my family together.

I ignored my pain. Because pain had become my destiny.

Though today was going to be different. Four and a half weeks after he had been shot, Osman was finally well enough to get out of his room, even if only for a trip around the hospital grounds.

"Are you ready to go?" I asked him when I reached the hospital that evening.

"Not yet. I am waiting for Aimy."

"Why? Did you want her to come with us?"

Not that I would have minded. The maroon-haired girl had spent nearly as much time by my brother's bedside as I had, and with her background, I'd come to depend on her to translate the barrage of medical jargon the doctors threw my way.

She had her quirks, for sure, but she was a sweet kid. And in the anxiety and uncertainty surrounding our family, her quirkiness was a distraction we all welcomed.

"No, she is bringing me the notes she took for me during the last few weeks. Exams are only a month away, Api. I have already lost so much time; I need to start studying right away."

He spoke slowly as he struggled to get up from the hospital bed. With everything his body had gone through, his muscles were so deconditioned he needed help getting to the bathroom.

I quickly reached out to steady him. "You can't be serious about taking that exam, Osman. You can barely walk on your own. Your doctors haven't even discharged you from the hospital."

He leaned on me as he made his way to the wheelchair that stood by the policeman guarding the entrance to his room. Constable Bilal, who was often stationed outside Osman's room, was a friendly man, but his presence was unnecessary, in my opinion. However, Inspector Junaid had insisted we let him stay there.

While Zain had fled the country, Osman was sure that it was the security guard next to Zain who had pulled the trigger. And that guard, whom we assumed to be on Ghazanfar's payroll, was yet to be found.

"I am making a steady recovery. If I don't take the exam, my graduation will be delayed. And I can't let that happen," my brother insisted.

"Why not? It will just be a few months."

"I made a promise to someone, Api. I am not delaying it for anything," he replied, grunting as he lowered himself into the wheelchair.

The ten steps he had taken had left him breathless. Yet, for the someone he was referring to, he would have run a marathon if it meant being able to fulfill his promise to her.

That someone, a girl whose name he whispered when he was asleep, may have lived on the opposite end of the world and been completely unaware of what he was going through, but her very essence had a home in my brother's heart. If there was one thing that had kept him going, it was his memories of her that I knew he relived during his most painful moments.

"Did you get my phone fixed?" he asked for the tenth time since he had woken up from being on the ventilator the second time around.

"I left it at the shop today to get the screen fixed. We should get it back in the next couple of days," I reassured him. Getting his phone fixed was the lowest priority on my to-do list. Though the frown on his face told me he didn't see it that way.

"Sanam probably thinks I've abandoned her," he pouted.

"Don't worry—she'll forgive you when she finds out what happened."

"Hello, hellooo." The cheerful voice of my youngest sister interrupted us. "Look who I met on the way up here."

"Assalamu Alaikum, Ms. Kiran." The deep voice I recognized all too well spoke from behind her.

Ugh. Why is he here again? I tried my best not to let my face contort with irritation.

It should have been the end of his workday, but his neatly brushed hair, trimmed beard, and crisp police uniform made him appear as if he had recently woken up, ready to face the world.

Not like me, who probably looked like a haggard old woman after having slept an average of five hours all of last month.

"Walaikum Assalam, Inspector Junaid. What brings you here?"

He smiled at me. "Oh, I was just passing by. I heard Osman was feeling much better, so I wanted to check in."

Before I could reply, Kaukab stepped in front of him. "Inspector Junaid, tell me one thing. You're the Additional Inspector General for *all* of Karachi. Correct?"

Dark brown eyes gazed at my sister curiously before he answered. "Umm . . . yes."

"Then how come you're always *just passing by* here? Does this part of the city have the highest crime rate or something?" she asked innocently.

I never expected that prim and proper man to get so flustered. His eyes shot up at me, then darted back to my sister. He gulped uncomfortably as he replied, "Actually, my office is close by, which is why I pass by here quite often."

He tried to step around her, but my sister was faster.

"Got it. So when Osman goes home, will your office move closer to my sister's apartment?"

Oh my God. My mouth dropped open when I realized what Kaukab was insinuating.

"What?" the inspector asked, still confused, even as the constable let out an audible chuckle.

I was breathing fire, with every intention of yanking my sister out of the room, but a peppy medical student stepped in and threw her arms up in the air. "There is a party going on here and no one invited me?" she pouted before laughing loudly at her own joke, with Kaukab joining in.

"What the heck is wrong with you?" I grabbed my sister's arm and whisper-yelled at her.

She squirmed, replying in a hushed voice, "His wife died ten years ago. He told me himself. Guy's a single dad, Kiran."

Why that piece of information made me pause, I had no idea—nor did I care.

"Come on, everyone, let's get a group photo with Osman. This is a big moment!" Ameerah called out, and slowly, the rest of us gathered around my brother. I glared at Kaukab when she asked the inspector to join us. She ignored me.

We smiled wide, even the inspector, and Ameerah snapped a picture.

None of us noticed the man in the corner, snapping a picture on his hidden phone.

ZAIN

I sat at the bar, nursing a glass of whiskey. The dim amber lighting flickered off the bottles lining the shelves. Distorted reflections stretched and bent like darkness teasing light, or perhaps it was evil teasing innocence.

Stop getting distracted, my father's voice echoed within, forcing me to take another sip of whiskey.

The clock on the wall grabbed my attention. *10 p.m.*

They should be here any minute now.

"Sorry to keep you waiting." A manicured hand slid over my bare forearm, making my skin crawl.

Another sip of whiskey, and I swallowed the disgust. Instead, I smiled at the woman with dark hair pulled back into a sleek ponytail.

"No worries, Yasmin. Are you here alone?"

"Sanam and Alice messaged. They're on the way, but I wanted a few moments alone with you." She batted her eyelids. I drank more whiskey, bracing myself for the flirting I would have to endure while waiting for the woman who would now be sober enough to threaten *my* way.

"Did you tell them I was treating them to dinner?"

"No. I told them I was." She smiled like the little puppet she was.

If only Sanam were this easy, but that woman had always had an impenetrable barrier around her heart. It would only have been fortified by that idiot cousin of mine.

Though, how fun would it be to see it shattered? The way her man had shattered my life.

"There they are!" Yasmin exclaimed, and I looked up to see those caramel-brown eyes fill with anger and disgust.

"What are you doing here?" she asked as soon as she was close enough.

"I invited him," Yasmin answered, and I sat back and watched the drama unfold. Waiting to make my move.

"I am going back to my room then," Sanam declared and turned to leave.

"Oh, come on Sanam, you've been stuck inside your room for the last forty-eight hours. I am getting claustrophobic just looking at you." Alice, her roommate, stepped behind her, blocking her exit.

Yasmin was on her feet now, her arm wrapped around Sanam's shoulder. "Zain wants the best for you, sweetheart. Just like Alice and I do. I know you miss that boy of yours, but until he comes off his surgery rotation or whatever, have a little bit of fun with us."

"I don't understand why he has to be here. Or why you are being so chummy with him," Sanam protested, her eyes narrowing at me.

"He's a friend." Yasmin defended herself.

Sanam knew that was a lie. "You only met him a few days ago. You know nothing about him. He is engaged, Yasmin. For God's sake, what are you doing?"

She glared at Sanam. "I don't see an engagement ring on his finger. And maybe you should quit being so judgmental. I bet Osman dumped you for someone less uptight."

Swords were drawn, heels dug in, blood as good as spilled. Alice tried to intervene, but neither of the other two women was ready to cede.

It was time for me to make my move.

"Maybe I could talk to Sanam—outside. Alone," I offered.

My prey was already retreating, and the puppet muttered, "Do whatever. I couldn't care less about her."

I followed the only woman I had intended to meet that night. "Sanam, hold on."

"Get lost, Zain." She quickened her pace, but her scurrying feet were no match for my lengthy strides. Neither were her dainty fingers, which tried to unravel my arm as it wrapped around her waist. A fact that she seemed to realize quickly.

"Let me go," she whispered frantically. "I am not the kind of woman you think I am."

"Oh, honey, you are exactly the kind of woman I want, though."

I kept walking, pulling her beside me on that dimly lit sidewalk. The few people who rushed by didn't bother giving a guy and a girl who looked intimate as much as a second glance.

She stared at me, aghast. "What are you talking about? You're with Maham and I with . . ."

I cut her off before she could say his name and I lost my cool. "Maham could never give me what you can."

"I-I don't understand." A hint of panic flitted across her face. I ignored the bile rising in the back of my throat and the small voice reminding me: *You're still in love with Maham.*

When we reached a secluded alley, I pulled Sanam in. The darkness shrouding her form quieted the dissenting voices. I was the hunter; she was the prey. That was the only thing that mattered.

"Your family name, Sanam Uzair, combined with my family's wealth, will let us rule the country for generations to come. And the two of us will get to enjoy the golden fruit of our union. How could I pass up such an offer?"

"An offer?" she questioned.

"Your father offered your hand in marriage. And I accepted. It's done, Sanam. You are mine, like you have always been. Maham was simply a phase."

A phase that will last a lifetime, you bastard, a voice spoke quietly.

Sanam's mirthless laugh drowned out that voice. "You want to marry me? What a joke! You're mistaken if you think I want anything to do with your wealth, or that my father owns me. I will only marry one man."

I wasn't surprised at her answer. Money was never going to attract her.

She started to walk out of the alley. I yanked her back, inadvertently slamming her body into the wall behind her. I didn't care. I had a job to do for my father. And revenge to take from a man, for myself.

With one hand holding her by her shoulder and the other fumbling in my pocket, I managed to take out my phone and show her the video from the weekend. She stared at the images of her drunk self dancing amidst a pack of equally intoxicated men and women, and then my face so close to hers it seemed we were kissing. Finally, it showed me taking her to her dorm room—all alone.

"Do you really think that man will marry you after he sees this?"

She pushed me back. "You tricked me. And, yes, he will. I'll tell him the truth, and he'll believe me."

Threaten her honor, Abu's words came to mind.

I tried another tactic and grabbed her arm before she could escape. "I'll release that video onto the internet. Everyone will know about your loose morals. Imagine what this will do for your uncle, or your stepfather and mother back home."

"There is only one person I care about, and he will never leave me. I stopped caring about everyone else a long time ago."

Even in the dark, I could see the fire in her eyes, matching the one that her lover had set in my heart.

I was running out of options. *Everyone either wants something or has a weakness you can exploit*, is what my father had always said.

Yet Sanam had no price. She didn't want anything, except the man she already had, and I couldn't figur e out her weakness.

I switched my phone's screen to another surveillance video.

"You give too much credit to my cousin. Osman was the one who ran away with Maham on our wedding day." My jaw clenched at the memories of that day and the man responsible. "Marry me, and together we can show them how little they mattered to us."

She stopped pushing back. Her eyes narrowed as she took in the video, her lips pursed, and a glimmer of hope ignited in me. But it didn't last long.

"So Maham left you? Good for her. I always knew you were a narcissistic asshole. Glad she saw it too. And I'm proud of Osman for helping her. You will never become even half the man he is."

How the hell does she know he was helping her?

"He's not helping her . . ."

"Yes, he is. I can read his body language." She stepped back from me, and I let her. "Give up, Zain. I don't know what has come over you, but you have no idea what Osman and I have. Nothing could ever come between us."

She kept stepping backwards, and I stood still, letting her escape. I was out of options. The trust she had in my cousin meant that she had no weakness—not her honor, not betrayal. Nothing I could say or do would convince her to doubt him.

You have no idea what Osman and I have, I repeated her words to myself. A realization struck like lightning. I started walking after her as I finished the thought in my head . . . *is each other.*

She had everything—because *he* was her everything.

This time, I dialed a number as soon as I reached her and thrust the phone in her face to show her a truth she was clearly not aware of. "Constable

Bilal, can you turn on your camera and show us what Mr. Osman is doing right now?"

Her gaze fixed on the live video feed of a doctor examining my cousin. His bullet-ridden torso might have healed, but the scars and the bandages covering him were unmistakable.

"What . . ." The terror in her eyes was reason enough for me to smile.

"Send me the pictures you've sent to Abu," I told the constable.

A moment later, I flipped through the pictures from the last four weeks—his body riddled with tubes and wires, the doctors racing in, his bed being wheeled out, the worried faces of his sisters, and the last one, where he sat in a wheelchair, pale and weak, with a pathetic smile on his face. By this time, Sanam seemed to have stopped breathing.

"I did this to him. Imagine what else I could do if I wanted to. You may trust him with everything you have, but you really shouldn't trust me with his life."

She swallowed hard. Her voice wavered. "I don't believe you."

A conversation I had overheard came to mind. I used it, even if I didn't understand it.

"Do you know that a vial of potassium can stop a man's heart? One word from me, and the constable will give him that injection." Her eyes widened; my voice dropped. "Quietly, when he is alone, and no one will be wiser."

She gasped. I glared at her, watching as the tides turned. The arrogance and stiff upper lip gave way to shaky breaths escaping her quivering mouth. Her eyes glistened under the full moon with tears she would only have shed for her former lab partner.

Finally, she whispered, "Wh-what do you want?"

Checkmate, sweetheart.

I had found her weakness—my poor little cousin, who used to sit in the corner and get beaten up in abandoned hallways. For him, she would do anything. Even be my puppet.

"Marry me."

"And you'll leave him alone?" A single tear made its way down her cheek.

"Yes. I will have no reason to harm him if I get what I want."

Her spine steeled as she wiped her eyes. "I will never love you."

"I don't fucking care."

Love had broken me once; I would be damned if I let it near me again. When she walked away, broken and dejected, I called my father.

"It's done."

"We'll arrange for the nikah for tomorrow afternoon," he replied.

Before ending the call, he said the words I had been wanting to hear my entire life. "Good work, Zain. I am so proud of you."

I was supposed to have won that night, both my father's love and the game of chess my life had become. Yet, no matter how hard I tried, I couldn't suppress the voice inside me.

You've lost, Zain. You've lost everything you ever had.

Well, so has that bastard Osman, I replied defiantly.

CHAPTER 24

Nikah

SANAM

The tears had long since dried up.

My heart was beating, my lungs were breathing, yet I might as well have been dead as I sat next to my father in front of the Imam (religious leader) at the mosque nearest to my college campus.

The images I had seen last night still haunted me. Though battered or bruised, he was still the man who held my heart.

Without him, I would be an unmarried widow. Thus, I had no choice but to save his life. To look into the murderous dark eyes of his cousin and give him what he wanted. No matter what it cost me.

An unfamiliar voice said something about accepting the marriage, and my father's hand squeezed my arm before replying, "She is shy."

"Answer the Imam's question, sweetheart," Abu whispered to me. His voice was soft, but if there was regret in it for putting me through this, I didn't hear it.

Just like I didn't hear the words that left my own lips.

"Qabool hai." (I accept.)

Or those said by Zain a few moments later.

"Qabool hai."

Or the congratulations said by the men in that room. I was dead. And corpses can't hear, feel, or see anything.

"I am going back to my dorm," I whispered, after aimlessly following others to the mosque's parking lot.

A hand grabbed my arm. "You're Zain's wife now. You'll go with him where *he* wants you to go."

I didn't bother looking up to see who that was or listen to the voice that spoke after that. They were all unrecognizable strangers to me anyway.

"Let her go. It's best she stays in her dorm. I am going to the bar anyway. I need a bloody drink."

OSMAN

"Here is your phone," Api said when she came to see me after work.

"Finally." I grabbed it like it was the air my lungs were deprived of. It some ways, it was.

If air was life, then so was Sanam. And this phone was my only connection to her.

There were hundreds of messages, none I cared about more than the ones listed under her name. At first, she was curious about my lack of replies. Then she became upset. Then worried that she had upset me.

"You could never upset me, Sanam," I muttered.

The last was a voicemail sent the day before.

"Hi, Osman . . ."

She greeted me the same as always, but it was her voice that made my eyebrows furrow—hoarse, steady, but slow.

"I hope you're doing well now. I heard from Zain that you were accidentally shot."

My heartbeat quickened as alarm bells rang.

She knew about the shooting?

Zain was in touch with her?

Why was her voice so monotonous?

As if me getting shot hadn't affected her at all.

Questions swirled, but I forced myself to listen further. There had to be an explanation. She cared for me like no one else ever could.

There was an explanation. But not one I could have ever imagined. Not after the promise we had made to each other, sitting in the lonely corner behind the school building, under a starlit sky. Or our guarded confessions when her Dado had passed away. Nor our string of text messages and infrequent but heartfelt phone calls.

All of that was supposed to have meant something. Something *eternal*. None of that prepared me for her emotionless words delivered with robotic precision.

"I wanted to inform you that Zain and I tied the knot yesterday. As you know, our families have worked together for decades, and I have known Zain for years. Our parents thought we would make a fine pair, given how similar our social setup is. I am sorry that we couldn't invite you to the nikah, but I wanted to say thank you for everything. And I hope you recover quickly."

If air was life, so was Sanam. If Sanam was gone, so was air.

The phone slipped from my palm.

Monitors started beeping.

Api rushed over. "Osman, what happened?" she asked.

I saw her worried face. I heard her call the doctors. I even felt her shake my shoulders. But what is a man to say when his life is no longer his?

"Zain . . . got married."

Kiran Api's eyes widened. "He found Maham?"

"No. He found . . ." My chest heaved. "He found *her*."

The doctors rushed in. "He is desatting," said one.

"Put the oxygen back on," said the second.

"Call for a stat chest X-ray," said the third.

The cool rush of oxygen flooded my nose and throat as the mask was strapped back on. Their voices blurred together, echoing through the cavern I was falling into.

I wanted to tell them to stop. To let me explain. That I didn't need oxygen. I didn't need a chest X-ray or their frantic energy. I needed her—my life.

But I couldn't find my voice. Instead, under the harsh fluorescent lights filling my vision, I wondered—was death the absence of breathing, or the absence of life?

KIRAN

It took me quite a while to realize what Osman was talking about. And why, after the doctors left, he was frantically calling Sanam and leaving voicemail after voicemail, or how he had suddenly found the strength to walk to the doctors' lounge to demand he be discharged from the hospital so he could catch a flight to the US, even though he was in no condition to leave his hospital bed.

I had witnessed this kind of gut-wrenching pain before—on my father's face, the day my mother died in the same damn hospital outside which I now sat at midnight, wiping away my tears, while my brother was inside getting sedatives so he could catch a few hours of sleep.

You have to be strong for him, I told myself over and over like a mantra, willing the words to sink in, to make me believe them.

Though where was I supposed to get the strength, day after day, year after year? I had no reserves left to tap into, no miraculous second wind to carry me forward.

It was just me, standing on the edge of exhaustion, feeling the guilt creep in again. If I had fought harder for what was ours, Sanam wouldn't have walked away with a man whose father had stolen it from us.

"Ms. Kiran?" A hushed voice spoke near me, forcing me to glance at the man dressed in blue jeans and a plain white T-shirt rather than his usual stiff uniform.

I scowled at him. "Inspector Junaid, why are you always popping up everywhere? It's midnight, for God's sake. I am not answering any more questions about my family."

He hesitated but clearly didn't get the hint. "May I sit?" he asked, and kept standing until I nodded, more out of annoyance than anything else.

"Be quick. I have to go back inside."

"You seem stressed," he said quietly, as if that was supposed to be surprising.

"My brother did everything right and yet had his heart shattered by a rich girl and her powerful family. What should I do—laugh at our fate?"

If my rudeness bothered him, he didn't show it. Instead, he pulled out a paper napkin and handed it to me, saying, "It's clean. In case you need it."

Leaning back on the bench, he sighed but stayed silent while I dabbed my eyes, unsure why he was here, but unwilling to admit that a familiar face was exactly what I needed right now.

Staring into the dark night, he eventually asked, "What does fate mean to you, Ms. Kiran?"

"The absence of choice in shaping one's future," I answered. If choices could be made, I would have chosen a vastly different future for my family.

"In my line of work, though, I often see fate being used as a convenient excuse for the devil's work."

My brows furrowed. "What are you saying?"

"I am saying that my son and your brother getting shot was not fate. Neither was the assault on you and your sisters all those years ago. It was the work of men who pretend to be God."

He was good with words, I had to admit. But words were not what I needed from him.

"I need justice, Inspector Junaid. Not a lecture on fate."

His gaze shifted towards me. Whether it was the glow of a nearby lamppost in his eyes or a warmth from within him, I couldn't look away.

"For the sake of our families, I have to be cautious, and it will take time, but I will not rest until I get justice for you, Ms. Kiran. That is my promise," he said, his voice so resolute, hope dared to flicker in my hardened heart.

He had stood up and said his goodbyes when I asked, "Why did you come here tonight?"

A small smile tugged at his lips. "I was just passing by."

Deal

ZAIN

"Married and Miserable" could have been the title of my life's show, written, directed, and produced by my father.

You're a fool, a voice chided.

I downed a glass of whiskey, and the voice shut up. For the past four weeks, it had been my foolproof method to dull the senses and bury the conscience. The only good thing to come out of that damn nikah were the videos sent to me by the constable, seemingly just after my cousin heard the message Sanam had sent.

Osman was writhing in agony, every scream clawing through the screen, his body crumbling under the weight of retribution. Bones shattered, muscles torn—like his life was being ripped apart, piece by piece. I recognized his pain because he had once inflicted it upon me.

His pain hasn't taken away yours. There was that stupid voice again.

"Give me another," I told the bartender and gulped down the golden liquid as soon as he slid it my way.

Ah. I smiled like a fool. Relief, even if temporary, flooded my mind.

"Osman brought this on himself," I said out loud for everyone to hear.

Yet, there was no one there. At 10 a.m. on a weekday, the bar lay vacant, except for me and the bartender, who was rearranging bottles on a shelf as he shook his head in disdain.

Abu glared at me when I walked into the living room at my father-in-law's house. "Where have you been? I told you to be here by 6 p.m. Zaviyar will arrive any minute."

"Class went overtime," I mumbled a lie. I had fallen asleep on the grass outside my class.

"Well, you look like shit," he remarked, turning his attention to my stone-faced wife, who sat alone on a sofa at the far end of the room. She had refused to move from her dorm, while I preferred to stay in the same guest suite I had occupied since arriving in Houston.

"Why the hell are you still sitting here? Get your husband some clean clothes," Abu told her.

Sanam didn't move, didn't even blink. Maybe she wasn't even breathing.

Another feminine voice answered instead. "It's okay. She isn't feeling well. Come, Zain, let's find you something nice to wear."

It was Zak Uncle's wife, Myla. She looked to be older than me by only a few years and had remained largely invisible since we got here—emerging only when her husband summoned her. Now, she stood at the entrance of the room, gesturing for me to follow her.

"Hurry up!" Abu's harsh tone was enough to send me scurrying towards his friend's wife.

"Thank you," I whispered to her.

She smiled warmly, and unexpectedly. "No worries. But, Zain, just because life is hard doesn't mean you shouldn't take care of yourself."

Life is hard? I silently scoffed. What would this woman, with her perfectly manicured nails and flawless makeup, know about a hard life? Or about being betrayed by your own flesh and blood?

"Actually, you know what, I don't need your help," I told her and walked away, ignoring the way her smile quickly faded.

Zaviyar Uzair's visit to Boston meant that Abu had him exactly where he wanted—in his tight grip. The man was a genius, after all. Though, as I got dressed, I realized that I, too, was my father's son. Any deal he made with the finance minister would fall apart if I announced the truth about my and Sanam's marriage.

Perhaps this was the time to make some deals of my own.

Back in the living room, my father-in-law had joined my father and my silent wife.

"This marriage will only be on paper. Do not expect us to be a normal couple. In fact, I want an apartment of my own in downtown Houston," I told them, in one breath.

Abu vehemently shook his head. "I need an heir to keep this family's name going, and you are my only son. You will live with her and get me that heir as soon as possible," he replied, his eyes so wide they seemed ready to pop.

One look at the disgust on Sanam's face was reminder enough of how much I loathed that woman.

"No," I heard myself say firmly, much to the surprise of the two men in front of me. "Neither of us is ready to live together. So you will use our marriage to get what you need from the Finance Ministry and keep our private business out of your plans. Otherwise, I will tell Zaviyar the truth about his niece's marriage. Then good luck trying to get him to back off ."

The doorbell rang. Abu shrugged and muttered, "Fine. Just keep your mouth shut."

I beamed, patting myself on the back, and turned to the woman in the corner. "Smile, sweetheart. Remember, we got married because we fell in love. Unless you want to fulfill my father's wishes and live with me. Or should we call the constable and see what your boyfriend's up to?"

The silent rage in her eyes extinguished as her lips slowly curled up, and she stood to greet her beloved Zavi Chachoo.

Yet I was no genius at all.

I might have won the battle, but the war was still to begin.

Dinner was civil, at least on the surface. Sanam kept a perfectly practiced smile on her face, and I mirrored her, playing my part. Zaviyar Uzair asked us questions, but Sanam—ever the daughter of her actress mother—handled them with seamless grace. I only needed to nod at the right moments.

When he inquired about our plans, I answered, "I'm pursuing a degree in finance. After that, I'll join GT Enterprise."

Sanam simply shrugged.

"And where will you two live after graduation?" he pressed.

"Houston," my father interjected smoothly, leaving no room for discussion.

The real drama began after dinner, once Sanam left to study for an upcoming test and Myla disappeared into the kitchen. The room grew heavier, the cordial pretense abandoned.

Abu leaned back in his chair, a smirk playing on his lips. Zak Uncle crossed his arms, his posture rigid, while the finance minister leaned forward, his elbows digging into the table. I was merely an observer, a fly on the wall.

"Nice of you to come all this way to check up on your niece," Abu said.

Zaviyar's frown deepened. "Only a bastard like you would stoop low enough to use an innocent girl as a bargaining chip."

My father got straight to the point. "Drop the cases against me and my company, and she'll lead a long, happy life."

The minister's nostrils flared, and his fist slammed against the table, making the cutlery tremble. But his fury wasn't directed at my father—it was aimed at his own brother.

"How could you let this happen, Zak?" Zaviyar spat, his voice laced with anguish. "She's your daughter, for God's sake!"

Zak Uncle glared back. "A daughter I had with the woman *you* were having an affair with."

Whoa. Zaviyar Uzair had an affair with Shabnam Murad.

I glanced at my father, who was gleefully looking on at the two men, almost as if they were acting out the very roles he had concocted for them —brothers, furious and feuding with each other.

Zaviyar's chest heaved. "I loved her," he said, his voice trembling. "And you treated her like shit."

Zak Uncle didn't miss a beat. "And then you loved her daughter like she was your own. So, I treated her like I treated her mother."

My father's smile stretched wider, the glint of triumph unmistakable in his eyes as he leaned forward over the dining table. "Well, Mr. Finance Minister, are you ready to make a deal? If not for the love of your niece, then perhaps for the skeletons rattling in your closet?"

Thick silence, brimming with tension, crackled in the air. Zaviyar's shoulders sagged ever so slightly. My father's gaze on the minister was as sharp as the knife he'd just twisted into his soul. Zak Uncle shifted in his seat, his eyes darting between his brother and his friend.

Zaviyar finally broke his silence. "What do you want?"

"Simple. Call off the tax evasion investigation. End the inquiries into our finances. Give a clean slate for me and my company."

"And if I refuse?"

My father's smile never faltered. "Then you'll see your career, your family, and your niece fall apart piece by piece. It's your move, Minister."

I watched in awe as Abu maneuvered the conversation, securing one reassurance after another. By the time Zaviyar finally stormed out, I couldn't help but marvel at how effortlessly my father had turned the tables. The man was a *frickin'* genius.

Though something still didn't make sense. I followed Abu out of the room to ask, "Why didn't you use his affair with Shabnam Murad to force him to drop the cases?"

He glanced at me, shaking his head. "Wouldn't have worked for long. A man's indiscretions are quickly forgotten—and forgiven—by our society, unlike what happens to women."

Then, as if savoring some private victory, he smirked. "Besides, why settle for one bird when you can bring down two with a single shot?"

I frowned, not fully grasping his meaning. "What are you talking about?"

His deep-throated chuckle sent a chill down my spine. "Zaviyar isn't the only threat against us. Neither is he the only one who'll do anything for his beloved Sanam."

It wasn't hard to decipher who he was referring to, yet that only raised more questions.

"Why are you so concerned about my cousins? Aren't they poor and powerless?"

When Abu kept walking without replying, I followed him and spoke again. "I mean, how can they possibly claim any part of GT Enterprise or our assets? That is all your hard-earned money."

This time, my father paused and turned around. "Don't fret, son. It's not like the shrewd minds of your cousins would make sense to your thick little brain." He took out his wallet and tossed me his Amex Black. "But you did well today in front of Zavi. Go out and treat yourself. Tonight, I'll speak to a realtor to get you that apartment I promised."

My cousins were shrewd, aka intelligent. I was simply stupid. My genius father's words echoed in my mind, relentless and haunting, even as I ordered the priciest bottle of whiskey at one of Houston's most exclusive clubrooms.

"My cousins are still piss poor!" I blurted out, loud enough to make several patrons turn their heads. The club manager approached, quietly but sternly warning me to keep it down and avoid causing a scene.

I ignored him, just as I ignored every other warning that followed in the months ahead. After all, I was stupid, wasn't I?

SANAM

My life felt like a never-ending reel of scenes, flicking from one to the next to a tune I had no control over. One moment, I was a senior in college, dreaming of a boy halfway across the world, and the next, I was a wife to a husband who wanted nothing to do with me—whom I loathed with every fiber of my being.

"You've tied my hands," Zavi Chachoo said, shaking his head in disappointment when we were alone for a moment.

"Being in love has tied mine too," I replied, though he never grasped the true meaning of my words.

Every waking moment after that fateful day four weeks ago, I had shed tears, mourning a present that was a living hell and a future that was nothing more than a mirage.

What I held on to with all my might was my past. That was where I had been loved—quietly and timidly—by a sweet boy who had grown into a wise man I respected as much as I adored.

His memories were my refuge whenever reality became unbearable. Behind my closed eyelids, in the darkness of my room, I still cradled the clay heart that he had once laid in my palms.

I could be that pretty girl who fell in love with the cute nerd.

The beauty who stole an orphan's heart, like he had once called me.

For a brief moment, I could let my guard down, unravel the barbed wire I had wrapped around my heart, and feel safe. Long enough to remember what it was like to be wanted by him, to give my soul a bit of light, and to ease the pain ever so slightly.

But sometimes, my pleasant memories of Osman would be invaded by more recent ones—the videos my father-in-law forced me to watch, like he had before Zavi Chachoo came to dinner. Whenever he sensed I might make a bold move to break free from the shackles he'd placed on me through his son, he'd remind me of the price I'd pay. Osman, the man I was still desperately in love with, was under constant surveillance by his team of paid thugs in Karachi.

It was torture knowing how close Osman was to bodily harm and being helpless to warn him. But my true agony came from seeing him—his life drained from his face—and knowing that I might be the reason for it.

My only solace came in the near-constant presence of a woman with maroon hair. It took me a while to realize who she was—the *Amorous Ameerah* I had teased Osman about. A part of me was filled with raging jealousy, but eventually, I found myself praying that Ameerah would bring him the peace I couldn't—even if she could never love him the way I did.

In those moments, my Dado's voice would echo in my mind: "There is good in every situation. But it takes patience to really see it."

I had no idea what good could possibly come from my warped reality, but her words had been sewn into my heart. And as I sat alone in my dorm room that night, somehow, I found the patience to keep waiting—and waiting and waiting.

OSMAN

"It will take a few weeks for you to start feeling like yourself again," the doctor had said when I was discharged from the hospital a week ago.

I had wanted to tell him that the man I once was had died the moment he'd heard her message. Nothing could resurrect him. Flesh can mend, and bones can heal. But when the soul is shattered, there are no drugs, no bandages, no physical therapy that can ever repair the gaping void left behind.

Instead, I told him I needed to go to Houston. He refused to clear me for a twenty-hour flight, and my sisters wouldn't even hear of it.

"You have to eat, Osman. How will you ever regain your strength if you only take two bites at a time?" Kaukab Baji's patience was waning as I stared at the plate of lentils and rice in front of me.

"I'm not hungry," I muttered.

Undeterred, Kauser Baji replaced the plate with a steaming bowl of chicken corn soup. "Then try this."

I scooped a single spoonful into my mouth before pushing the bowl away. "There, I tried it. Happy? Can I go to my room now?"

Kiran Api gave me a long, measured look before speaking. "No, Osman. You may not go lock yourself in that room for hours on end. I know it's hard, but it's been a month. Life has to go on. It has for her, I'm sure."

"You have no idea what she's going through," I snapped, my frustration breaking through the haze of my exhaustion.

"Osman, she left you for a billionaire's family," Kiran Api said. Her words, I knew, were intended to break through the wall I'd built around myself.

"She didn't leave me. She was snatched away," I countered, my voice rising.

When all three of my sisters exchanged knowing glances, I practically heard their unspoken thoughts. They had warned me countless times about the rich and powerful—their games, their lack of loyalty. But Sanam wasn't one of them. No matter how many times I replayed her message or reread the texts from the past three years, nothing could convince me that her marriage to Zain had been of her own free will.

Kauser Baji lay a gentle hand on my arm. "You're grieving. We get that. But even if this is all a power play of some sort, you not eating isn't going to help anyone."

They were such typical Pakistani mothers. The world could be ending, and they'd be stuffing your mouth with food. It was driving me insane.

"If you don't eat, you can't take your meds."

"How will you get better if you don't take your meds?"

Their questions kept coming. Ignoring them, I started to get up from my chair and stumbled. All three rushed forward to hold me—as if I was still a child.

"Leave me alone." I glared at them.

They moved aside without a word, but their gazes pierced my back as I trudged to my room. Once inside, I shut the door and collapsed onto the bed, out of breath from just walking from the dining table to my room.

Outside, the doorbell rang, and new but familiar voices filtered in: the loud, shrill one of a classmate who was turning into a nuisance, and the deep resonant one of the inspector who seemed to have forgotten he had a whole city to take care of.

I blocked it all out and grabbed my phone, praying she had received my messages. But there it was, that single tick under the hundreds of messages I had sent, mocking me with its dull gray, the color of my life. Suddenly, a new message appeared on my screen. It was from a US number, one I didn't recognize.

Unknown: Feeling better, boy?

What the heck? I quickly typed out a reply.

Me: Who is this?

No reply came for a few moments before a picture showed up on my phone with a caption: guess.

It was a picture of Sanam—sunken eyes, sagging cheeks, slumped shoulders. She sat like a statue between her Zavi Chachoo and that bloody cousin of mine. With my heart thumping, I called the number.

"Let me talk to her."

A gruff voice I instantly recognized replied, "No, but if you stay away from her and do as I say, I'll spare her, even though she is more my type than Maham was."

Spare her. His type. The vile words Asif Ghazanfar had used for Maham echoed in my mind.

"Don't you dare lay a finger on her!" I yelled into the phone with all my strength.

"Boy, you are in no position to call the shots here," he retorted. "Your only option is to make a deal with me."

"What deal?"

"Tell Kiran to accept her reality. Your grandfather may have started this company, but it's *mine* now. If she tries to go to court again or makes a statement to the press, Sanam is fair game."

"What company?" I found myself asking.

Asif scoffed. "Don't tell me she hasn't told you how she stupidly signed over all your shares in Tariq Enterprise to me."

I had no idea what he was talking about, but I was beginning to understand. The T in GT Enterprise stood for Tariq. Which meant it must have once been in my grandfather's or father's name. After their death, my sisters and I should have inherited it. As the cogwheels turned, another realization sank in.

We hadn't been born middle-class or powerless. but had lost our wealth and power. Both of which could have saved Sanam.

Was Kiran Api responsible for it all?

"Well, let me not stop you from digging up the truth, *boy*. But while you're at it, tell Inspector Junaid to release my man, will you? And ask him how his son is doing."

The call ended, but the questions it raised had me jolting from my bed and hobbling out of my room once again.

Kiran Api sat in the living room with the others, drinking chai. There was chatter about an arrest made, and evidence of Asif's and Zain's involvement in my shooting. Neither concerned me at the moment.

"Did you sign over my shares in Dada's company to Asif Ghazanfar?" I asked my sister.

Silence descended on the room as quickly as the question left my lips. Kiran Api froze, her hand tightening around the teacup she held, while my other two sisters exchanged a worried glance.

"What are you talking about, Osman?" Kiran Api replied calmly. But it wasn't convincing enough to mask the guilt flashing in her eyes.

"You heard me," I said sharply. "Did you or did you not sign over my shares?"

Kaukab Baji tried to reply. "Osman, maybe we should talk about this later—"

"No," I interrupted, my frustration spilling over. "We're talking about it *now*. Did you do it?"

Kiran Api sighed, putting down her cup. "It wasn't a decision I made lightly, Osman. I had no choice."

"There is *always* a choice. Isn't that what you taught us?"

In the corner of the room, the inspector shifted in his seat. "She did it to save your life," he said as he held my gaze, clearly not pleased with me.

"It's true." Kauser Baji added, recalling the details, making Aimy gasp.

I glanced at my sisters. The eldest sat distraught with her head in her hands; the other two looked at each other uncomfortably. These were the women who had always stood beside me. It's not that I doubted their intentions. It was that I couldn't stop thinking how different Sanam and my relationship could have been had we stood in the Ghazanfars' place.

How ironic it was that I was the reason we were in the place we were. Just like I was the reason we were orphans.

"Should have let me die," I muttered.

Kiran Api's gaze shot up. "Don't you dare say that again." She frowned.

Aimy scrambled from her seat. "Come sit down, Osman. You shouldn't be standing for so long," she said, reaching for my arm.

I yanked my arm back and shot her a glare. "Why do you keep showing up? I told you, I don't need you." My words must have stung, but being the stubborn woman she was, she remained by my side, scowling.

Softening my tone, I apologized to my sisters before telling them about the phone call. "Whatever you were planning to do, drop it."

Complete resignation had set in as I turned to the inspector and delivered Asif's message. "I don't care who you've arrested or what evidence you have against Zain and his father—*close* the case."

"But, Osman," Kiran Api interjected, "we were just starting to make progress. We can't back down now—"

I couldn't meet her gaze. The image of Sanam trapped in a nightmare I couldn't even begin to fathom clouded my vision.

"Unless someone can guarantee that Asif won't hurt her, I am begging you, let it go," I pleaded with the room full of people.

No one answered. How could they? They knew that Asif had won, again.

Inspector Junaid broke the silence. "You all should know, I don't go back on my promises. I am not closing this case, but I'll be more discreet and wait until Asif Ghazanfar makes a mistake. Because he will—every criminal does."

His reassurance felt hollow to me. All I could hear was Asif's triumph echoing in my mind, drowning out whatever hope the inspector's words were meant to inspire.

Without another word, I turned and headed towards my bedroom.

My heavy footsteps must have masked the soft ones that had been following me. To my equal parts surprise and irritation, when I turned to close my bedroom door, there stood Aimy with a backpack in hand.

"Good God, Aimy, can't you take a hint?"

She pushed the door all the way open. "Oh, I took the hint, alright. You're a self-centered fool who can't see how much you're hurting your sisters by being rude to them every chance you get, as if they haven't gone through hell themselves for the last two months."

"They need to stop babying me."

"Then grow up." She had the audacity to step forward and poke me in the chest. "You lost the love of your life to a deranged man, we get it. But starving yourself and refusing your meds isn't about to bring her back."

If I hadn't been so engrossed in rage at the universe, I might have thought twice before blurting out, "You've never been in love, Aimy. What the heck do you know?"

Her face fell, and the anger in her eyes disappeared, replaced by pain. A pain I was too familiar with to not recognize.

"Aimy..." I tried to take back my words but that's not how life works, is it?

She took out two folders full of papers and tossed them onto my bed. "Shut up and listen to me. Those are the notes from the last two months. Go over them tonight—we'll start studying *together* tomorrow. You're graduating on time, whether you like it or not."

When she turned to leave, I said what I should have said a long time ago. "I have nothing to offer you except friendship."

"I didn't ask you for anything," she mumbled, without meeting my gaze.

"Then why bother with me?"

She turned to face me, and I caught the glimmer of tears in her eyes. "I had a brother who died from sheer hopelessness," she said, her voice trembling. "I see that same hopelessness in you sometimes, and it terrifies me. So, no matter what you say or how much you try to push me away, I will keep showing up."

Tears spilled onto her cheeks. "I can't help it," she whispered.

A wave of guilt washed over me. There was no doubt that I had much to thank her for. "I am sorry. I didn't mean to make you cry."

"It's okay." She gave me a feeble smile, wiping her eyes. "Crying is good for the soul, far better than anger. You should try it, if you haven't already."

As she retreated, I closed the door behind her and sank onto my bed.

Isn't it strange how you can see some people every day and feel nothing at all? And then there's that one person—you meet them once, share a lollipop, and somehow, you're bound to them forever by an invisible, unbreakable thread.

Thoughts of *her* surged through me again. The familiar crushing ache in my chest returned, making me want to scream, to rip apart the walls, to smash everything fragile within reach.

Instead, I reached for the bedside table and opened the drawer stuffed with lollipops—all of one flavor, strawberry.

Ripping the wrapper off one, I shoved it in my mouth, the sweet, tangy taste coating my tongue as tears streaked down my cheeks. The harder I sucked on the candy, the harder the sobs came. One lollipop finished, and I unwrapped another. And another.

Yet, the tears never stopped.

I grabbed my phone and sent her another message that I knew she might never read.

Me: When I said I was yours, I meant for now and forever. In this world and the next. I will only ever be yours, Sanam. Even if you can't be mine.

That was my promise to her, as I prayed for a 'mistake' to happen.

239

PART THREE

Six months passed. Still no peace.

CHAPTER 26

Graduation-I

ZAIN

Well, here it was. My graduation day.

The day I was supposed to marry the woman of my dreams.

The first day of the rest of my life.

Instead, I was married to a woman I couldn't even look at anymore. My life had crumbled, my dreams and aspirations buried under an impenetrable mountain of regret.

I used to seek solace in a woman. Her thoughts, her words—her mere presence—were the elixir to my mental persecution. But then she left me and took with her my last thread of sanity.

I still sought solace. Not in a woman anymore, though, because the one betrothed to me was as lifeless as a puppet herself. She offered nothing; I took nothing. She despised me; I detested her. She was the innocent victim; I was the foolish villain.

More than six months into our marriage, we still lived separately. Eager to do so, because while she sought solace in work, I sought solace in intoxication. And I didn't need a 'wife' constantly deriding me. We were both graduating, but she was at the top of her class, and I was near the bottom. Thus, like a matchstick and gasoline, we were best kept apart.

I sat among a sea of fellow graduates, all clad in black gowns over formal dresses and suits, wearing black graduation caps. The Texan summer sun beat down on that football field as relentlessly as the waves of pain that wracked my body and soul. I couldn't even tell what the pain was from: a night spent drowning in hard liquor or my soul twisting on itself as it tried to escape its sins.

Yet the pain was a distraction from my reality, as well as the faces of my father and in-laws. Masked behind a coating of civility, they pretended that all was well with their son and daughter. We were a happy family that had gathered for the graduation of a young couple.

The truth was understood, but not spoken of. What was done was done, Sanam and I had been told. Ours was a match with widespread repercussions: more funding for Zaviyar Uzair's election campaign to be the next Prime Minister of Pakistan, more prominence for Zakariya Uzair after being unofficially exiled from the country, and a clean slate with even more power for Asif Ghazanfar.

Everyone was a winner. Except us.

"Zain Ghazanfar." A woman called out my name, gesturing for me to line up. It was almost time for me to get my degree.

I glanced around, looking for my 'wife,' more out of curiosity and boredom than anything else. She was sitting, waiting for her turn; her last name was still Uzair, which meant she wouldn't come onto the stage for a while. Her eyes remained downcast, and even from a distance, I could see the pain on her pretty face as she wiped her eyes, and the gentle heaving of her chest as she silently suffered a loss that, ironically, I understood far too well.

Look what you've done, a voice said, and I quickly tore my eyes away.

"It wasn't me," I muttered. It was the man she loved who had started it all.

My name was called, and I walked onto the stage, collected a piece of paper—the only evidence I had of doing a Bachelor of Business Administration—and walked back off. Not that the degree held much value for my father. He had insisted I stay in the US and gain some work experience before he gave me a position at GT Enterprise.

The only work I could find was as an accountant at my father-in-law's indie production company.

A while later, Sanam repeated my steps. A loud whistle pierced the air, followed by hooting as she received her degree, and the slightest of smiles that had graced her lips in over a year disappeared quickly.

Shabnam Murad. I rolled my eyes as several heads turned to look at the actress.

Sanam's mom was at it again. A daughter's moment to shine was over-shadowed by an attention-grabbing mother. If I weren't her husband, I would have commiserated with her, like I used to back in the day when we were young and innocent. I had once been her friend. Now, I was the enemy. So, I sat still, leaving her to fight her own battles.

I had no more fight left in me anyway.

Whatever was left, I drowned out with the golden liquid coursing down my throat, gulped from an unassuming flask.

SANAM

I almost made an excuse to skip out on the graduation ceremony. That day was supposed to have marked the yearlong countdown to the moment when he, whose name was too painful to say, and I could finally fulfill the promise we had made to each other.

Yet, while that promise could no longer become reality, the sentiments behind them remained.

At least for me.

I was caught in a web now, but my past still fueled the life I had left in me. For even in the depths of despair, I found hope in his memories. Like the one from the coffee shop, when he had said, "I think we owe it to ourselves to tread our paths alone, to grow and become the people we have always wanted to become, before we get together."

He was heartbreakingly wrong about us being together, but he had been right about one thing. I owed this to myself. To grow and make something of the teenager who had sat with him that day.

I had once been a girl who took biology for a cute boy who gave me lollipops. I was now a woman graduating with a Bachelor of Science, majoring in Psychology, but there was no one to give me a lollipop.

This graduation was supposed to be a small victory solely for me.

Mama ruined it anyway, but she was easily ignored—a skill I had ironically acquired from her and now applied to everyone in my life. Even my 'husband.'

"Where is he?" I muttered, looking around the football ground for Zain.

"Let go, pervert." A woman's voice grabbed my attention.

A fellow graduate with dark curls, wearing a midnight blue dress, was pulling her hand away from the man of my nightmares. Even from a distance, I could tell he wasn't sober, and I knew exactly why he had gone after that woman. I couldn't care less about him, but a quick glance at my father-in-law's scowling expression spurred me into action.

The more Zain angered his father, the more Asif felt the need to show his power and control over our lives, threatening the status quo that we had miraculously managed to maintain over the last six months. And today, of all days, I needed him to be in a good mood. I was going to request something I was sure he wouldn't be happy about.

"Zain, come on. Get a grip on yourself. That's not Maham," I told him, pulling him away from the woman and her friends, who were now crowding around him. I even apologized to the girl on his behalf.

"You have no right . . ." He started to protest despite his slurred speech, but stumbled backward, straight into the arms of his father instead.

"What stupidity is this, Zain? You're a married man. Have some shame, at least." Asif Ghazanfar glared at his son, as if he himself was the epitome of purity.

"Married?" Zain scoffed. "We don't even live together. Did you know that she is still in love with my cousin dearest?"

My parents had joined us by now, and of course, my mother had to give her unwanted opinion. "That is not true, Zain. Sanam is your wife, and she was only living apart because you guys had such busy schedules. Now that you are both done, we should set up that fancy apartment of yours properly," she said excitedly.

I gulped. *It's now or never, Sanam.*

"Actually, I got into the PhD program here for child psychology. I'll stay in campus housing—it's convenient for getting to classes."

There was a calculated strategy behind diving straight into the program, but it was more than just that. The deeper I delved into understanding how the mind works and how it's shaped by its surroundings, the more I realized how vulnerable children are during their formative years. I was fortunate enough to have Dado, my personal psychologist and best friend, all in one. But not every child has someone like that. I was determined to change that for as many children as I could.

"Who is going to pay for this degree? Because I am not," said my father, who had made it amply clear that I was not his problem after graduation.

"Money is not an issue for our family. She can do whatever she wants as long as she minds her own fucking business," Zain said with unexpected clarity, catching everyone by surprise. Except me.

In a weirdly warped way, I had begun to understand my 'husband' better than anyone else did. Turns out, we had plenty in common between us—broken hearts, trampled dreams, and a relationship neither of us had wanted.

Though Zain was a battle I was bound to win, it was his father who scared me. He was the war with no rules. And the way he was studying his son at that exact moment sent a shiver down my spine.

My mother and father were chiding me for not acting like a proper wife. But in typical divorced-couple style, they were arguing more about their past than they were advising me on my future.

Not that I cared. I was singularly focused on my father-in-law, who stood there with his lips pursed and eyes hooded, still staring at his son.

What is he thinking?

"It's okay," he said, turning towards Abu and Mama. "Sanam should do that PhD. As my daughter-in-law, I am more than happy to pay her expenses as well."

"Are you sure?" I had to ask. This had been terrifyingly easy.

He nodded slowly. "But how about we all go to Pakistan first and throw a grand party? After all, this relationship between the Ghazanfars and Uzairs isn't something to hide. The world needs to know about our powerful alliance . . ."

". . . and what that means for the future of our country," Abu finished his sentence and nodded along.

Call it intuition or anxiety, but nothing was ever what it seemed with Asif Ghazanfar. A grand party to celebrate our unholy union was not what he really wanted. He had bigger plans for me. I decided to delay them, even before I knew what they were.

"Classes start right away for the summer course, and as soon as that ends, the fall semester begins," I interjected.

Dark, hooded eyes were now watching me. "Then we'll do it in December. What do you say, my lovely daughter-in-law? Will you give me what I want?"

Zain started walking away from us, muttering, "It's only a stupid dinner. Do it whenever, who the hell cares?"

My parents followed, now arguing about the venue for the dinner, while I hung back.

"A trip to Pakistan is not what you really want from me, is it?" I asked my father-in-law.

"Smart girl," he replied with a crooked grin.

"What is it then?"

"A grandson."

"Absolutely not." I stood my ground, cloaking my trembling heart in defiant words and unblinking eyes. "Zain and I are not ready—"

"Darling . . ." He brought his hand to my cheek, making me recoil in disgust. "It's so cute how you think you can deny me what I ask of you."

"But Zain—" I started to say.

"Is a drunkard. His kind are the easiest to manipulate." He leaned towards me. "Just like it is easy to manipulate a woman in love."

His dark, beady eyes didn't leave me when he stepped back again.

"Dean Nadir tells me my nephew is enjoying his pediatric rotation in the newly built ward these days. It would be a shame if he didn't show up to the hospital one day, wouldn't it?"

ZAIN

"I need to speak with you," Sanam said, walking into my apartment late at night.

This was the place I had negotiated with my father for. In one of Houston's newest high-rises, it would have been the ideal place for any young couple to be celebrating their graduation.

We were not that couple.

Her gaze flicked to the golden liquid in my glass, and she rolled her eyes. Without breaking eye contact, I downed it all in one go just to spite her before asking, "Why? Was Osman not picking up the phone?"

Eyes flaring with indignation glared at me. "I am not having an affair with him, if that is what you are trying to imply."

"But you still think about him." That was not a question, but a statement I didn't need her to confirm—and she didn't.

"After what you did with that girl at graduation, you are no one to judge me."

I scowled as the truth stung more than I cared to admit. "Why are you here?"

"Your father wants us to have a baby—"

"So you want me to fuck you?"

"*No!* I want you to be a man and tell your father that we are not ready. And that he has no right to tell us what to do in our private life, or threaten Osman whenever he wants to."

Anger, like a raging wildfire, burned in her eyes, but all I could think about were the words spit in my face by my father earlier that day.

"You're a loser for life, can't even be man enough to take from her what is your right."

"She will never agree," I told him.

His dark eyes, like black holes that usurped all light in this world, bored into mine. "What are you? A wimp like your cousin? Use your fucking strength to make her agree."

"I-I can't," I dared to say. It's not like the thought hadn't crossed my mind, but the coward in me froze every time I neared her.

"Fine, then be a complete failure. You are useless to me. Your mother wants nothing to do with you. She couldn't even come to your graduation. The only person you have left in this world is Sanam. And I can bet she'll leave you too, unless . . ."

Every word he spoke felt like a dagger, plunging deeper. Nothing in my life had turned out the way I had envisioned. But, my father was right about one thing—Sanam would eventually leave me too, unless she had something to stay for.

A child we shared.

I prowled closer, pushing her against the wall until I was so close I could feel her rapid breaths on me. "The way I see it, Ms. Uzair, the only rights we should be talking about are mine over you."

She tried to fight, but I was much stronger than her. "Give up, Sanam. You know very well how this ends. Either you do what my father says, or he does what he said he would do."

"You don't want this, Zain," she implored.

"*Stop* telling me what I do and do not want!" I yelled in her face.

She raised her voice too. "I am not bringing a child into this world when I don't love its father."

Love. For a brief moment, the alcohol coursing through my veins wasn't enough to numb me. And in that moment, I felt it—the gut-wrenching pain, the betrayal from the woman I loved with everything I had, and then some more. And I hated it.

"Love has destroyed both of us, Sanam. Why do you still believe in it?" I hissed.

"Love is not what destroyed me, Zain. *You* did."

Her accusation cut through me, but she didn't stop. "*You're* the man who doesn't know how to love, so don't you dare taint what I had with Osman."

Had. That's what she said. Not *have.*

She and Osman were in the past tense.

Her present was different. She was alone, and obviously angry, just like me.

It gave me pause. Enough to ask, "In all these months, why haven't you asked me for a divorce?"

Pushing me away, she scoffed and took out her phone. "You think I am staying with you willingly?"

A picture of a smiling young girl, dressed in uniform, standing outside the middle school building of Kingston Academy was thrust into my face. "Who is this?" I asked.

"Aliyah, Osman's niece. Your father sent it to me. It was taken by one of the guards at her school. One move from me, and she would disappear."

"Why would he do that? She's a child."

"He is a sick bastard. That's why."

I had always known my father was ruthless. But threatening children? *No*, I couldn't believe it—it had to be a bluff.

Yet the way Sanam sighed at that picture before tucking the phone away told me that it was a bluff she had already fallen for.

A smirk tugged at my lips. Abu was wrong; I didn't need to force myself to do anything to her. She was forcing herself to stay with me.

Genius.

"Glad you understand what's at stake. I don't know who all is on Abu's payroll among the security forces in Pakistan, but there are plenty, so there's no point in reaching out to them."

"I am not going to. But you better man up and tell your father to forget he'll ever have grandchildren," she replied and headed towards the door.

"And why would I do that?" I called out.

"Because I hate you!" she yelled, slamming the door shut behind her.

"Well, I hate you too," I muttered to the empty apartment.

In the few seconds it took to walk from the front door to the kitchen and pour another glass, the oppressive silence of my apartment threatened to consume me whole. Every footstep on the tiled floor grew louder, and the low hum of the refrigerator droned incessantly, until the loneliness wrapped around me like a stifling shroud.

Living alone was starting to feel like a prison sentence. Though who would take in a loser like me?

"I am not a failure," I said defiantly for the walls to hear. Sanam wasn't leaving.

The bell rang again a short while later. "Now what is it?" I asked, flinging the door open.

But it wasn't Sanam.

Myla stood there, impeccably dressed, with her blow-dried hair and flawless makeup, holding a glass dish neatly wrapped in foil.

"It's almost midnight. What do you want?" I frowned at the woman who was technically my mother-in-law, but never acted like one.

She didn't make a move to step in. "I made lasagna. Zak's chauffeur is downstairs, but I thought you might want some," she said in a hushed voice.

"Thank you. But I don't," I said firmly and started to close the door, but she held it open with her foot.

"Wait, Zain, umm . . . how are your cousins?" she blurted out.

What? I blamed it on lack of sleep, but nothing made sense. Why would this woman, dressed like a runway model, be standing at my doorstep at midnight, asking about my bloodsucking cousins?

"Ask your husband's friend. He has them under constant surveillance." I tried to close the door again. This time, she shifted to stand in the doorway itself.

"I-I meant the *other* cousins. On your father's side."

Now I knew I was going bonkers. I hadn't met those cousins for as long as I could remember. *In fact, did I even have cousins on Abu's side?* I couldn't recall.

"No idea. Never met them. Don't care. Leave now, please."

She sighed, her shoulders sagging under some invisible weight, but still, she stepped forward and placed the lasagna in my hands. "Eat this, Zain. You need to take care of yourself."

Without waiting for a response, she turned and left, disappearing as quickly as she'd arrived. I stood there, holding the dish, baffled and trying to make sense of what had just happened. But my eyelids were getting heavy and my brain felt foggy.

I tossed the dish aside, mumbled, "She is so stupid," and dragged myself to bed.

Though, Myla wasn't stupid at all. She was being incredibly brave.

CHAPTER 27

Tales of the Past

KIRAN

About nine months had passed since the day Osman got the phone call that shattered his world.

"Ten lakh rupees?" Kaukab frowned at the news report playing on the TV in my living room. "That is all he has to pay the government for bribing the Karachi Land Development Authority? Doesn't this government have a spine?"

"When the finance minister's niece is married to the man's son, what did you expect?" I remarked with disdain for everyone in power, including Zaviyar Uzair, who was a popular politician in the country. The financial investigation unit he had established had recovered millions from tax evaders and white-collar criminals. Yet, he refused to go after the biggest fish in the pond.

And now, he was bidding to become the next Prime Minister of Pakistan.

"Well, soon it seems our Phuppa will have the Prime Minister under his control too. And then absolutely nothing will touch him," Kauser said, sharing my despondency.

My phone rang, interrupting our conversation. Kaukab lunged for it, her face breaking out into a huge grin. When she handed it to me, she had already accepted the call and it was on speaker. A deep, familiar voice I had only rarely heard in over a year called out my name, making my heart sink. Or maybe it was fluttering, or racing, or skipping a beat.

Whatever it was, it was irritating. I was too old to be affected like this by a mere phone call.

"You can blush all you want later. Answer him first," Kauser whispered.

"Be quiet," I hissed, but was stuck answering the man.

"Yes. Walaikum assalam, Inspector Junaid. What can I do for you?"

"Are you at home? I need to speak with you about something important."

Kaukab replied without waiting for me, "Yes, sir, she is at home. You can come by anytime."

I am going to kill her one of these days, even if Junaid has to put me in handcuffs, I told myself. But unfortunately, that was the wrong image to have in your head when, out of the blue, your body had decided it would start reacting to a middle-aged police officer with warm brown eyes.

"Okay, I'll be there in ten minutes," that police officer was saying when I blinked away the unwanted images from my mind.

He had already hung up, but I wasn't done with my sisters. In fact, I was furious at them for acting like little schoolgirls.

"You two need to start respecting me more."

"Well, he respects you quite a lot. Then what's your problem with him?" one of them replied between giggles.

"I don't have any problem with him. But he is a police officer doing his job. And I am your older sister, who you have started to talk back to far too often." I glared at them like I used to when they were younger. They instinctively straightened up like they always had.

The bell rang soon after, and I opened the door before anyone else could move, ignoring my racing heart at the sight of the man in black and khaki uniform who stood at my doorstep.

"We should leave, Kaukab. I have to pick up Aliyah from her friend's house." Kauser gestured to her sister. I was about to discreetly chide them when the inspector spoke.

"Please stay. I need to tell you all something. And it's best that you have each other when you hear this."

A lump appeared in my throat. "Did something happen to Osman?"

"No, he's okay. It's actually about your father."

The three of us sat together on a sofa opposite him. He sucked in a breath and met our gaze, the usual warmth in his eyes replaced with trepidation.

"I believe he was murdered," he said quietly.

Murdered?

There was absolute silence in the room for a moment before one of my sisters replied to him. "No. That's not true. He was in an accident. The doctor said he was under so much stress that he had a heart attack while driving."

The other argued fervently that our father had no enemies. So, who could have murdered him?

I felt numb. I should have felt angry and betrayed, or at least confused. But I felt nothing. Not when he told us how he had spent the last year discreetly digging through the police records from two decades ago. Nor when he revealed that he'd uncovered two reports from separate mechanics referencing diagnostic tests on Abu's car. One report had cleared the car and was filed in the official case file, while a carbon copy of another noted something chilling: the brakes had been cut.

He had even tried to investigate the mechanic who had given a clean chit to Abu's car. But the man had been arrested soon after Abu's death when the police broke apart a drug smuggling cartel, and since then had mysteriously died in police custody. The other mechanic had no criminal record.

"One of these reports is true," I heard the inspector say. "I am inclined to believe that it's the one put together by the man who *wasn't* arrested with drugs in his pockets."

"Kiran." I felt someone tug my arm. "Do you have any idea why a drug smuggler would have something against Abu?"

I simply shook my head.

"Ms. Kiran?" The deep, low voice was addressing me again, forcing me to clear my head.

"Yes?" I looked up to see the warmth permeate back into his eyes. A warmth that was starting to melt my frozen heart and, with it, make me feel things I couldn't afford to feel: hopelessness, fear, pain. I looked away and squared my shoulders, waiting for him to ask more questions.

"Do you remember if anything unusual happened in the weeks before or after your father's death?"

"No," I told him, keeping my voice steady. "I had been married for about a year at that time, and Kauser, Kaukab, and Osman lived with Abu and Dada. Phuppo went over to help sometimes, but nothing happened out of the usual."

"And after?" His gentle voice coaxed further as he scribbled something in his notebook.

The "after" was a nightmare that I had tried hard to forget. But at that moment, as my sisters looked at me with despair, their own memories probably coming back to them, I knew I would have to be the one to put into words what we had faced.

"Nothing happened in the first six months after Abu passed away other than Phuppo and Zain moving into our house so she could take care of all the kids. Asif visited too, but only intermittently. He seemed to travel a lot for his own business. Then Dada had a massive heart attack. He slept one night and never woke up again."

I glanced at my sisters, the solemn look on their faces a reflection of what had followed Dada's death.

"A few months later, one night, Phuppo woke up Kauser, Kaukab, and Osman and told them to leave her house immediately. With nothing but the clothes on their backs and a few hundred rupees, they showed up at my doorstep, alone and shivering from the cold at 4 a.m. that morning."

Kaukab filled in more details, her voice wavering at times. "We started to walk, taking turns to carry Osman, since he was just four, but we kept getting lost. Finally, a rickshaw driver took pity on us and helped us find Api's home."

"Do you need to take a break?" Junaid asked softly.

I wanted to say yes to him and stop talking altogether, but this was not the first time we were telling this story. This was just the first time someone was listening.

"We can continue," I told him, and my sisters nodded.

"Do you know if Asif was in the house the day your grandfather had a heart attack?"

Kaukab shrugged, but I couldn't help noticing how Kauser tightened her grip on the sofa cushion and closed her eyes before looking at the inspector again.

"He was there that day. I remember," she said quietly.

Realization dawned on me, and my stomach churned with disgust. She had always known when he was around.

"And something out of the ordinary did happen before Abu died," Kauser admitted in a mellow voice, her breaths quickening.

"I told Abu that Asif had come to my room and sexually assaulted me, and that he had threatened me, saying that if I didn't keep that a secret, he would show everyone my pictures . . ." She heaved a breath.

I told Junaid the rest of it. "He threatened her with pictures that would destroy her reputation if anyone saw them. She was a teenager, so of course she was worried. But the thing is, she never saw those pictures, and has no idea when they were taken or *if* they were taken at all. So, she didn't say anything to anyone for almost three years."

I glanced at the inspector while keeping my arm around my sister. Kauser had told her story before, but each time in the past, the next question had been, "Do you have any proof for what you're saying?"

Of course, we didn't have any proof. It was the police's and the lawyer's job to find that, not ours. Yet every time, we had been turned away with the words, "Look at Asif Ghazanfar's status, and look at yours. There is nothing we can do without evidence."

This policeman said none of that. Instead, his brows furrowed, and he simply scribbled something in his notebook before looking at Kauser again.

"What did your father say?"

"He was angry. So angry. I remember he stormed out of my room, saying something about killing Asif. But that evening, he came back to my room and made me promise not to say anything to anyone else. He said he had a plan and told me to trust him."

"Do you think he may have been trying to expose Asif?" I asked.

"Maybe. And maybe Asif found out and decided he had to do something about it," Inspector Junaid replied.

Kauser gasped. "So Abu was killed because of me?"

He leaned forward quickly. "Your father was killed because of a criminal. Don't *ever* blame yourself."

If there was any doubt in his mind about the validity of our story, he did not show it. Instead, he put down his notebook and ran his fingers through his hair. A thoughtfulness reflected off his face that allowed me to relax my shoulders a bit.

"I am so sorry that no one has ever given you the help that you needed or listened to your complaints," he started slowly. "That was probably a function of corrupt people in law enforcement and plain cowardice against a powerful man. But I believe every word you've said, and while I can't go out and arrest Asif just yet, I would not be surprised if there was a link between the drug smuggling group that the mechanic worked for, the men who showed up at Ms. Kiran's house, and Asif himself."

"How are you going to find any evidence for that link when all this happened about twenty years ago?" I had to ask.

"It's hard, I agree. But I know this for sure: rats like Asif Ghazanfar never cut down their illegal activity or suddenly stop becoming sexual predators. And with every crime they commit, there is evidence gathering somewhere. We just have to find it."

In that moment, something shifted within me as I released the heavy burden I'd carried for years—a burden I now shared with the determined man before me. For the first time, justice felt possible, however improbable, because he had said the words we had longed to hear: *I believe in every word you've said.*

In doing so, he had earned my absolute trust and respect. I couldn't deny it: he was a good man, even when I saw him through my lens of distrust and deception.

Kauser and Kaukab went to get some water for our guest, leaving me alone with him, which, for once, I was thankful for, because I needed to say something without my sisters misinterpreting my words.

"Inspector Junaid, I don't even know how to thank you for believing us. We've had a hard life and have learnt to rely only on ourselves. But I've always hoped that one day we could get justice. If for nothing else, for closure."

"Please, call me Junaid," he said with a smile, forcing me to look away from him.

"And you don't have to thank me. I am just doing what should have been done decades ago." His voice dipped, and my heart did those irritating things again. "But I have to say, I am in awe of you, Ms. Kiran. I've never met a person braver than you. Probably never will."

I dared to glance at him just as my sisters entered again. A part of me instantly wanted them to go back to the kitchen. But I stopped myself, ashamed of the reason behind that thought, and the way I kept letting this man affect me.

"Anyway, I must take my leave now." He got off the sofa and turned towards me. "Ms. Kiran, I'll also send you the contact of a lawyer friend of mine. She is one of the best in the country, and I have never doubted her integrity. If there is a way for you to get back what was taken from you because you signed under duress, she will find it."

He has a she-friend who is a hotshot lawyer? Despite the circumstances, a jealous voice reared its head, surprising me.

"You can call me Kiran," I blurted out.

He smiled, nodding slowly, while my sisters' hands flew to their mouths and their shoulders shook with silent laughter despite me glaring at them. Something shifted within me again, but I promptly put it back in place.

Some things were not meant to change.

Like my single status.

CHAPTER 28

Pediatric Cardiologist

OSMAN

"One of my friends from medical college is a pediatric cardiologist in Boston. He's visiting the hospital today to set up teleconsultation services between our hospitals. Interested in meeting him?" Iftikhar Bhai asked when he met me in the cafeteria early one October morning.

After spending the entire summer immersed in childhood diseases during our fifth and final year of medical college, I was convinced that taking care of the most vulnerable was my calling. Or maybe it was simply that the innocence of children was the only pure thing left in my world.

"Sure, I'd love to. Maybe I could even ask him about the path to a pediatric residency in the US," I told him. It had never been my intention to leave Pakistan for further medical training because Sanam and I had always seen ourselves living here, but now. . .

The thought alone made my chest tighten.

"I want to go to the US too," said a perky voice, interrupting my despair.

"I'm sure he'd be excited to meet both of you," Iftikhar Bhai said before leaving.

"Since when have you been interested in peds? You wanted to become a cardiac surgeon," I asked Aimy.

She rolled her eyes and slapped her forehead. "I gave up on being a cardiac surgeon the day I got kicked out of the OR by one for asking too many questions. And I have been telling you I want to do peds ever since we started this rotation. Where is your head at, dude?"

Trying to block you out, I wanted to tell her. But that would have been rude, and as reluctant as I was to admit it, Aimy didn't deserve to be spoken to condescendingly after all she had done for me over the past six months. Like my sisters, she had pushed and prodded until I started finishing my assignments and showing up to the clinical rotations simply to avoid listening to her shrill voice berating me.

Yet, I was no less wary of her. She was too close to me and my family, and despite plenty of other men paying attention to her, some even confessing their romantic feelings, she kept pushing everyone away. Nor did she ever talk about the purported reason behind her helping me: her brother's death.

"Let's make a deal. I don't talk about my baggage, and you don't talk about yours," she had said when we'd first start studying together. And that was a deal we had stuck to ever since.

Of course, Aimy did whatever Aimy wanted.

She broke the deal as soon as we met Dr. Saeed Qureshi later that day, and he asked me which school I had gone to.

"Kingston Academy."

"Did you know my niece, Maham Qureshi? She did her A-Levels there," he replied.

My eyes widened, but it was Aimy's mouth that opened. "Does he *know* her?" she began, and didn't stop until the man I had met just a few minutes ago knew everything—from my love life to my family drama, and even my brush with death.

No matter how much I glared at her, the woman kept talking until Dr. Qureshi was shaking his head and thanking me profusely for saving his niece from a maniac.

"I am so sorry for everything you have gone through. I will let Maham know, but if there is anything I can ever do for you, please do let me know."

"Oh, no need to tell Maham. None of what happened was her fault. I am just glad she is okay," I told him. Her family had moved to the UK, where she had completed her undergraduate degree in journalism.

That should have been the end of the conversation, but an idea had been slowly forming in my mind as Dr. Qureshi spoke about his work. They say only fools let fear chain their hands when opportunity comes knocking. I was no fool. I took the opportunity.

"Actually, Dr. Qureshi," I called out as he was leaving. "It would be really helpful for me if there was a research project I could work on with you to boost my CV."

He didn't hesitate before replying, "Of course. I love working with medical students. There is a project I've been thinking about, but it would require at least two students."

A slow smile spread across Aimy's face. Mine disappeared altogether. Still, I managed to choke out the words—or call it a self-inflicted wound.

"Aimy and I can work together."

And that is how I found myself spending every spare moment over the next few months analyzing data from pediatric patients with cardiac infections at our hospital and comparing them to those at Children's Hospital of Boston.

Our task—to identify shared and unique risk factors at both institutions that would inform patient care—was made infinitely harder because of the incessant yapping of my research partner, Ms. Ameerah Sheikh.

CHAPTER 29

Meeting

OSMAN

"Hey, give me one of your lollipops," Aimy said on the chilly Saturday afternoon in late December, when we were wrapping up yet another marathon session of collating results from the research study we'd started a few weeks ago.

I handed her an apple-flavored one from my bag without looking away from my laptop.

"I want a strawberry one," I heard her say.

My fingers froze over the keyboard. Someone with a soft voice and caramel eyes used to ask me for strawberry lollipops. The memory hit like a wrecking ball, her absence tearing through me with a crushing ache that made it impossible to keep up the pretense that life could simply move on.

"Sorry, those are only for me," I replied, my voice wavering.

Aimy's gaze settled on me for an uncomfortably long moment before she asked, "Just like that pen in your pocket is only for you?"

That pen, with a name engraved on its sleek dark gray metal casing, was never too far from me. Call it a talisman or a lifeline, it was the only tangible piece of her I had left. How could I ever let go of it?

I shut the laptop and shoved it into my bag. "I think we're done for the day," I told her then walked out of the library.

She followed. "It's been almost a year, Osman. You can't keep hanging on to the past."

I stopped and swung around. "How long has it been since your brother died?"

Her irritation morphed into pain. Nothing that I was proud of, but it was the only way to nip this conversation before it started. "We don't talk about our baggage. Those are the rules *you* made, Aimy," I pointed out.

Her jaw clenched, her eyes narrowing for a brief moment before she muttered, "You're such an ass, Osman," and walked away.

Standing alone in the college courtyard, I was trapped in a familiar limbo once again—clinging to the past, feeling guilt over the present, and treading cautiously toward an uncertain future.

A full year had passed since I'd heard her message on my phone, yet the pain felt as raw as it had back then. Perhaps some gaping wounds can never truly be healed.

KIRAN

"Isn't Aimy coming? I told her I would take you both to lunch," I asked Osman when I picked him up from college.

"She has better things to do, Api," he grunted.

He was in such a foul mood all the way to the restaurant that I didn't have it in me to broach the subject again. To us sisters, he and Aimy together made so much sense. Yet he wouldn't hear even a word of it, let alone consider her as an option.

Falling in love was such a nuisance. *At least at my age, I am wise enough to stay away from it*, I reassured myself.

I was instantly questioning my wisdom when I noticed a certain inspector and a teenage boy walking towards us at the restaurant.

"Assalamu Alaikum, Kiran. I didn't expect to see you here." His baritone voice reverberated across the table.

"We're celebrating her promotion to section head of O-Level. Why don't you join us?" Osman spoke before I could kick him under the table.

Much to my dismay, the inspector agreed and pointed towards the polite boy who shared his father's eyes and smile. "I don't think you've met my son, Nael."

"Assalamu Alaikum, Aunty."

Putting a smile on my face, I greeted the boy. "Walaikum Assalam, Nael. Do you know Danish and Daniyal?" I asked, noticing that my sons had already shaken hands with him.

"Yes, our schools are football rivals. Though I have to admit, I don't think we have anyone who matches Daniyal's skills."

Daniyal's face lit up immediately. "Thanks, bro. You're pretty good yourself."

Ugh. That's what was left—our sons fan-boying over each other.

"Our sons seem to be getting along quite well," Junaid said in a hushed voice as he took the seat opposite me.

"That doesn't mean anything," I replied before I could stop myself.

He looked amused. "When did I say it did?"

I mentally slapped myself.

Thankfully, the food came quickly, and I'd ordered enough to feed our uninvited guests too. Osman went to use the restroom, leaving Junaid and me alone with the boys, who were now discussing cheat codes for some game. Before things could get awkward again, I brought up something that I had meant to call him about.

"I've decided to visit Phuppo and tell her about Abu's possible murder. They always had a great relationship. I can't imagine that she would knowingly be involved in his death, but maybe she remembers something from that day."

"I already spoke to her in detail when Osman was shot, and I don't think she knows much about what goes on in that house." He leaned across the table, and I caught a whiff of his smokey sandalwood cologne.

For the love of God! I sat back in my chair, trying to increase the distance between us. I was too old to get distracted by a mere masculine scent.

"Yes, but there is a difference between me talking to her like her niece and you interrogating her like a policeman."

He smiled, the kind that was almost a smirk but mirthful enough that it turned up the heat in my cheeks rather than offending me, and asked, "Tou aap keh rahin hai ke agar koi pyaar se sawaal poochay tou jawaab bhi pyaar se hi milta hai?" (So, you're saying if someone asks a question with love, the answer is also given with love?)

But I, too, was stubborn, and the inspector with flirty eyes had nothing on my decades of experience with ignoring men like him.

"Not necessarily. Sometimes you get a slap in return too."

He burst out laughing, irritating me even more because I couldn't stop a smile from creeping onto my own face, when I should have been complaining to him about the lack of progress his department had made.

"Anyway," I continued with a straight face, "Bua told me that Phuppo is throwing a graduation party for Zain and Sanam tonight. I am going to talk to her before then."

Junaid raised his eyebrow. "Who is Bua?"

"The nanny who raised us. She still lives with Phuppo, and I call her sometimes to check up on her."

"That's really nice of you. But how will you get into a mansion that is guarded from all sides? I doubt Asif Ghazanfar will just let you walk in."

"I have my ways, which may or may not include disguising myself as an event manager for their party, one who just happens to be sick and needs to wear a mask."

Junaid stared back. I wasn't sure if he was surprised, appalled, or thought I was a fool for coming up with such plans. Not that I cared or needed his opinion. What I needed was a moment alone with Phuppo. Finally, he chuckled. "When did you become Nancy Drew?"

"It is my family that was wronged. I'll do anything to make it right."

"It could get dangerous for you."

"I can take care of myself."

"I'd rather you let me take care of you," he said with that slight smile that kept making my stomach flip.

I ignored the flipping and frowned. "And why would I do that?"

He straightened up and cleared his throat. "I meant, you shouldn't be going on your own. I'll come with you."

"Your face is plastered all over the news. Even strangers easily recognize you."

"Then take Osman."

"No. Absolutely not." I shook my head. I couldn't risk my poor brother running into Sanam at that house.

"Take me where?" Osman asked. *Darn.*

"Your sister wants to play detective and crash your cousin and his wife's graduation party," Junaid said before I could stop him.

Osman's eyes widened. "She's in Karachi?" he whispered.

"I'll go on my own. You don't have to be anywhere near Sanam," I reassured him.

Osman's gaze hardened. "I am not letting you go to that house alone, Api. Besides, I am over her."

He wasn't over her; he couldn't even bring himself to say her name. But I knew my brother well. That determined look in his eyes told me that nothing could sway him from the decision he had already made.

"Fine. But you're staying in the car outside the house," I told my brother.

SANAM

Karachi, the city I once called home, now felt like the graveyard of my dreams. Everywhere I turned, there were remnants of a life snatched from me. My only solace came in the form of retail therapy.

Zain, on the other hand, sought his escape in the company of old friends and the vices they brought with them—a temporary reprieve he was foolish enough to seek again and again. But today, it worked to my advantage.

Asif Ghazanfar made sure I never left his house alone in Karachi. Zain took me to the mall to buy clothes for tonight's fancy dinner, but on the way back, he picked up our old classmate Farhan. In their rush to get to a booze and drug-fueled party, they dropped me off at the corner of the Ghazanfar mansion's massive boundary wall.

"Don't try anything stupid. There are guards everywhere," Zain warned and took off, leaving me alone with a handful of bags but not a soul in sight, except for an old Suzuki Cultus that was parked at some distance from the main gate.

What if I ran away? I wondered. *To a place where no one could find me.*

They'd find him instead, a voice reminded me. Images of him in the hospital, frail and broken, flashed through my mind, and my feet carried me toward the front gate without hesitation. Loving him had come at a price, but it was a price I would always be willing to pay.

A car door shut behind me, and the sound of footsteps that followed grew louder. If I had cared about myself, I would have turned around to see who it was. But now, if kidnapping was in my destiny, well then, so be it.

"Sanam . . ." The wind carried my name.

I stopped dead in my tracks. A bag dropped from my hand.

Only one person ever said my name like that. Like he was breathing it out rather than speaking it. As if his soul was calling out to mine. I swung around and saw him standing a few feet away.

Time stopped ticking.

I watched him as he watched me, the distance between us too great to read the expression in his hazel eyes, yet not nearly enough to stop my heart from pounding wildly against my ribs or my breath from catching in my throat.

In that fleeting moment, I wasn't the wife of a business tycoon's son. I was just a girl hopelessly in love with a boy who had once handed her a bag of lollipops. And he was the boy to whom I had promised my forever as we sat beneath a starlit sky.

"Osman," I whispered.

There was that silence again. A thousand unsaid words. A story of two hearts ripped apart. A tale which had ended too soon. All forgotten in a moment of temporary tranquility in each other's presence.

He took a few hesitant steps forward. It took every ounce of my strength not to rush into his arms, just like I had two years ago at Dado's funeral. And just like that day, I knew he was the elixir my heart so desperately craved.

I knew, because I could see his truth the moment I laid eyes on him.

He hadn't moved on. He couldn't.

"How are you?" he asked, his voice so quiet and humble, unlike his cousin's, which was always so loud and obnoxious.

Not good.

"I am fine," I told him instead.

Footsteps interrupted the silence again, forcing me to tear my gaze away from him, focusing on the guard instead that had circled around us and now stood behind Osman, his hand on his holster, his eyes cold and calculated.

Damn it.

I stepped back, but Osman only moved closer. The guard pulled out his handgun. His eyes, those of an assassin, followed Osman's every move. Yet Osman was so focused on me that he hadn't even noticed the man standing behind him.

"You don't look fine," he said.

Of course I didn't. My life was a nightmare, and the only man who could alleviate my suffering was one I couldn't reach out to, not anymore. "I am fine. You shouldn't be here, Osman. Please go," I pleaded.

A car screeched to a halt next to us, and out stepped two men.

"Well, well, well. No one told us we were having a high school reunion," an irritating voice from my past spoke out. Farhan walked up to Osman and slapped him on the back.

"Our boy has become a man, I see," he sneered.

Osman curled his fingers, ready to punch him, but was held back because of his eldest sister, who seemed to have appeared out of nowhere.

"Let's go, Osman." She reached out for his hand.

He pulled away from her. "Not until I talk to Sanam."

I felt an arm wrap around my waist. A familiar, pungent smell inundated my senses, nauseating me.

"And who the fuck are you to talk to my wife?" Zain growled.

Osman ignored him, his intense gaze never leaving mine. Like he was studying me, deciphering my secrets, answering his own questions.

I knew then that he knew my truth.

I hadn't moved on. I couldn't.

Before I could stop him, he lunged at Zain. "Get your hands off her!" His fist connected with my husband's jaw, sending him sprawling to the ground.

Ms. Kiran's scream pierced the late evening air as the guard thrust his gun into the back of Osman's head.

Everyone stilled.

"Tch tch tch . . ." Zain clicked his tongue as he slowly got up and dusted himself off, his movements slow and deliberate. "Oh, dear cousin, I've done far more than simply put my hands on her."

"What?" I turned to face him. *What the hell was he talking about?*

Zain pulled me closer, his arm snaking around my waist again. His fingers caressed the bare skin of my neck, and his rough lips kissed my temple, trailing down to my cheek.

"And you always come to me so willingly too, don't you, sweetheart?" he said, loud enough for all to hear.

I understood what he was doing.

The agony on Osman's face ripped through my heart, but the inferno in Zain's eyes had only just been lit. The man he blamed for knocking down the first domino of his shattered life was standing in front of him. This was not an opportunity he would let go of.

"Zain, please, stop it," I begged, struggling to push him away, but his grip only tightened, pulling me harder against his unyielding frame.

More armed men appeared. In the midst of them stormed my father-in-law.

"What is going on here?" he demanded to know.

Zain's lips curled into a cruel smile, his hand splaying possessively over my lower abdomen, a gesture as calculated as it was suffocating.

"We have an announcement to make, Abu," he said, his voice dripping with mockery and triumph.

"Zain, don't," I whispered in desperation, but he didn't even flinch. His need for vengeance had obliterated any humanity left in him. His father, standing nearby with a cold, expectant gaze, had none to lose in the first place.

Neither did the man still holding a gun to Osman's head.

My chest tightened as I squeezed my eyes shut, unable to face the agony etched on Osman's face as my husband's cold, merciless lie echoed around me.

"Sanam is pregnant with *my* child."

Silence.

Stillness.

Quietude.

Even the birds stopped chirping, in solidarity with the man who must have felt so betrayed by me. Me, a woman who had promised her life to him, now ensnared in a web so tight, every move only tightened it further.

If someone said something, I shut it all out, until a whispered breath reached my ears.

"Sanam . . ."

I opened my eyes, fearing the worst. Yet all I saw was his hazel ones gazing at me with familiar tenderness and infinite fidelity.

"As long as I live, I promise, I will always be there for you."

Peace.

Comfort.

Tranquility.

In an instant, the web of lies disappeared, replaced by a love so real and undeniable it became the air that kept me alive as I was taken away into the mansion, leaving behind the man who held my heart.

Chaos erupted within those gilded walls, yet I remained unfazed. The deafening threats, the thunderous berating—none of it broke me. What did, was the bag of newly bought clothes I had dropped, which Bua later brought to my room.

Tucked in the corner of one of them lay a small paper bag, stuffed with strawberry-flavored lollipops.

CHAPTER 30

Flight

ZAIN

As long as I live, I promise I will always be there for you.

Those words echoed in my mind as I sat next to her now, on our flight back to the US, just as they had all of last week. Said by my cousin to my wife as the two stood in front of each other.

He'd had a gun pointed at his head.

She'd had my arm wrapped around her, her eyes shut in embarrassment, or agony, I wasn't sure.

The lie I had concocted for the woman he was so desperately in love with was supposed to have driven him insane. It was meant to turn him away from her in disgust and revulsion. She was supposed to be a tainted woman, willingly touched by another man.

I had thought he would at least cower in fear after having already been shot once by my men. Yet all he did was stand tall and look at her, his eyes filled with some indiscernible emotion, before whispering her name and uttering those words.

Sanam, as long as I live, I promise I will always be here for you.

Glancing at her sleeping form, I asked myself again. *What was it that bound them together so strongly that nothing seemed to make a dent? How could they look at each other so longingly after everything that had been done to them? It couldn't simply be love.*

No. I had been in love. Part of me was still in love with a woman I could no longer have. Love is maddening, irrational, and selfish all at the same time. I know, because I burned everything down around me when I couldn't get her.

So how could he stand there calmly, gazing at Sanam as she opened her eyes at his words? Why did her whole body seem to relax as she gazed back at him? Where was his outrage? His resentment?

And why, after all was said and done, had he turned towards me and implored, "Take care of her," like she was the most precious part of his life—one he had been forced to entrust me with.

The rustle of a blanket brought me out of my thoughts, and I looked over at my wife again. Her blanket had slipped as she straightened her legs on the flattened business class seat. I reached out and pulled it back over her. My hand brushed against her soft hair, and I couldn't help pushing it away from her face.

Sanam was a beautiful woman. There was no denying it.

She is not yours, a small voice inside me said.

She is not his, either. She is married to me, I countered, vehemently.

Yet, for once, no matter how hard I tried to argue with myself, I had to accept that some truths could not be bought or forced. Neither could the lie I had concocted be magically turned into a truth without me growing a pair of balls, like my father would say.

The night we met Osman, I thought I had gathered the courage.

It was supposed to be easy. Forced to sleep in the same room as me under my father's roof, she was supposed to have caved, accepted her reality and reluctantly agreed. After all, I was the good guy. No one else would have given Sanam this much time to accept our marriage.

Now, there was only one way left to deal with the arrogant woman.

Yet, when I saw her curled up on the sofa, tears flowing down her cheeks as she sucked on a lollipop, the coward in me emerged again.

"What the heck is wrong with you?" I asked, keeping my voice firm.

"Leave me alone," she whimpered.

With Abu still raging outside, I had no intention of leaving the room. Instead, I slumped on the bed. "Well, I guess pregnant women are emotional creatures, so your crying or whatever is good."

Despite the tears, she scowled at me. "Why would you tell that lie in front of everyone?"

I didn't tell her that watching my cousin die inside was worth twisting my own soul. Though that wasn't my only excuse.

"Didn't you see my father's face? He is convinced that he is about to be a grandfather."

"And what is going to happen in a few months when there is no baby?"

A smart man, like my cousin, would have known how to answer that question. He probably wouldn't ever have had to make up a lie in the first place. But I was not smart.

I emptied my glass of Chardonnay and pressed the flight attendant call button again. When a woman appeared, I told her, "I'll take a glass of vodka."

You have to stop drinking, a voice chided me.

It's for the flight, I told myself. Surely, I could stop whenever I wanted.

CHAPTER 31

Warning

KIRAN

The dark night was slowly giving way to the light of day, blacks and blues fading into oblivion as crimson hues took over the horizon, bathing God's land with renewed hope. A new day, a new opportunity, a do-over.

With a steaming cup of chai in my hand, I sat alone in my living room, still in my pajamas, with my legs tucked under me. Ever since I had been on my own, this was how I preferred to spend my time on lazy weekend mornings while the rest of my house slept in.

A week had passed since the day I had ventured into Phuppo's house. Obviously, Bua was in on it and had vouched for me when the guard stopped me at the entrance.

Phuppo was in the TV lounge, wearing an elegant white saree and a string of pearls when I met her and told her about Junaid's suspicions. Her expression went from apathetic to astonished, but she did not utter a word. Instead, she got up and left the room when I asked her if she remembered anything from the day Abu died. Which is why what lay in my hand made no sense at all.

Written in pencil with haphazard letters, the crumpled piece of paper had been quietly handed to me by Bua as I was about to leave.

Give me time, it simply said.

I mentioned it to Junaid as soon as I reached home, but he hadn't been able to find anything new on our Phuppo other than what we already knew. She was a simple housewife. Didn't even have a bank account to her name. So what did she need time for?

A door opened and closed, and the rushing footsteps that followed made me look up at Daniyal's panicked face. "Mama, you forgot to wake me up. I have to be at the football field in half an hour. We're playing our archrivals."

Great, I groaned. Nael Razzak played for Daniyal's archrival team.

Getting anywhere on time was the daily miracle I pulled off. That's why, when we made a mad dash to the football field and reached with a minute to spare, it irked me to no end when my gaze landed on a certain inspector dressed in a black monochrome shirt and tracksuit bottoms. He was sitting on the bleachers, smirking at me as he pointed towards his watch and mouthed, "You are late."

I ignored him and looked around to find an empty seat. The place was completely packed. Fortunately, I found one. Unfortunately, it was right next to the inspector himself.

But I was born stubborn too. Ignoring my thumping heart, I trudged up the bleachers and made my way to the seat next to Junaid.

"Couldn't find anyone to sit next to you? Try dressing better next time." I couldn't help taking a jab at him as I sat down. Or maybe that was just my way of justifying why my gaze kept going back to the bulge of his biceps, visible through his half-sleeve shirt.

He let out a low chuckle and leaned in, close enough for his smoky sandalwood scent to engulf me. "Oh, there were plenty who were dying to sit here. I told them I was saving it for my wife."

"What?" I literally jumped out of my seat, and his chuckle turned into full-blown laughter, attracting the attention of those around us. He composed himself quickly and gestured towards the seat.

"Don't worry, I wasn't talking about you," he said, his eyes still sparkling with amusement.

I stood rooted in spot, debating whether I should be offended by his frankness or ask the question that I hated to admit was bothering me: was there someone he wanted to make his wife?

Ugh. I huffed instead.

The whistle blew, and the crowd started cheering. He nodded again towards the seat, and his expression suddenly became stoic. "Sit, Ms. Kiran. I did save the seat for you, but only because I needed to tell you something important."

"And why couldn't you just call me?" I sat down gingerly, careful to keep as many inches between us as possible.

He sighed and rubbed his chin, and that is when I noticed the redness in his eyes, like he hadn't slept much. "Because I am afraid your phone might be tapped."

The whistle sounded again. A player on the field had been kicked by his opponent.

I moved my attention back to the inspector. "What is that supposed to mean?"

"One of my detectives has been keeping an eye on you—" he said.

"Excuse me? You have someone following me?" I interrupted, aghast at the unconsented invasion of my privacy.

He looked at me sideways, that cocky smile playing on his lips again. "Everything is fair in love and war, isn't it, Kiran?"

"Junaid, you . . ." Incredulous, I jumped out of my seat for a second time, determined to give him a piece of my mind. But he spoke up before I could gather my raging words.

"Now what's the problem? Are we not at war against your Phuppa?" he asked with a straight face, even though the wicked glint in his eyes gave him away.

I hate him so much.

He grabbed my hand, pulling me onto the seat next to him again. "Stop jumping up, please, and let me finish. While following you, for your *own* safety, Detective Iqbal noted that someone else was also following you and Osman."

"Who?" This time, I stayed in my seat.

"Bilal."

My heart sank at the implication of that news. "Constable Bilal? As in the man who stood guard over my brother all those weeks?"

His voice dipped as he leaned in again. "Yes. I have been interrogating him all night. It seems that Asif paid him off to keep an eye on Osman and you. He especially kept asking Bilal about you being in touch with lawyers."

"He's been checking to see if we followed the instructions he sent to Osman last year," I guessed. That probably also explained why Asif's men had let Osman and me go relatively easily when they had caught us outside his house. We hadn't made any major moves against him.

Junaid nodded, but our attention was diverted by *ooh*s and *aah*s from the crowd again.

"Goallllll!" Cheers rang out on one end of the field, while the other side vehemently argued with the referee about the validity of that goal.

"It didn't cross the line!" someone yelled from the sideline.

This was a high school match, so there were no instant replays, and the referee stuck to his call. Tensions ran visibly high on the field when a player from Daniyal's team shoved one from Nael's as they stood in formation for the game to start again. The coaches and referee separated the two, and both were given a warning. The game started, and the ball was kicked around like my mind had been with Junaid's revelations.

"We haven't been in touch with a lawyer, but you and I have met. What did Bilal think about that?" I asked.

Junaid didn't meet my gaze when he said, "He thought we were in a romantic relationship."

"What?" I gaped at him.

"I told him we were."

"What?"

He faced me, raising a brow. "Did you want me to tell him we were digging through his boss's past?"

Of course I didn't. But Junaid's rapid shift from flirty to serious to dead serious was giving me a whiplash headache. Meanwhile, he remained unfazed as he leaned towards me again.

"I think there is something much bigger going on. This is not just about a real estate company and a mansion, or your family."

"What else could it be?" I asked.

Junaid nodded. "I am not sure, but we have been combing through surveillance videos, news reports, and social media clips of Asif. He seems to have some association or another with people who we have been interested in for every crime imaginable."

"Maybe Asif Ghazanfar just attracts the criminal kind of crowd."

"Maybe, but all of them have bought large properties through GT Enterprise, and in my line of work, there are no coincidences."

My pulse quickened, this time not because of the proximity of a handsome inspector dressed in black, but because of what his words meant for us. My siblings and I had been leading a comfortable, albeit cash-strapped, existence ever since our parents died. Never did it occur to me that the company that our father and grandfather had built would be used for criminal activity.

A commotion on the field diverted our attention to the game again. It seemed that this time a player from Daniyal's team was injured, and a player from Nael's team had been benched for injuring him. Daniyal and Nael were among the only handful of players who hung back and did not engage in what looked like a fistfight that had broken out among the rest of the players.

"What is wrong with these kids? It's only a game," I lamented.

Junaid agreed. "Nael said there was a lot of smack talk going on over social media between the two schools. I am not surprised these kids are so on edge now."

His phone went off. "That was my police detail," he said after hanging up. "Seems like some kids and their personal security guards are threatening each other. I'd better go check. Could you keep an eye on Nael?"

"Of course." I smiled.

Given all the commotion, I wasn't surprised when the coaches decided to cancel the game altogether. Not wanting to leave Nael alone, I stood at the bottom of the bleachers waiting for Junaid as dozens of dejected students and their families swarmed out. In the midst of that crowd, however, something odd caught my eye.

A student in our school's uniform was walking back towards the field instead of away from it. His face was partially covered by a baseball cap pulled low over his eyes. I continued to watch him—perhaps it was my overactive sixth sense, but this student seemed to have the long strides of a man on a mission.

A few feet away from us, he suddenly bumped into one of the coaches, which knocked off his cap.

I gasped.

He was the guard who had held a gun to Osman's head outside Phuppo's house.

My shocked eyes met his cold, heartless ones for a millisecond before he looked out onto the field where my twins were standing, chatting with Junaid's son. I looked back at the man, my legs already sprinting towards him as my brain caught up.

He pointed a gun straight at the boys.

I yelled, the loudest I had ever yelled.

"Boys . . . get down!!"

BOOM

The gun went off.

CHAPTER 32

Bravery

KIRAN

I sat on the ground, dazed. For a moment, nothing made sense. Why did I have an intense throbbing pain at the back of my head? Why did my knuckles feel like I had punched a wall? Why were the contents of my purse strewn on the ground all around me?

And who kept yelling, "Mama, Mama, Mama"?

Then there were those familiar dark brown eyes shrouded in concern. "Kiran, look at me," the man repeatedly said, his hands gently cupping my face.

A younger, excited voice interrupted him. "Abu, you should have seen Kiran Aunty. She literally flew into that man, like Superwoman."

Nael?

Suddenly, it all made sense.

"Oh God, Junaid, the boys . . ." I tried to get up, but the pain in the back of my head intensified, almost blinding me.

"Take it easy." Rough hands clasped both my bare forearms; the warmth of their touch was enough to make me forget the pain.

"All three boys are fine. But I think you have a concussion, Superwoman." Junaid's mirthful eyes met mine, even though his voice remained calm and collected, like any senior police officer at a crime scene.

Danish and Daniyal appeared next to me, and Junaid let go. *Too soon,* I wanted to protest, but caught myself. My sons needed my attention more than my fluttering heart did.

"Mama, where did you learn to throw punches like that?" asked one of the twins, wrapping his arms around my waist from one side.

Not to be left behind, the other one joined in the group hug. "Yeah, Mama. I think you broke his nose."

The throbbing in my head had dulled, and I remembered more of what had happened. The man, with an innocent-looking face but the cold, ruthless eyes of an assassin, had raised a gun towards my sons and Nael. I had yelled out to all three, and saw Nael pulling the other two to the ground, while I slammed into the short man's muscular body, catching him by surprise.

The gun went off. But I kept hitting the man in every way I could. Knee in his groin, fists on his face, clawing at his eyes.

"Tell Asif Ghazanfar to stay away from my boys," I remembered hissing at him before he threw me off, and my body slammed against the concrete pillar. Then, everything had gone dark.

My mom-gaze gave my sons a quick once-over. Satisfied, I looked up from them to meet the gaze of another young boy standing awkwardly next to his father, who was busy giving instructions to his subordinates. In the crowd of black and khaki uniformed men, the solemn look in his eyes and the subtle shaking of his shoulders confirmed what I was afraid of.

This wasn't the first time Nael had been shot at. He was safe now, but as the adrenaline rush subsided, he would likely relive his earlier trauma. And even though his father was right next to him, the boy needed more.

"Daniyal, Danish, go sit down on the bleachers. I'll be right back."

As I approached Nael, I saw tears pooling in his eyes. He deftly wiped them away and gave me a small smile.

"Are you okay, Nael? I hope you didn't get hurt."

"I am fine, thank you," he replied quietly.

His eyes told a different story, though. "It's okay to be afraid, but you're not alone. We're in this together," I told the sweet boy.

I asked him to sit with my twins and was about to follow when I felt that same rough hand as before clasp my wrist.

"Thank you for taking care of Nael. You have no idea what that means to me right now," Junaid whispered, still holding on to me. If it wasn't his breathy voice trying to hide the angst beneath his tough exterior, it surely was the gratitude in his eyes that melted my heart.

It couldn't be easy to have your son targeted twice because of what your job entailed. Though whether my sons had been the target or Nael, I suppose it was hard to tell at this point.

"Of course," I smiled. "He is no different from my sons."

Junaid nodded, a slight smile breaking through his worried expression. "When you tackled the man, he dropped his gun. I need to make sure it gets to the right place so we can use it for evidence."

I remembered then that I hadn't told him an important detail about that man yet. "He was one of Asif's men. I saw him outside his house last week."

"Hmm. I should have known he would try to hit us where it hurt most."

The flurry of activity around us continued unabated as Junaid and I parted ways. Detective Iqbal, a kind-looking man not much older than me, interviewed us and the other witnesses in that stadium. When an ambulance arrived, the paramedics insisted on taking me to the ER.

"I can't leave the boys alone," I told them.

"They won't be alone. They'll be with me," Junaid said from behind me.

"But—"

"No buts, Ms. Kiran. You blacked out and were confused after that. That earns you a trip to the doctor."

Without leaving any room for debate, he told me we would be spending the night at the police safe house. "It's a hut along the beach and is heavily guarded. Until we are sure there are no other assassins targeting them, it's best that you all stay there."

He had also ordered increased protection for the rest of my family.

As he helped me into the ambulance, he whispered, "I am telling you, there is something much bigger going on. And the closer we get to finding out what that is, the more desperate Asif is getting."

I'd known Junaid for over a year now. Never had I seen him so tense before. Yet, never had I felt so calm before either. When he shut the doors of the ambulance and I watched his silhouette fade through the small back windows, I had an inkling why that might be.

ZAIN

Myla, along with my father-in-law's chauffeur, had picked us up from the airport and brought us to her house.

"Come in, come in. I am so happy you guys are back." She gestured as I pulled in my bag and tried to pull in Sanam's before she snatched the handle from me and took it in herself.

"I had the chef make your favorite dishes," she was telling Sanam as I quietly followed behind.

Always stylishly dressed, Myla was still an enigma to me. No matter what time of the day I met her, she always had a wide smile plastered on her make-up-painted face. *How could someone be so happy all the time?* I wondered.

When she left us in the living room, I tried to speak. "Sanam . . ."

"What do you want?" she immediately scowled.

"I am sorry," I blurted out.

"About what?"

"Everything."

That is what I had willed myself to say after spending twenty hours on my journey from Pakistan to the US, with a woman bound to me in a marriage whose very foundation was built on lies and deceit. And with whom I was now supposedly having a child—a lie I still wasn't sure how to explain away.

"I am sorry about everything," I repeated.

"No, Zain." She shook her head defiantly. "You do not get to say a simple 'sorry' after everything you have done to me and expect me to forgive you."

She stomped away, and I let her, knowing full well that my road to redemption was never going to be easy. Or maybe I was so far gone that the only road left for me to travel was the one going straight to hell.

I was starting to get a headache, the kind that could only be alleviated by my father-in-law's liquor cabinet. Myla was nowhere to be found, and Sanam had stepped into the restroom, so I decided to help myself and headed towards the study, where the golden goodness was kept.

However, raised voices coming from the room through a door left slightly ajar made me pause. A voice I recognized intrigued me further. Inching closer, I tried to listen in on a conversation I had not been invited too.

"How did you even know they would be there?" Zak Uncle said.

Abu scoffed at the speaker. "Social media accounts. These dumb kids display their whole lives online."

"Targeting their children was a dumb move too."

I had no idea who they were talking about, but the picture of Osman's niece on Sanam's phone didn't seem like a bluff anymore.

My father went on. "They needed to be taught a lesson. Kiran had the audacity to come into *my* house, speak to *my* wife, and think that I wouldn't find out. And that police officer arrested Bilal. Unlike my coward son, I don't take invasion of my property or my people lightly."

"She spoke to Zarine? What did she say?"

"I asked my men, but no one saw Zarine say anything to her. The stupid woman was probably high on her pills."

"Well, your man failed to scare them, and now the whole country's police force is looking for him," Zak Uncle pointed out.

"Don't worry. I've gotten rid of all evidence linking him to me. Besides, they won't find him anyway."

"How can you be so sure?"

Abu let out a throaty laugh. "That failure is lying six feet under the ground." Much to my disgust, my father-in-law joined in.

"Well, I suppose congratulations are in order. You're going to be a grandfather," Zak Uncle said.

"Just in time. I was starting to think we would have to get rid of that daughter of yours."

Get rid of Sanam? A chill ran through me. My stomach recoiled when her father agreed.

"This is why I told you not to include her. Zain may be stupid and self-destructive. But Sanam is stubborn and smart. What if she figures it all out?"

My father's voice lowered. "As long as she gives me a grandson, you can shut her up however you like."

The sharp click of heels echoed down the hallway, making me instinctively step back from the door, but I wasn't quick enough.

"There you are." Myla's cheerful voice rang out, ceasing all talk coming from the study. Zak Uncle came out immediately, pinning me in place with his piercing gaze.

"How long have you been standing here?"

"I . . ."

"Oh, Zak, leave the poor boy alone. He's been on a long flight," Myla interrupted, draping an arm over my shoulders. Without waiting for a response, she guided me towards the dining room, where Sanam sat, avoiding my gaze entirely.

Dinner passed in a blur. Afterwards, I offered to drop Sanam off at her apartment near the college campus, but she called a cab instead. It wasn't until I returned to my own apartment that Abu's call came, his voice dripping with venom.

"If you know what is best for your wife and unborn child, forget everything you heard back at Zak's house. Otherwise, you know exactly what I am capable of."

His words repeated themselves in my mind long after the call ended. I stared at my phone, trying to understand how a man who wielded so much power could wield it with so little conscience. How could he justify threatening his own daughter-in-law, a pregnant woman carrying his grandchild, even if fake, without so much as a flicker of remorse?

You've done some things without remorse too, a voice spoke out.

I am not the bad guy, I defiantly shut it down and poured myself the glass of whiskey I had been craving.

It had been a long flight . . . and an even longer evening.

As I sipped on the golden elixir, I wondered: *What was Sanam smart enough to figure out?*

CHAPTER 33

The Hut

KIRAN

The two-bedroom police hut was sparsely furnished, which is the nicest way to put it. Half the lights didn't work, the beds might as well have been wooden planks, and only one of the four burners on the gas stove lit a fire. Which was, obviously, a problem as I tried to cook breakfast for three hungry teenage boys.

But somehow, I managed. I always did. Working with the bare minimum was nothing new for me.

With breakfast done, the lack of internet and TV had the boys rummaging through the closets for board games to play while I took a break outside on the porch, facing the white sand beach and the vast ocean in front of me. If it hadn't been for the reason that brought me here, I would have found my surroundings quite peaceful. Right now, it felt like the calm before chaos.

I am not sure how long I sat on that porch, my legs tucked under me on an old wicker sofa, when I heard the door to the house creak open and looked up to meet the gaze of an inspector with tired eyes, ruffled hair, and crumpled clothes, all of which somehow made him look more real. Even likable.

More importantly, he had what I was craving most at that moment but had run out of ingredients to make: two cups of hot, steaming chai.

"Just what I wanted." I grinned.

Junaid smiled back, and I ignored the butterflies that gesture always caused.

"My men told me you fed them breakfast as well and were out of supplies, so I stopped at home to pick up some more," he said, handing me one cup as he sat on the opposite end of the sofa with the other.

"It's no big deal. I figured they would be hungry, and I didn't see any way they could make breakfast for themselves."

"Yet, you're sitting here hungry yourself."

"How did you . . ."

"I am beginning to understand quite well how the KT action plan works," he interjected.

"The Kiran-Tariq action plan?" I couldn't help laughing, though the mirth in his gaze had been replaced by something else.

"Yes. The plan where you keep filling everyone else's coffers, even when yours are empty." He was looking at me as if he could see right through every barrier I had ever constructed around myself.

"Tell me something, Kiran." His voice deepened as his gaze intensified. "Why are you so reckless when it comes to yourself?"

I forced myself to look away from those dark brown eyes, as if that could stop his gaze from penetrating my walls. But I might as well have been made of glass.

Stop looking at me like that, I wanted to say. With heat creeping into my cheeks, I opted for silence, lest my words give him the key to unlock more of my secrets.

Yet, he was relentless.

"You raise five youngsters all by yourself, you work like there is no tomorrow, you fling yourself at assassins without a thought for your own safety. How long will you keep doing that, Kiran? What if you had gotten shot last night? What if he had taken you hostage? What if—"

I ignored the growing distress in his voice and the deepening frown. Instead, I shot back, "Okay, I get it!"

My defenses were fortified with the primal urge to protect my family, and now his.

"I did what I had to do to protect my sons *and* yours."

He pursed his lips and replied, "So, you see the dilemma that puts me in?"

I met his gaze again in an attempt to put a stop to whatever he was trying to do.

"Fine. I am reckless when it comes to myself. But what choice have I ever had, Junaid? My mother died, leaving me with a baby brother. My father died, leaving me with my young sisters. My husband walked away, leaving me with newborn twins. I've never had a choice, so don't you dare sit here and patronize me."

My voice cracked, and the moisture in my eyes threatened to give way to a deluge of pain. But I didn't care. This man had no right to lecture me.

He must have realized it too, because he finally sat back and shifted his gaze to the ocean. For the next few minutes, there was nothing but the soothing sound of the waves gently lapping at the sand, coming forth only to retreat just as quickly, akin to the inspector next to me.

His jaw clenched as he spoke again. "Why did that bastard leave you?" he asked.

"Who?"

"Your ex-husband. No sane man would ever have left a woman like you."

A woman like me. That sentence shouldn't have affected me the way it did, neither should the concern in his voice have made my pulse quicken. For the last twenty years of my life, I had been a nobody. Just a woman struggling to take care of her family.

But here I was, under the worst of circumstances, sitting next to a man who seemed to care. I gave in to the temptation to let him unlock my secret. Only one, for now, so that I could retreat quickly and bury the hurt if I had to.

"He married the eldest daughter of a family that was worth millions. Then she became nothing but a lonely, ordinary housewife. I guess he lost interest."

Junaid put down his cup of chai and turned towards me, closing the distance between us slightly.

"You are anything but ordinary," he said slowly. "Neither are you alone anymore. I don't know where this investigation will go, but I promise to protect you and your family."

I should have looked away from him then. Away from the emotions in his eyes and the devotion they held. But I didn't want to. I stayed rooted in that spot and took in his compassion and gentle demeanor till they obliterated the scars in my heart.

For the past two decades, it felt like I had been searching for something. And in that moment, I stopped.

I had no need to search any more.

Or to bear my own burdens or swallow my own fear as I stood alone, sheltering my family from the storm always threatening to engulf us.

"I will always have your back, Kiran," he said softly, the words filled with such candor and sincerity that the last bit of ice around my heart melted.

In him, I had found an ally.

Maybe even more.

CHAPTER 34

Acceptance

KIRAN

The twins and I were back at our own apartment after staying at the beach hut for close to a week. The bell rang as I was about to step out of the house to pick up the boys from their afterschool activities. I glanced at the newly installed security camera and saw a man in a black and khaki uniform standing there. This time, I didn't bother trying to hide the smile on my face as I opened the door.

"Assalamu Alaikum, Junaid."

"Walaikum Assalam, Kiran," he replied, his lips turning up into that slight smile I was starting to recognize meant a lot more than what met the eye.

"Were you leaving to go somewhere?" he asked.

"Yes. To pick up the boys."

"I'll walk you to your car, then."

I had no idea when our relationship had turned from a strictly professional one to one where he would show up at my apartment unannounced and then walk me to my car. Maybe it was the day when we had sat together outside the beach hut, or when he'd told me that he had believed every word

I'd said. Whatever it may be, here I was—so comfortable in his presence, it felt like I had known him my whole life.

"What brings you here?" I asked as we walked down the stairs.

"Well, I have good news and bad news. Which do you prefer first?" he asked.

I chose the bad news. Might as well get disappointed first.

"Unfortunately, the man who shot at our boys was found dead. We were able to get a search warrant for Asif's house and interviewed everyone, but no one admitted to seeing that man on the premises. The security camera at the front gate was also conveniently broken, so there is no footage of him holding a gun to Osman's head."

"So, once again, we hit a dead end." The pun wasn't intended.

"Not quite." Junaid perked up. "We were able to identify the man as Akbar Jafri. He's a low-level criminal who was jailed when one of the largest drug-smuggling cartels in the history of Pakistan was busted two decades ago."

The man had been released five years back. But his lack of remorse was not what had Junaid excited when he asked, "Guess who else worked for the same cartel?"

"The mechanic who found nothing wrong with my father's car?"

He beamed like I was his trainee detective. "Exactly! And there's the connection between your father's death and his brother-in-law."

This was a lead we didn't have before. Junaid's team was now pulling up all the files for that case. That gave me some hope, yet it didn't answer the obvious question.

"Why didn't you call me?"

He raked his hands through his hair, his gaze shifting between me and his shuffling feet. Almost like he was shy.

"There was something else I wanted to tell you in person. I got promoted to be the next Inspector General of Sindh. I'll be the youngest one in the department's history," he said, before quickly adding, "Don't tell anyone yet. It is not supposed to be public knowledge for another few months."

Then why are you telling me? I wanted to ask, but didn't.

"That's awesome, Junaid! Congratulations, I am so proud of you." He grinned like one of my students who had received a gold star for a job done well. So adorable.

"Well, I should get going. I was supposed to be at the Chief Minister's house ten minutes ago."

Seriously? I gaped at him. "You made the Chief Minister wait because you wanted to tell me about your promotion? What is wrong with you?"

He shrugged. "I've been asking myself the same question, Ms. Kiran. All I know is . . ." His signature smile spread across his face. "Dil ko aap se milne ki talab ho rahi thi. Mein uss ko manaa nahi kar saka." (My heart was craving to meet you. I couldn't say no to it.)

My heart nearly stopped.

"*Junaid.*" I scowled instinctively.

Stop flirting with me, is what I should have said next, but I didn't.

He laughed—a sound that made me want to douse the fury he had fueled. "You are so easy to rile up. I was kidding. I was just passing by."

He didn't wait for me to reply. Though what could I have said anyway? He was a man who seemed to freely cross lines whenever and however he wanted, letting me glimpse pieces of his inner self, only to retreat as quickly behind a veneer of jest and witty denials.

What do you want from me? was a question I wished I could ask him, but I didn't.

Are you ready for his answer? a solemn voice asked. I sighed, because I wasn't.

Before I could pretend to be a woman who got butterflies in the presence of the next Inspector General of Sindh, I was a mother, an older sister, a woman with a demanding career. All of which came with responsibilities and expectations.

I glanced at my watch and muttered, "Oh shoot," before jumping into my car. I was supposed to be at my sons' school ten minutes ago.

OSMAN

It had been a couple of weeks since I had last seen her. Dressed in a simple light pink kurti and straight white pants, the soft brown waves of her hair, let loose over her shoulders, caught the early evening sun, as it descended from the clear blue sky to make way for the darkness of the night.

She was just as I had always seen her. Caramel brown eyes with their familiar warmth, now overshadowed by an aching desire. Pink lips slightly parted like they always did when she said my name. The glow of her complexion that no amount of makeup could ever duplicate.

So beautifully innocent.

So exquisitely graceful.

Until I walked closer and noticed the sunken cheeks and sagging shoulders, making one thing painfully clear: the reality that exists is never the same as the dreams we dream.

I could have asked her to come away with me. I could have punched her husband harder. He could have gotten angrier. He could have taken it out on her.

So many *ifs* and *buts*, *coulds* and *woulds*. Yet, the only thing that mattered was her, and now, her unborn.

Her silent emotions, the pain in her face as she closed her eyes, spoke volumes more than her husband's taunts ever could. He was easily ignored, but she would always be the woman I had made promises to.

The first, while we sat in a coffee shop—that I would always be there for her.

The second, while we sat under the stars—that one day I would marry her.

Destiny had snatched away my dream to fulfill the second promise, but the first was one I could never give up on.

"Osman, are you ready to present your data?" Dr. Qureshi's voice over the video call cut through the nightmare I lived every day.

"Yes, all set," Aimy replied for me.

We spent the hour in that conference room presenting our data on risk factors for cardiac infections. Some findings were obvious, but there were others that neither of us had expected.

At one point, Dean Nadir poked his head in.

"Busy at work?" he asked, while I was talking to the doctor online.

"Yes, sir. On an international call," Aimy quickly whispered, and the man left. I never gave it a second thought.

"Good job, guys," Dr. Qureshi said when we ended the presentation. "I think this data will be really helpful as we in Boston prepare to accept some of the complex pediatric cardiology patients who need surgery."

He was talking about the international patient referral program being set up between our institutions, but that's not what had me thanking the doctor profusely. It was his promise to mention our work to the resident recruitment committee there.

"You're exactly the kind of hardworking pediatricians we want to train at Children's Hospital of Boston," he said.

When he ended the call, Aimy beamed. "A peds residency in the US would be so frickin' amazing."

I mustered a smile the best I could.

'Amazing' was not what came to mind when I thought about my real reason for pursuing a residency in the US.

"Yup," I mumbled and gathered my things, ignoring her questioning gaze on me.

"Are you still mad at me?" she asked.

"No, Aimy. I was never mad at you to begin with."

That wasn't supposed to be a segue into more questions, but Aimy never needed permission anyway. "Why wallow in misery for a past that will never lead to the future you want?"

The question she asked me was one I had asked myself many times over the past year: *Why couldn't I let go of Sanam?*

I'd found the answer when I'd seen her last week. She was pregnant with his child. It had shredded the last vestige of hope I had. And yet, there she was, standing in front of me—the woman I'd given my heart to.

"I can't move on from her, because I do not trust Zain. If he lets her fall, and there is no one to catch her, I will never forgive myself."

Aimy watched me for a long moment before her voice cut through the quiet. "How far is Houston from Boston?"

"Five hours by plane."

"You could go in the morning and come back in the evening."

I pursed my lips and nodded faintly, trying to steady the ache rising in my chest. The truth was, I had no plan—only a hope.

A hope that if Sanam ever needed me, I'd be near. Not across an ocean. Not lost to her forever. Just a few hours away, waiting.

"What if she never comes back to you?" Aimy asked.

"Then I will take my last breath still loving her."

CHAPTER 35

Dream

ZAIN

Three nights in a row, I had the same dream.

A little boy with hazel eyes peppered with flecks of gray, and a head full of silky black hair climbed onto a bike.

"Look at me, Baba," he squealed as he rode up and down a paved driveway.

"I am, beta. I am looking. And I'm so incredibly proud of you," I declared when he got off the bike and ran towards me.

He jumped straight into my outstretched arms, and we spun in dizzying circles. Trees merged into a blur; flower beds transformed into a rainbow of colors. Yet, we continued to go round and round until we tumbled into a heap of happiness.

His soft lips pecked my cheek, and he said, "I love you, Baba."

That's when I would wake up, in darkness, engulfed by a haunting silence. Alone, with no one in sight and nothing but the weight of my own regrets to keep me company.

For three days now, I hadn't stopped thinking about that little boy, or the smile on his face when he looked at me. I wasn't a father, perhaps didn't even deserve to be one. So why did I find myself yearning for that little boy who kept showing up in my dreams?

Because he told you he loved you.

How sad and pathetic, a voice inside me mocked, and I let it. After all, wasn't I the textbook definition of a sad and pathetic man with daddy issues?

"What can I get for you today?" the barista asked, pulling me back from my dream and into the coffee shop where I stood.

"Twenty-ounce black coffee, please," I told her, paid for the drink, and stepped towards the pickup counter.

A toddler with chocolate-brown eyes and a mop of dark curls stood on tiptoe, reaching for the container of paper napkins on the counter.

"Here you go," I said, smiling as I slid the container closer to him.

He hesitated for a moment, then, without meeting my gaze, mumbled something about a new baby sister. Before I could respond, a woman called out, "Joey, come back here."

But Joey's small fingers had already wrapped around mine, gently tugging me towards her. Without a second thought, I followed him to where the woman sat cradling a tiny baby in her arms.

I crouched down beside Joey, who was gazing at the baby, and said, "Your sister is adorable. You must be so proud of her."

He still didn't look at me, but a faint smile graced his face.

The woman straightened abruptly, her eyes darting between Joey and me. Her expression shifted to something between shock and wonder.

"How did you do that?" she asked.

"Do what?" I replied, puzzled.

"Make Joey smile. He's on the autism spectrum. He's never smiled before."

I had no idea why he had smiled, or why this little boy, who she said avoided interaction, had chosen to take my hand and lead me to meet his baby sister. As I sat in my car, all I could think about were the words his mother had said.

You'll make a fine father one day.

It seemed impossible. Yet, I couldn't stop myself from wondering—*what if?*

Though I knew those thoughts had to stop. They only made my oppressive reality more depressing. Reaching into my backpack, I pulled out a plain flask and discreetly poured a splash of its contents into my coffee.

Only to get rid of these stupid thoughts, I reassured myself.

There were plenty of ways a woman could become un-pregnant. But there was one problem: the fake pregnant woman betrothed to me refused to answer my texts and calls.

Today, I was determined to get off work early enough to track her down on campus and make her talk to me. Armed with my coffee and loaded up on ibuprofen to dull my morning headache, I reached the offices of ZakU Productions at 8 a.m. sharp, almost two hours before my usual time. It was early enough that only a handful of people had arrived, one of them being my father-in-law, the company's CEO.

His office door was ajar. I knocked and entered, meaning to ask him about his daughter's class schedule.

"Zak Uncle, do you . . ." I began, then stopped. His chair was empty, illuminated only by the glow of his computer screens, which displayed the student portal on the Texas University's page.

I had been a student there; I knew exactly how to look up a class schedule on that portal. Whether driven by plain stupidity or spurred on by the few drops of alcohol in my coffee, I glanced around to see if there was any sign of him, then proceeded towards the desk.

The username and password auto-populated, making me wonder how many times he had logged into the portal. And why would he be doing that when he showed such disdain for her?

When I pulled up her schedule, even more questions arose.

Every hour of her day was booked with a class.

"Statistical Physics. Child Development. Social Psychology. Quantum Mechanics. Electrodynamics. Adolescent Cognition," I read out the list of the courses she was enrolled in. The psychology ones made sense, but physics?

Just then, a notification popped up on the screen. It had the TU logo on it, prompting me to open it.

"Dear Ms. Sanam Uzair. We have received your request for withdrawal from the Master's in Physics program. You will receive your refund in seven business days."

What the heck? She was enrolled in a PhD program for Child Psychology.

A quick search of her emails confirmed that she had been enrolled in the Physics program last month, at the beginning of the current semester.

On the surface, it seemed like a mistake, yet, I couldn't shake the feeling of déjà vu. I was once a student at the University of Los Angeles who had been accidentally enrolled in extra courses that required a refund to my father's US account.

Coincidence?

"What the hell do you think you're doing?" a voice bellowed, startling me. I swung around to see Zak Uncle looming with a scowl on his face.

"Oh, I uh . . . I wanted to see Sanam's schedule," I mumbled, scurrying out of his seat.

Eyes narrowing dangerously, he prowled towards me. "And you thought snooping around my office and poking through my computer was the way to do it?"

I stammered, "I'm sorry. I didn't mean to, but your screen was open—"

"*Shut up*. The only reason I am babysitting you here is because you're my son-in-law. Stay in your bloody lane, and no one will get hurt."

What was it with him and my father and their cryptic threats? I swallowed hard, wishing I had my mug of coffee for some semblance of composure.

Maybe then I wouldn't have been stupid enough to say, "Which account does Sanam's course refund go to? Because if it's American, and the money trail started in Pakistan—"

Before I could finish, the gap between us disappeared. His fingers gripped my collar, yanking me forward until his dark, piercing eyes bored into mine.

"Listen closely, boy," he hissed. "Your father isn't the only one pulling your strings. Whatever you think you've figured out, shove it out of that pea-sized brain of yours if you want your pretty, *pregnant* wife to stay safe."

He let go abruptly, stepping back, but his gaze did not wander. "And unlike your father, I don't bluff."

I couldn't contain my disgust anymore. "She is your daughter. How can you threaten her?"

"She is her mother's daughter. For me, she has been nothing but a burden."

"Burden? You've hardly even been in her life. How is she a burden to you?" I retorted to the man who wasn't fit to be called a father.

"Look at you," he sneered, his face inches from mine again. "The mighty Zain, coming to the rescue of his wife." His dark eyes glinted with mockery as he leaned in further. "Go back to your parties, boy. Leave the real work to us men."

With that, he shoved me towards the door, his laughter ringing out behind me.

"Oh, and Zain," he called out. "Be careful. If you keep defending your wife like that, you might actually fall in love with her."

Back at my desk, I was sure it wasn't "love." That entity didn't exist, as far as I was concerned. But it was solidarity. Sanam's father treated her the same way my father treated me.

I gulped down my coffee to calm my jittery nerves and made a vow to myself. When Sanam and I did have a child, I would never treat them this way.

SANAM

Finished with my last class of the day, I stared at a screenshot on my phone as I walked back to my apartment. It was of an email sent by a journalist, Sikander Ahmed.

He had sent it to my university email account with the subject line: *Can we talk?* The rest of the email introduced him as an investigative journalist who had been contacted by a friend of mine. No names were given, but the friend was concerned about me being abused in the Ghazanfar house. He had provided a phone number as well, asking me to contact him in any way possible.

That email no longer existed in my inbox. All I had left was the screenshot I had instinctively taken during class. This would not be the first email that had mysteriously disappeared. The last one had the subject line: Bank account for refund.

At first, I thought it was my mistake, but now it was obvious what was happening to my emails—and who the journalist's 'friend' was.

Asif Ghazanfar had promptly sent me a dashcam video of the journalist being trampled by a car a few years ago, along with a news report of how he had barely survived. And then there were the pictures of Osman, sitting in a conference room next to his maroon-haired classmate, appearing to speak to the computer in front of him.

He appeared so content, so immersed in his work, while I struggled to keep sadness from overwhelming me again. Could I truly blame him for moving on if he believed I was pregnant?

No. The only thing I could do was to preserve that image of him, living his life the way he deserved to.

When I was still a block away from my apartment, a car sped past me, swerving dangerously close to a couple that was crossing the street and screeched to a halt in front of the main entrance of my building.

Out came the buffoon I actively avoided.

Instinct told me to turn and disappear, but the man had already seen me and was now gesturing wildly as he yelled, "Why the hell aren't you picking up your phone?"

"Maybe I don't want to deal with you," I hissed, walking past him. After the stunt he had pulled in Pakistan, I had nothing but pure hatred for the man.

With a travel mug in hand, he followed me up the stairs. "Well, unless you've magically become pregnant, we both have a problem to deal with."

"Both?" I swung around outside my door. "You're the one who created that mess—you clean it up."

He took a long sip from his mug before meeting my gaze again. His voice lowered as he took a step closer and said, "I am much stronger than you, Sanam, and well within my rights to fuck you right now, *if* I wanted to. So, don't you dare try to play cocky with me. Because I can stop playing nice."

This was him playing nice? I silently scoffed at the delusional man.

Still, standing alone with him on that landing, caution prevailed. "What do you want?" I asked, keeping my tone steady.

"Open the door. Let's go in and talk."

Zain unnerved me—there was no doubt about that—but at that moment, he was calmly sipping from his coffee mug again and scrolling through his phone. I did as told and let him in, but stayed near the front door.

"Did you know about the physics classes you were enrolled in this semester?" he asked.

"I did, but I don't know how that happened. Or why your father even paid for them."

Slowly, he nodded. "Same thing happened to me when I went to ULA," he noted. "Why did you choose to come to Texas University, Houston, of all places?"

Weird question, but he wasn't threatening me, so I answered, "Abu insisted that it was the only university he would pay for."

Another sip from his coffee mug. "Well, something weird is going on for sure. If Zak Uncle is such a penny-pincher, why insist on sending you to the most expensive college in the state? And my father isn't one to pay for things so carelessly. Like in what universe did he think you'd be taking physics?"

I tried to not get offended. I could take any subject I wanted to. Instead, I remarked, "You've started drinking a lot of coffee."

"I haven't been sleeping well," he replied quietly.

Serves him right. Sleep had eluded me ever since that morning I woke in my dorm room, haunted by hazy memories of him carrying me, and the disturbing sight of my shirt ripped open.

But I'd be damned if I ever let him see how deeply he had scarred me. Indifference had been my shield for over a year, and I wasn't about to let it slip now.

"Are you done?" I asked curtly.

His response was just as short. "No. You're still supposedly pregnant."

"Then admit to your father you're a liar."

"And lose the time I was smart enough to buy us?"

Him? Smart? I wanted to laugh, but he had slumped on the sofa and had his head buried in his hands. Things were getting weirder.

"Both our fathers keep threatening you. Neither of them thinks I am worth anything at all. If we stay here, I am not sure we'll ever be able to escape their clutches," he eventually said.

Dark eyes met my gaze, not filled with malice but something else altogether—*hope*—catching me completely off guard.

"Let's run away from here, Sanam. Just the two of us," he said softly.

Nothing made sense. Since when had there been the *two of us*? It had always been me and him, on our separate paths. That's the only way this relationship was supposed to exist.

"Where would we go?" I asked cautiously.

"Boston."

I immediately frowned. "Because Maha—"

"No." He shook his head vehemently. "Don't say her name. She doesn't mean anything. Never did."

He was lying. His voice said it. His heaving chest said it. The hurt in his eyes said it.

Yet, he went on, "Abu gave me money to buy an apartment there last year for . . . myself. No one knows where it is but me. It can be ours now."

A set of keys jingled in his hand as he got up and approached me.

"Zain—"

Without letting me finish, he grabbed my hand and placed the keys in it. "I know you don't trust me, Sanam, but I am not lying."

He gave me the address of an apartment in Boston, in a building called Crimson Commons near Harvard Square. The gold keys resting in my palm bore the CC emblem. Could they open some other random locks? Possibly. But something about the way he stood before me—soft eyes, hands at his sides, shoulders slouched—told me that, for once, he was telling the truth.

Yet, it was a truth I wanted no part of.

"A marriage cannot be built on treachery and deceit, Zain," I said flatly.

In an instant, the softness in his eyes vanished. His fists clenched, and through gritted teeth, he spat, "Then call it a fucking living arrangement."

I knew I should've stopped there, maybe spared myself the brunt of his rising fury. But why should I? What about my own anger at his audacity to trap me and then act like everything could somehow become normal?

"A living arrangement like your father and mother have? Where he disrespects her whenever he wants, and she hides in the shadows?"

Zain fully morphed into the nightmare that haunted my darkest hours. He snatched the heavy crystal vase from the coffee table and hurled it at me. I barely had time to raise my arm over my face before it struck me hard. The force of the impact sent pain shooting through my forearm.

The vase fell to the ground and shattered, glass exploding around me like gunfire, ripping a scream from my throat.

Before I could react, his fingers clamped around my throbbing wrist in a vice-like grip. He twisted my arm, and pain shot through me in waves until it numbed everything else.

"I am *not* like my father. I am the good guy," he growled, his breath reeking of alcohol. "You want to leave me for that bastard boyfriend of yours, don't you?"

A pained whimper escaped me as I willed my tears not to show themselves. "You're hurting me."

His jaw clenched, and for a moment, he hesitated before releasing my wrist. "I can do far worse than this, Sanam," he warned. "Don't push me."

The travel mug he had set aside temporarily was at his lips again. This time he was close enough for me to smell its contents. It wasn't coffee he was drinking.

Standing there in my apartment alone with him, my back pressed against the front door, my heart raced from fear as much as from fury and pain. How was I supposed to be okay living with a man as erratic and volatile as Zain? Did a marriage contract signed under duress strip me of the right to feel safe in my own home?

Even if I hadn't spent four years majoring in psychology, two things were abundantly clear. The first, I said out loud.

"You're an alcoholic, Zain. You have no idea what your reality even looks like. Get help before it's too late."

He smirked, stepping closer again, his rough finger tracing my jaw, making my skin crawl. "Aww, you care about me," he drawled, his tone laced with mockery.

I didn't tell him that by help I meant get locked in a residential facility, never to be seen again.

The second was more personal. I refused to be the woman who stayed silent while her husband used her as a punching bag to vent his anger. *That is not going to be my destiny*, I vowed.

I reached behind me and opened the front door. "Leave, before I call the police," I told him firmly.

"You wouldn't dare do that," he laughed, but thankfully stepped outside. I slammed the door shut, finally letting myself sink to the ground and allowing my breaths to shudder as the façade of bravery and indifference shattered.

Perhaps I should have followed him down and told him he was too drunk to drive. But I was distracted—by the keys in my hand, the gnarly bruise developing on my wrist, and a plan formulating in my mind. The Children's Hospital of Boston was listed on my PhD program's website.

When the sharp pain radiating up my arm became too much to ignore, I glanced at it again. My wrist was already swollen, and I could barely flex my fingers.

In the midst of deciding whether I should seek medical help, I never heard the screeching tires, the loud crash that followed, or the sirens piercing the peace of my neighborhood.

CHAPTER 36

Regret

ZAIN

Sterile walls. The sharp scent of antiseptic. Bright fluorescent lights. Nurses in scrubs with unreadable expressions and curt voices judging me. Machines beeping, monitors flashing—cold, unfeeling witnesses to my failure.

My left arm was in a sling, and my right was handcuffed to the railing of the hospital bed—under arrest for driving under the influence.

That was my tangible reality.

Regret. Loathing. Hatred. Blame—on myself, my destiny, my upbringing. A broken, beaten-down, nameless soul with dulled senses and purposeless existence.

That was the storm raging inside me, tearing apart every shred of who I thought I was.

I had become who I was destined to be: the very man I vowed never to become. A failure as a husband. A devil disguised as a human.

"Zain Ghazanfar," a burly man in uniform called out from the doorway of the hospital room. "Your wife is here to see you."

The police officer disappeared. Instead, there she stood—the woman who was supposed to be my path to redemption—wearing a sweater several sizes too big, its long sleeves swallowing her hands.

She had been crying, I could tell. Though I doubted a single tear had been shed for me.

"I am so sorry," I whispered.

Silence.

"It won't happen again. I promise. I'll get help," I said, a bit louder.

Silence again, until a nurse walked past her and whispered something. "I am fine," she said to the woman.

"I am so—" I started to say again, but she interjected.

"The doctor said you dislocated your shoulder, but they've fixed it. Keep the sling on, even when they take you to jail. The pain meds will wear off soon. If it hurts, it is your right to ask for more."

Each word fell from her lips with mechanical precision, as if pre-rehearsed to strip away any trace of emotion. She had always been a good actor, but I understood now that this wasn't an act. This was what she truly felt for me: absolutely nothing.

"Please, Sanam. Please, yell at me or scream. Curse me all you want. I deserve it," I pleaded, hoping it would lessen my guilt.

There was nothing but deafening silence. When she did glance at me, her eyes did not hold disappointment or anger. And I knew why. Like my parents, she had never expected anything from me.

"I am going to Boston," she finally said. "My PhD program partners with some pediatric hospitals to provide us with clinical and research experience in child psychology. The best one is in Boston."

"That's perfect. You can stay in our apartment."

Relief crept in; she was following my original plan.

But she shook her head, walked towards me, opened my palm, and placed in it the keys I had given to her. "I will never need anything from you.

Just tell your father you approve of me being in Boston and that I am staying in your apartment, so he stays off my back. Or else, I *will* go to the police."

"Done," I said quickly. "I'll send you some money too. Your PhD stipend won't cover the cost of living in Boston."

She didn't even glance at me when she replied, "Don't bother. I'll get a part-time job."

When she turned to leave, I caught her wrist. She winced. The dagger of self-loathing twisted deeper within me when I realized why she was in pain—a rigid white cast encasing her wrist peeked out from under the long sleeves of her sweater.

I had meant to tell her that she was all I had left. Instead, my voice caught as I asked, "Did I break your wrist?"

Silence was the only reply she gave before pulling her arm away and walking out of the room, sealing the final nail in the coffin of my shattered dreams.

One day after the accident, I lay on the cold, hard floor of the jail cell, writhing in pain as my body craved the alcohol it had become so accustomed to.

Two days after that, I was in court for DUI. My driving license was revoked for six months, and I was asked to pay a hefty bail if I wanted to be a free man.

I didn't want to be a free man.

Three days after court, I was being escorted out of jail.

"Who posted my bail? I didn't call anyone," I said to the officer.

"How the hell am I supposed to know?" he scowled, handing me a bag with my belongings and shoving me out the door.

There was no one there I recognized, until my gaze landed on a woman standing next to a BMW, while her chauffeur stayed in the car.

"What are you doing here, Myla?" I asked, walking towards her.

Suddenly, her arms were around me as she hugged me so tightly my shoulder hurt. "You are such an idiot, Zain," she whispered.

"I am my father's son." I pulled back. "Why would I be anything but an idiot?"

Kohl-lined brown eyes peered at me for a moment as her persistent smile disappeared. She placed a gentle palm on my cheek and said in a hushed voice, "You are not like your father. Trust me."

"Why are we whispering?"

Her gaze darted to her chauffeur, who quickly looked away.

"No reason." She smiled widely as the cadence of her voice increased slightly. She hooked her arm into mine and led me to the car.

"Where are we going?" I questioned.

"The place where people go when they hit rock bottom, Zain. I can't stand by and watch you destroy yourself anymore."

Curiosity got the better of me, as I pulled my arm free from hers. "Myla, why do you even care? You're my mother-in-law. You should have figured out by now how useless I am."

She shrugged, and murmured, "Because you're all I have left."

CHAPTER 37

Sunday Bazaar

KIRAN

Fancier people might call the place I stood in a farmer's market. For middle-class families like mine, where every rupee mattered, this place was simply Sunday Bazaar. Under the open February sky, vendors shouted over one another, calling out prices and showcasing their goods. While women, and a few men, haggled fiercely, their hands gesturing animatedly as they bargained for fresh fruits and vegetables piled high on wooden carts.

In that chaos, getting jostled around by the crowd was not unexpected. However, when two women clad in burqas, with their faces fully covered, shoved me from behind, I had to turn around and give them a piece of my mind.

"Can't you look where you're going?"

"We can. Now you look at this too," a familiar voice replied as a hand snaked out from under the black robe and handed me something wrapped in a plastic bag.

"Phuppo?" I raised a brow.

"And Bua," the second voice replied.

I took the bag and quickly placed it in my purse. "What are you two doing here?"

"Keeping my promise," Phuppo replied.

After Dada and Abu died, Phuppo's husband had gathered all the documents from Tariq Enterprise, put them in Abu's old study, and locked the door. No one had gone there in over two decades. But spurred on by my recent visit, Phuppo had decided to reopen that room.

"And your husband let you?" I asked.

Bua chuckled. "That man loves his koftas—the spicier, the better."

Koftas, as in meatballs? It didn't make sense until Phuppo explained. "Bua doesn't cook much, except every Sunday when she makes her special koftas that Asif has always loved. For the last month, they may or may not have been laced with Valium."

"Fool licks every last morsel off his plate and then snores like a train the whole night," Bua added.

I stood in awe of these two women, attempting to bring down the mighty business tycoon with spicy balls of meat.

Though the reunion was quickly cut short when Phuppo said, "I have to be at a luncheon with Asif soon, but these are sale deeds for a hundred acres of property that Mustafa sold to a man called Basaam Sadiq, only to cancel the sale three days before he died."

She thought it was a weird coincidence, as did Junaid when I told him later that day.

"You know, I could have come by myself to the meeting with your lawyer friend. You didn't have to come as well," I said to a certain inspector after we both stepped into the elevator at the law firm run by Yusra Azam, Junaid's childhood friend.

I ignored the pangs of jealousy that flared when he kept praising her and focused instead on the fact that she had a national reputation for taking on the hardest cases, and never losing. Exactly the kind of person we needed to go up against Asif Ghazanfar.

"Who said I've come because of you? This is a police matter. I need to be present," he replied as we got off the elevator.

"You're not the only police officer in Karachi. As the next Inspector General of Sindh, you really need to start delegating tasks to your juniors as well."

I noted the room numbers as I walked along the tiled corridor with fancy recessed lighting and artwork.

"You're not my teacher, Ms. Kiran. Don't boss me around," I heard him chuckle behind me.

We reached the room I was looking for.

"I am not bossing you. Just being observant. You'll burn out if you don't pace yourself." I paused and knocked on the door.

"Then I'll burn for you," he whispered, his warm breath fanning the shell of my ear.

My breath caught in my throat. I swung around to face him. But we weren't alone. The door had opened, and a woman dressed in sleek black pants and a white silk shirt stepped out.

"Junaid, so good to see you," she exclaimed, reaching out to give him a quick hug.

"Likewise, Yusra. How are your parents doing?" the man said with a straight face, as if he hadn't just set me on fire.

"Very well." She smiled at him before turning towards me. "You must be Kiran."

With my composure decimated, all I could do was gape at her, then him.

"Yes. This is Kiran." Junaid answered for me, with a slight smile on his lips, even as his eyes danced with mirthful humor. "Give her a second. She sometimes forgets how to speak."

Damn him . . . and his eyes, and his voice, and his words.

Oh, how I hate him.

I was seething as Yusra led us into her office suite. *How dare he mess with my head whenever he wants. And then have the audacity to stand there smirking at me.*

"I can speak for myself. Thank you very much." I glared at my nemesis.

"Have you two known each other for long?" the pretty lawyer asked when we sat down at her desk.

"Yes . . ." he started to answer.

"*No,*" I interrupted firmly. "I don't tend to interact with random policemen."

Junaid's smirk was back, but his head lowered. For now, I knew I had won the game he played, though the tournament continued.

"Let's get down to business, shall we?" I said.

"Absolutely." Yusra put her hair up in a bun and turned towards her computer. It looked like a scene out of a legal drama, and whether it was the air of confidence around her or the comforting smile she gave me, something told me I was in good hands with this woman.

Thankfully, the man in the room largely kept quiet while I narrated my life's story to my lawyer, only speaking once I was done.

"Basaam Sadiq, whose land sale was canceled by Mustafa Tariq, was apparently very close to Asif."

Yusra's eyes widened. Junaid silently nodded to her. I was clueless. "What does that name mean?" I asked.

The lawyer explained, "Basaam Sadiq was a notorious drug smuggler a couple of decades ago. He had a rap sheet the size of the Indus River, but somehow, he always managed to escape arrest."

Junaid added further, "Evidence collected against him would disappear. Lawyers prosecuting him would have their families threatened. Key witnesses would show up dead, even while in police custody."

"Where is he now?"

"In jail, serving a life sentence. An envelope had been mailed anonymously to the then head of Karachi police with all his hidden financial details. Money trails that originated from illegal drug sales and ended up in real estate around the country, as well as in offshore accounts. That was the key evidence that finally put him behind bars."

Yusra was typing something on her computer when she suddenly looked up.

"He was arrested only forty-eight hours after your father's death."

My heart sank. "You think Abu found out about Basaam's illegal money when he bought that large piece of land from him, and mailed evidence to the police?"

I wasn't sure when he had moved closer, but Junaid grasped my hand as he looked at me with such conviction, I felt my chest tighten. "It's plausible, Kiran. But I will not rest till I find out for sure. This didn't only affect your father."

"What do you mean?"

"Basaam Sadiq was the head of the cartel that Akbar Jafri once worked for."

That meant the man who shot at our boys might have spent over a decade in jail because of my father. A chill went down my spine at how complicated and interconnected my past and present seemed to be.

A question came to mind. "Where does Asif come into all of this?"

Yusra, who had been clicking away on her computer, furrowed her forehead. "I pulled up the defense lawyer's statements. It looks like they were trying to argue that Basaam wasn't alone in his dealings. Other high-profile individuals were involved as well. But there was no incriminating evidence against anyone else."

She scoffed a moment later after scanning that statement. "Guess who was named as an accomplice by Basaam."

I knew the answer even before she finished her sentence.

"Asif Ghazanfar."

CHAPTER 38

Photo

OSMAN

"Here is the reason I didn't want to meet at your college," said Sikander Ahmed, as he sat across from me at a nondescript tea shop several kilometers away from Karachi Medical Center.

The image on his phone was a picture of another phone displaying a photo of Aimy and me in a conference room, doing a presentation on my laptop.

Frowning, I asked, "Who sent this?"

"Someone in the US who is afraid of using their own phone to communicate with me," he replied.

There could only be one person: Sanam. "Well, call her. Let me talk to her. Come on, do it now," I pleaded with the journalist, who promptly placed a gentle hand on my arm.

"Calm down, Osman. I already called the number, but it was disconnected. She probably used a burner phone to send this picture."

I sank into the chair, feeling the weight of guilt and helplessness bearing down on my chest. I'd always believed she hadn't married into that family willingly, but knowing the lengths she had gone to in order to send this message drove that truth even deeper into my heart.

What must she be enduring? And here I was, sitting at a *frickin'* tea shop, living my life.

Tugging at my hair, I asked, "Who sent her that photo?"

"She said it was Asif Ghazanfar."

"Why would he do that?" I frowned.

Sikander paused before answering. "For the same reason he sent you a photo of her when she first got married. To let her know that he is watching you, so she'll stay quiet."

He slid his phone in front of me with her text message displayed on the screen. Every breath felt tortured as I read her words.

Dear Sikander. Please let your friend know he doesn't have to worry about me. Sometimes what we think of as our destiny, is only a beautiful dream. But that's okay. Life still has to go on.

"None of this is okay, Sikander." I rose from my chair, struggling to contain the anger surging within. "I am going to Houston. I have to get her out of this."

He shook his head. "No, Osman. You're not looking at the bigger picture. As long as Asif Ghazanfar is a free man, she will always be stuck."

As frustrating as it was, I recognized the truth in his words. When my gaze fell on Sikander's phone and the picture Sanam had sent to him, I realized that she recognized the same truth too.

"I know why she sent that picture. There were only two of us in the room," I noted.

"Then who took the picture?"

I remembered the exact moment he had interrupted our online meeting with Dr. Qureshi and given Aimy a sleazy smile. *That bastard.*

"Dean Nadir did."

CHAPTER 39

Dharko

KIRAN

"Dean Nadir lawyered up faster than I could say the man's name," Junaid was telling Yusra and Detective Iqbal when Osman and I entered his office at police headquarters in Karachi.

The cool air conditioning was a welcome respite from the warm March air outside. But it did nothing to calm my anxiety. How many more people around us did we have to worry about being on Asif's payroll?

"There is definitely something up with the dean, though," Yusra replied. "His assets, even those declared by him, don't match his income."

"How so?" I asked.

"He owns almost fifty acres in the town of Dharko, in interior Sindh, supposedly acquired as part of a deal with the Sindh government to build a hospital. The hospital itself is not-for-profit, but the legal documents my team acquired showed that close to a hundred million rupees were spent on its construction by none other than GT Enterprise. And he has multiple similar-sized land holdings in Baluchistan, Punjab, and Sindh. All bought through GT Enterprise."

"There is no way he can afford all of that on an academic salary, even as the Dean of the institution," Osman noted.

"Where did you say the hospital was built?" the detective asked as he scrolled through his phone.

"Dharko, Sindh."

A moment later, he looked up. "Dharko is a ghost town. Its entire population moved out ten years ago when the nearby coal mine shut down and all the jobs dried up."

"Why does a ghost town need a hundred-million-rupee hospital?" Osman asked the question on everyone's mind.

Junaid's eyes narrowed. "It doesn't. It's a bloody sham hospital, similar to a shell company. A way for him to hide his illegal money under the cover of a legal-sounding asset which only exists on paper."

A flurry of conversations happened between Junaid and the detective, after which the detective left the room to accompany a team to Dharko to confirm our suspicions.

"We'll also need to look into the rest of his finances, and those of this mystery hospital, to figure out where the money is coming from and where it is going, right?" I asked.

Junaid nodded, but the solemn look in his eyes did not change. "Yes, but we'll need a warrant. If I file that, he will know we're after him, and so will Asif Ghazanfar. Surprise is our most potent weapon against that man. I am hesitant to lose that advantage."

Yusra, though, had a sly smile on her face. "I agree, the dean might end up dead or worse. But who said we have to file a warrant to look at his financial record?" She turned towards me. "Kiran, what did you do before you became a teacher at Kingston Academy?"

"I was a bank teller," I replied. It was the first job I had held after my divorce.

"Then you know your way around bank accounts. How would you like to take a trip to Al-Faisal Bank, where the dean's and his hospital's bank accounts are?"

"Uhh, sure." I could guess what was going on in her head, even as Junaid covered his ears.

"I didn't hear any of that," he said quickly.

"Why would you? I didn't say anything, did I, Kiran?" Yusra winked at me and got up from her chair.

"Nope." I backed her up with a chuckle. She asked Osman and me to meet her at the Al-Faisal Bank after she had scouted the place. Meanwhile, Osman sat down to answer the questions Junaid had for him.

"How much have you interacted with Dean Nadir?"

"He is our dean. I see him around often."

"So, he is popular among students?"

"Oh, he is *very* popular, especially among female students. Aimy said he even invites them over to his house sometimes."

"Has Aimy ever gone?"

"I doubt it. She thinks he's creepy."

I didn't like where any of this was going. "What are you trying to say, Junaid?"

"There was an anonymous sexual harassment complaint against Dean Nadir a year ago. It was superficially investigated, and the case closed. It never came across my desk back then, but it resurfaced when Iqbal was looking into the dean's past. We are investigating it further now."

"Do you think it is linked to whatever illegal business he has?"

"I don't know. But I am not ready to disregard any theory."

The magnitude of what our uncle was involved in gave me goosebumps. I wasn't scared, but at every turn of this investigation, it felt like I was getting sucked deeper and deeper into an abyss filled with lustful, power-hungry, money-grabbing monsters. I was tough, but this was a little nerve-wracking.

I could feel Junaid looking at me in silence, and when our gazes met, I knew he had deciphered my emotions without me saying anything.

"I'm here, Kiran. Everything will be alright," he said softly.

He held my gaze for a tad bit too long, or maybe the relaxed feeling that had come over me was too obvious. Whatever it was, I heard Osman clear his throat and speak in a tone I had never heard from him before.

"What exactly are your intentions with my sister, Inspector Junaid?"

I swung my head around. "Osman!"

But the boy who had suddenly become a man kept his gaze firmly fixed on Junaid. "Let him answer, Api," he said.

A faint smile flickered across Junaid's face—a quiet acknowledgment of the authority Osman now commanded in the room. "My intentions are nothing but honorable. I assure you of that," he told my brother.

"Good. Because if I hear any complaints, you'll have me to deal with."

Honestly, I didn't know whether to laugh at how the baby whose diapers I used to change was now squaring his shoulders and standing up for me in front of the highest ranked police officer in Sindh, or cry because it felt like just yesterday when I was holding him tightly in my arms, telling him that if anyone was mean to him, they'd have me to deal with.

"I promise, you won't hear any complaints," I heard Junaid say.

"Quit it, you two," I said. "I am quite capable of taking care of myself."

"But having us by your side can't hurt either, right?" Osman grinned and gave me a side hug.

He shook Junaid's hand, and the two joked about older sisters. Apparently, Junaid had one too. I stood there, looking at them with a smile on my face, questioning why that sight made me so happy.

OSMAN

It had taken Yusra less than thirty seconds of batting her eyelashes at the manager of Al-Faisal Bank to get him to abandon everything he was doing and follow her out of his office to help her open her non-existent locker in the basement of the building.

Meanwhile, Api had discreetly slipped into the manager's office, while I stood on lookout duty. By the time I spotted the manager ascending the stairs from the locker room, Api had already secured the financial records we needed on a USB and was heading out through the bank's front entrance.

Soon after, the three of us met in Yusra's office.

"That is interesting. Osman, did something big happen at the hospital about a year and a half ago—sometime in November?" Yusra asked, as she and Kiran Api pored over a screen full of numbers.

"That's when work on the Ghazanfar Pavilion began."

"And one year ago, in July?"

"Construction on the new pediatric ward started."

Api's eyes lit up as if a switch had flipped in her mind. "I bet the dean received kickbacks for those projects," she said, pointing to his financial records. "Look at this—each time one of those projects went through, millions were deposited into the Dharko hospital's account."

"Except there is no hospital there at all. Detective Iqbal confirmed it," Yusra updated us.

"So, Dean Nadir obtains money illegally by facilitating the approval of large and expensive projects, then hides it in an account that belongs to a fake hospital. Where does the money go from there?" I asked.

"Can't say for sure," Yusra replied. "But I am going to bet most of it goes to GT Enterprise, since they are listed as the builders of that fake hospital, and they, in turn, transfer it to other offshore accounts."

"It's money laundering 101," she explained. "Obtain illegal funds, pass it through a legitimate business, like a real estate company, a.k.a. GT Enterprise, that engages in illegal activity on the side. The money is layered by transferring it through a number of bank accounts or shell companies, so that it is extremely difficult to trace its origins. And finally, once it is untraceable and sitting in some foreign account, you can take it out and buy yourself a nice luxury apartment in central London."

"Or bring it back into the country as legitimate money and buy multiple large plots in Baluchistan, Punjab, and Sindh," Api added.

"Do you think Abu found out that Basaam Sadiq was trying to use laundered drug money to buy those hundred acres of land outside of Karachi?" I asked Api the only question that mattered to me in that moment.

"Yes, I'm sure of it," she replied solemnly. "Abu never compromised on his principles. If he had realized that the money was obtained illegally, he would have done everything he could to report it."

And gotten killed for it in the process. I sighed. For some people, it was so easy to sin, while others would lay down their lives for the truth.

"What do we do next?" Api asked Yusra.

She smiled, her eyes literally glowing with eager anticipation. "Now we go make a deal with Basaam Sadiq. The man had plenty to say about Asif Ghazanfar all those years ago—I am sure he hasn't forgotten those tales."

CHAPTER 40

Graduation-II

OSMAN

The day that I and dozens of my other classmates had waited for, worked towards, and poured our sweat and blood into was finally here. Our class would graduate with an MBBS degree, and we could call ourselves "Doctors" in the real sense of the word.

It was all so surreal.

Until reality struck as I sat with my classmates in the sports field, which had been covered with a canopy to protect us from the sweltering May sun of Karachi, waiting for the Chief Guest to arrive. There was a sea of people around us—everyone from our teachers and physicians to friends, family, and the hospital's support staff—all of whom had made us into the men and women we were today.

Yet, for me, there might as well have been no one there at all.

"She was supposed to be here, wasn't she?" a voice whispered in my ear. I didn't have to ask who Aimy was referring to.

"Yes."

"I am sorry," she replied solemnly.

I kept quiet. What is one supposed to say or do when your most precious dream was left unfulfilled? A year after her own graduation, Sanam was supposed to be at mine. I was supposed to propose to her that night after we celebrated with my family, along the beach, under the starlit sky. She was supposed to have said yes.

We were supposed to have our happily ever after.

But whether I took a wrong turn along my path, or like a hyperbole, our paths were only meant to briefly touch before separating again, I guess I would never know. All I knew was that my life was not what I had envisioned it to be.

"Osman, Osman . . ." My friend excitedly shook my arm.

"*What*, Aimy?"

"Check your email. *Now*."

"Why?" I frowned at her.

"Just check it, dude. The residency match results are out."

Before I could respond, she grabbed my phone and quickly pulled up my email herself. Handing it back with a huge grin, she said, "Looks like you're stuck with me for another three years, buddy."

Dear Dr. Osman Tariq,

Congratulations on matching with our pediatric residency program at Children's Hospital of Boston. As one of the best pediatric programs in the country, we strive to maintain excellence in teaching the next generation of pediatricians and look forward to welcoming you as a part of our family.

"I got into Children's Hospital of Boston?" I exclaimed, hardly able to believe the words on the screen.

"We *both* got in."

My excitement instantly vanished. "You matched there too?"

"How many times do I have to repeat myself?" She hooked her arm into mine and squeezed it while grinning from ear to ear. "It's our *lucky* kismet, my friend."

Unlucky kismet was more like it, I wanted to tell her, but for now, I politely pulled my arm away from her grasp and looked up at the sky. *Dear God, I keep asking You for a girl with brown hair and caramel eyes, and You keep giving me a girl with maroon hair and gray eyes. What's up with that?*

"You know, you could thank me instead of looking like you got a death sentence. I was the one who forced you to study for your USMLE exams and helped you finish our project with Dr. Qureshi. That's probably the only reason we got in."

"Okay. Thanks, I guess. . ." I started to reply, but my words were cut short by the announcement of our Chief Guest's arrival and the start of the national anthem. I stood up with everyone else, and that's when I saw him.

Our Chief Guest: Asif Ghazanfar.

KIRAN

"Why is he here?" Kaukab exclaimed as soon as we caught sight of a particular relative of ours at our brother's graduation.

"He is a businessman—why is he at a medical school graduation?" Hussain, Kaukab's husband, asked.

"The health minister was supposed to be here, not him," Iftikhar added, while Kauser and I shrugged.

The other four started whispering amongst themselves, but call it intuition or this constant sense of impending doom, I could feel that something was off. It was a feeling strong enough that I immediately messaged Junaid.

Me: Guess what? Asif Ghazanfar is the Chief Guest at Osman's graduation. Last-minute change from the health minister.

Junaid: That's odd. What is he doing?

Me: He is up on the stage, giving a speech.

A few moments passed before my phone buzzed.

Junaid: Checked with Iqbal. Asif was supposed to be in a closed-door session with the Karachi Traders' Association. Looking into why he is at a graduation ceremony instead.

I put my phone away and focused my attention back on the stage. Shoving my anxiety deep down inside, I was determined to enjoy this moment of motherly-sisterly pride in a young man who had accomplished the impossible against all odds. From being shot and having to spend weeks in the hospital to having his heart irrevocably broken, fate had left no stone unturned in trying to tear him down. Yet he stood tall and confident as he strode onto that stage and took his degree.

I was still smiling with the same pride when my phone buzzed with a text message that made my heart sink immediately.

Junaid: Basaam Sadiq was found dead in his cell.

Bloody hell. I never cussed, but I couldn't help it now. I'd seen parts of the video recording from the time Yusra had interviewed Basaam. He had more than a few things to say about the business partner who had betrayed him.

"Asif told me to buy that hundred acres of land through Tariq Enterprise. It was the fastest way to convert our drug money into an asset that no one would question," the prisoner with silver-gray hair said.

"Except Mustafa found out about the origins of that money, canceled the sales deed, and you decided to get him killed?" Yusra questioned.

Basaam vigorously shook his head. "Why would I do that when I could have gone to another real estate company?"

Yusra raised an eyebrow. "Then who had him killed?"

Basaam's eyes narrowed. "Asif Ghazanfar, who else? The man had been obsessed with taking over Tariq Enterprise ever since the day his father-in-law kicked him out of his house because of his huge ego."

"*Nice theory.*" *Yusra crossed her arms over her chest.* "*But explain to me why Asif is scot-free today and you have been in here for almost seventeen years.*"

"*That's because that backstabbing son of a bitch somehow wiped off all evidence of his dealings with me. The property papers that were sent to the police and revenue bureau had only my name on them, even though we had bought them as joint property.*"

"*Are you willing to say all this in court?*" *Yusra asked.*

Basaam Sadiq sat back, a gleeful expression spreading across his face.

"*That depends. What do I get out of it?*"

It had taken weeks of intense negotiations with the criminal mastermind to secure his testimony against Asif. While we lacked sufficient evidence for a criminal case, Yusra believed that with Basaam's statement, we could build a compelling civil case for the unlawful possession of Tariq Enterprise to bring before a judge.

The court date had been set for tomorrow.

Today, Basaam Sadiq had conveniently died.

I glanced at the stage and caught my uncle's gaze fixed on me, a smirk tugging at his lips. That's when it all clicked. I understood why he had chosen to attend this graduation ceremony instead of being behind closed doors at a meeting with the Traders' Association.

We should have been gathered in my living room to celebrate Osman's big day, but instead my family, along with Junaid and Yusra, were gathered around the coffee table, discussing the day's events.

"He died of a heart attack," Junaid reported, reading off his autopsy report. "According to the jail doctor, he was known to have high blood pressure and was on medication for it. But the timing is far too suspicious."

"Did they check for toxins in his blood or any signs of poisoning?" Yusra asked.

"Yes, but all reports were clean, except for an elevated potassium level in his blood, which can also result from red blood cells breaking down after death."

Junaid met my gaze, and for the first time I saw a hint of uncertainty in his eyes. "Even if they were positive, no one could blame Asif Ghazanfar for his demise. He was in plain sight of hundreds of people at a graduation ceremony. His alibi and defense are rock solid."

"What if we handed over the financial documents to FIU?" Hussain asked.

"Zaviyar Uzair still heads it. They won't do anything," his wife replied.

A heavy, frustrated silence blanketed the room. Junaid leaned forward, elbows on his knees, his face buried in his hands. Yusra stared blankly at the files in her lap. But for my family and me, this was all too familiar—the endless cycle of seeking justice, only to watch it slip through our fingers.

"Mob justice," Yusra mumbled out of the blue.

"Isn't that a bad thing?" Iftikhar asked.

Yusra's gaze hardened. "Asif Ghazanfar existing is a bad thing."

Junaid, too, was sitting up now. "Yusra is not wrong. Sometimes breaking the rules is more important than upholding them." He quickly added, "You never heard me say that."

Yusra chuckled and told him. "I don't even know who you are."

To the rest of us, she explained what she had meant earlier.

"Typically, bank statements, land holdings, and other financial documents are confidential. But I say we put all our findings, including Basaam's statement, on the internet. Let the people see the truth behind the billionaires who steal from them and fill their own coffers."

"Zaviyar Uzair will be on the ballot for Pakistan's next prime minister in two months. Imagine the scandal that will erupt when his own brainchild, the FIU, refuses to prosecute his niece's father-in-law," Junaid noted.

Osman spoke for all of us. "Why imagine it when we can watch the drama unfold in real time?"

Not a single forlorn face remained in the room thereafter.

OSMAN

"By the way, Aimy called," Api said when my sisters and I were alone in her living room.

"Of course, she did," I groaned. The woman had been jumping with excitement all day.

"What's the problem? This is what you wanted," Kauser Baji remarked.

"I know. But there is so much going on here too."

It wasn't reluctance holding me back, but a sense of duty to my sisters, who had always had my back. What kind of a brother would I be if I left the country now, knowing Asif Ghazanfar might retaliate once Yusra went public with the evidence she had gathered?

Kiran Api held up a hand, her resolute gaze fixed on me. "You are accepting that position and making something of yourself. We'll be fine here. End of discussion." She stood abruptly and walked out of the room, leaving me staring at her back.

"Did she just kick me out of the house?" I asked my other two sisters.

"Her house, her rules. She found nice boys for us and kicked us out too," Kaukab Baji laughed and patted my cheek. "Better start packing your bags, kid."

"Besides, we know why you're really going to the US," Kauser Baji added with a soft smile. "With Asif distracted by what Yusra is about to unleash, this may be your only chance to find her and make sure she's safe."

My sisters weren't wrong. For too long, we had been the pawns in a game of chess we had no control over. Now, it was time to make our own moves.

Later that night, I replied to the dozen messages Aimy had sent.

Me: Thank you. I will look up the flight information myself. Stop blowing up my phone please.

Then I wondered how *she* was feeling, how her pregnancy was going, whether she was excited about her newborn, and if Zain was treating her right.

I tried not to think about her. The crushing pain in my chest that came with thoughts of her had a way of becoming unbearable, with no way to soothe it.

I had tried not to, but here I was, thinking about not thinking about her. And that crushing pain in my chest was back.

Getting up from my bed, I did the only thing that brought me some peace. I prayed. For her, for her child, for both to get the love and care that they deserved, even if I wasn't the one to give it to them.

CHAPTER 41

Calculated Move

SANAM

Moving to Boston was never going to be easy; I knew that when I handed the apartment keys back to Zain three months ago. Or maybe I was the spoiled rich kid who had never held a real job in her life. Whatever the reason, reality hit hard the moment I landed in Boston.

The cost of living was exorbitant compared to Houston, and the pace of life relentless. Everyone was hustling all the time, while I barely managed to put one foot ahead of the other. Between a part-time job as a cashier at a nearby coffee shop where I worked the early morning hours, and the long days at the hospital learning from the best child psychologists in the country, it became painfully clear how far out of my comfort zone I really was.

"Why do you look like someone died?" a voice startled me as I sat in the corner of my coffee shop after my morning shift had ended and before going into the hospital.

"Oh God, Mama. You scared me."

"Oops, sorry," she replied, without any expression on her face. Somewhere in her heart, she was probably smiling, but her perfectly Botox-injected exterior never let me feel her maternal warmth.

Mr. Malik was at a high-level government meeting in Washington DC. After doing all the sightseeing she could there, Mama was visiting me in Boston. Though I would soon wish she had stayed in DC.

Her gaze shifted between my form and the cinnamon roll on my plate as she sipped on her own herbal tea. "You might have kept your figure for now, but keep eating like that during your pregnancy, and you'll turn into a cow. And trust me, no man appreciates being married to a cow."

This was my mother in a nutshell. Obsessed with the world at large, unable to see the reality right in front of her.

"I am not pregnant," I told her.

She gawked at me. "*What?* But Zain said—"

"Zain is a liar. How can you still not see that?"

She ignored my question. "You two have been married for over a year. It's high time you had a baby. Poor Zain probably thinks you're infertile or something."

Poor Zain? I would have thought my hearing had gone bad, but she was dead serious.

"First you insist on living separately. Then you move to Boston and live like a pauper. That boy is going to get sick of you and send you packing one of these days."

"It'd be the happiest day of my life," I muttered.

For a moment, she remained silent, sipping her tea with impeccable posture, her fingers delicately poised like the British might have taught my ancestors generations ago.

"You still have a thing for that middle-class doctor, don't you?" she asked.

"Osman, and how I feel about him are not the problem, Mama," I retorted. "I haven't even contacted him since I got married. *Zain* is the problem. Besides, I make my own money. I don't need anyone, least of all a deceitful husband."

She let out a mirthless laugh. "Wait till the loneliness sets in, Sanam. When you're all alone, talking to the walls, unable to tell the difference between the shadows in your house and the darkness inside you—the kind that drives you to make stupid decisions—then come and tell me how awesome it is to not need anyone."

I had always suspected that she regretted my birth, but I never had the courage to ask directly, unsure of my own ability to withstand the hurt that comes from feeling so unwanted by your own mother. Today, I didn't hold back.

"Stupid decision? That's what I was for you, right?"

She stayed silent; her gaze remained averted.

"Answer me, Mama. After all these years, you still regret having me, don't you?"

Slowly, she looked at me again with eyes so cold that even her paralyzed facial muscles gave way to her icy soul.

"You were a calculated move, Sanam. I was married to a charismatic man who wielded power with such confidence that the world fell at his feet. There was only one way for me to keep him from wandering away."

Her words hit me like a sledgehammer. There is indeed something worse than being unwanted—it's being used as a pawn by your own mother to trap a man who didn't have an ounce of fatherhood in him. And to think that I had always considered Asif Ghazanfar to be the biggest villain of my story. Turns out, the betrayal had started even before I was born.

I steadied my voice and asked, "What was the stupid decision?"

My mother's unflinching gaze didn't waver. "Calling Zavi when I sat all alone at home after being rejected from the biggest role of my life, because I became a mother to you."

At first, it didn't make sense. He was my uncle, her then-husband's brother. What could have gone wrong if she called Zavi Chachoo? Then I noticed her sigh as her gaze softened, and she looked away. The same things I did when I remembered the "middle-class doctor."

"You loved Zavi Chachoo." The words barely came out.

"He loved me too. But love is useless in this world," Mama muttered.

"*How?*" I gaped at her. "How could it be worse than living with a man who treated you so badly?"

When she looked at me, it was obvious she had zero regrets. "Zavi was twenty, with nothing to offer other than his heart. Zak was ten years older than him, and well established as a producer. He was widely considered to be the next Chairman of AWP after your grandfather. Who would you have chosen?"

"The man who *loves* me," I replied instantly. What other choice could one possibly make?

"See, that's why you are so naïve. Love doesn't support your career, or your lifestyle. Money and power do. That is why I chose Zak. When he found out I'd called Zavi, he was angry, but my transgressions were nothing compared to the list of affairs I knew he'd had. And for as long as it lasted, our staying together was mutually beneficial. I was the trophy wife, and his name attached to mine eventually got me the acting roles I wanted."

She reached out and placed a hand on mine, the only motherly gesture she'd made in years, and lowered her voice. "Look at where both of us are today. Despite everything, we *both* still won. That's the point, Sanam. So, forget about your first love. Make a calculated move with Zain, be the bahu that Asif Ghazanfar wants, and watch as you soar—because with the money and power that family has, even the sky will not be a limit for you."

In a heartbeat, she transitioned to her usual self-indulgent ways and proudly gave me a rundown of all the important events she was invited to. There was a dinner at the White House on Friday, the Pakistani embassy was hosting their annual May charity ball on Saturday, and on Sunday, she and her husband were flying to Cancun for a much-needed break from their busy lives before heading back to Pakistan.

All that while, I sat silently, remembering the moments when I felt like nothing could stop me. Those were the moments when I lay in my dorm room, warm and comfy under the duvet, listening to his quiet voice paint a future, where my dreams weren't just dreams—they were plans, tangible and achievable. A world where every step forward felt lighter because I wasn't walking the path alone.

That night, when I lay down to sleep in a studio barely large enough to hold a single mattress, I knew what my mother meant about loneliness setting in. It was when the walls seemed to close in, the silence became deafening, and the darkness outside the windows merged seamlessly with the shadows in my heart. This place I lived in, because it was all I could afford, wasn't just empty. It was hollow.

Still, I could never be my mother. For when I closed my eyes and held a clay heart close to my own, everything else disappeared.

The tears flowed.

The cold seeped in.

Yet I soared.

On the wings of a love I once shared with a man who told me, *"As long as I live, I will always be there for you,"* I left this ugly world behind, and soared beyond the blue sky and the darkness of the universe, until I reached my heaven, where beautiful dreams came true, hope was not lost, and there was a kind boy who gave me lollipops.

Some days, that was enough to keep the nightmares away. On others, I would wake up drenched in sweat, frantically checking to see if my clothes were still on.

CHAPTER 42

Hard Questions

ZAIN

I was a vulnerable narcissist, which, according to some experts, is the true form of narcissism, because those with grandiose ideas are psychopaths—at least, that is what my Google search told me.

When I first started therapy, my psychiatrist, Dr. Tan, insisted on not putting a label on my demons. *Wimp,* I had silently replied.

"Alcoholism is a disease, Zain. But like any other disease, underlying issues will exacerbate it. And unless we drill down and expose those underlying issues, treating your alcoholism will be difficult," the man had said.

When I asked him about my underlying issues, he simply smiled and said I had to figure them out myself. But the only thing I excelled at was failing. How did he expect me to succeed at understanding my own problems?

Yet, week after week, my mother-in-law showed up at my apartment at 9 a.m. on Saturday mornings and dragged me off to my therapy sessions.

At thirty-two days sober, I told Dr. Tan that life sucked. Though craving alcohol was only a part of it. What I hated most was how the world around me had become so much clearer. The silence of my apartment, the chatter in the office, the suffocating weight of my own thoughts—I couldn't stand it.

At sixty-six days sober, I complained to Dr. Tan that a new liquor store had opened along my running route.

"What will you do now?" he had asked.

I felt like suing the damn city government and boarding up the place. Instead, I shook my head and told him what I knew a normal person would do—change my running route.

Today, after being more than three months sober, Dr. Tan greeted me as soon as I got off the elevator. "Good morning, Zain."

"It's June in Houston and burning out there. What's good about this morning?" I snapped at first.

But when the man's smile didn't falter as he gestured toward his office, I felt compelled to explain the reason behind my foul mood.

"Sorry, I didn't mean to be so curt out there," I said, taking a seat. "It's just that the production house released a new movie today, and there was this huge party—with alcohol everywhere. I even poured myself a drink . . ."

"And?" the doctor asked with a neutral expression.

"I saw a little boy and his parents," I replied, fully realizing how ridiculous that sounded.

But how was I to explain to a stranger about the little boy with hazel eyes flecked with gray and silky black hair who appeared in my dreams and told me he loved me? It was only a dream—an unattainable, unrealistic dream. That's all.

Besides, there was never a mother in those visions.

Dr. Tan didn't ask if I drank that glass or not. Instead, he said, "Tell me what you found so special about this family."

"They were happy."

So happy that first the father played with the toddler, throwing him up in the air until he squealed with delight, and then his mother wrapped her arms around him when he sat in her lap. Picture-perfect, I'd call it.

"And how did that make you feel?"

"Like a failure."

"You use that word a lot to describe yourself," the doctor noted.

"Because it's true," I replied. I could be honest about that much.

I fully expected the man to give me a lecture on how no human is a failure, we all have our strengths, *blah blah blah*. It didn't happen.

"When was the earliest you remember feeling like a failure?"

Whether it was the unexpected question or a memory that had never quite faded, I found myself telling him about the time I was six years old and had returned from a trip to the beach with my father. "My mother was standing at the top of the stairs when I entered the house. I ran straight to her and tried to put my arms around her because I hadn't seen her for a whole day. But she pushed me away and told me to get lost."

Why I still felt humiliated, I couldn't quite understand.

At the end of the session, Dr. Tan asked, "How many days have you been sober now, Zain?"

"One hundred and thirty-two."

He smiled and said, "You should be proud of yourself."

For the first time in months, I felt a smile creep onto my face.

"Good morning, Dr. Tan," I said as I stepped into his office a month later.

"Good morning, Zain," he replied. "Ready for today's session?"

"Bring it on."

Where had the eagerness in my voice come from? No idea. Yet, I couldn't deny that these sessions were becoming the part of my week I looked forward to the most. If for nothing else, to proudly tell the doctor how many days I had been sober.

"One hundred and sixty-four," I reported today.

"Well done." He nodded and picked up his writing pad. "Let's start by talking about why you began drinking alcohol."

It was a tale told easily in the beginning. My father drank, mostly socially. He offered me my first drink when I was sixteen. But then the harder questions started.

"When was the first time you felt like you couldn't stop drinking?"

Pausing, I took a deep breath. The hesitation wasn't because I didn't remember, but because it would force me to accept another truth. I hadn't started abusing alcohol since my sham of a marriage. I started the day I gave Maham a phone with a tracker installed on it—more than five years ago.

"I had to quieten the voice inside me," I explained.

Dr. Tan raised a brow. "The voice, as in your conscience?"

"It's a pesky little thing, isn't it?"

Dr. Tan chuckled. "Depends on the situation, I suppose. When has it bothered you?"

How many instances can one list in an hour-long session? From the moment I stalked Maham to the moment I showed Sanam a video of Osman, and then the final nail in the coffin of my virtues, my conscience had screamed till it was hoarse. Sometimes I listened. Often, I didn't.

The doctor leaned forward. "Why try to shut out the voice?"

"Because it interferes," I replied.

"With what?"

"With doing things others can do so easily."

"Who are these 'others'?" he pressed further.

"My father," I admitted, the words slipping out before I could stop them.

Oh shit. It hit me then. For all my claims of detesting my father, of claiming that I was nothing like him, I had been chasing his shadow all along. Trying to emulate the very personality I accused of destroying my life.

When Dr. Tan asked why that might be, the answer was painfully clear.

"He always gets what he wants. And I never do."

Sanam had been right. I was my father—not just in the way I had behaved in her apartment but in every other way that mattered. Abu embodied power, and I had been craving it my entire life.

As I sat there talking with Dr. Tan, I realized something else too—my father must have known this all along. He used to say that everyone has a price: it's either a weakness to be exploited or something they want. When Maham left, Abu knew my price.

My weakness was my need for power, and I had wanted revenge. No matter how much I regretted it now, back then, blinded by hatred, I had been foolish enough to hand him my strings and let him use me as his own puppet. And now, as the pieces fell into place, I was left with nothing but the cold, hard truth: I had always blamed my father for destroying my life, yet I had played no less of a part in it myself.

Rising from my seat, I told the doctor that I would have to skip the next week's session. "I'll be in Boston with Sanam. There is so much I need to make right with her."

Redemption seemed possible as I exited the doctor's office. I wasn't the good guy—I accepted that now—but I was absolutely willing to become one. If I admitted I was wrong and told her she was right, perhaps together we could fix our broken marriage and create the family neither of us had.

Hope is a terrible thing to have, though.

PART FOUR

We came out of the shadows—more astute, less innocent.

CHAPTER 43

Rolex

KIRAN

In May, shortly after Osman's graduation, my state of euphoria was vastly different from what it became by the following August. And that wasn't because anything had gone wrong in the investigation against Asif Ghazanfar. In fact, it had been quite a success.

Yusra had reached out to the FIU with what we had found on Dean Nadir, the fake hospital in Dharko, and the involvement of GT Enterprise. As we expected, they had dragged their feet. Then the astute lawyer released the information we had on social media, openly challenging the finance minister, Zaviyar Uzair, who was still heading the FIU back then, on why he was not going after Asif Ghazanfar despite the overwhelming evidence against him.

Her exact words in a viral video were: "We know you have a family relationship with Mr. Asif Ghazanfar. Is that why you are not investigating GT Enterprise?"

In another she taunted: "It seriously puts into doubt your claim that you will ensure all corruption will be eliminated from Pakistan when you become the prime minister."

It all resulted in Zaviyar Uzair having to come on TV and reassure the public that he would apply the law of the land evenly to everyone, even if his niece was married into the family in question.

Since then, every day brought forth new information about Asif Ghazanfar's illegal financial dealings. From bribery and tax evasion to shell companies in Pakistan and abroad, it became increasingly clear that GT Enterprise was involved in extensive money laundering activities.

With Osman having moved to Boston a few weeks ago and my sons busy with their final year of A-Levels, I didn't hesitate when Junaid asked if I wanted to accompany him to Yusra's office that Saturday afternoon.

"Pre-arrest bail for Asif Ghazanfar," Yusra muttered in frustration.

Despite all the good news, *that* was the problem.

All of what he and others like him, including the former dean, were being accused of fell under the definition of white-collar crime, which was notoriously difficult to prosecute. Especially when the crimes were committed by a large corporation such as GT Enterprise. There was evidence of fraud, but most of it was buried under otherwise legitimate business activity, and parsing it out would require the resources and manpower that FIU simply did not have.

So, while Asif Ghazanfar had been placed on the country's exit control list and was heavily fined, and many of GT Enterprise's assets were seized and their offices shut down, he was still a free man living a life of relative luxury in a mansion.

He was down, but not out by any means, which was infuriating, because we knew he wasn't just a white-collar criminal. He was also a sexual predator and murderer.

"Where do we go from here?" I asked the other two.

"Back to the evidence," Junaid answered, pulling out several khaki envelopes from his briefcase.

"We knew the investigation report we had on your father's death wasn't complete, so Iqbal has been digging through a mountain of old paper records. He discovered additional evidence that had been collected when your father died. Whether it was deliberate or a mistake, it never made it into the formal report that was filed."

He laid out a number of photos on the desk.

"And here is a timeline we came up with between your father's accident and that of Basaam Sadiq's arrest."

He laid out another printed paper on the table. Yusra summarized what we knew so far.

"So, Mustafa Tariq figures out that Basaam Sadiq is using drug money to buy land through his company. He then finds out his daughter has been abused by Asif Ghazanfar, but wants Kauser to keep quiet about it."

"Exactly," Junaid continued, "Mustafa Tariq was killed while heading to an unknown destination. We don't know where he was going, but we assume he was mailing evidence to the police, because a guard at your former house reported seeing an envelope in your father's hand and overheard him telling Bua that he was going to the post office. However, the evidence didn't reach Karachi police until a day later, and it was sent anonymously."

"You know, the anonymous part has never made sense to me. Abu was not the kind to hide his face, especially when it came to standing up against wrongdoers."

"What if your father was not the one who mailed those documents?" Yusra asked.

Junaid nodded thoughtfully. "Before he died, Basaam did say he suspected Asif had sent them."

I was still mulling over that new angle of investigation when Yusra hummed.

"This is weird. Look at that man." She pointed to one of the pictures from the crash site. "He looks like a homeless person loitering around, but he is wearing a Rolex."

I honestly couldn't tell one luxury brand from another, but I had no doubt that Yusra could recognize them even with her eyes closed. Instead, my gaze wandered to the man's face.

Oh God. My stomach dropped, and I had to grip the edge of the table to steady myself.

"Kiran?" Junaid's firm hand gripped my shoulder. "What happened?"

"That man . . ." I pointed to the homeless person.

"Do you recognize him?" he asked.

I had shared my most intimate moments with him, and then he had destroyed me. Of course I would recognize him anywhere, anytime.

"That is my ex-husband."

ZAIN

"Hi, I'm Zain, and I'm an alcoholic," I admitted to the group of mostly unfamiliar faces seated in a circle on their plastic chairs.

"Hi, Zain," they replied in chorus.

I took a deep breath, shut everything out, and said whatever came to mind. "I've been sober for 192 days. I wish I could say that I haven't thought about drinking every day, but that would be a lie. One day, I even stood outside the bar near my building, watching people drink inside. They seemed so happy, and I desperately wanted that for myself. But it had rained earlier in the day, and a car passed through a puddle, drenching me head to toe in rainwater. I cursed at the driver and forgot about the alcohol."

A few people chuckled. Some nodded knowingly. One said, "There is no better planner than God."

I wondered what plan He had for me, because happiness sure wasn't a part of it.

When the Alcoholics Anonymous meeting ended, I stepped out of the drab building and spotted a stylishly dressed woman standing by a BMW.

Her chauffeur, as usual, remained in the car. She extended a plastic container towards me and smiled. "The chef made some delicious sandwiches today. I thought you might enjoy them."

"Thank you," I said, taking the container despite myself. "But you don't have to keep feeding me, Myla."

Though I was sure her visit wasn't about the food at all. It was to ensure that I was attending the meetings as I'd promised. Why she cared, I still couldn't figure out. But hey, if a woman not even related to me wanted to hover around and make sure I didn't stray, who was I to argue? Clearly, I was incapable of making my own decisions.

"There's a park around the corner. You want to sit with me while I eat?"

"Sure," she replied and gestured to the chauffeur, who promptly got out and followed us, keeping his distance.

"Does that guy double as your bodyguard too?" I asked.

Her smile diminished. "Something like that."

Just as quickly, it widened again as she glanced at my wrist. "Nice watch. Is that a Rolex?"

"Rolex Daytona, year 2000 edition. I forgot to charge my smartwatch last night, so I picked this up."

"Oh, I like classics way more than the fancy new ones."

I couldn't have cared less about watches, certainly not one that my father had given me on my sixteenth birthday, but it was a collectible now, and watches seemed to be a decent enough topic to discuss with a woman I didn't have much in common with.

"Yours is nice too," I told her, glancing at her diamond-encrusted watch.

Her voice lowered when she said, "It was a wedding anniversary gift."

Myla being married to Sanam's father had always intrigued me. There was an obvious and significant age difference between them, but more than that, I couldn't understand how she had fallen for him. The two were poles apart. Perhaps it had been an arranged marriage.

"How did you meet Zak Uncle?"

Her gaze abruptly shifted to the chauffeur trailing behind us. "I, uh . . . was a model for a brand that shot a commercial in his studio. We met there and hit it off immediately. It was quite the whirlwind romance, and we got married a couple of weeks later."

With the arranged marriage theory out the window, I asked, "How many years have you been married?"

"Nineteen."

Nineteen? Suddenly, the mundane conversation wasn't so mundane anymore.

"How old were you when you got married?"

"Twenty-five," she said quickly. A little too quickly.

I glanced at her, skepticism creeping in. She couldn't have been older than her mid-thirties. The math didn't add up, and neither did her story. She must have realized the slip of her tongue at the same time, because she suddenly turned pale and flustered.

"I meant *tenth* anniversary."

Without meeting my gaze, she continued to speak. "I really just came to check up on you. Sanam said you haven't gone to Boston in a while. I really think you should. She is your wife, after all."

I ignored her words. Thoughts of that woman would pull me into a place I had only managed to escape because of an asshole speeding through a puddle. There was something more pressing at the moment anyway.

"Myla, were you a teenager when you got married to Zak Uncle? Or were you really twenty-five?" I asked in a hushed voice. "You can tell me."

She swung towards me. "*Twenty-five*," she replied emphatically, before turning around and hurrying back to her car, the chauffeur walking almost in step with her.

As the car sped away, I stood wondering: *had Myla been a child when she'd married Zakariya Uzair?*

CHAPTER 44

Coffee Shop

SANAM

It was 6:30 a.m. on a September morning when she walked into the coffee shop. The maroon hair was gone. Her shoulder-length sleek hair was now a dark, almost black color. But she was still the woman who was always with him in the pictures sent to my phone, only far prettier in person.

"Good morning. Two lattes. No sugar," she said without sparing me a glance as she focused on the phone in her hand. "And two egg sandwiches as well."

"With or without bacon?" I asked—a force of habit.

The woman chuckled, finally meeting my gaze. "Without, please. I am not in the mood to get a lecture from Osman about eating halal food."

"Osman?" The name caught in my throat.

Before I could stop myself, I was scanning the crowd gathered there for their morning caffeine fix, searching for the hazel eyes that used to hold a whole world in them just for me. But not a trace of him existed. None, other than the woman with gray eyes looking at me curiously as I forced myself to breathe.

"Are you going to charge me for my order?" she asked, much more politely than many others might have.

"Y-yes. I am sorry." I shook my head, rang her up, and placed two egg sandwiches, *without* bacon, into the toaster.

Her phone rang as she walked towards the pickup counter. A second later, she slapped her forehead and said, "Uff, Osman. You're *not* committing a crime. You can stay in the no-parking zone and move the car if someone comes. I'll be there in a few minutes."

My gaze drifted on its own once again, out to the road, through the glass window and the pedestrians on the walkway. And then I saw him— waiting in a blue sedan, for *Amorous Ameerah*.

He seemed thinner, his cheeks slightly hollow, and his longer hair fell over his forehead in untamed strands. Something on the car's dashboard had caught his attention. That's all I could make out. Yet, my sinking heart knew he had changed at his very core.

How could he not have? He and I were never the endgame we had naively dreamt of being.

Though I suppose he had kept true to his word. He never gave girls a ride on his bike.

He'd simply rewritten the rules for his car.

OSMAN

"What took you so long?" I frowned at Aimy when she finally climbed into the car.

"It's not my fault. The cashier was stoned or something."

I glanced inside the coffee shop. The place was brimming with the morning rush, but there was no one at the cashier's counter.

"Next time, make your coffee at home," I told her and started the car.

"Next time, take the frickin' bus," she shot back.

"Excuse me." I swung to face her. "You're the one who asked me to drive your car because it was making a funny noise, which, by the way, is coming from the stereo. I was perfectly happy taking the bus."

She grumbled and shoved a sandwich into her mouth, and I silently thanked whoever had made it. They'd saved me from a whole lot of arguing with a woman who had only gotten more hyper as the rigors of being a pediatric intern bore down on us.

The relief didn't last long. The bite she took had been swallowed, and words started pouring out again.

"How is your cardiac rotation going?" she asked.

"Fine."

"See anything interesting?"

In only the first week of this rotation, my third one of residency, I had seen some fascinating cases, from rare congenital heart diseases to innovative treatment methods for pediatric hypertension. On any other day, I would have told Aimy about them too. She was smart, and we would have had an engaging discussion. But today, I was driving her car on the opposite side of the road from what I was used to and still learning to navigate Boston's streets.

Today, I chose to keep my answer simple.

"Not really. Just a bunch of kids worried about their hearts."

Aimy jumped in her seat anyway.

"Do a child psych consult for them. We did it for one of my patients with cystic fibrosis, and I swear, those people really know how to talk to children and calm them down."

"Will do, Aimy. Thanks for the suggestion." I sighed and smiled.

"Anytime." She winked and smiled back.

It was supposed to be a simple conversation with a quirky co-intern. I never thought it would end up changing my life forever.

Princess

OSMAN

With Dr. Qureshi as our attending on service, the last week of cardiac rotation had come so quickly that I was sure the calendar had skipped more than a few days in September. He was an excellent physician but drove his trainees *hard*. Between daily patient rounds, the presentations he had us do, and the procedures he involved us in, I barely had enough time to eat, drink, or sleep.

Thoughts of *her* had been relinquished to the back of my mind, but, it seemed, not deep enough to be forgotten by my subconscious.

"Are you sad?" a small voice asked me as I listened to my seven-year-old patient's chest while she sat on her bed, clutching a doll.

I forced a smile. "What makes you say that, Stacy?"

"You're the only doctor who never tells me jokes," she said, her big brown eyes fixed on me, their depth almost making the nasal cannula on her face disappear. "I figured you're either really sad or you don't like kids."

"I love kids."

"Then you're sad. Why?"

I straightened up after examining her for signs of heart failure following her recent surgery to replace the valve between her left atrium and ventricle. Born with congenital mitral stenosis, her condition had caused blood to pool in her lungs, depriving the rest of her body of much-needed oxygen.

"It's a big person problem," I admitted to the astute little girl, "but forget about me. Why don't you tell me more about your doll?"

The girl immediately grinned like a Cheshire cat with missing front teeth. "Her name is Princess Jasmine, and she is the most beautiful girl in the world."

"Well, I am really happy to meet Princess Jasmine."

But she is not the most beautiful girl in the world, I wanted to add.

"Have you ever met a real-life princess?" Stacy asked.

Whether it was the way she sat with her legs tucked under her or the fact that, after a month of caring for her, this was the first time she smiled like a child should, I found myself pulling up a chair to sit next to her.

Or perhaps, in that hospital with brightly painted walls and children who had all kinds of illnesses yet never lost their wondrous innocence or gave up on the magic of life, I too wanted to escape my adult problems. And, for a moment, pretend that I lived in a fairy tale with a happy ending.

"Funny you should ask. I have actually met a princess."

"Really?" The girl squealed and clapped her hands. "What was her name?"

"Princess Sanam." Despite the pain that name conjured, there were memories too that had me smiling.

"What was she like?" Stacy's eagerness had me diving deeper into my fairy tale.

"Well, she was more beautiful than any other princess. She had big brown eyes like you, and when she smiled, it was like a thousand stars lighting up the night sky. And when she spoke, it sounded like the nightingales singing in the morning. But do you know what the best part about her was?"

The little girl looked at me with eager anticipation. "What?"

"Her heart."

My vision blurred, and a sudden lump rose in my throat, but for the sake of the wide-eyed girl in front of me, I continued. "You see, she wasn't just the most beautiful princess in the world, she was also the kindest and the friendliest and the most generous of all the people in the world."

The little girl stayed silent for the next few moments, which was good, because if I had to keep talking, I would not have been able to stop my voice from cracking.

Stacy might be small for her age, but her mind was sharper than most seven-year-olds. A life as tough as the one she had led was bound to have taught a lesson or two about human emotions.

"Are you missing Princess Sanam?" she asked quietly. "Is that why you're sad all the time?"

I sighed. Even a child could see my inner turmoil. Then how was I supposed to move on, like my family and friends wanted me to? She was a part of me. Her essence pulsed through me with every beat of my heart. How was I supposed to ignore the perpetual pain of her absence?

No, that pain was good, I had decided a long time ago. Because when the pain diminished, so would her essence, and I couldn't let that happen.

A small hand squeezed mine, and I heard Stacy murmur softly, "I'll tell Princess Sanam you're missing her."

Glancing at her, my already shattered heart splintered even more.

Way to go, Osman. Making sick kids sad because of your miserable life. Swallowing my pain, I put on a smile for her. "She isn't real. I was making up a story. But how about we focus on you getting better so you can celebrate your birthday tonight?"

The girl frowned as I got up from my seat. "She *is* real. I met her yesterday, and she promised to come to my princess birthday tonight."

Hyperactive imagination, medication-induced hallucinations, or psychosis after prolonged hospitalization? My mind ran through a list of differential diagnoses as I made a mental note to inform my senior resident. Maybe this also warranted a call to the child psychologist who had seen her.

Truth never made it onto the list. What else could you expect from a hopeless nerd?

"Where do you think you're going, Osman?" asked a voice I had come to dread in this rotation. It was 7 p.m., and I was supposed to have left the hospital two hours ago.

"Home," I gingerly replied.

"To have dinner alone?" Dr. Qureshi raised a brow.

When did he become my sister? I thought to myself as he insisted that I follow him to Stacy's birthday party that the nurses were throwing for her that evening. "It's not good to be alone when you're under so much work stress," he said.

"I like being alone," I muttered.

"You must have some other hobbies?" he asked.

"Sleeping."

"And?"

"Working."

"Well, we're going to change that today." He grinned. "Otherwise, I will never hear the end of it from my niece."

His niece? That caught me off guard, but there was no time to process it. We'd arrived at Stacy's room, where the atmosphere was anything but somber. Her parents stood by her bedside, her siblings crowded around, and nearly every nurse on the floor, along with a handful of residents on call, had gathered. Pink streamers crisscrossed the doorway, and Mylar balloons shaped like Disney princesses floated gently above.

Birthdays were celebrated with serious fanfare in this place—a testament to the resilience of human spirit in the face of life's fragility.

In the middle of it all sat Stacy, her nasal cannula still delivering oxygen and IV drips running into her tiny, frail arms. Yet her smile outshone everything else in the room, brighter than the balloons and decorations. Her joy was infectious—no tubes, monitors, or hospital walls could dull it.

Her face lit up even more when she saw me. "You came, Dr. Osman!" She clapped her hands with glee.

"I wouldn't miss this for the world," I replied, stepping closer to her bedside, grateful to Dr. Qureshi for dragging me here.

Then her gaze shifted, locking onto someone behind me. She let out a delighted squeal. "Princess Sanam, you came too!"

Stacy glanced back at me triumphantly. "See, I told you she was real!"

It's a coincidence; I tried to convince myself, ignoring the hope that had dared to rekindle itself as I slowly pivoted—before I froze.

Turns out, it was destiny.

There she stood, framed by the doorway as if she had stepped straight out of a fairy tale. Caramel-brown eyes brimming with warmth, soft pink lips curved into a gentle smile, a glittering tiara perched atop her wavy hair—the most beautiful girl in the world.

Princess Sanam.

Why the room fell silent and faded away might defy science itself, but all I heard was the sound of blood rushing through my pounding heart. The laughter, the chatter, the clinking of plates—it all blurred into an unrecognizable hum. All I saw were her eyes finding mine and her chest heaving as she drew a sharp breath, her lips parting as if words were meant to come out, but none ever did.

For a second, I wondered what it must feel like to be her prince. To take her hand and run away to a faraway land. To love her freely, to my heart's content.

Yet, we weren't in a fairy tale, and neither was this a dream. She wore a wedding ring, and we stood in a room full of medicine, machines, and people celebrating a little girl's birthday. I wasn't her prince, and she wasn't my princess. This was a warped reality where nothing made sense, and yet I refrained from asking questions, lest it all disappeared—lest *she* disappeared.

"Come in, Sanam." Dr. Qureshi gestured to her. She stepped in, smiled, and greeted the girl. I didn't question how my attending knew Sanam.

"Where is the cake?" Stacy's mother asked.

A nurse brought it in, setting it in front of the little girl. A chorus of "Happy Birthday" echoed through the room. Plates of cakes were passed around. Unfiltered jubilation filled the air.

I barely moved; she never came close. A bite of cake later, after placing an affectionate pat on Stacy's head, she headed towards the door. I finally moved.

After all, some dreams are worth chasing.

SANAM

Stacy didn't understand why she had to stay in the hospital and couldn't play outside with her siblings and friends. As her hospital stay prolonged, the child was becoming more and more withdrawn. Dr. Lopez, the child psychologist I was working with, was asked to evaluate her.

"She likes princesses, so if you need an icebreaker, you can use that," the senior resident had told us. As a friendly gesture, I picked up a tiara from the gift shop before we headed there.

"Are you Princess Jasmine?" Stacy had asked when we had entered her room.

"I am just Sanam," I replied. Princess Jasmine had a happy ending. I had never-ending misery. How could I possibly be her?

"Okay." The girl had smiled. "I'll call you Princess Sanam then."

That's all it was supposed to be. A sad little girl's figment of imagination. Something Dr. Lopez and I could use to show her that when life doesn't go as we want, it's okay to be sad, while not losing hope. Lessons I didn't quite believe in myself.

I wasn't supposed to have run into him at a princess-themed birthday party. Or force myself to swallow a bite of cake, ignoring his hazel eyes as they followed me, drinking me in until I couldn't bear it anymore.

My footsteps resonated in the empty corridor, and another pair joined mine, closing the distance. *Why were the damn elevators so far?*

"Sanam . . ." he breathed out my name, like always.

A hand reached out, encircling my wrist, forcing me to stop before I could press the elevator button. The muscles of his arm twitched as it brushed against mine. An electric bolt shot through me at the mere touch of his skin.

"Wh-what . . ." his voice caught. Hazel eyes searched mine for answers that were hidden so deep, even I hadn't figured them out.

He let go of my hand and tried again. "What are you doing here?"

"Working with a child psychologist for my PhD," I replied through parched lips.

His gaze dropped to my abdomen, and I knew why. "False alarm," I blurted out.

"Oh," he whispered. "You're okay?"

I nodded.

So much had changed, yet the silence remained. Still comforting, still safe, filling the space between us when words couldn't. Where would I even begin?

There was silence until it was pierced by a woman who said, "Oye, Osman. You're still here?"

The answers I'd been searching for came tumbling out. She was here with him; I'd seen them together a few times in the cafeteria. The woman who had been with him all along was loud but caring, animated but kind. She joked; he rolled his eyes. But in the end, he always smiled.

They were friends of the best kind, teetering on the edge of something more profound.

And who was I? Fractured, bruised, and hollow.

Let them be, my conscience spoke, as she walked closer to him.

I pressed the elevator button and forced a smile. "It was good to see you, Osman. But I've got to run. Zain is waiting for me downstairs."

The elevator's door opened, and I stepped inside. If I had turned around, he would have seen the tears flooding my eyes. If I had turned around, I would have seen the gut-wrenching pain in his eyes.

"If" is a cruel word. But no more than "destiny" is.

CHAPTER 46

Ex-husband

KIRAN

The sun still seemed shy of the morning twilight, but the fauna that lived on my sliver of earth had already started to wake up on this cool fall morning. I could hear the birds chirping without a care in the world, and a rooster crowing in the distance, hellbent on making sure that no one stayed asleep. Ordinarily, these were the sights and sounds I would find solace in. Alone with my thoughts, a cup of chai in my hand, is when I was in my element.

That had not been the case recently. Seeing my ex-husband, Shafiq Irfan, at the site of my father's car crash, and his possible involvement in his death, hadn't made any sense initially. The man had literally disappeared after he had divorced me. Even his parents had never reached out to meet their grandsons.

But the more I thought about how I had gotten married to him, and our time together, the more I realized that perhaps he had always been the kind that would associate with Asif Ghazanfar. I had just been fooled by this thing he called 'love'.

He had an uncanny effect on me whenever he was near. I knew why that happened to me: he was the high school boy that girls flung themselves at. Tall and handsome with an impeccable style. Dark brown eyes that were as mysterious as they were enchanting. A smile that could earn him a spot in a toothpaste commercial. He was the epitome of confidence. The captain of the basketball team. The apple of every teacher's eye.

What I could never understand was why he had paid attention to me.

Sure, I met the standards of being a pretty girl. People said my hazel eyes were my best feature. Others praised my luscious locks and rosy complexion. But I wasn't popular by any means. I was the nerd who sat in the corner, surrounded by my own small group of friends.

In my naïveté, enamored by a handsome boy, I had chosen to ignore my own alarm bells when we got to college.

When I was nineteen, we sat in the college cafeteria as he lamented, "Kiran, I haven't seen you in a whole week."

"I am sorry, Shafiq. Osman has an ear infection and Abu had to travel for work. It's been really busy at home," I replied to him while stifling a yawn.

"You know what they are doing to you, right?"

"What?"

"You're essentially a housewife, Kiran. Ever since your mother passed away, your father has forgotten that you are still young, a college student. Instead, you have all these responsibilities on your shoulders when you should be enjoying your own life."

"I don't have a choice," I said. How was I supposed to say no to my father? Who would take care of my siblings if not me?

"You do, Kiran. You have a choice. Get married to me. Come home with me and let me take care of you."

"But we are nineteen."

"So what if we are young? We can build a life together. Besides, I am in love with you. Maybe the only one who truly loves you right now."

On my twentieth birthday, he sent a proposal.

"He is not compatible with you," my father had tried explaining, but I was having none of it.

"Why? Because he does not live in a mansion like us?" I replied spitefully.

"No, because his values are different. I have no problem with you marrying anyone you like, but when his family brought the marriage proposal, they were more interested in what kind of car I would give you for your wedding."

He placed a hand on my cheek. "I don't have a problem with their social status. I have a problem with their greediness."

I argued and eventually Abu agreed, but warned me, "If that is what you want, I can't stop you. But I am not caving to that family's demands."

"That is fine. Our love will be enough for us," I told him defiantly.

But love was never enough.

"I am graduating next year. What kind of a job does your father have lined up for me?" he asked when I was twenty-one.

"Shafiq, he has already told you to apply for a job like everyone else. He detests nepotism. He will never hire you simply because you are his son-in-law," I replied, trying to fight an intense bout of nausea.

But that nausea only got worse when I felt his breath, reeking of cigarette smoke, on my face as he grabbed my chin, forcing me to look into his dark, threatening eyes. "But see, I am his son-in-law. In fact, I am the husband of his lovely daughter. Tell him that if he wants to see you lead a happy life, he had better start practicing nepotism like a good man."

I pulled back, doing my best to glare at him and retain that last bit of dignity I had left.

"He has already given you a house, a car, and sent multiple gold sets to your mother and sister. When will it ever be enough for you?" I asked, choking back my tears.

"When I become as rich as him," he replied in a hushed voice that chilled me to the bones.

Two weeks later, Abu died in a car crash, and I found out I was pregnant.

There was a reason why I was vehemently against Osman giving his life away to Sanam before he had made something of himself. I had done exactly that, and regretted it every day of my life thereafter.

Lost in my past, my chai had gone cold, so I got up to warm it again. Instead, the doorbell rang, forcing me to make a detour to my front door. A certain inspector stood there, clad in an all-black tracksuit.

"Junaid? What are you doing here at six in the morning? Is everything okay?"

Nodding slowly, he said, "I just, uh . . . wanted to see if you could come by my office after school today. We uncovered some new information on Shafiq Irfan that I wanted to share with you."

I couldn't help smiling. "You could have called."

"Actually, I was . . ." he started to say before I interjected.

"Don't say I was passing by. I know that your house and office are nowhere near here, and it is too early for you to be going to a meeting."

"I just wanted to check on you... make sure you were okay," he replied with a sheepish smile.

"I'm fine," I reassured him, but he didn't buy it.

"You're not, Kiran. And I know that because . . ." His fingers wrapped around mine that were holding the cup of chai. "You like your chai steaming hot, but right now your cup is full, and your chai is cold. And when you get lost in your thoughts, you always forget to eat and drink." He stepped back. "And I know you were lost in your thoughts because you recently found out that your bastard ex-husband may have had something to do with your father's death."

I stood looking at him, dumbfounded, which was becoming a norm now. I tried, but I couldn't figure this man out. He would say these things that would induce butterflies in me and make my heart gallop, but then just as easily step away like nothing had ever mattered to him.

He was a riddle, one that I understood but couldn't quite solve.

"Go warm up your chai. And this time, have it hot. Let *me* worry about your past."

With that, he said goodbye and left, and I headed to the kitchen and enjoyed my hot chai as I pondered a fact of life: there was no need to let your past taint your present, or one man, taint another.

National elections were two weeks away, and Karachi's already horrendous traffic was compounded by the multitude of rallies in the city. I would have given up, but curiosity about my ex-husband compelled me to finish the journey I had started.

When I arrived, Junaid gestured for me to take a seat and said, "I wanted to talk to you in my office because I didn't want the boys to accidentally overhear this."

"Danish and Daniyal haven't had contact with their father since they were born. I am not really sure if they care at all."

He cleared his throat. "Well, after he divorced you, he seems to have disappeared altogether for several years. We are not sure what he was doing or where he was. But he resurfaced ten years later and came on our radar when a raid was conducted on a farmhouse near Hyderabad, almost an hour outside of Karachi. The police had received a tip that a prostitution ring was operating out of it, but by the time they got there, everything had been cleaned out. The farmhouse's owner was Shafiq Irfan. He was questioned, he denied everything, threatened to sue the department, etc. etc., so he was let go."

"He owned a whole farmhouse?" I frowned. He couldn't even afford to buy his own house when we were married.

"Still owns it. Along with a fleet of luxury cars, a sugar mill, and multiple land holdings."

"Where is all his money coming from?"

"The ANF team investigating him thinks it's from selling designer drugs like Ecstasy, meth, and Rohypnol, also called roofies."

The ANF, or the Anti-Narcotics Force is a federal executive bureau and a paramilitary force of the Government of Pakistan, tasked with combating narcotics smuggling and use within the country. But that wasn't the only thing that had piqued Junaid's interest.

"ANF has evidence that at least a couple of locations from where these drugs are being sold are guest houses owned by GT Enterprise. They had initially written it off as a case where the owner was unaware of what the guests were doing, but I doubt that anything happens at GT Enterprise without Asif's approval."

"Does the ANF know where Shafiq is getting these drugs from?"

Junaid shook his head. "Not yet. That's why they haven't made a move on him. There's no point in simply nabbing the middleman."

I knew we both had the same question on our minds: Could Asif Ghazanfar be the supplier? If so, GT Enterprise wasn't being used as a front for money laundering alone. It was a front for a drug cartel too.

CHAPTER 47

Care Conference

SANAM

A care conference is meant to bring together the entire team caring for a patient with complex medical needs—physicians, allied health professionals, and bedside nurses. When Stacy got sick with high fevers and an infection in her heart, her care team gathered in a conference room.

"Do I have to be there?" I asked Dr. Lopez. "I don't understand half of what these doctors say."

That was a lie. I understood diseases of the heart like any other trainee on that team. All thanks to a boy who was now a doctor, waiting in the conference room I hesitantly stood outside of.

"Saeed specifically asked us to come, Sanam. And I agree. You can't fix the mind without knowing what's going on in the rest of the body, and vice versa."

She held the door open, leaving me no choice but to walk into the room full of people already gathered. Only one pair of eyes looked up when I walked in. I ignored them and found a place in the corner of the room farthest from him.

When the discussion began, he presented the case. "Seven-year-old with a history of mitral stenosis . . ." The rest all blended into background noise as his voice resonated in the room, settling in my chest like a steady rhythm. Intelligent, calm, humble. Nothing about him had changed.

"Echo images have been uploaded," the senior resident told the group.

The heart surgeon spouted out some medical terms. Prosthetic valve. Thrombus. Endocarditis. Surgical removal.

"Sorry, what does all of this mean in layman's terms?" Dr. Lopez asked.

"Osman, would you like to explain?" Dr. Saeed Qureshi asked his intern, just like he had probably asked countless other interns.

But this time was different. This intern had a point to make.

"A prosthetic valve is a foreign material which increases the risk of blood clotting around it. When the blood clots, it causes what is called a vegetation on the valve, so the valve doesn't close properly. That clot can also become infected."

"That is—" the senior resident started to speak, but the intern wasn't done.

"I know that foreign material inside your body can get infected, because I was shot and retained bullet fragments in my lung."

A collective gasp went around the group.

Across the room, his gaze held me captive. "Those fragments got infected, and I had to be put in a medically induced coma for several weeks while I underwent two surgeries to repair all the damage done."

"Wow, Osman, that is horrible. Are you okay now?" someone asked from the periphery of the room.

His gaze didn't leave mine. "No. I woke up from the coma and my entire world had collapsed. I never even got a chance to ask why."

Everyone else remained silent and confused, while I tried to fight the moisture in my eyes and the knot in my stomach. I had no idea how sick he had truly been. But the agonizing pain in his voice told me more than his words ever could. It wasn't him being shot or the sickness that followed which had broken him.

It was the voicemail I had left.

If only he knew. I kept quiet in a desperate attempt to leave our past behind.

He finally looked away and continued, "The fevers, combined with the echo results, show Stacy likely has a condition called endocarditis. As a precaution, we have already sent blood tests to identify the exact bacteria that is causing the infection and have started her on broad-spectrum antibiotics. At some point, if the clot doesn't resolve, she'll need another surgery."

"Thank you, Osman. That was a good explanation of endocarditis," Dr. Qureshi told him.

When the care conference ended, I tried to sneak out with the rest of the crowd, but Dr. Qureshi stopped us again. "In case you want to talk to Stacy about her condition, I can draw a simplified diagram of the heart's anatomy for you."

Dr. Lopez smiled. I froze.

"Oh, that won't be necessary," she said. "Sanam already has a clay model of a heart that we've been using to explain procedures and diseases to children."

No, we'll use a diagram, I wanted to scream, but judging by the way Osman swung around, I knew it was too late.

"I heard Stacy mention it," the senior resident standing near us said. "Do you have it with you now?"

Of course, I did. I never came to the hospital without it. Though it had initially served a practical purpose, it had become my daily reminder of the times when I had truly been at peace.

Wrapped in Bubble Wrap, it lay securely in my bag. But the expectant faces around me forced my hand, so I took it out, unwrapped it, and handed it to the resident.

"Be careful with it," I instinctively cautioned.

"It's so cool," she said. "Did you make it yourself?"

I had never been good at lying. And right now, not a single word was coming to my mind.

But I didn't have to reply. Osman did it for me.

"She didn't. I did. On my eighteenth birthday, I stayed up the whole night to make this for her, so she would remember the heart's anatomy for our biology test."

There it was. The public declaration of our past. The undeniable link between us, which I had tried to hide but found impossible to erase.

Dr. Lopez smiled at me. "Is he the lab partner you always talk about?"

"I don't . . ." My voice caught again. *Damn it. Why couldn't I lie?*

I averted my gaze from him. But not for long.

"She gave me a gift too," he said, pulling out something from his shirt pocket. I stared at him in disbelief.

"You still have my pen?" I whispered.

His gaze met mine. We stood at a distance, in front of strangers, but none of that mattered. Our defenses slipped away. The armor came off, our naked truths laid bare. The past briefly became our present.

"How could I not," he said quietly, "when you've been holding my heart in your hands all this time."

Too tangled in that moment, I was barely aware of Dr. Qureshi ushering the others out of the room. And just like that, it was me and him in an empty conference room. Alone. Enraptured. Engulfed in unanswered queries—but unquestionable emotions.

He stepped closer. I stood rooted to the spot.

"Sanam," he breathed my name.

"I have to go," I whispered, though my feet refused to move.

"Why do you keep running away?"

It tears me apart to be near you, I wanted to say. He was so close, yet impossibly far.

Instead, I stayed silent, the words locked in my throat. My heart screamed for me to stay and tell him my truth, but my mind warned of the storm that would follow if I did.

His pager went off.

The door opened, and attendants for the next meeting walked in.

Life doesn't stop, even when old wounds in your heart tear open once more.

"I am not running away," I told him, steadying my voice. "I am simply walking the path I am destined to walk. You should walk your own path too."

Almost two years ago, I had steeled my heart and done what loving him had forced me to do. Who said I couldn't do it again?

OSMAN

"Why didn't you come to the noon teaching conference?" Aimy asked when she walked into the resident workroom.

"I am busy," I muttered, not bothering to hide what I was searching for on my computer.

"Busy trying to find Sanam on the internet?"

It wasn't her that I was trying to search. It was Zain. That no-good cousin of mine seemed to be nowhere in the news, despite there being dozens of daily reports about his father and his company.

"I don't care what she says. Sanam is not okay. And if she won't talk to me about it, I need to find the idiot who married her," I told Aimy.

Shaking her head, she pulled up a seat next to me, and I knew what was coming. "If you're going to tell me to forget about her, *don't*," I told her pre-emptively.

She frowned, then lowered her voice and replied, "I was going to agree with you. Something isn't right. She is the daughter-in-law of a billionaire, and the niece of Pakistan's likely next prime minister. Then why is she working as a cashier in a coffee shop, along with whatever she is doing at the hospital?"

Coffee shop? I stopped searching online. "Why didn't you tell me this before?"

Aimy hadn't recognized Sanam, and I couldn't blame her. The pictures she had seen of her were from the political rallies Sanam used to attend. That girl had a smile which, even when forced, was radiant and full of life. The woman she had seen had hollow cheeks and sunken eyes—a shadow of her former self.

And there was only one person to blame—the man I was intent on finding because I had a promise to keep.

SANAM

"Bye, Sanam. See you tomorrow," Dr. Lopez said after we finished visiting our last patient for the day.

"Goodbye," I replied, swallowing the urge to walk away from this clinical rotation I had once believed would be my escape from the nightmare I was trapped in. Instead, it had added more dimensions to my hellish life.

That late September evening in Boston, I chose to walk back to my apartment instead of taking the train. The crisp fall air hinted at the approaching chill, but for now, it was exactly what I needed to clear my mind . . . and my heart. In the span of an hour, I passed hundreds of people—some hurrying home, others heading to evening shifts, and a few with no home or job to return to.

How many of these faces have loved and lost? How many have surrendered to the idea that love isn't worth the pain?

Yet, as I walked, I doubted that many among them had experienced a love so profound, so consuming, that it could sustain them for a lifetime, even in its absence.

By the time I stood in front of my apartment building, fumbling through my purse for the keys, I had convinced myself that destiny had shown me some kindness too. Coming to Boston, seeing him thrive, was the closure I desperately needed.

"Is this where you live?" a familiar voice said, startling me enough to drop my keys.

He picked them up and handed them back. "Doesn't quite strike me as a place Zain would choose."

Annoyance was a good cover for a heart hellbent on drawing its own conclusions. "Now you're going to resort to judging my life? That's real rich, coming from you."

Hazel eyes didn't even blink when he replied, "Not judging—just curious about the path you're walking."

"How'd you find my place?" I tried to change the subject.

"I walked right behind you."

For a whole hour? I wanted to ask, but he had come here with an agenda, and nothing was about to distract him.

"Where is your husband, Sanam?" he asked so resolutely that I could feel the weight of his determination pressing into me.

"Why do you care?" I countered, trying to mask the tremor in my voice.

His eyes narrowed. "Because I need to understand why the woman who once had the world at her feet is living like this. And why the man who is supposed to be her husband isn't here."

The truth dangled on the tip of my tongue, but I swallowed it, my defenses snapping into place. "You've always been good at asking questions, Osman. Maybe one day you'll figure out the answers too."

"Oh, I will find the answers, alright. Just tell me this—did Zain hurt you? Are you hiding here from him?"

More lies tumbled out. "No, of course not."

But there was something unfamiliar about the man standing in front of me, with his fists clenched and jaw tight, as if he was ready to wage a battle. He couldn't have known how hard I'd fought for the peace I had now.

"Where is he then?" he asked, his voice low.

"He works in Houston for my father," I replied quickly, meeting his gaze with equal intensity. My acting skills hadn't faltered over the years. "And if you must know, I'll be going back there as soon as my rotation is over."

I barely got the last word out before he turned and walked away, leaving me standing in the dim hallway, clutching my keys.

Perhaps I should have gone after him, because when he visited my apartment again, he already knew my truth.

Prime Minister

KIRAN

Shafiq Irfan had been asked to come in for questioning by the police on the same day I had made my famous almond halwa and decided to visit Junaid during lunch hour. The halwa and the sentiments behind it were quickly forgotten when I heard the inspector and his detective speak.

At first, it seemed Shafiq had insisted on involving his lawyer, but on the day of the interview, he showed up smug and alone.

"You have to admit that is weird, Junaid. Why don't you let me watch the interview? I know him better than any of you. Maybe I'll catch something you won't," I offered.

"You are not going anywhere near him," came the instant reply.

"I won't. I'll stay in the side room with the one-way window. He won't be able to see me."

He was shaking his head emphatically when Detective Iqbal chimed in, much to his boss's obvious displeasure. "She helped ID him in the first place, sir. She's not just his ex—she's the reason we brought him in. Besides, she'll be secure in the observation room."

It was against protocol, but these were extenuating circumstances. Reluctantly, Junaid led me to the side room a while later and stayed with me. Our room was dimly lit, but on the other side of the one-way tinted glass window sat my ex-husband at a single table, surrounded by a couple of chairs.

It was strange seeing him after nearly two decades. His receding hairline had dampened his charm somewhat, but those dark eyes and aristocratic features were still a reminder of why I had fallen for him. He was one of the handsomest men I had ever seen, and when he started to talk and gave you that smile, it was hard not to melt.

I was about to make a comment on how relaxed Shafiq seemed, when a hushed voice spoke next to me.

"I know the guy is good-looking, but you don't have to stare at him like that."

"Are you jealous, Inspector Junaid?" I chuckled.

"Nope," he replied, continuing to stare at the room through the window—though his puffed cheeks and pouting lips revealed his truth.

"Sure, my ex-husband may have ruggedly handsome features, but you're kind of cute too."

"Cute?" He swung around, not a bit pleased, which made me laugh even more. "Babies are cute. Not grown men. Besides, I'll have you know, I have been called ruggedly handsome too."

"By whom?"

"My late wife."

That slammed the brakes on our conversation. We had never spoken about her. All I knew was that she had passed away years ago from ovarian cancer. Though I had always wondered what kind of a woman she was, and if he had loved her in a way a wife should be loved.

Was I now being the jealous one? Maybe. But I wasn't the one who had opened that door. And while we waited for the detective to start his interrogation, I found myself quelling my own uneasiness.

"How did you meet her?"

"Through our parents. We had a typical desi arranged marriage."

"A strangers-to-lovers kind of story? That is sweet."

He turned to look at me, and even in that dim light, it wasn't difficult to make out the dreamy look in his eyes. It was enough to make me look away from him, lest the disappointment in my heart become obvious on my face.

But I couldn't escape his words.

"Something like that. I was the grumpy policeman who wasn't ready to get married, but my parents found a nice girl, so I did what every obedient son does. Turned out Mariam wasn't anyone I had ever expected. She was so full of life all the time; it was impossible not to fall in love with her."

I swallowed my emotions. Of course, he would have had a whole life before I had met him, and it wasn't fair of me to expect anything different. If my marriage had imploded, it didn't mean his had also.

"You must have been devastated when she passed away."

"I was." He sighed. "It was so quick. One week, we were on vacation, and she started to have stomach pains. The next week, she went to the doctor, and within two days, she was diagnosed with stage four ovarian cancer. The doctors told us there was nothing that could be done. A month later, she passed away at home, leaving me alone with eight-year-old Nael."

My heart broke for him and his son. "I am sorry, Junaid."

He shrugged. "There isn't much you can do in front of *kismet*, can you?"

"No. I suppose not."

Just like it was my kismet that I met Shafiq all those years ago and not the man who was still in love with his wife, I thought to myself and looked away.

His gaze stayed on me, studying me like he was trying to decipher something.

"Kiran, it was almost ten years ago," he said softly.

"I didn't—" I was going to say that his love life didn't matter to me, but suddenly the door of the interrogation room opened and in walked a man in a business suit.

"What the hell?" Junaid exclaimed.

"Who is that?"

"Aslam Sheikh, the new Director of FIU."

"Wait here," Junaid told me and stormed out of the room and into the one on the other side of the window. Shafiq was grinning and shaking the new man's hand when Junaid entered and asked them what the Director of the FIU was doing there.

"Mr. Shafiq's association with GT Enterprise is a case of money laundering, Inspector Junaid. Not a criminal one. Therefore, it falls under the jurisdiction of FIU, not the Karachi Police."

The detective had entered by now, carrying a file. "I am sorry, sir," he said to Junaid. "I got a call from the Prime Minister's Office asking me to hand over the case to FIU."

Junaid frowned and grabbed the file from the detective. "This *is* a criminal matter. We are investigating the death of a man, and Mr. Shafiq here was found at the crime scene."

He showed the men pictures that I had seen as well, but the FIU director scoffed. "That man looks nothing like Mr. Shafiq."

"He's in disguise," the detective told him.

The director looked squarely at him. "Then get me a warrant for his arrest. Until then, Mr. Shafiq is coming with me."

Junaid glanced in my direction through the window. I knew he couldn't see me, but I understood the frustration in his eyes. What I didn't notice was Shafiq studying Junaid at the same time.

"If you want me, Inspector Junaid, tell my lovely Kiran to come talk to me. You work closely with her, don't you?" he said.

Suddenly, the frustration in Junaid's eyes morphed into anger, and he lunged at my ex-husband. "Keep her name out of your filthy mouth."

He was quickly held back by the detective.

A smug smile adorned the director's face. "Assaulting a citizen doesn't suit you, Inspector. The next time I hear about you or anyone from your police force harassing Mr. Shafiq, I will personally file a complaint against you with the Sindh Governor. Then you can forget about your promotion."

I watched as he led Shafiq out of the room, but not before my ex-husband turned in my direction through the one-way window. "Your Shafiq will be waiting for you, Kiran," he smirked.

A moment later, Junaid burst into the side room. "I know what you are thinking," he said, holding me by my shoulders. "But you are not going to meet him. Do you understand that?"

"What if he has something important to say, though? I can handle him."

"I don't care. He is far more dangerous than you think he is."

"How can you say that?"

"Prime Minister Zaviyar Uzair's first order of business was to protect him," he replied solemnly.

That evening, I sat at home watching the news with my sisters, their husbands, and the kids. While Daniyal and Danish were busy entertaining Aliyah, Kauser's daughter, the rest of us watched the TV with a mix of emotions.

New cabinet members were being sworn in. Interviews and news clips of the new prime minister were being shown on a loop. There was an air of jubilation in the country. A new party, a new face, was taking the helm of a struggling nation.

Yet I questioned if anything had changed at all.

The man who had won the elections on a mantle of accountability and honesty was now protecting a man who I was sure had something to do with my father's death. Not only that, but the family bond between him and Asif Ghazanfar meant that he was going to protect him too. And all our efforts to prove our allegations against him would go to waste.

I glanced at Kauser, who was staring at the TV screen stone-faced, and I knew she was thinking of the same. Reaching over, I squeezed her hand in an attempt to reassure her.

"We will get him somehow."

She shook her head. "We'll spend our whole lives trying to catch up with him, Kiran."

"We have the best policeman in the city and an excellent lawyer on the case. There will be a breakthrough," I assured her again.

However, something had shifted in Kauser. Rather than the resignation that usually filled her eyes, she maintained an unwavering gaze on the screen. Instead of her shoulders slumping, she squared them as she sat up.

"I am done waiting. I am going to take matters into my own hands."

"What are you going to do?" I asked.

"I am going public with my story."

Her voice was no longer a hushed mumble. Instead, it was loud and reverberated across my small living room. Iftikhar looked at her and nodded. Kaukab's mouth fell open, and her husband, Hussain, looked simply clueless.

I was in awe of her courage, though I was still the cautious older sister.

"Are you sure, Kauser? There will be consequences."

"I am absolutely sure. Junaid said it himself: if Asif sexually assaulted me, he would have assaulted others too. And each one of us is probably thinking that we are all alone. But I want to tell my story to the world, so if anyone else is out there, they might get the courage to speak out too."

Iftikhar quickly put an arm around her.

"You're okay with this?" I asked him.

Jaw clenched, he nodded. "If I had it my way, the man would be dead. So if she wants to go public now, of course I will stand by her. And if someone wants to come after her, they'll have to go through me first," he said defiantly.

Kaukab must have updated her husband on the side, because Hussain locked hands with her and said, "I am so sorry to hear that, Kauser, but we, too, will stand with you."

"You don't have to, Hussain," Kauser said immediately. "Asif Ghazanfar is very popular among the business community, and you've just started a new business. Any association with me could hurt you."

"Doesn't matter. Taking a public stand against a sexual abuser is my duty as a citizen of this country. Everything else can be dealt with later," he replied without hesitation.

The potential for this move to disrupt our lives was immense. As someone instinctively driven to protect her family, it gave me pause. But when I looked at our next generation—my sons and niece—I knew, deep down, that we had to be the ones to take this brave step. For their sake. So they would learn that even when the stakes are high, demanding justice is their right, and the courage to do so is in their blood.

"We will all be there to support you, Kauser," I told her.

So far, we had been chipping away at the walls of criminal silence that Asif Ghazanfar, and men like him, had surrounded themselves with. And that had gotten us nowhere. But even a king's castle will collapse if its foundations are weak. In my living room, at that moment, the first domino in that castle's foundation finally fell.

CHAPTER 49

Press Conference

KIRAN

The first Saturday of October was the day everything changed for our family.

We stood in front of the Press Club, surrounded by a slew of reporters. Joined by Yusra, her lawyer, on one side, and Iftikhar on the other side, Kauser stood tall at the podium, crowded with mics and under the glare of dozens of cameras.

Kaukab, Hussain, and I stood behind her. Junaid stood in line with us, at a respectable distance for a non-family member. I glanced at him as Kauser started to speak. He gave me a solemn nod, but his eyes said what his lips didn't: *I will always have your back, Kiran.*

His was the support I needed as I watched my younger sister relive the trauma she had endured for so many years, and then had been forced to suffer in silence, while the man who had made her childhood a nightmare roamed free without any repercussions.

"Asif Ghazanfar came into my room that night . . ." She reached out to hold Iftikhar's hand. He immediately grasped it, squeezing it gently. His strength became her courage, and her voice steadied as she described in detail what Asif Ghazanfar had done to her.

A collective gasp escaped the audience.

"Do you know who you are accusing, Ms. Kauser? He is one of the biggest philanthropists in our country and funds everything from orphanages to schools. It seems unbelievable that he would do what you accuse him of," one of the reporters asked.

Yusra spoke up for her. "Sir, you are only here to listen and report what Ms. Kauser has to say, not to give your worthless opinions."

She stepped back; the man sulked. A female chuckle was heard from another corner. I didn't look in the direction of that female reporter.

I should have. I would have immediately recognized those dark curls.

For now, I was singularly focused on my sister as she started to recount all the times we had sought justice but were denied. On Yusra's insistence, we had gone back and pulled out all the records I had of reaching out to lawyers and trying to record a statement against Asif at the police station.

As the lawyer, she took over once Kauser finished narrating her story. And that is when it became obvious to everyone in the audience that we were not backing down from these accusations. Names were proclaimed of prominent lawyers and police personnel who had ignored us. Records of phone calls and text messages were held up as evidence. Police reports that were registered but never acted upon, only discovered now by Detective Iqbal on the orders of his boss, were passed around for the reporters to see.

The entire system had failed my sister, and the only way to get her the justice she deserved was to take down the very people who made up that system.

"We have now filed another report with the police. The fifth one over the last two decades. And this time, we hope that the police will fully investigate Mr. Asif Ghazanfar," Yusra said, throwing a glance towards Junaid, who promptly stepped up to the mic.

"Thank you, Ms. Yusra. I publicly acknowledge that many in the police have failed Ms. Kauser previously, but as the incoming Inspector General of Sindh, I assure her and her family that this time, all the allegations against Mr. Ghazanfar will be thoroughly investigated."

Questions were thrown out by the reporters as soon as Junaid finished his statement.

"What proof do you have?" the first male reporter asked.

Junaid answered, "I cannot comment on the specifics of an ongoing investigation."

"Mr. Ghazanfar is a billionaire. Is this an attempt to sue him for money?" the second male reporter asked.

Yusra responded, "No woman would put her honor on the line for the sake of money. Certainly not my client, Ms. Kauser. So no, we are not interested in settling this case for money—we want Mr. Ghazanfar to be tried in court for sexual abuse."

"What if Mr. Asif says that you are being paid by someone else to ruin his reputation? He has enough enemies surrounding him," the third male reporter asked.

Yusra answered with a frown. "My client will not dignify that question by answering it."

Finally, a female reporter spoke up. "How did that childhood experience affect you as an adult?"

Kauser stepped forward, Iftikhar staying close. "I had nightmares for a long time and was almost always depressed in my young adulthood. I was lucky that my sisters supported me and that I was able to get the therapy I needed. I was luckier that my husband believed me when I told him about my past. I came forward today because so many girls and women like me never get that kind of support."

On and on it went. Questions about our personal lives, that of our children, our careers. Many were thwarted by Yusra and Junaid. As I had expected of our patriarchal society, all the focus was on Kauser and her family, and almost none on the man being accused.

By the end of it, my family felt like we were living in a glass house with one-way windows, where the entire world could see us while we were sitting ducks, waiting for the fallout from what Kauser had done today.

We gathered at Kauser's home a few hours after the press conference, not just to support her, but also to recover from the emotional rollercoaster that our morning had been.

"I am so proud of you, Kauser Baji. I wish I could have been there with you," Osman was telling her on the phone when the doorbell rang, and Junaid and Yusra walked in.

"How is Kauser holding up?" Junaid whispered as he took a seat next to me.

"Pretty good, considering that the ridiculous press ripped her apart. Thank you for your help, though."

"Of course. It looked like Iftikhar was going to punch some of the reporters if I hadn't threatened to arrest them for harassing his wife."

I had to admit, it was heartening to see the way Iftikhar was protecting his wife. Not many men would do that. Neither would most brothers-in-law put out public statements in support of a woman accusing the stalwart of his business community of sexual abuse.

"What are you smiling about?" a voice asked in the middle of my rare happy thoughts.

"Just that I am so glad my sisters have found such amazing husbands," I replied.

I felt his eyes on me again, studying me with quiet intensity, before the smoky sandalwood of his cologne teased my senses. "Don't lose hope for yourself, Ms. Kiran."

When I turned to meet his enigmatic eyes, swimming with emotions I couldn't decipher, I dared to ask, "What does that mean?"

"Nothing." He shook his head quickly and stammered, "I just . . . you know what, forget about what I said."

Without a breath in between, he turned towards the rest of the room and declared that he had important news, leaving me confused but also highly irritated. How long was he going to keep doing this back-and-forth?

I had a good mind to pull him aside and ask him that, but my attention was diverted to his important news.

"We received a tip that there is an exclusive party at Shafiq Irfan's farmhouse today. Rumor has it, it won't just be a gathering of his family and friends. Our informant will be in attendance and will pass along any information she gets."

"Since when have you had an informant in Shafiq's home?" I asked.

"Started today. She's been working with Sikander Ahmed to investigate Asif. She wants to go undercover now," Junaid replied without looking at me, like he was avoiding me altogether.

My phone buzzed in my lap. I glanced down and saw a text message on it that I should have told Junaid about. But when I looked at him again, he was standing in the corner, talking on the phone with his back towards me.

My defiant side took over. The cautious part lost. *I can take care of myself,* I thought with contempt. Besides, if the FIU was going to protect my ex-husband, perhaps it was time to approach him unofficially.

Scowling at Junaid, I replied to Shafiq's text message.

CHAPTER 50

Party

KIRAN

"You are going to get me into so much trouble with Junaid," Yusra complained as we sat in her car on the outskirts of the expansive farmland that surrounded Shafiq's house.

"I don't think he cares."

"He cares a *lot*." She laughed. "How do you not know that?"

"He sure has a way of irritating me, then. But forget about him. Help me put on this wire."

The wire had been Yusra's idea when I told her that I was going to meet Shafiq at his house during a party he was throwing for his old friends. His text message that afternoon included an Evite, a calligraphy font on a pretty white, gold, and pink background, promising a party with good music and delicious food. But the message that came with it wasn't pretty at all.

Shafiq: Be my guest tonight for old time's sake. I think it's time we have a chat.

That was the mellow part.

Shafiq: And if you bring your inspector boyfriend or any of his men, you'll be signing their death sentence yourself.

That was the part that sent a shiver down my spine and was the reason why I couldn't have told Junaid even if I'd wanted to.

The wire threaded under my shirt was meant to record any conversation I had with Shafiq. The pepper spray in my bag was for my defense. And Yusra, sitting in the car outside the house, was to be my getaway, if needed.

Prepared as well as I could be, and with all the confidence I could muster, I slipped on my heels, let down my hair, checked my lipstick, and made my way towards the farmhouse. If Shafiq wanted to meet his ex-wife, he sure as hell wasn't going to meet the woman he had abandoned two decades ago.

The place was lit up like a dance club. Techno music blared, young men and women huddled together, laughing and drinking, while others danced in the middle of the courtyard. In my modest silk dress shirt and straight pants, I stuck out like a sore thumb.

Two men in black, with AR-15s slung over their shoulders, stopped me. I only had to tell them about my relationship to their boss for them to escort me to the inner lounge area and ask me to wait.

As soon as they left, a woman whispered from behind. "Ms. Kiran?"

I instantly recognized that voice. "Maham? What in the world are you doing here?"

She put a finger to her lips, shushing me. "I am undercover for a story I am doing. But what are *you* doing here? Don't tell me Detective Iqbal sent you."

She knows Iqbal? Things clicked into place.

"Are you the informant Junaid was talking about?"

"I am. Never thought I would become one when I entered journalism school." She grinned with a youthful excitement that I was, in that moment, completely lacking.

"It's dangerous, Maham. You have to get out of here."

She waved her hand in dismissal. "Don't worry. I know what I am doing."

The sound of shuffling footsteps came closer, and a man called out for her in a slurred voice. "Mahi, are you there?"

"I have to go," she whispered. "My fake date awaits me."

The young man who draped his arm around her came into focus before the couple turned to leave, and I gasped. I knew him too. He had been my student once upon a time and Osman's nemesis. Also, I remembered with disgust that he was Zain's supposed best friend who was now "dating" his ex-fiancé.

"Farhan?" His name escaped from my lips, though thankfully, he was too drunk or high on something to respond.

I stood in that room for another few minutes, taking in my surroundings and trying to understand what was happening. It seemed more like a drug fest than an actual party.

"Well, well, well. Looking beautiful as ever, *my* Kiran." The voice I dreaded from my past made me turn around. He walked closer. So close that I could smell the alcohol on his breath when he reached out and caressed my cheek.

"Soft and exquisite."

I jerked his hand away. "Keep your hands to yourself, Shafiq. Just tell me what you want."

"Let's go somewhere private." He smirked and grabbed my arm.

"No." I tried to pull back, but he tightened his grip and let out a throaty laugh.

"Still as defiant as before, I see."

As he led me down a twisting corridor away from the main lounge, I committed the route to memory. Finally, we reached a set of double doors. He swung them open and shoved me inside. I found myself in a bedroom.

The rapid beating of my heart and the sweating of my palms were enough of an indication that even my subconscious knew that I had gotten myself into quite a mess. But I stood tall. I would be damned if I let fear show on my face. Especially in front of this man who had tormented me for so many years.

"*What* do you want?" I asked through gritted teeth.

"You." He stalked closer, his fingers tangling in my hair.

"Get lost." I shoved him aside for the second time.

He laughed, but a murderous look clouded his eyes. "My sons."

My stomach dropped; it made total sense now. "I would rather die than let you come near my sons," I spat out at him.

He pushed me against the wall, a menacing smile creeping across his face. "They are mine too, or have you forgotten those moments of passion where you begged me to touch you? Because I would be glad to reenact them right now. Me, you, and that bed."

I am not sure where I got the courage from, but I did. I slapped him—so hard he went tumbling back, the imprint of my hand visible even from where I stood at a distance. Whether that was a mistake or not, it was done now. I could only brace myself for my ex-husband's wrath.

It wouldn't be the first time I had been subjected to it. But I hadn't forgotten that in becoming a slave to his anger, he lost all his senses.

His lips curled as his face contorted with fury. Before I knew it, his hands were wrapped around my neck, and his voice thundered in that empty room. "You will pay a very heavy price for that slap, bitch."

Give another push, my brain ordered despite losing oxygen as his fingers constricted my airway.

"What will you do? Kill me? Like you killed my father?" I gasped as defiantly as I could.

He bared his teeth, his eyes nearly popping out of their sockets.

"I killed your father because I was paid to do it. You, on the other hand, I will take pleasure in killing slowly and painfully, in front of our sons, so they'll know what a weak and pathetic woman you are."

Weak and pathetic, my ass.

I smiled at him, closed my eyes, and held my breath. At least I wasn't stupid like my ex-husband.

Then I released the pepper spray straight into his face. He cursed loudly, and immediately dropped to the ground. And I *ran*, like my life depended on it—through the twisting corridor, through the lounge, and out of that house.

A red Mercedes skidded to a halt in front of me, and the passenger door flew open just as men in black came running out of the house, followed by their stumbling boss.

Yusra gunned the car before I'd even shut the door. In seconds, we were well out of reach of those men, who were left shouting empty threats into the cool Saturday night.

"Who the hell are you?" She turned towards me with wide eyes.

"My father's daughter." I grinned back. "And I just got the evidence I needed to avenge his death."

Even if my ex-husband had only been the hitman, there was no way he would be spared with the evidence I had now. All we had to do was turn over the recording of Shafiq's confession to the police.

CHAPTER 51

After the Party

KIRAN

I had gotten home around midnight after Yusra and I met with Junaid and Detective Iqbal to go over the confession that my ex-husband had unwittingly said out loud, and was now recorded on tape to be submitted as evidence. Though my father's murder was not the only crime Shafiq had been booked for that night.

He was also charged with my attempted murder. I had his threat on tape and the strangle marks around my neck to prove it.

The full-length mirror in my room gave me a view of what had transpired between me and the man I had once been in love with. The bruises, now turning into a gnarly blueish-purple down the length of my neck, were a reminder of how close I had to come to meeting my Maker last night.

Yet, it wasn't their sight that bothered me so much. It was the look on Junaid's face when he had seen them and when he'd heard everything on that tape. His jaw had clenched, a deep frown etched across his forehead, and I could sense his fists curling as he restrained himself from saying anything to me, or even looking at me.

Instead, he had asked the detective to file an urgent warrant for my ex-husband's arrest before barking orders to his subordinates to take me home with a police escort, depriving me of an opportunity to explain myself to him. Though why I had felt the need to explain myself at all escaped me.

He was not my keeper, and I was no one's responsibility.

A knock on my bedroom door forced me to quickly wrap a scarf around my bruises to hide them. The impatient tapping and whispered arguments outside my door told me exactly who required my immediate presence. Like they always did.

Might as well get over with it, I told myself as I headed towards the door. It was time to tell my sons the truth about their father. Though it seemed I hadn't accounted for their deepening connection with a friend from their rival school.

"Mama, what happened last night?" Danish asked as soon as I opened the door.

"Nael called. He said Junaid Uncle was very upset because you went into a criminal's house without telling anyone, and that man hurt you," Daniyal added.

Both boys stood there looking at me, their young faces marred by confusion and worry. While I tried not to show my vexation at their friend's father, who apparently found it appropriate to talk to everyone but me— even his own son.

But now that he had forced my hand, I proceeded to tell them the whole truth.

"He wasn't just any criminal—he was your father."

Their hardened expressions at the mention of their father did not change as I narrated to them everything I knew about the man who had abandoned them, and what had happened last night.

"Mama, can I say something very frankly?" Danish asked.

"Of course."

"I know that while we were growing up it was hard for you to handle everything with us, Mani, and our aunts. But I am so glad our father left us. We are much better off without him."

Daniyal reached out to hold my hand. "This is the only time in my life I will agree with Danish." He gave his brother a smirk before continuing. "But our family will always be enough for us. You taught us that, Mama. Thank you for being our strength and not giving up on us."

I had moisture in my eyes when I reached out to hug my sons, but that turned into a full-blown deluge of tears when Danish whispered, "It's okay, Mama. You can cry. We are here for you."

My life had come full circle. From the time I held my twins in my arms, whispering to them that their boo-boos would stop hurting soon and that it was okay to cry, to this moment, where my sons became my unwavering supporters.

"I love you both," I told them, wiping my tears.

"We love you too, Mama," they replied with goofy grins on their adorable teenage faces.

I still had someone else to deal with, but for now, I let go of his thoughts and enjoyed a nice breakfast with my boys. He would raise my blood pressure anyway.

When afternoon came, I tried to leave my house for some errands but ran into a policeman standing outside my door.

"Sorry, Ms. Kiran, but Inspector Junaid said that you are not allowed to leave this house without his explicit permission. Would you like me to call him?"

"You have got to be kidding me." I glared at the policeman.

Of course, his boss didn't pick up his desk phone when the officer called him or his cell phone when I called him myself.

"Forget it. I am going to his office. I have had enough of this ridiculous behavior." I attempted to stomp off, only to be blocked again by the officer.

"Actually, ma'am, he said not to let you drive anywhere. But I can take you to police headquarters in the car he sent."

With my blood pressure now literally through the roof and curses in both Urdu and English at the tip of my tongue, I followed the man down the stairs to the waiting police car.

The officer ignored my rants as I got in. *Who does his boss think he is anyway?* I scowled at the officer's back.

"I am in the middle of a meeting, Ms. Kiran," the inspector scowled as soon as I barged into his office.

"I can go, sir." Detective Iqbal stood up.

"*Sit* down." The man promptly did as told when his boss threw him a deadly stare.

"Ms. Kiran, you are apparently very hard of hearing. So let me repeat myself. I. Am. In. A. Meeting," the inspector repeated slowly, in a deliberate attempt to rile me up. I was sure of it.

"You can wait outside." He waved me out of the room. I turned on my heels and left, shutting the door behind me.

Fortunately for me, though, he didn't notice when the door was left slightly ajar. With a bit of straining, I could easily make out the conversation inside.

"I've interrogated him as much as I could, sir," the detective said.

"He really has no clue who gave him the order to cut Mustafa Tariq's brakes?" That was the inspector's defeated voice.

"No, sir. He said the call was made from an untraceable phone, and his payment was dropped off at a random place under the Korangi Bridge."

"Did he take an envelope from the crime scene?"

"He did, but it was sealed, and he didn't look inside. He mailed it to the address he was instructed to. I visited that place. It's an abandoned house along the Super Highway."

"Who was it addressed to?"

"He doesn't remember the name."

I imagined Junaid sighing before he spoke again. "Where did he get the drugs being sold at his party?"

"This time it was someone called Abbas," the detective answered, before adding, "but for years his contact had been Akbar Jafri."

My ears pricked, and Junaid's must have too, because Akbar was the man who had been sent to kill our sons but had been found dead soon after. A hushed conversation I didn't understand ensued. The detective must have walked closer to the door in that time, because a moment later I heard his loud voice say, "Sir, what should I do about that father who came yesterday?"

"Open his case again. We should not let Ms. Kauser's bravery go in vain. If anyone comes in accusing Asif Ghazanfar of abuse, I want you to take it very seriously."

"That case is more than nineteen years old. It will take some time to go through all the records."

"Don't care . . ." was the last thing I dared to hear before quickly stepping back when footsteps headed my way.

The detective exited, red-faced and apologetic to me, while Junaid stood in his office doorway, gesturing. "You can come in now."

I should have left, but I had had enough of this man's ambiguities. It was time to put an end to whatever he was doing, or not doing.

"Had your fun?" I huffed and walked past him into his office.

He followed, clearly not pleased by my presence. "You think this is fun for me?"

I whirled around to face him. "Then what else is it? A chance for you to flex your muscles and show everyone that you're the big boss who can trap people whenever and wherever you want?"

"And when exactly did I trap you?" he scowled.

The time you filed a report against the son of the most powerful businessman in Pakistan. The time you told me and my sisters that you believed us. The time you sat with me on a seaside porch and told me that you would always be there for me. The times you flirted with me and made my heart race and my mind go numb.

There wasn't a single moment I could have chosen to answer his question with, so I stayed quiet and glared at him.

"If you're referring to me stationing officers outside your apartment, that was for you and your sons' protection. You can't bulldoze your way through a hornet's nest and not expect them to come after you."

"You could have asked me if I wanted that protection," I retorted.

"You would have said no. And excuse me for thinking about your safety before indulging in formalities. Maybe I wouldn't have to be so worried about you if you knew how to listen once in a while."

I instinctively dug my heels in. "I am an adult woman with free will who can do whatever she wants, whenever she wants. So maybe you need to quit thinking about me."

He *hmphed* but stayed quiet. That's when I noticed the large bruise over the knuckles of his right hand.

"What happened to your hand?"

"I injured it."

"Doing what?"

He paused and looked up at me. His jaw ticked. "Punching your ex-husband."

"You punched him so hard you hurt yourself?" I frowned. "What is wrong with you? Or do you go around punching every criminal in your custody?" The absurdity of his actions was beyond me, not to mention borderline illegal.

"None of the other criminals have laid a hand on you or threatened your honor. So, sorry if I lost my cool," he snapped.

I crossed my arms over my chest. "Thank you, but I don't need special treatment from you. In case you have forgotten, you and I have no relationship at all."

The deep brown of his irises darkened further when he swung his head around. "How can you say that after everything we have been through?"

"At least I am saying it out loud. Unlike you, who prefers to either speak in riddles or not at all."

His voice lowered. "Kiran, what we have doesn't need words. Can you not feel it in your heart?"

What does that even mean?

"See, there you go again. Throwing out these riddles as if I don't matter to you at all."

Those words were spoken in frustration, but once they were out in the open, they became the reason the tide turned on me. I was no longer the fearless woman standing in front of a man who vexed her. Instead, I held my breath, trepidation laced with anticipation, as a wave of emotion swept across his admittedly handsome visage.

He walked closer. I stepped back until my rear hit his office desk.

His hands rested at the edge of his desk on either side of me, truly trapping me this time, in his arms.

"You matter to me," he growled, just inches away from my face.

"But if you want me to be clear, then fine. I'll be clear." His fiery, unflinching gaze and the smoky sandalwood scent that engulfed me made my heart race and nearly took my breath away.

"You consume me, Kiran. Day after day, you consume my thoughts, my dreams, even my nightmares. Awake or asleep, all I want is to be near you. You think you don't matter to me, yet for almost two years, I've tried and failed to stay away."

He backed away, leaving a void that I never expected to bother me as much as it did. I told myself that at least now I could take a breath and try to break the spell he had me under. But he continued, robbing me of even that.

"I wish you could see me when I am standing at the corner of your street, debating with myself whether or not to step into your life. And feel the fear I feel when my heart gives in—every . . . single . . . time—and I ring your doorbell. Then maybe you'd know what it is you're doing to me."

The onslaught of his words left me dazed, yet I gathered myself enough to ask, "What do you fear?"

A softness permeated his demeanor for the first time that afternoon.

"That I am an afterthought for you. A means to an end," he replied quietly.

He wasn't. He was so much more.

A knock on the door interrupted us. Detective Iqbal announced that he had some news. Junaid told him to come in. The door opened, and the two men discussed something about a liquid that their informant from Shafiq's residence had sent in for analysis. A drink she said had been served to her by the man she was with.

I wasn't one who could switch emotions that quickly. Perhaps that was a special skill taught in the police academy. I remained silent in the corner, hardly listening to the two men's discussion, instead letting my mind process what had happened in that room earlier.

The detective left, and Junaid closed the door behind him. "I need to go with Iqbal to the chemistry analysis lab, but you should go home. And please try not to meet criminals on your own next time or throw yourself at assassins."

He gave me a small smile. "Or at least call me before you do."

That was an endearment, which meant he expected me to ignore his plea. Turns out, he did know me quite well.

"I'll think about it." I smiled back.

"Well, think hard." His hand brushed against mine. "Because I really need you."

My heart fluttered uncontrollably, and I wished I could have told him what he did to me too. But unlike him, my emotions always seemed to get stuck in my throat at moments like these.

As the junior police officer drove me home, I ruminated on Junaid's words, and then I felt it: that feeling he had talked about. Maybe the warmth that infused my soul in his presence was because of a special relationship my heart had with his.

I couldn't stop a grin from spreading across my face. Despite the complexities of our individual lives and the circumstances that had brought us together, there was one thing I was sure of now:

Inspector Junaid was quite smitten with me.

And I didn't mind that at all.

CHAPTER 52

Houston

ZAIN

Closure. Dr. Tan said it was the full stop to the final sentence of a story before the next chapter could be written. For too long, I had ignored the part of my story that was the hardest to forget. It was high time I faced it.

"Hi, I'm Zain, and I'm an alcoholic," I admitted to the group of mostly familiar faces seated in a circle on their plastic chairs on a Saturday afternoon.

"Hi, Zain," they replied in a chorus.

Glancing around the room, I took a sip of my coffee and started speaking. "My last drink was 245 days ago. I am getting to the point where the cravings fade into the background, as long as I keep myself busy. But there is something I have to do that I am afraid might make me start drinking again."

Another sip of coffee flowed down my throat, but then I forced the words out. "I was in love with a girl, and then she left me. I know now that I forced her to leave, but I feel like I cannot move on with my life unless I meet her one last time and apologize. I am going to try to do that soon."

"Good luck, Zain," said Steve, whose story wasn't that different from mine. "But remember if she doesn't want to meet you, that's okay too. The important thing is that you have to move forward."

This group of people, so diverse in race, religion, color, and profession, seemed an unlikely assembly at first glance. Yet, what we shared transcended all that. We had demons that fed off a disease, a relentless foe that we battled daily, a fight that was both deeply personal and profoundly collective.

For me, that collective spirit—the voices wishing me luck, urging me to stay strong—were the reason I found myself in the office of the private investigator who had helped Abu track down Maham when I had first arrived in Houston.

"I need to see the pictures of Maham you sent to my father."

He raised a brow. I explained further. "I need to apologize to her, but I don't know where she is. If I can figure out who her husband is, I might be able to find her too."

After I offered to pay, the man finally pulled up the pictures he had found. They were nothing like the ones I had seen. Those had her having dinner and laughing late at night with a young man. These had her father and another older man in the same shot as well.

Bewildered, I asked, "Where is the one with her and the young guy sitting alone?"

The investigator was just as confused as I was. "These are the only ones I found. She was at a conference with her father, and the other men are her father's colleagues."

"You sent my father a nikahnama of Maham with this guy, Ahad Tanvir."

When he responded, "Who the heck is Ahad Tanvir, and what's a nikahnama?" I could only stare at him, momentarily stunned. Flashbacks flooded my mind—seeing pictures of her with him, convinced they were married, and the fury that had utterly consumed me. Those images, and my father's words, were the reason I had destroyed my cousin's life.

Now, sitting in that cramped office, a fresh wave of anger surged within me. This time, however, the targets had shifted. Irrepressible fury was directed towards my father, and I needed to hear the truth from my cousin.

"Can you find the contact number of a doctor who works at Children's Hospital of Boston?" I asked the investigator.

On the Sunday that followed, I had no need for that number. The doctor showed up unannounced at my doorstep.

"Osman? What are you doing here?"

He pushed his way past me. "Maybe I should be asking you the same question."

"Huh?"

He scowled. "Only an idiot like you could forget about her so easily."

I was thoroughly confused by so many things right now. "What are you talking about, man? Who have I forgotten?"

"Your *wife*. You know, the woman who is your responsibility because you signed a nikahnama with her."

Oh.

The smile that spread slowly across my face wasn't intentional. It just happened as realization sank in. Plus, it was a little funny to see my once-wimpy cousin all grown up and become a man.

He frowned again. "What are you smiling at?"

"At how stupid you are."

Pot calling the kettle black, a voice laughed inside me.

He told me to shut up, and I told him he couldn't make me. Yet, when I motioned for him to follow me into my living room, he stepped right into the apartment.

"How did you find my place?" I asked.

"Someone at the ZakU office gave me the address. You'd be surprised how trustworthy people think doctors are," he replied as he used his pinky finger to move the clothes strewn across my sofa and make space for himself.

Still a sissy. I shook my head.

"Are you here to kill me or something?"

With his gaze fixed on me, he replied, "As much as I'd love to, killing assholes goes against the Hippocratic Oath I took. But, Zain, do not underestimate my ability to make your life hell if you don't step up and be the husband Sanam deserves."

His voice did not waver, and the scowl had returned to his face. Yet, the calmness he portrayed was betrayed by his tightly clasped hands and the breaths he heaved as he sat before me. Sure, I could have been nice and put him out of his misery, but no amount of therapy makes your cousin suddenly less irritating.

I leaned back on the sofa. What was the harm in playing a little game before we got down to business? "You know that pain scale you doctors love to use?"

"What about it?"

"How painful was it for you to come here and ask me to go back to Sanam?"

"A hundred," he replied with a straight face.

On a pain scale of 1-10, where ten was the worst pain you had ever felt in your life, this man described his pain as a hundred. *Unbelievable.*

"Then why the fuck should I go back to her?" I glared at him.

"Because she refuses my help," he replied, clenching his jaw like his soul was being extracted from his body, slowly and agonizingly.

"She is miserable and exhausted, working God knows how many hours a day, and then she goes back to this tiny apartment in a shady neighborhood, while you're sitting here in this luxurious condo. How could you discard her like that?"

He was looking at me, yet his mind was somewhere else, a place where she was, and he had to helplessly watch her because the stubborn woman refused any assistance.

Un-fucking-believable.

Blazing eyes glared at me, but he couldn't hide the desperate plea in his voice when he said, "For once, do the right thing and be the man she deserves."

So, this is what it is. I finally saw it—Sanam and Osman's selfless love.

This was why she could never let go of him. And why, no matter how far I took her from him, she would always return to him. This was what love was supposed to be: magnanimous, altruistic, sacrificial.

They say life has a way of teaching you lessons when you least expect them. Sitting in my messy living room, opposite a man who was my blood yet couldn't be more different than me, wasn't how I had imagined I would witness the purity of an emotion I had to admit I had never truly understood before.

The awkward silence had stretched long enough, and Osman was peering at me, expecting an answer, so I stammered a reply the best I could. "I-I can't go to Boston. I have to go to Pakistan to take care of some unfinished business there."

He frowned. "What could be more important than your own family, Zain?"

"The part of my family I never asked for. My father—who altered pictures of Maham to convince me that she was having an affair with someone."

"Maham wasn't having an affair. She ran from you because you turned into a narcissist and made her life hell. The same way you're doing to Sanam."

"I know that already."

His eyes narrowed. "You do?"

So irritating. "Will you fix your face? I know I made grave mistakes, but I am not a monster like my father, or like those people your sister accuses of not believing her."

I'd seen those clips of Kauser's press conference and knew for sure that my father had done to her exactly what she had described.

He crossed his arms over his chest. "And your going to Pakistan is supposed to do what, exactly?"

"Put an end to his tyranny, once and for all. I am the only one who lived with the man, and contrary to what you think, I am not that stupid. I know things about him that no one else does, like the fact that he killed someone."

Osman sat up. "My father?"

"I don't know. But Abu once used a vial of potassium to stop someone's heart. I overheard him talking about it with Zakariya."

That couldn't have been Osman's father, he pointed out; he had been killed when his car crashed after his brakes were cut.

"But do you know who did die of a heart attack and had high levels of potassium in his blood? Basaam Sadiq, the man who was going to testify against your father."

I hadn't known that, but Basaam Sadiq had died a few months ago, and I had overheard their conversation a year ago. Someone else came to mind as I sat with my cousin.

"Our grandfather died of a heart attack, too, didn't he?" I asked Osman, though I didn't quite understand what my father's motive might have been back then.

He nodded slowly, like pieces of some story were starting to fit together. "That would make total sense. My father is killed, then my grandfather, and Kiran Api is left all alone to fend for three young siblings and her own newborns. Perfect opportunity for Asif Ghazanfar to swoop in and steal what wasn't his."

It was my turn to frown at him. "What wasn't his?"

Osman's gaze locked onto mine. "Tariq Enterprise, the house you grew up in—your entire life was stolen from me and my sisters."

Turns out I really had no clue who the fuck I was. The rich kid born to a business tycoon, or an imposter raised on wealth usurped from my unsuspecting cousins, forced to leave the mansion in the middle of a cold, rainy night.

Basaam Sadiq, my mamoo's death, an unnamed dead man, altered pictures, and fake documents of a woman I once loved, were all forgotten the moment the basis of my existence unraveled, as my cousin laid out one truth after another, all that made perfect sense in retrospect.

A lesser man would have reveled in the agony of my crumbling world. But Osman wasn't that man. It was clear that he didn't even care about his stolen wealth. His focus was singularly on the woman he was undeniably in love with.

"I'll relay what you heard about the potassium to the inspector overseeing our case against your father. But you need to come to Boston with me and make things right for Sanam."

"What if I don't want to?"

"Then set her free," he demanded.

There it was—the only thing he truly wanted from me. Not his family's wealth or insider information to solve his father's murder, but the part of his life most precious to him—my ex-wife.

"I am surprised she hasn't told you. You forced me to divorce her three months ago."

The Journalist

KIRAN

The coffee shop near my school held plenty of memories for our family, including sad ones, like the time I sat on the dusty steps, consoling my baby brother after he watched Sanam walk away. On the Monday after Shafiq's party, I stood at the same spot, waiting for a former student of mine who had sent me a text message earlier that day.

"Hello, Ms. Kiran," the young woman said, quickly walking up the stairs while she threw suspicious glances behind her.

"Maham, what is going on?"

"Sorry for the secrecy, but I leave for Islamabad in a few hours, and I wanted to meet you before going. Inspector Junaid doesn't think it is safe for me to stay here anymore," she said when we reached a secluded corner of the coffee shop.

"Are you in trouble because you were seen at Shafiq's place? I told Junaid he shouldn't have roped you in. I don't know what he was thinking."

"Actually, it was my mentor, Sikander Ahmed, who suggested that I should attend it."

I raised a brow, and she explained further. "It started off as a thesis project on the freedom of press in Pakistan for my Master's in Journalism. I never thought it would lead me to Zain's father."

She had sought out Sikander Ahmed, given his award-winning career in investigative journalism. Both had quickly realized that they had a common enemy: Asif Ghazanfar. Though Maham's interest in that man wasn't only because of her ex-fiancé. It was also because of a memory that hadn't made sense to her initially, but then shed new light on Zain's father after she and Sikander started digging into GT Enterprise's illegal activities.

"We had an end-of-semester party at Zain's house the first year I was here," she started. I remembered that party because of how hurt Osman had seemed at being the only student from their class to be left out.

"Zain told me he loved me that night, and I was on an absolute high from that itself. I remember Zain's father congratulating me on us being such a lovely couple, and in his charming way, he offered to show me Zain's baby pictures in his study."

She paused to take a shaky breath.

"Before I followed him, he handed me a glass of lemonade and told me to keep myself hydrated. Not thinking much of it, I had probably finished half the glass by the time we reached the hallway outside his study, but Zain met us there and insisted that he wanted to take a walk with me outside. Until that point, his dad had been really sweet, but the moment Zain met us, his dad became so aggressive against him, telling him that he would always be useless and that he couldn't believe that a girl like me loved him. Thankfully, Zain grabbed my hand and walked me out of the house. That probably saved my life, because a few moments later, I started to feel dizzy, and my legs became heavy."

Zain had taken her home, thinking that she was coming down with something, and—the youngster she was—it had never occurred to her that her boyfriend's father might have drugged her until she heard about Asif Ghazanfar's alleged involvement with drugs such as roofies.

And then she had attended Kauser's press conference.

"I realized why I might have subconsciously pushed that whole episode to the back of my mind. I was seventeen. Asif Ghazanfar was a business tycoon. Who would have believed me, even if I told someone about it?"

"Is that why you decided to become an informant for the police?" I asked.

She nodded. "How could I not, after your sister showed such bravery in public? Going undercover was the easy part."

"Besides," she laughed, "Farhan is stupider now than he was in school. He tried to get handsy with me, like I knew he would. Just like I knew he would try to drug me when I refused. So, I switched my drink with his when he wasn't looking, and he fell asleep in the middle of the dance floor."

"So the liquid that was submitted to Junaid was . . ."

"Yes. That's what he gave me, and it contained traces of roofies."

The date rape drug? My stomach knotted at how badly things could have gone for this young woman, but she seemed unfazed. Instead, she said, "Neither of those facts is why I wanted to meet you, Ms. Kiran."

Her shoulders slumped, despair and guilt suddenly clouding her eyes. "I am so sorry that I ran away and messed up your lives so much."

"Oh, Maham." I reached over and squeezed her hand.

"If I hadn't abandoned Zain . . ."

"He would have made your life a living hell. And even if he hadn't, there was no way for any of us to have predicted what would happen with Osman and Sanam."

"I know." She nodded slowly. The determination in her voice was unmistakable when she said, "That's why I will keep doing whatever I can to bring Asif down. I owe it to Osman and Sanam, and even to Zain, for that matter."

A smile briefly lit her face. "Don't tell your brother this, but I told Saeed Chachoo about Osman and Sanam's history. Now that they're together in Boston, maybe there is some hope for their relationship too."

Osman had mentioned seeing Sanam at his hospital, but the pain in his voice had been so gut-wrenching to hear, even sitting all the way across the world that I hadn't had the heart to ask him for more details. I could only pray that whatever destiny had in store for those two, it brought peace to their souls.

When Maham left, I took a moment to call Kauser and tell her about Maham's story. That young girl might have escaped Asif by sheer luck, but I was sure there would be others who hadn't.

A reminder I had set went off on my phone. It was time to get back to my motherly duties.

For once, we arrived five minutes early at the stadium for Daniyal's match against their archrivals. After the last time, when this match had devolved into fistfights, the organizers had strictly prohibited more than two family members per player. That meant most of the stadium seats now lay unoccupied.

I chose a secluded place under the canopy for shade, put on my sunglasses, and pulled out the papers for the math test I had given my students the day before. Grading papers while watching my son's match: peak multitasking for a teacher.

But if I thought that hiding behind my glasses and burying myself in papers or sitting away from everyone else would spare me an interaction with the inspector, whose words still rang in my ears, I was very mistaken.

"See, this is the difference between you and me." His baritone voice made me look up at his dark figure, framed by the afternoon sun.

"What difference?"

He took a seat next to me and gave me a small smile. "You sat next to me only when you were forced to do so in a packed stadium. I am choosing to sit next to you among rows of empty seats."

I stared at his profile for a second before looking away, trying to decipher the meaning behind his words. Did he think I wouldn't choose him if I had a choice?

If I were an articulate romantic, I might have been able to come up with something coherent in that moment, but I was a math teacher who had never really been good at language arts.

"Okay, stop buttering me up. Is there something you need?" I asked instead.

Disappointment flitted across his face, but it disappeared quickly when he took out a folded piece of paper from his pocket and handed it to me.

"I have another riddle for you."

The paper was a photocopy of a book with some legal language on it and a heading that read "Code of Conduct."

"It's from the police academy's handbook. These are rules that apply to everyone uniformly, from the lowest-ranking officer to the Inspector General of Sindh."

I was thoroughly confused.

"Read clause 15.2," he said.

"'No law enforcement officer shall investigate any crime that is committed by, alleged against, or otherwise involves, in any capacity, an immediate family member or spouse, in order to prevent a conflict of interest. Any officer found to be interfering in such an investigation shall be subject to immediate disciplinary action, which may include unpaid administrative leave or termination from the department,'" I read aloud before questioning him again.

"What does this have to do with me?"

He leaned in ever so slightly. "I cannot investigate the murder of my *wife's* father. Or her own attempted murder. And I do not trust anyone else to do it as thoroughly as I will. That is why it may seem like there is no purpose behind all the words I have ever said to you, but in reality, time and rules simply don't permit me to say more."

Getting up from his seat, he continued. "For now, I want you to think about this riddle while I finish the investigation, and then I will seek your answer."

My heart lurched.

He walked a few steps away but turned again. "You will always have a choice, Kiran. But I hope you decide to take the seat next to me, even when there are empty rows around us."

The sound of his retreating steps faded quickly into the excited cheers from the field below us. Yet I sat still, buried under the weight of his words despite the subtlety with which he had said them.

The implication of the riddle sank in. So did how real this relationship had suddenly become in the last few days. We weren't just two lonely adults who sought solace in each other's company.

He had dared to think of our future. A together forever kind of future.

Also . . . had that been a proposal?

"Huh." I sat up, another smile creeping onto my face.

I think it was—kind of.

CHAPTER 54

Destiny

OSMAN

There are some conversations that play on repeat in your head forever. The one I had with my cousin last weekend was one of them.

"Why did you divorce her?" I asked.

"You wouldn't be asking me that question if you knew how we got married in the first place."

"Sanam said your families forced you."

He scoffed. "Trust her to protect you and your feelings."

His disdain for me was loud and clear, like it had always been, but there was something else too. Regret, maybe even jealousy.

"Most of our family didn't even know. I was the one who forced her, by threatening to kill you. And she was so in love with you, she signed her life away to protect yours."

The shock that had come with those words still reverberated through me today, almost a week after I had returned from Houston. But that had since given way to something else: a dread that had been gnawing away at me from the inside.

Did she not want me anymore?

It was a question I had asked myself again and again, as my harried days turned into sleepless nights. Why would she keep a clay heart I had given her so many years ago, yet not tell me that she was divorced?

No matter how hard I tried, I could not answer those questions. The only one who could, lived in the apartment building I now stood in front of, zipping up my fleece jacket as the nighttime fall air made its presence felt through the thin shirt of my scrubs.

I took a deep breath and pressed the button for the apartment that listed her name. The intercom crackled, and her voice came through. "Who is it?"

"It's me, Sanam. We need to talk."

"I don't want to—" she started to say.

"I went to Houston to meet Zain," I blurted out.

The crackling went silent, but a few seconds later, the building's door was flung open, and she stood there wearing blue pajamas. The usual defiance in her eyes had morphed into trepidation. "Why would you do that?" She gaped at me.

"You were hurting, Sanam, and you refused to let me help. So I thought I would talk some sense into your husband."

"He's not . . ." she started to say but stopped.

"I know. He told me everything."

For a moment, she stood still, staring at me, before stepping out and sitting on the front steps. I took it as a win and sat down next to her.

The quiet of the night engulfed us, only interrupted by the faint hum of the occasional car passing by. I wished I could put my arm around, pull her closer, tuck that brown lock of hair caressing her cheek behind her ear, and just . . . hold her.

I did nothing, because in that moment, there was a wall between us, built with regret, cemented with uncertainty. I felt it. She felt it. We were a far cry from the teenagers who always felt a warm comfort in each other's presence.

"You shouldn't have bargained your life for mine," I told her, breaking the silence.

She turned to face me. "Would you have done it for me?"

"I would do anything for you. But that's different."

"How?" she shot back. "Because you loved me more than I loved you? You know very well that was never true, Osman."

"Because I was supposed to protect you. *Not* the other way around. I would have died for you without giving it a second thought. You should have known that."

There, I had said it—the pain that had been eating at me since Zain's words. How could I live with myself, knowing the woman I loved had paid such a heavy price for that love?

"Don't give me that bullshit, Osman. I did what I had to do, and I would do it again." She looked away, but I didn't. Because I saw it: the moisture building in her eyes. The first sign that it wasn't over between us.

It couldn't be, not with the way she gazed at me when I turned her face towards mine and wiped her tears, her eyes filled with so much longing that if my heart had belonged to me, I would have served it to her on a silver platter. But I had already done that a long time ago.

"I made a promise to you. You should have let me keep it."

Her pink lips curled into a small smile. "I haven't forgotten. But some promises are simply teenage fantasies."

I glanced at the woman beside me. She wasn't the beautiful, innocent girl I had obsessed over as a teenager. She had lived a life that no one should have to endure. Yet I could tell that nothing had changed in the way she saw me, just as nothing had changed in the way I still longed for her with every breath.

"We were never a fantasy, Sanam. And while you don't have to say yes, I will still keep my promise to you."

I moved to get down on one knee, just like I had told her I would. "Sanam, will you . . ."

"No! Get up, Osman." Her hand gripped my arm, stopping me, even as her voice quivered. "Please, get up. Why don't you understand? We were never destined to be together. If we were, I wouldn't have gotten married to Zain."

She got up and walked down a couple of stairs, rubbing her arms against the cold. I followed close behind, unzipping my fleece.

"Besides, you don't need me," she said, turning around. "You're a doctor now, living the life you always dreamt of."

I draped my jacket over her shivering shoulders, closing the distance between us.

"I dream of you."

SANAM

For a moment, my guard slipped at the tenderness of his words and the affection in his actions. The warmth of his proximity was too much to bear. It kept pulling me towards him, towards a life that I used to dream of, before I became who I was now—a woman who was still tethered to her past through a web of lies and the nightmares that wouldn't leave me alone.

I backed away, shaking my head to clear my own haze more than anything else. "You can't say these kinds of things to me anymore."

"Why not, Sanam?"

"Stop saying my name like that," I pleaded.

"Like how, Sanam?"

"Like that . . ." My voice caught, desires and reality clashing, locked in a battle within me, threatening to buckle my knees if he breathed my name out again—the way only he did.

If he saw the dilemma in my eyes, he chose to ignore it altogether. Instead, his warm palms rested against my cold cheeks.

"Like I am in love with you?" His husky voice kept its hold on me as much as his hands cupping my face. "I am, Sanam. I'm more in love with you today than I ever was before. And I know you love me too, because you say my name the same way I say yours."

I forced myself to pull away, increasing the distance between us, despite my soul craving his. Convinced that he wasn't seeing clearly in the heat of the moment, I attempted to reason with him. Even if it meant putting a dagger through my own chest.

"My life is a mess, Osman. You have Ameerah. She's beautiful and witty, and she makes you smile. She's perfect for you."

My plea meant nothing. Instead of the quiet resignation in his hazel eyes when he had last walked away, there was now an unbridled ardor that lashed dangerously against the fortress encasing my heart—chipping away at my defenses.

"I don't want perfect," he said, his gaze steady on me. "I want *us*— our mess, our memories, even when it hurts, even when it's far from perfect. I want you, just as you are. I'm done faking smiles for the world. I want to laugh again—with you."

His warm fingers caressed the back of my hand. The simplicity of his touch, his hushed confessions, stunned my senses, taking away any ability to ignore our blatant truth.

"Please let me love you, Sanam. The way you *should* be loved. Fully, honestly—with everything I have."

The desperation in his voice cut through me. But perhaps if he understood the lies I was surrounded by, he'd change his mind.

"It's not that simple. Zain and I have kept our divorce a secret because if word gets out, our fathers will raise hell. Their first target will be you and your family, and the second may very well be me and Zain. They've made enough threats against all of us."

He stepped back, and for a second, I thought I had been able to get through to him. But then he said, "I get it. Things are complicated now. But I've waited seven years for you, Sanam. I can wait however many more it takes."

"No, Osman, I am destined to be alone. Please, don't wait."

"That's not your choice to make," he replied with a slight smile. Defiance clouded his eyes instead of desperation when he backed away towards the street before pausing once again.

"You know this destiny you keep talking about. What do you call this moment, right now? After everything we have been through on our separate paths, in two different countries, on opposite sides of the world—why am I here, under the stars like the day we left school, telling you that I want to marry you? Tell me what this is if it's not our destiny bringing us together?"

I didn't have an answer for him, and he didn't wait for one.

Standing outside my building, I watched his retreating form until it blended into the dark night, kept warm by a piece of him he had left behind—his fleece jacket, that he hadn't asked for and which I hadn't offered to return.

That night, I fell asleep wearing his jacket. It smelled of him, fresh and earthy, and felt like him, comfy and mine, and it hardly came off in the following days and nights.

It was enough to comfort my heart, even when Osman disappeared for two straight weeks.

CHAPTER 55

Planning Phase

OSMAN

The night I walked home from Sanam's apartment, I called Kiran Api for an update on the investigation. Then I told her about the plan that had been forming in my mind since my trip to Houston.

"Asif is a cunning man, Osman. Let Junaid handle it," she warned.

"He's not handling it fast enough. Besides, how cunning could Asif be if we've figured out his playbook?" I told her.

Hanging up, I sent a text message I never imagined I would.

Me: Still looking to seek revenge from your father?

Zain: Yes. Why?

Me: I have a plan.

The enemy of my enemy is my friend.

I could never forgive Zain for what he had done to Sanam, but I could make sure that I used him to complete what my sisters had started—destruction of the infallible king's castle, one manipulative move at a time.

"Alright, let's hear this amazing plan of yours so I can point out how it will spectacularly fail," Zain said when I video-called him a couple of days later. It was a good thing he was in Houston and I in Boston. Else, I was sure I would be punching his smug face.

Reminding myself that this was a business call, with a singular purpose, I answered with a straight face. "Junaid Bhai wants to talk to you. He's the Additional Inspector General leading the investigation against Asif Ghazanfar."

Zain raised a brow. "And you call him *Bhai*? How much are you bribing him?"

"*Shut up*. He's almost family."

Fortunately, Junaid Bhai and Detective Iqbal joined the call right after I'd let my sister's secret slip, giving me an excuse to avoid Zain's curious gaze.

"I am conflicted, Mr. Zain." Junaid Bhai immediately took over the conversation. "You are the son of Asif Ghazanfar, a man notorious for using any means possible to escape justice. But your cousin seems to think that you are not the prodigal son that you are often considered to be. Would that be true?"

Zain's reply was sober. "Yes, sir. I could not choose my father, unfortunately. But I can choose to help you bring him down."

"And why would you do that?"

My cousin's brows furrowed. "Because he took everything from me. And now I have nothing to lose and everything to gain by watching him burn."

"Careful, son," the inspector's deep voice cautioned. "Seeking revenge will get you nowhere; it is only justice that brings with it peace and healing."

"Call it whatever you want. Just tell me how I can help," Zain insisted.

The inspector must have picked up on my cousin's impatience, because the life lessons ceased, and we got down to business. They wanted to know more about the "vial of potassium" that Zain had overheard about.

"Administering IV potassium makes sense, as it can induce a heart attack without immediate suspicion, and elevated potassium levels in a post-mortem analysis can be easily attributed to the natural process of cell lysis after death. But are you sure it was Zakariya Uzair who bought the vial of potassium and not your father?" the detective asked Zain.

"A hundred percent sure. Why?"

There were whispers in the background before Junaid Bhai spoke again. "It's odd that Zakariya had anything to do with the potassium vials, since we don't have much evidence of the two having a criminal partnership. Or really any relationship at all until you married Sanam."

They might not have had evidence in Pakistan, but from what Zain had observed, his father and Zakariya seemed like the best of friends. That might have been a subjective observation, but he had an objective one too.

"You need to dig deeper for more evidence, then," he told the police men, "because Abu has been sending money to US colleges and then immediately getting refunds for it."

"And where does the money go?" the detective asked.

"Into a US account. I don't know in whose name it is, but I know for sure that Zakariya Uzair is aware of it."

Another moment of hushed whispers passed, and then the inspector spoke again, "That is new information. We'll officially ask the US authorities to look into possible money laundering through these colleges."

In the brief pause that followed, I brought up the plan I had already discussed with Junaid Bhai.

"The police think your father is involved in trafficking drugs," I told Zain.

He wasn't surprised. "So?"

"So, with him under so much scrutiny by law enforcement, he would need to find new ways to get the drugs and the money out of the country. I am happy to provide my services—"

Zain laughed so hard that the phone seemed to have tumbled to the ground. For a moment, all I could see were his bare, ugly feet. When he picked it up, he was still laughing like the fool he was.

"That wasn't a joke," I muttered.

"We're serious," Junaid Bhai's deep voice backed me up.

Still, Zain's chest shook slightly as he made a show of wiping his eyes, pretending to catch his breath before asking, "What makes you think he'd ever trust you to carry out his dirty work? You've spent all your life hating him."

"That's where you come in, idiot. You've always dreamt of being a criminal like your father. In fact, you've learnt the art of manipulation from him. And just like he used Sanam and me to get what he wanted, you're going to use us to get back into business with your father."

"You're the idiot," Zain retorted.

Junaid Bhai shook his head, trying to keep us on track. "Quit the name-calling, boys. Act like men."

"Sorry," my cousin muttered. "But I *hate* my father."

"You can act pretty well," I pointed out.

Another cocky smile appeared on his face. "Look at that—the great Osman Tariq praising me."

The guy had always known how to get under my skin. Back in school, I ignored him because I'd been taught to stay out of trouble. I wasn't a schoolboy anymore. And I'd learned that the path to justice was paved with the good kind of trouble.

Ignoring Junaid Bhai, who sat back and sighed, I raised my voice just enough for Zain's smile to disappear. "Listen to me carefully. I didn't reach out to you for fun, nor is this forgiveness for what you did to Sanam. This is an opportunity for you to do something right for once in your sorry excuse for a life. So, you either get your effing act together and take it, or I walk away, and you keep wallowing in misery and hatred."

He stared straight at me through the phone for a long, silent moment. The Zain I knew in school would have gone on an expletive-laced rant. But he, it seemed, was no longer the schoolboy I once knew.

"How am I supposed to use you?" he finally asked, without a hint of ridicule.

Detective Iqbal didn't waste any time in laying out the plan.

"Asif still thinks that you and Sanam are married. He also knows that Osman would do anything for her. So, you pretend to strike a deal with Osman—Sanam's freedom in exchange for his help in using the healthcare system to do what Dean Nadir used to do for him, and more."

We went over the details. He grumbled about some parts but was surprisingly useful in figuring out others. An hour later, Junaid Bhai and the detective had hung up.

I was about to end the call too when Zain called out.

"Hey, Osman, can I ask you something?"

"Sure," I replied. I couldn't ever have anticipated his question.

"When Sanam left you, why didn't you burn down the world?"

I could have reminded him that she didn't leave me, she was snatched away. But there was something about his hushed voice that made me give a completely different answer—the one he was probably looking for.

"I love her. But I don't own her. If she left of her own free will, burning the world wouldn't have bought her back. It would only have proven she was right to leave."

He nodded slowly and ended the call.

CHAPTER 56

L-word

ZAIN

Two weeks after I had spoken to Osman, I had to swallow my pride and visit Boston one last time—to give Sanam the finalized copies of our divorce papers and then catch the only flight to Pakistan available at such a short notice.

The city held so many memories for me, all of which made my heart sink when I thought about them. A reminder of how vastly different my life was now from the first time I had landed here. Doe-eyed, a lover boy, with dreams of making a life for myself and the girl I was going to spend the rest of my days with.

That girl was gone, mostly because of me. A fact that I had accepted now.

But that was nowhere as painful as what had come after.

What is done is done, I told myself as I waited outside the Children's Hospital of Boston for Sanam.

To distract myself from the elixir my brain was craving, I dialed Myla's number. I needed a favor from her anyway.

"I left the keys to my apartment under the doormat. The lease will be up next month. Can you turn them in for me, please?"

"You're giving up your apartment? Why?" Myla's high-pitched voice came over the phone as I walked to a secluded corner near the hospital's back entrance.

"There is nothing left for me in Houston. But do me a favor and keep this to yourself till I tell you. I haven't officially resigned from ZakU."

"You won't come back to Houston at all?"

"No, I am sorry I couldn't say a proper goodbye."

That was probably the only regret I had about leaving Houston. Myla and her friendship—or whatever you call the relationship you develop with your ex-mother-in-law who is only a decade older than you—was something I would never forget. That woman had become the big sister I never had or thought I needed.

"That's okay," she replied in a soft, dejected voice, very unlike her. It reminded me of the one other time she had let her sunshine-and-rainbows façade slip.

"Myla, if you ever want to tell me the truth about your past or feel the need to do something about it, you know how to get a hold of me, right?"

She didn't protest this time. She simply said, "I know," and hung up.

I took a deep breath, telling myself it was time to focus solely on the future. Perhaps letting the past stay buried was the only way forward for someone as broken as I was. I might have even believed that, if a woman's voice hadn't suddenly broken through my thoughts, startling me.

"How many lives are you going to destroy? Maham, Sanam, now this Myla person? Who is next?"

I swung around to see a woman in scrubs, hair pulled back in a ponytail, striking gray eyes that I instantly remembered. Because they still held the same defiance in them as the first time I had met her, outside the men's locker room at her medical college.

"You smoke in hidden corners now?" I noted, glancing down at what she was holding in her hand.

She scowled. "You're one to speak. Hostage taker. Homewrecker. Wife abandoner. Alcoholic."

"*Recovering* alcoholic," I pointed out reflexively.

Footsteps interrupted us, and an angry voice made the woman pale in the face.

"*Dr. Ameerah Sheikh*, what do you think you're doing hiding behind the building and smoking," the man's voice boomed.

Panicked, her eyes wide, she started to say, "Uh, Dr. Qureshi, I . . ."

I reached out and took the cigarette from her. "It's actually mine, doc. She found me smoking here despite the 'No Smoking' sign and took it away from me."

The woman's gaze burned into my side as the doctor redirected his anger at me. "Then you should be ashamed of yourself. Smoking near a children's hospital! Get rid of it and don't ever let me see you with that thing again." He scowled as he watched me stamp on the cigarette butt. Satisfied, he left the two of us standing there alone.

"What the hell did you do that for?" the Dr. Sheikh woman hissed.

"Trying to make up for pulling your hair. Something told me a 'sorry' wouldn't have been enough," I retorted.

"*Nothing* is enough to make up for what you've done to so many of us."

"I know," I sighed. What could I do? Even she, a relative stranger, who I only knew because she had been there when I had let my anger dictate my actions, knew how badly I had messed up my life.

She pursed her lips. "What are you doing here?"

"None of your business," I told her and started to walk away.

She followed. "Are you here to apologize to Osman? Because let me tell you, you owe that man two full years of his life."

I stopped in my tracks and swung around. "I didn't ask you to tell me anything, okay? So be quiet."

Walking away from that highly irritating woman once more, I thought I was done with the conversation, but like a freaking mosquito buzzing in my ear, she started following me again.

"Are you here to meet Sanam?"

"None of your business."

"She's right there, if you wanted to."

For a second time, I stopped in my tracks. This time, my gaze locked onto the woman who sat at a bench outside the main entrance of the hospital, wearing a puffer jacket as she rubbed her hands together and brought them up to her lips. I might have gathered the courage to approach her, if another figure in scrubs hadn't shown up first.

She glanced up at him; he handed her a cup of coffee. She gave him a grateful smile. He lingered for a moment before disappearing back into the building.

As long as I live, I will always be there for you. His words echoed in my mind. It was surreal to watch them play out in front of me.

"He's always had everything in life."

I didn't realize the jealous voice from within me had spoken out loud until the woman next to me asked, "How can you say that? You're the one who grew up as a billionaire's son."

The burst of clarity that had hit me stayed. "He's had everything that matters," I replied and averted my gaze from the woman sipping her coffee.

But no matter where I looked, or even closed my eyes, that image was back in my mind; the last time I had seen her.

It was supposed to be my one shot at redemption, at the happy ending I always searched for. So, there I was, standing at the front reception desk of the hospital with a bouquet of red roses for my wife in one hand and a bag full of gifts in the other.

"Where is the child psychology department?" I asked one of the two people at the entrance desk and gave him Sanam's full name. The man

was looking something up on his computer when the older woman next to him, with her arm in a sling, called out to someone behind me.

"Good morning, Doctor."

"Good morning, Mrs. Andrew," a man replied.

I froze.

It was a voice from my past. A little gruffer, but unmistakably him.

"Which one is he?" the man asked the woman as footsteps rushed away from us

"Foreign kid. Can't remember his name," the woman replied with a chuckle. "But he's been raised right. He stopped at the entrance the other day when he saw me struggle and helped me carry my bags all the way back to the office."

I wasn't listening to them anymore, nor was I reaching for the visitor's badge the man was handing me. My attention was fixed on the figure hurrying down the hall, raking his fingers through that familiar mop of dark hair.

"Wh-who is that?" I stammered.

"A brand-new pediatric intern."

I did make it to the psychology department, despite the raging battle within me. I even made it to the office where the interns sat and took in the vision in front of me without showing any emotion at all.

My beautiful wife.

My saving grace.

My second chance.

The woman I hoped to one day have a family with.

"Zain?" The voice I had been dying to have a real conversation with and beg for forgiveness, spoke through the storm engulfing me.

"You brought me flowers?" she asked.

It was just a question, though. There was no relief in her eyes, no happiness on her face. A simple transaction of facts.

I could see it then. The moment she would lay eyes on my cousin—the man who was raised right—if she hadn't already, and her heart would flutter with the emotions she held so dearly only for him. It would be a moment that was the exact opposite of the one I was living through right now. With both of them in the same city, in the same hospital, perhaps even caring for the same patients, how could I ever stop that moment from happening?

I stood rooted at the entrance of the office, ignoring my own thoughts. A step forward would have been a step too close to her.

"I need to ask you something, Sanam."

"What?"

"Could you ever love me the way you've loved Osman?"

She stilled, staring at me, her expression going from baffled to defiant, then bitter. "No, Zain! You forced me to marry you, broke my wrist, and then emotionally abused me. You even came close to sexually abusing me. I wake up with nightmares on a regular basis and jump at the sound of something crashing. I am an utter mess because of you. In which world do you think I could ever fall in love with you?"

I had been right. My prayers that she would forgive me weren't going to be answered. My only option now was to choose differently, or else history would repeat itself. And I couldn't let that happen. I said my next words quickly, before I could stop myself and change my mind, or go down the regretful path I had gone before.

"I am so sorry, Sanam. For everything." My voice wavered.

"Apologies are not what I need from you."

"Then I'll give you a divorce," I blurted out.

Her eyes brimmed with rage again. "Then what? You'll run to your father and ask him to carry out every threat he's ever made?"

"Osman . . ." I tried to explain.

But she was having none of it. "I am not having an affair with him, so leave him out of this. This is about you being the selfish, self-centered coward that you have always been."

She had hated me at the core of her being, even if she remained civil. Perhaps I should have been thankful for that. I kept quiet and obliged when she asked me to leave and never show her my face again. I didn't think I could face her anyway.

I could only pray that his path would cross hers quickly, so that she got what she deserved—his unconditional love.

"Holy smokes, you were in love with her," the woman who hadn't moved exclaimed. "Like, Sanam has *two* men completely crazy over her, and then there is me." She chuckled. "Man, my kismet sucks."

"I am not in love with anyone. I don't believe in that crap," I shot at her.

She squinted her eyes at me. "Then you would have eventually fallen for her." Her gaze drifted back to the woman drinking coffee. "You did the right thing, though. With the way those two love each other, ain't nothing coming in their way. I know, I tried."

There was a reluctant acceptance in her voice when she said that last sentence, but it was quickly replaced by a smirk that lit up her face as she slapped a hand on my shoulder, her gray eyes boring into mine like my soul had already divulged all its secrets.

"You didn't abandon your wife; you got out of her way. I take that part back. But you're still an idiot."

Who the hell does she think she is? I couldn't believe I was still standing here with her, and on top of that, she had the audacity to use that *L*-word in front of me.

"I have to go." I stepped around her.

She was faster. "Don't you want to finish what you came here to do?"

"No." I took out the khaki envelope from my bag and handed it to her. "Since you like playing desi aunty so much, why don't you go and give this to her? I have a flight to catch to Pakistan. And tell Osman to make sure he doesn't miss his own flight next week."

She took the envelope and said she would be dropping my cousin off at the airport, but when I tried to leave, she was standing like a brick wall in front of me again. This time, her voice lowered. "Recovering alcoholic, huh? How many days sober have you been?"

"262. Can I leave now?" I asked, not that it mattered to her.

"Planning to start drinking again? Divorce can be rough," she said, as if I didn't know that already. Though something told me that this insane woman wouldn't let me go unless I gave her the answer she wanted.

"No, Doc—"

"Call me, Ameerah," she interjected.

"No, *Ameerah*. Alcoholics don't *plan* to drink. It just happens. But I've figured out my triggers and learnt to deal with them. How about you worry about your own smoking habits and let me be?"

"Hey, don't judge me." She frowned. "I had a tough adolescence."

Suddenly, she held her hand out. "Let's make a deal. You never take another drink, and I never smoke again."

Why I gave in and shook her hand, I had no idea. Perhaps her relentless energy was the distraction I needed to fight my cravings, or there was something about her that felt oddly comforting on that cold October day.

Whatever it was, it convinced me to stand there a few minutes longer and ask, "Osman mentioned an international patient referral program between the Boston and Karachi hospitals for peds cardiology patients. Have patients really been brought over here through that service?"

"A couple came for heart surgeries last month. But it costs a lot of money, and transporting those sick children is not easy. Why?"

"Just curious," I said casually, admitting to myself that Osman's plan to gain my father's trust might actually work.

Before I left, I noticed something about the woman that made me pause.

"You have black, silky hair now."

It was maroon the last time I had seen her.

"And you look like you have got a mop dipped in charcoal for hair. What's your point?"

Cackling, she walked away, leaving me alone to push a dream back where it belonged—in the part of my life reserved for things that would never come true.

CHAPTER 57

King's Castle

OSMAN

The morning after I landed in Karachi, Zain and I were in a meeting with the men spearheading the investigation against Asif Ghazanfar. Detective Iqbal launched into a summary of what they had so far.

Asif had been charged with money laundering; however, he had secured pre-arrest bail and was essentially a free man at home. Basaam Sadiq, one of the men willing to testify against Asif, was dead. Shafiq Irfan, a man who would do anything for money—whether selling designer drugs or committing murder—was currently in custody. Akbar Jafri, the only man linking all three, had been killed by Asif after a failed assassination attempt on my nephews and Nael.

"Basaam's drug cartel was dismantled once he was arrested, but Asif had done business with him, so he must have been aware of the smuggling routes, clients, officers willing to be bribed, and so on," Junaid Bhai said.

Zain had been listening with his head bowed when he asked, "Is my father's drug business a reincarnation of Basaam's cartel from two decades ago?"

"Partially," the detective answered. "He's obviously added new routes, brought in designer products, and built a new clientele of the country's elite."

For weeks, a select team of highly trusted officers from the Karachi Police and the federal ANF had been meticulously combing through records from Basaam's time in the business, alongside current surveillance footage and social media activity of the city's influencers known to live life on the edge. What once seemed like unrelated events was starting to reveal clear patterns.

A certain car showing up at the port when the same port authority guard was on duty.

Raves happening at Shafiq's farmhouses and property owned by GT Enterprise soon after consignments of particular goods arrived at the airport.

Yet all of it was circumstantial evidence at best.

"Like money laundering, the most sophisticated drug cartels evade prosecution by using complex networks of intermediaries and front organizations to obscure the trail between the drugs' origin and their final destination, making it nearly impossible to get to the cartel leadership," Junaid Bhai explained.

"Unless the family of the cartel's leader is on your side." I glanced at my cousin, reluctantly accepting how prominent his role was about to be, as long as he didn't mess it up.

"Are you both all set then?" Detective Iqbal asked.

Zain nodded. "I am."

"Me too," I added.

ZAIN

Osman was right about one thing—I could be a darn good actor. Today, it wouldn't just be a hobby, but a weapon. Every lie he fed me, every string he pulled, had taught me exactly how to play my part. And now, I'd use the role he'd written for me to bring him down.

Game face on, I walked into the study my father had been spending a lot of time in lately. The TV was on, the smell of cigar smoke choked the air, and papers littered his desk. But he sat on the leather chair with a spine of steel, as usual, his black-dyed hair gelled back, wearing one of his signature tailored Armani suits.

This was not a man who was prepared to lose. He had all his bases covered. Yet, he had overlooked a measly detail.

A son he had been using as a puppet.

"Hello, Abu." My voice was surprisingly cool and collected. Battle-hardened, one could say.

"What do you want?" he muttered without looking up from the file in front of him.

"Your blessing to run GT Enterprises' businesses."

His head snapped up as his gaze locked onto mine. "*You're* going to run *my* business?" he scoffed.

"I mean, you clearly can't. You know, with the FIU breathing down your neck and all."

"Get lost," he waved me away. "You're a drunkard in *therapy*. You're useless to me."

I didn't get lost. Instead, I walked further into the room and took a seat across from him.

"Therapy, being drunk . . ." I smiled slowly. "It was all a ruse, Abu. An excuse for the authorities to overlook me. Unlike you, I was able to tell that GT Enterprise was going to go down soon, and all its associates investigated."

He tipped his head. "You're lying."

"I am not. You kept thinking that Zaviyar Uzair would stay away from you as long as you kept his niece a hostage, because she was his weakness. But his weakness is, and will always be, his own reputation. When that lawyer challenged him openly, I knew he would cave. And he did."

My father stared at me; I kept my smile on.

"You're not an alcoholic?"

"*No*. It simply gave me the perfect cover," I lied, but he wouldn't know the extent of what I had gone through. He had never bothered to check on me. All he knew was what Zakariya Uzair had told him, which wasn't much at all, since he and I hadn't even spoken after our spat in his office.

Piercing eyes gazed at me. "Cover for what?"

"Every one of your associates was investigated. Even Ami was questioned. Guess who has never been questioned about your finances or even suspected of being involved?"

It took a while for him to say it, but eventually, he did.

"You," my father said quietly, with a tinge of reverence. He was seeing what I wanted him to see.

A way out.

"Exactly. As far as the police know, I am innocent. So, let me take over your business."

The cogwheels in his brain were starting to move, but trust was still lacking. I showed him a clearer mirage.

"I know of a much easier and safer way to send both the drugs and the money abroad."

He drew a sharp breath and looked away. "I don't know what you're talking about."

"Oh, Abu," I said, leaning toward the table. "You think I don't know where all the drugs at those epic parties you threw came from? Or that you used Sanam's and my universities to launder drug money into the U.S.?"

For a moment, I worried that he wasn't going to buy it, as I had never questioned those drugs before. Nor had I ever brought up his involvement in money laundering. But the thought of returning to a life steeped in fame and power was tempting beyond doubt.

Curiosity had gotten the better of him, even as he looked at me suspiciously. "You're my family. They're keeping an eye on all of us, even if they haven't found anything on you yet."

"Then we'll use the part of your family no one will ever suspect."

I ignored his questioning gaze and rose from the seat, heading toward the door. In the hallway outside stood Osman, holding a khaki envelope and pacing like he was about to take an exam he hadn't studied for.

"Relax, will you? My father can literally smell fear," I told him, keeping my voice low.

"I am not afraid," came the hushed reply.

"You're sweating like a pig."

"It's hot outside."

"It's almost December."

Osman scowled. "Be quiet and stick with the plan."

Despite his glistening face, I gestured for him to follow me. Abu nearly jumped out of his seat when he saw Osman.

"What the hell is he doing here?" His voice bellowed across the room.

I half expected Osman to whimper and run away. But he didn't. He squared his shoulders and met my father's unflinching gaze.

"Assalamu Alaikum, Phuppa. I'm here to make a deal," he replied, his voice impressively calm.

Abu's fury redirected to me. "Is this a fucking joke to you?" he asked, picking up his phone.

Before my father could call his guards to get Osman thrown out, I interjected. "Not a joke at all, Abu. This is called preying on a man's weakness to turn him into a puppet, just like *you* taught me to."

His hand stilled. I answered his unasked question.

"My dear cousin *wants* a woman he can't have, and his *weakness* is his honest reputation, which I fully intend to exploit. He's agreed to do what

Dean Nadir did for you in exchange for me divorcing that pathetic, useless woman who can't even get pregnant."

Osman opened his mouth for a split second, before drawing in a sharp breath and shutting it again. It was almost fun watching him control his anger at the words I used for his beloved. But my father's silence had me focusing on him again.

I knew what he was thinking. The world would have to be nearing its end before Osman and I worked together. But the thing was, my father's world, as he knew it, was coming to an end.

Slowly, he turned towards Osman. "Why would you want to ruin your reputation, forget everything your sister taught you, and live the life of a criminal for a woman who can't even give you a child?"

"I love her," Osman replied.

His voice was so full of raw conviction that it was all he needed to say. If words could change a destiny, the three he said while standing tall in front of my father would be it. Even Abu accepted them without question.

He put his phone away and sat back down. "Alright, Mr. Osman, let's hear your brilliant plan to save my daughter-in-law from my son."

It was funny how my father, the master manipulator, hadn't been able to see through the lies I'd told him about Sanam and me. As I watched Osman pull a set of printouts from the khaki envelope he was holding, I realized why—it hadn't even occurred to him that I might have a conscience that was still alive.

I took out my phone and watched my cousin put on the most important show of his life.

"Karachi Medical Center has set up a program with Children's Hospital of Boston through which sick children needing heart surgeries are sent abroad," Osman explained and pointed to the names on the list in front of my father. "These are real patients who will need real accounts in the US into which large sums of money will be deposited, often by philanthropic organizations to help them with these surgeries."

He stepped back and met my father's gaze. "I can open a fake philanthropic account and use that to send money abroad."

My father laughed loudly and shoved the papers away. "You are a bloody orphan. No one will believe—"

"I am the rightful heir of GT Enterprise."

There he was again, leaving my father at a loss for words, without raising his voice by even a decibel.

He's a good actor, I thought to myself at first. But then I understood where his confidence came from—he was yet to utter a lie. I scoffed internally. Isn't it funny how easily truth can decimate a lifetime built on lies?

Taking a cue from my father's silence, Osman went on. "FIU has reassured me that once their investigation is complete and the company's debts are paid, the remaining assets, including this house, will be returned to me and my sisters."

Abu was on his feet again, leaning across his desk as he glared at his nephew. "You wouldn't dare—"

"I would, actually—dare. Unless you make a deal with me and tell your son to let go of Sanam."

That was my cue. I stepped towards my father, placing a hand on his shoulder. "I don't mind taking the deal, Abu. Haven't you always said that one should keep your friends close, but your enemies closer?"

I might not be speaking the truth, but I was a good actor.

"Besides, Sanam is an awful fuck. She just lies there—"

Osman's fist connected with my jaw.

I stumbled back.

He pinned me to the wall.

Fire blazed in his eyes, his breath heaving like a man on the verge of losing control. When he spoke, it was a low, threatening rumble.

"Don't ever talk about her like that again. Understood?"

He was not acting.

I licked the blood from my busted lip while Abu yanked him back.

"Get the hell out of here before I call my men to throw you out."

"Fine." He straightened up. "But remember this, *Phuppa*. I will make sure Sanam is free of this wretched life you two have imprisoned her in, even if I have to give up my life for it."

He stormed out of the room, slamming the door shut behind him. Abu paced the room in silence, occasionally rubbing his temples. The cogwheels were turning again, analyzing every situation in fifty different ways. I knew him well enough to not disturb him.

There was only one conclusion he could reach anyway. His troubles ran far deeper than he would ever admit, and the risk of him losing his entire illegal empire was very real—even without Osman's threats.

"What made you think of using Osman?" he eventually asked me.

"I read a news article about the cardiology program, and it mentioned Osman's name because of some research he'd done."

Abu's eyes narrowed. "Since when do you read the news?"

"It was in the Boston Herald. I never canceled my subscription after Maham. . ." my voice trailed off. It was a deliberate act, yet a lump grew in my throat anyway.

Had I ever loved Maham the way Osman loves Sanam? I wondered.

Shaking my head, I got back in character, gritted my teeth and looked at my father.

"I will never forget what he did to me, Abu. He thinks he is so innocent and honest. Imagine him leading the life of a criminal. Poetic justice at its finest, I'd say."

My father nodded, and trust in me—I could tell—was slowly developing. When he resumed his silent pacing, I walked out of the room.

To the inspector and his team, who were listening through the device in my pocket, it may have seemed like a failed mission. But I knew better.

Even my father's silence was deliberate—a calculated move that gave him time to carefully examine the records Osman had presented and convince himself that my plan was worthy of his trust.

Three days later, he asked me to meet him in his study. The cigar smoke, the Armani suit, his piercing gaze—nothing had changed, except for his voice. It no longer cut through me like before.

"I think we have more than $500,000 lying at the stash house, with no way to move it because FIU is everywhere."

The stash house? The inspector would be delighted to hear that word. But he would have to wait a bit longer.

Smirking, I pointed at one of the patient records. "Luckily, Afreen Nisar has . . . patent ductus art-something." I silently cursed Osman for using the most difficult medical terms he could possibly find.

But it didn't matter to my father. A hint of a smile, a single pat on my hand, his head nodding with acceptance—the plan was working.

I knew it. I bet Inspector Junaid, listening in on our conversation, could sense it too.

"No one will ever suspect anything if we use a fake philanthropy in Osman's name to send money for the surgeries of sick children. We can keep the warehouse functional, and the income from it hidden," my father admitted.

A subtle smile appeared on his face when he said, "It's kind of brilliant."

"I am your son, Abu. Of course my plan will be brilliant." I grinned, more at myself than anything. Victory was indeed sweet, and I was almost there. I just needed to feed the fire of his ego a bit more.

"I am sorry that I haven't appreciated your genius till now. No other man could have risen from a humble background and run such an extensive operation for so many years."

Walking around the table, I knelt in front of him. "Take me under your wing, Abu. Make me like yourself. I promise, I will not disappoint you."

He chuckled at being called a genius. I was sure of it. *Such an egotistical bastard.*

"You better not disappoint me," he replied, his voice mellow like it had never been before. "Just make sure that you can keep Osman under control, even after you divorce that stupid girl."

"Don't worry about that. I learnt from the best," I told him and pulled out my phone. "I made a video of his conversation with you. He's literally begging you to help him commit a crime. We can use this to force him to become a drug mule for us too. With all his hospital charity work, he'll be going back and forth with sick children several times a year. And if anything goes sideways, I'll release it to the police."

My father's smile widened. "Good. I've taught you well."

Turns out, I had figured out his weakness too: he, himself, and his name.

My father wasn't a fool, he still hadn't confessed that he actually ran a drug cartel. Yet, his ego was proving to be exactly what I needed to cloud his judgement.

A little more patience, and I was certain the untouchable Asif Ghazanfar would be completely outsmarted by a couple of twenty-four-year-olds.

A week later, the first installment of funds from the 'stash house' had been successfully transferred to an account under Osman's supposed philanthropy that he had set up before coming to Karachi. And I was pretending to go through with divorcing my ex-wife.

That should have put my father at ease. Instead, he had been awake since the crack of dawn, and his phone had been ringing almost nonstop. He still didn't trust me enough to let me in on what Inspector Junaid suspected was happening: a major shipment of drugs was to be moved, given that a particular port authority guard was scheduled for the night shift again, and a new cargo ship was about to dock.

But he was comfortable enough with me now that he didn't stop his conversation when I entered his study to offer him a cup of morning chai.

"I will be there tonight at exactly ten. If you're even a minute late, your dead body will go home," he said.

What is happening at ten? I wondered, but didn't ask him yet. Instead, I was going to try something else—manipulate the bastard like he had manipulated me.

"Abu, if you have to be somewhere at ten, should I ask Bua to serve dinner at eight?" I asked him innocently.

"Fine," he replied, and waved me away.

I smiled as I left the room.

Abu deserved his last meal as a free man to be the one he loved most: koftas, made by Bua.

"Where is your mother?" Abu asked as we sat down for dinner.

"She is sleeping," I lied. Detective Iqbal had already sneaked her away to keep her safe.

"What else can you expect from a useless woman like her?" he scoffed.

Oh, you have no idea, murderous monster.

"Exactly." I joined him in ridiculing my mother while he ate one, two, three, and then four koftas. With gravy dripping off his fingers, he devoured one naan after another, washing it down with beer. Not once did he suspect what was in those koftas: a very strong laxative.

Not even when he was clutching his stomach and running to the bathroom, the first, second, third, and then fourth time in the span of half an hour. Or when he suddenly became so weak and dehydrated, he could barely stand up.

"The meat must have been bad," I told him as I helped him to the bed and felt his forehead, which was damp and cool. I was about to call the doctor when he stopped me.

"No, don't call anyone. I have to go for a very important business deal."

It was time to turn on my charm and get a confession.

"Is this about your drug business?" I asked calmly.

When he didn't answer, I pushed a bit more. "I am sure you have an impressively large business, anything else would be beneath you. Can't you find someone else to go?"

A subtle smile tugged at his dry lips. "Someday, I'll tell you about it. But today, I need to handle this myself."

"No way, Abu. I can't let you go." I placed my palm gently on his cheek, giving him the tender look that I used to wish he would give me.

"I am your son. Trust me, *today*. Let me go in your place."

"But . . ." he started to protest.

"How long will you keep working yourself into the ground, Abu? This is your time to relax and pass the baton to me. I'm no longer the naïve teenager who once lived in this house. I promise—I won't let you down."

I had never considered myself to be a good actor. But in that moment, I swear, even Shah Rukh Khan was nothing compared to me.

Abu took a long, hard look at me. My inner disgust at him stayed hidden deep inside as I held his gaze and kept that look of absolute adoration on my face, until he finally conceded. And I took a deep breath.

"Fine. We're shipping out fifty kilograms of Ecstasy and a hundred of Rohypnol tonight. The idiots at the warehouse always mess up the shipment, and I am sure they are also stealing from me. You'll have to oversee it all."

I nodded; he kept talking. "It's an old, abandoned house along the Super Highway. When you enter it, it will look empty, but go to the kitchen, open the walk-in pantry, and you'll see a broken shelf. Remove that, and behind it, you'll see a keypad. The code is 83728. That will open the door to the basement, where we operate from."

Detective Iqbal had mentioned that house before. It was where the envelope Shafiq had taken from Mustafa Tariq's car had been mailed to.

Unfortunately, it seemed the police had missed the entrance to the basement the first time around.

"Wow, that does sound like a huge operation." I gave him my best doe-eyed expression. "How many men are there?"

He gave a feeble smile. "It is huge. Twenty people in the house alone, five chemists who manufacture the drugs, ten who move them to other dealers, and twenty who are heavily armed and stand guard. Then there are all our dealers spread across the country."

I put an arm around his shoulders and helped him lie back in bed. "I think we've talked enough. You should rest, and I will take care of the shipment tonight."

After calling the doctor, I gave him some water, like any good son would do for a father. Except that Inspector Junaid and Detective Iqbal had heard every word my father had uttered. And while I was pulling the blanket over my father and making him comfortable in bed for the last time in a *long* time, the ANF and the Karachi Police, with backup from the Karachi Rangers, were already on their way to the stash house.

"I am glad you came home. I am so proud of who you've become—a real man," my father said, when I was about to leave.

There was a time when I had been desperate for those words. But today, as I looked at him, I could clearly see through the smokescreen he had always enveloped me in.

It had taken me a long, arduous road to realize that real men don't use and abuse others at their own whim. They listen to their conscience instead of the devil.

So yeah, Abu should be proud because I had finally become a real man.

One who had just brought down the king's castle.

Osman came up with the idea, my inner voice was back.

How I hated my conscience sometimes.

It's Done

KIRAN

I'd had a restless night; I wasn't even sure why. Maybe it was the frustration of being so close to nabbing Asif Ghazanfar. Or the fact that my future, in so many ways, depended on this investigation being over.

After saying my morning prayers, even though it was only 5 a.m., I decided to turn on the TV, hoping to catch a random drama's rerun. Instead, I nearly dropped my chai when the news channel came on.

"Breaking News," a reporter announced, as a video of a police raid ran in the background.

"Asif Ghazanfar, the former business tycoon, already entangled in a money laundering case, has been caught running a massive drug cartel. The operation against the smugglers was led by Inspector Junaid Razzak just before midnight."

The camera went live to the scene, and my heart nearly stopped when I caught a glimpse of Junaid swamped by members of the press. With streaks of mud on his face, glazed eyes, and obvious blood on his left arm, he looked like he had been engaged in battle himself.

"It was a tough operation, but it is now complete," he said in front of the cameras, but there was something about his voice that worried me.

"I can confirm that three criminals are dead and the rest have been arrested. I can also confirm that we have arrested their mastermind, Asif Ghazanfar, at his home. Unfortunately, two of our brave young officers were injured and have been rushed to the hospital."

Every reporter started talking at the same time, but Junaid held his hand up. "I will let Detective Iqbal take over; I have to go somewhere."

He left, and the detective came on the screen. The camera panned back to the TV reporter. "I believe the inspector is headed to the hospital. We have eyewitness reports that he was shot while trying to rescue one of his injured men . . ."

He was shot?

I couldn't listen to the rest of the report—all I wanted to do was reach out to him, to quell my desperate need to know that he was okay.

This couldn't be happening again. Another man in my life, who I deeply cared about, shot again because of Asif Ghazanfar. Even if my Phuppa and his legacy disappeared forever, the damage he had done to us would last for a long, long time.

"Please, please pick up," I whispered into the phone, while frantically dialing Junaid's number. No one answered.

I went back to the TV; the detective was still fielding questions from the press. I switched channels, hoping to get a word about the injured policemen. I scoured social media for any live updates.

Nothing.

So I did the only thing I could. With my heart racing in panic and a sinking feeling in the pit of my stomach, I prayed. Like I had prayed for my brother, my sisters, and my sons. All the people I loved and cherished.

I prayed for Junaid.

Please let him be okay, I pleaded with Him, tears streaming down my cheeks.

The bell rang as soon as I finished. Wiping my face, I ran, stumbling on my way, sure that it was one of my sisters, who had heard the same news as I had.

Instead, there he stood. In his uniform, disheveled like I had never seen him before—a blood-soaked arm held stiffly at his side, deep grazes on the other, and scrapes on his face that still carried mud stains.

"Junaid . . ."

"Will you marry me?" he blurted out.

I gaped at him, barely managing to say, "What?"

I wasn't sure if my voice was caught because of what I saw or what he said, but nothing seemed to faze him.

He took a step closer and reached out to hold my hand, leaving only a few inches between us. His chest still heaved from running up the stairs, but it was his eyes that held me hostage. Dark, enigmatic, brimming with raw emotion. They were an amalgamation of angst, hope, a burning ache, and—

Love.

A boundless pool of pure devotion.

I saw it. I felt it. In the way his eyes desperately searched mine, and in the way his hand tightly gripped mine. Like he was afraid of letting me go.

"Marry me, Kiran," he said, his voice a hoarse plea. "It's done. The police operation, putting Asif Ghazanfar behind bars, the threat to our families—it's all over. I don't have to wait anymore. I can't wait anymore."

But the blood trickling down his arm, the report of him getting shot, and the panic that I had felt just a few moments ago were far more distracting. I tore my gaze away from him and looked at the bloody flesh on his bicep, barely covered by the torn and tattered shirt.

"What is wrong with you? You're bleeding. Go to the hospital, for God's sake."

"Look at me." His fingers, resting on my cheek, leaving a trail of searing heat, forced me to turn away from his injury.

"It's only a bullet graze," he said gently. "I'll be fine. But I need you to answer my question."

"I-I . . ." I couldn't find the words.

It wasn't like I hadn't thought about it since the stadium. I had . . . every day. But there were so many things to consider: my sons, their school, our finances, their future.

His hand dropped to his side, dejection clouding his eyes, breaking my heart. He was too good of a man for me to hesitate. I knew that. And if I were alone, I wouldn't have. But I wasn't.

Before everything else, I was a mother.

"I am forty-one years old, Junaid. I have two sons. I just . . ."

I stopped talking as his shoulders slumped and he looked away, raking his fingers through his hair, then running his palm over his sorrowful face.

"I just . . ." I started to explain myself again when his gaze shifted to the room behind me. The prayer mat on the floor. The TV on silent but still running headlines on the deadly midnight raid and a rerun of his press conference. Then he looked back at me.

He took in the scarf wrapped around my head, the prayer beads in my hand, the tearstains on my cheeks. His lips parted and a look of confusion skimmed across his face.

"Were you praying for me?"

Jumbled thoughts came out as mumbled words. "You weren't picking up and—and they said you were shot, and I thought you were hurt."

In complete contrast to the tears brimming in my eyes again, a cocky smile slowly spread across his face. He started laughing, like the kind of belly laugh where he had to hold his side, annoying me.

"Why in the world are you laughing?" I quickly wiped my tears and frowned.

"I am laughing at myself." Mirth had replaced trepidation in his dark brown eyes. "I was so afraid that you would reject me. But clearly, you want exactly what I want."

"And how do you know that?"

"I have flirted with you. I have told you exactly how I feel about you. I have proposed to you. And instead of saying, 'How could you even think about me like that?' you prayed for me and made excuses like *I am forty-one and I have two sons.*" He gave me a lopsided grin and narrowed the distance between us.

"I pray for you too every day. I am forty-five and have one son. You know we are perfect for each other. So think about what is really holding you back," he whispered, "because it's not your lack of feelings for me, Mrs. Kiran."

Mrs. A title I hadn't held for over a decade, but which made my skin tingle when he said it. His words held so much conviction, like our union was inevitable, written in the stars as much as it was in our hearts.

For a silent moment, he held my gaze again before his lips curved into a smile. With his eyes oozing of flirtatious humor, like usual, he backed away.

"I should go to the hospital before this wound gets infected. Your silence has answered my question anyway. When you find your voice, give me a call, and I'll come . . ."

". . . with the *baraat.*" He winked. (Groom's wedding party)

My mouth dropped open, but he had already disappeared down the stairs as quickly as he had appeared, leaving me stunned, speechless, breathless.

What just happened?

A voice answered, *he read you like an open book, silly.*

And he sure knew how to read me.

I went through the rest of that day with my heartbeat repeating every syllable he had muttered. My heart, it seemed, had already decided—like he had said it had. What other option did I have anyway? If you've felt someone's intense longing, their love that consumes you wholly and unapologetically, been a part of their daily prayers, you'd have to be a fool to say no to them.

My heart knew it, my soul knew it, my mind accepted it. The man was one big green flag waving itself in my face.

There was only one thing left to do. In the days to come, I debated on how to broach the subject with my twins, when one weekend morning, I was woken up by impatient knocking at the door.

The rest, as they say, became history—and the beginning of our future.

CHAPTER 59

Closure

ZAIN

It was surreal coming to the police station to record my statement about everything that had happened in the last few days. From flying back to Pakistan to getting Abu to reveal his illegal drug business, and then watching the defiant hatred in his eyes as he was arrested in front of me, life had been anything but ordinary.

The shark lawyer Abu had hired tried to get him out of jail while awaiting trial, but the evidence against him was so overwhelming, there was nothing he could do.

My phone started pinging as I walked out of Detective Iqbal's office.

Unknown: Heard about the stunt you pulled off. Like OMG!!!

Unknown: Are you good? Do you have someone to talk to?

Me: Who is this?

Unknown: Your worst nightmare! Haha.

Unknown: Your evil subconscious!

Pranksters. I shook my head and put my phone away as I exited the building. But it buzzed again a few seconds later.

Unknown: Okay, okay. Don't ignore me. It's Ameerah. Your voice of reason!

Ameerah? The crazy woman I met in Boston?

Me: How did you get my number and what do you want?

Ameerah: Your ex-wife gave it to me, and I just wanted to remind you of our deal. If you need to blow off steam, go to the gym. Call up an old friend or scream into an empty room. Don't drink. Please. It's not worth it.

I stood outside the building, reading that text. The last few days had been stressful for sure, but I had managed to steer clear of alcohol. Yet, the plea in that text was odd. I read it again. It was unexpected, and unnecessary, from a woman I barely knew.

Though . . . not unwanted? a voice within me asked.

I was forced to ignore that inner voice when it was drowned out by another that called out my name. A voice I recognized instantly. It was the melody my heart had once sung to, until it had left me to wallow in my own misery and become a slave to my demons.

"Maham? Wh-what are you doing here?" I stuttered.

"I was here to record my statement for the Asif Ghazanfar case."

Nothing made sense until she explained that she was the journalist who had gone undercover to prove Shafiq's involvement with selling drugs. A possessiveness I had always felt took over.

"What were you thinking, Maham? Do you know how dangerous things could have gotten?"

"Don't worry, my fiancé was sitting in the car, anxiously waiting for me." She smiled slightly.

Fiancé? The word landed like a punch to the gut. After all this time, knowing how badly I had messed up, it still hit me hard.

She had moved on, built a life, while I was still stuck at square one. Alone, lost, and haunted by the shadows of this thing called love that wasn't in my destiny.

I forced a smile, masking the ache clawing at my chest. "That's . . . great. I'm happy for you. Sorry for how badly I behaved."

The words tasted bitter, but what else could I say? This was the closure I was looking for.

She shrugged and sighed. "Sometimes you have to hit rock bottom before finding your way back up."

As she turned to leave, I couldn't hold back the question that had been gnawing at me. "Was any of it real?"

She paused, her gaze meeting mine. "All of it was, Zain. But you chose not to see the parts where you were hurting me."

Her words cut deep, because I remembered those parts all too clearly. Vivid snapshots of moments where I had failed her, where I had made excuses for my behavior until there were none left, and then resorted to outright coercion.

Her phone rang and she told whoever was on the line to come pick her up. She offered to introduce me to her fiancé, but I made an excuse. Facing my failures wasn't something I was strong enough to do yet.

All I had in me was to follow the suggestions made by a persistent woman who lived on the other side of the world—punish my body in the gym and scream into empty rooms. There were plenty of those now, fitting reminders of the hollowness I couldn't escape.

I replied to that woman first.

Me: Stop bothering me. Don't you have lives to save or something?

Ameerah: I am saving yours, aren't I?

I scoffed and put my phone away. What would she know about saving a lowlife like me? Nothing at all.

CHAPTER 60

The Sons

KIRAN

Two weekends after Junaid's proposal, having considered every possible scenario, I had vowed to discuss the matter with my sons. But my carefully curated plans unraveled early in the morning while I was still in bed.

"Mama, Mama, Mama!" One of my twins began impatiently knocking on my door.

I opened it, blurry-eyed and ready to give them a piece of my mind, when I realized that the boys had a guest over.

"Nael? Is everything okay?"

The three boys looked at each other awkwardly. Daniyal seemed annoyed, Danish was shuffling his feet, and poor Nael stood there blushing, looking like he regretted his life's choices.

"Uh . . . Nael wanted to talk to you," Danish finally said.

"No, no. Aunty, it was Danish's idea," Nael said, stepping back.

Daniyal huffed and stepped into my room, glaring at the other two. "Ugh, fine. I'll speak. You two are so useless."

He turned towards me. "Mama, we heard that Junaid Uncle proposed to you, and we wanted to know what your decision is?"

He said it so casually that, for a moment, I thought he was talking about his football schedule. But as his words registered, my jaw nearly dropped in disbelief.

"Who told you about that?"

The twins pointed at a crimson-faced Nael, who was trying his best to hide behind the door.

"Uh, Abu just told me," he replied in a small voice. "But he didn't tell me not to tell these guys. So, I kind of mentioned it to them, and now they are fighting."

My heart sank. "Fighting about what?" I asked, assuming the worst, wondering if they would hate me forever for bringing another man and his son into their lives.

But that wasn't it.

Daniyal stuck his tongue out at his brother. "Nael said they have three extra rooms in their house, and we could each take one and leave one for guests. But I want to take the bigger one because of all my sports stuff. Danish has *books*."

Danish shoved his brother. "My books take up more space than your stupid gear."

Eyes wide, I was trying to comprehend what was happening, when Nael interjected, "Guys, one of you can take my room. I'll take the smaller one. I don't mind."

"Time-out, please."

I stepped into a conversation that was light-years ahead of where I was. "Junaid did propose, but I haven't said yes yet."

All three boys glanced at me simultaneously.

"Why not?" Daniyal asked.

"Yeah, you're both old but not *that* old, and you get along well, so what's the problem?" Danish followed with a straight face.

"Abu already said yes," Nael offered helpfully.

Daniyal slapped his shoulder. "Dude, the person who proposes obviously says yes."

"Oh, right, right." Nael gave the twins a sheepish grin.

I wasn't sure whether to laugh or worry that things were so out of my control. Gone was the speech I had prepared for my sons to ease them into the idea of Junaid and me. Or the list of questions I had braced myself for.

No. All these boys were concerned about was which room they would get in their new home, and that I was happy.

"Say yes, Mama. You're always smiling when he's around," Danish urged, while his brother chuckled.

Nael broke out in a grin. "Abu sings old love songs all the time at home these days."

The three of them burst into laughter as I ushered them out of my room. Their voices trailed off down the hall, still laughing and plotting how to spend their day, while my heart swelled at how effortlessly their lives had intertwined.

My phone rang. I snatched it up eagerly, hoping it was the call I had been about to make myself. Instead, the screen displayed an unfamiliar number.

"Umm . . . hello. Kiran Api? Ms. Kiran? This is Zain." A hesitant voice came from the other side.

I hadn't spoken to him in a long time, and the last time I did was as his teacher. Though, as soon as he said her name, I understood why he was calling me, of all people.

"Could I talk to you about Sanam?"

CHAPTER 61

Surprise Visitor

SANAM

A month had passed since Asif Ghazanfar was arrested. Zain and I had announced our divorce soon after. Irreconcilable differences was the reason stated—such a tidy phrase for the relentless devastation that clung to me, even when the world of the man who had turned my life into a nightmare was supposed to have fallen apart.

That day, even the coffee shop resembled the chaos of my life.

The morning rush had hit hard, with the line snaking out the door and customers growing visibly impatient. Behind the counter, the espresso machine sputtered and hissed in protest, spilling milk everywhere as a barista frantically jabbed at the buttons. Another barista dropped a tray of porcelain mugs. The sound, sharp and violent, was too close, too familiar, sending my heart into a frenzy. This was not the time to have flashbacks of a vase breaking my wrist before shattering on the ground, but it happened anyway.

"Hey, lady. Are you going to take my order or what?" barked a man as I stood frozen at the cash counter.

"Y-yes. I am so sorry," I managed to stutter.

An order was called out, only to be claimed by the wrong customer. The rightful one approached, but the first refused to cede the drink in his hand. With short tempers and uncaffeinated brains, one thing led to another, and soon the two men were punching each other. No one budged, except for the female barista who went to break them apart. I tried to help, but was shoved by one of the customers.

Suddenly, I wasn't in the coffee shop anymore.

I was back in that apartment, my rear hitting the door instead of the wooden counter, his voice snarling in my ear instead of distant shouts. My hands clutched at nothing. My chest seized.

This isn't my apartment. This isn't my husband, I repeated to myself, yet my heart wouldn't stop racing. Still, with sweaty palms and shaky breaths, I pushed myself back to work. What other choice did I have?

"I need a break, please," I finally told the manager.

"Two minutes, Sanam. No more," he said, as more customers poured into the shop.

Wearing only the coffee shop uniform, I stepped out into the December cold, hoping the freezing winds would reset my soul. *I'll be fine*, I told myself. *It'll just take time.*

As a psychologist-in-training, I could diagnose myself, treat my own brain, but how long it would take—I had no idea.

"Sanam?" a voice called out.

Dressed in a heavy jacket with a woolen scarf wrapped around her head, I almost didn't recognize the woman walking towards me. Or perhaps I'd been a high school student a lifetime ago.

"Ms. Kiran? What are you doing here?"

"Visiting Osman," she said with a smile before her hazel eyes, much like her brother's, filled with concern. "Why are you out here without a jacket?"

"I was taking a quick break," I told her.

She wrapped her own scarf around my shoulders and asked, "Mind if we chat later this evening?"

How could I say no?

KIRAN

She profusely apologized for the state of her apartment when she invited me in, but all I could do was smile. The laundry was draped over a couple of chairs in the corner, books and papers scattered on the mattress, mismatched dishes in the kitchenette—it all reminded me of when I was young and struggling, but determined to stand on my own two feet.

"I've lived through worse, Sanam. Don't worry about me," I told her. "I won't be long, just wanted to see how you were doing."

Sighing, she glanced around. "Not good, as you can see, but . . ." She straightened her shoulders. "But I am managing."

I followed her gaze. "All I see is a courageous woman facing the challenges of life."

She gave a slight smile. "Thank you. That's really kind."

And then I saw it—what my brother had seen in her. She was a pretty woman, but her true beauty came from within. The quiet strength and grace she exuded, even now, as she sat down on the only other chair in that apartment. Defiant in the face of all she had been through.

It was mesmerizing.

"You're wearing my brother's jacket," I noted with amusement.

She immediately blushed. "Oh, he, uh, gave it to me a few weeks ago, and it's very comfortable."

It was a thin jacket, two sizes too big, and sure didn't look particularly comfortable or warm. It even had lint on it. But it had my brother's name embroidered on the chest, just above her heart. And that was probably all the comfort she needed.

So cute. I couldn't help chuckling.

She offered me chai, but I declined, because I was here for a very specific reason. "Who is your person, Sanam? The one you feel comfortable picking up the phone and talking to in the middle of the night, or when life gets too tough to handle on your own?"

Her lips parted, then she looked away. This was why Zain had called, whether to atone for his past or out of pity, I didn't ask.

When she didn't answer, I spoke again.

"Zain told me how his father used threats of physical violence and mind games against you. I know that feeling, because he did exactly the same to me when I was your age. I was forced to isolate myself and swallow my pain just to protect the people I loved so much. And I know what that does to your mind. There were so many nights where I would lay awake, unable to numb my mind, only to force myself to get up next morning and pretend that I was okay."

Her gaze dropped to the ground. I reached out to lift her chin. "I see the walls you've built around yourself . . . because I had built them too. They might keep out the despair and let you function, but they also shut out joy, comfort, and love. That's no way to go through life, Sanam."

"No one deserves to be dragged into my mess," she said softly.

Dismay was easy to see in her eyes, and I thought about that innocent teenager who used to sit in the front row in math class, looking at me wide-eyed and with a goofy smile on her face. To her, I represented the boy she was falling in love with.

That boy still loved her more than his own life, and she wasn't even aware of the depths of her love for him.

"Sweetheart, there are people who don't see another's mess. They only see a home in the person they love so dearly."

"I am not who I used to be in school," she said, and I knew she understood what I was trying to say.

"My brother has loved you against reason—even when the whole world told him he was a fool for not letting you go. I know he will love whatever version of you he finds, Sanam."

"What if I can't love him back? I feel so exhausted," she said, her voice barely above a whisper.

"I remember when I was living from day to day and constantly bracing myself for something to go wrong. You're right. It is absolutely exhausting. But I've also realized that love is not a constant. It ebbs and flows, and that's okay. It's trust that has to be constant between partners for any relationship to work. So you have to ask yourself how much you trust Osman."

She looked away into the distance. I had a feeling she already knew the answer to that question, and the only thing holding her back was the burden she carried, one that she was reluctant to share with my brother. Even though he, I knew, would embrace it with open arms and an infinitely loving heart.

"He kind of proposed to me," she said after a while, and her cheeks flushed.

"I know." I smiled.

"I said no, but . . ."

"He gets off work soon."

She only paused for a moment, and then it seemed that a whole palette of color had been infused in her black and white world. Jumping up, she grabbed her jacket and the two of us walked out together.

I made my way back to Osman's apartment.

She made her way back to him.

CHAPTER 62

Simple

OSMAN

I was still signing out my patients to the overnight team when I saw her message.

Sanam: Meet me at the Harborwalk near the Children's Museum when you get done.

She didn't say why, and I didn't ask. If a single moment with her was all she was willing to grant me, I would take it. No questions asked.

By the time I finished and reached the Boston Harborwalk, the sun had already set. The night sky was illuminated by a half-moon, and the city's lights danced across the harbor's water. It was a beautiful view from the bench where she sat.

Though nothing compared to the view I had of her—her hair cascading in waves past her shoulders, her skin glowing despite the dim light.

What made my heart flip was what she was wearing. Visible through her open puffer jacket was my fleece jacket. The collar was turned up to protect her from the cold, her hands hidden in its long sleeves.

When she looked up and spotted me, her lips curved into a smile. "Thank you for coming," she said softly.

"I could never say no."

We sat on the bench under the starlit sky in silence until she quietly asked, "Why didn't you ever give up on me?"

I shrugged. "I had faith in my prayers and trust in you."

She shook her head. "Osman, I wasn't yours for a long time. You could have moved on."

"How could I, when I was always yours?" I replied.

She sighed. "But we were so young when all this started."

That was true. We were young. Never in my wildest imagination had I thought that I would be sitting here next to a woman as alluring and graceful as her, who had once been just a girl with brown wavy hair, a kind heart, and a lollipop in her backpack.

"Do you know when I fell in love with you?" I asked. She shook her head again.

"Neither do I. From the moment I saw you in eighth grade, you have always been special to me. Like you were put on earth just for me. And you're right. It couldn't have been love back then; we were kids. We barely even spoke to each other. But sometimes, I wonder if my soul fell in love with yours when we were still in heaven. And every moment since has been a promise we kept to each other."

She closed her eyes.

"I don't know if I can ever love you in entirety the way you love me. I try to put on this brave face, but sometimes I feel so empty inside. I know I am supposed to move on and forget about what happened. But part of me never will. And maybe I will never feel whole."

"I'll wait, then. However long you—"

She didn't let me finish.

"But see, the thing is . . ." Her chest heaved. "I still want you so badly, it hurts."

Her lips quivered when she turned to face me. "You told me you dreamt of me. But I've thought about your words during the most painful moments of my life. I held on to our memories when everything around me was crashing and burning, because they were the only thing that gave me the space to breathe. I imagined that you were holding me when I was all alone, crying myself to sleep."

Moonlight shone off her tears before she wiped them away. "So, maybe I am being selfish. And maybe I'll never be able to love you the way you deserve to be loved, but—"

I knew where she was going with this. "Do you trust me?" I asked her.

Trust was the only thing that mattered. It was the unwavering, constant foundation on which our relationship had always stood, from mere classmates to lab partners and then lovers.

"With everything I have," she replied without hesitation.

I wasn't sure when I had moved closer to her, but somewhere between her spilling the raw emotions she hid so well under her calm exterior and the gut-wrenching pain in her eyes, I couldn't stop myself from closing the distance between us on that bench.

Or from tucking her hair behind her ears and saying, "Then trust that I have enough love in my heart for both of us."

Or from telling her, "Ask me what you came to ask?"

"Are you sure?" Her moist, caramel eyes searched mine. "There is no turning back."

"Turning back was never an option." I smiled and wiped away the remnants of her sorrow.

"Ask me, Sanam," I urged.

Her lips curved up; her cheeks glowed. A tender, irresistible smile spread across her face.

She said she couldn't love me enough, but at that moment, all I felt was her overpowering love—love that gave me strength and made me who I was. I had been a boy when I met her. I would be a man when I held her and fulfilled her every dream, wish, and desire.

I felt her love course through me with every heartbeat. And if this was only the beginning, just a small proportion of what she held in her heart, then God had made me the luckiest man in the heavens and the earth.

"Osman, will you marry me?" she asked softly, shyly.

I took her in my arms and whispered, "I already said yes when our souls met in heaven."

I had always loved her.

I will always love her.

Our story was that *simple*.

CHAPTER 63

Nuptials

KIRAN

Osman's wedding was like none I had planned before. Yet three months after I returned to Pakistan, I was getting ready to fulfill my brother's wishes, the only time he had openly asked me for something.

"Api, I have never asked you for anything big, and you know I am a simple man, but I am going to ask you for something today," he said hesitantly the night after I had met Sanam.

"Of course—anything," I told him.

"After what happened to her the last time, Sanam deserves her dream wedding. You know, pretty dresses, a nicely decorated venue, surrounded by her family and friends. I know that will be expensive, but I've saved up money."

Something told me that Osman was the only part of her dream wedding she really cared about, but I could never say no to my brother. So here we were, his three sisters, the two brothers-in-law, and an inspector whose status was still in limbo, all tasked with different duties for a wedding that needed to be grand enough for the prime minister's niece and a famous actress's daughter.

We couldn't afford to put on an extravaganza, so we went with exquisite elegance, where less was more. And YouTube videos, Pinterest boards, and online shopping saved our souls . . . and our pockets.

"Can someone explain to me why Junaid Bhai gets to roam the city in his air-conditioned car while we are out here doing manual labor? I could have gone to pick up the flower bouquets too, you know," Kaukab complained.

"Kiran loses her focus when he's around," Kauser laughed, as the two put the finishing touches on the centerpieces.

"And she can't be as scary either," Iftikhar muttered in all seriousness, making his wife giggle while he put up the dozens of fairy lights that I was hoping would give the outdoor venue the perfect magical glow in the night's darkness.

Hussain couldn't stay quiet either. "Guys, all I know is, we better save all these decorations. My prediction is that in a few days, we will need them again—in this very venue."

Junaid had pulled some strings to get this place, though I now regretted telling my family about his proposal. Not that I'd had a choice after I had come to a decision about our future, which, for now, had to be shoved to the back of my mind. Osman's wedding had taken up every waking moment since my return.

"Stop it," I chided them. "This is not the time to make jokes. Sanam and her family are coming from Islamabad this afternoon, and Osman lands in exactly one hour."

"Let me guess, one groom is going to pick up the other one from the airport," one of my sisters chuckled.

Trying to distance myself from the chaos, I stepped away from them. I couldn't allow myself to drown in the surge of emotions his name always stirred within me—not yet. But after tomorrow, when my big sister duties were fulfilled, I promised myself it would finally be my turn to choose happiness.

SANAM

We arrived at the wedding venue, a beautifully decorated space nestled within the manicured lawns of one of Karachi's prestigious social clubs. My mother had fussed that it wasn't a five-star hotel, but to me, this place looked enchanting. Even from the entrance, I could make out how the white and muted gold theme was perfectly harmonized in every detail. Fairy lights twinkled like stars, and paper lanterns cast a soft glow as the delicate fragrance of Arabian jasmine lingered in the air.

Simple, elegant, breathtaking.

A far cry from the drab mosque interiors where I'd once sat like a live corpse and signed papers the last time I was getting married. This was the kind of wedding I had always dreamt of, without the flashy nonsense my mother would have insisted on had I let her keep this event in Islamabad.

Standing there in my lehnga, adorned with jewelry and bridal makeup, it felt almost surreal—like I was on the brink of fulfilling a destiny written in the stars.

I noticed the beautiful woman in a timeless, elegant dark green chiffon saree walking towards me like the queen she was.

"Sanam, sweetheart, you look so gorgeous," she exclaimed. "I am a little afraid my brother will faint on the stage."

Chuckling, I hugged my sister-in-law. "Thank you, Kiran Api. You look absolutely stunning too."

She greeted my mother, who only gave her a half-smile and then complained, "Well, I suppose the place is . . . adequate. Not exactly my choice, but I guess it'll do for *your* kind of wedding."

Kiran Api ignored her, as did I. My mother's choices didn't matter anymore. All that did was Osman, and his wonderful family, which was excitedly waiting to make me theirs.

"Is Zavi Chachoo coming?" I asked my mother about the only living family member who had ever really cared about me.

"He said he'll be late, but he'll try his best to be here. He is flying out of the country tomorrow morning and is still in a meeting for that trip."

I had outright refused to invite my father but had secretly hoped Chachoo would attend. Still, I understood that for a prime minister, his niece's wedding might rank low on a list of pressing national priorities.

What I didn't realize was that neither his leadership position nor his busy schedule was the real reason for his absence. It was the groom and his family—tied to a secret I could never have imagined.

OSMAN

"Why are they taking so long to come in? Has something happened? I am going to go check." I would have walked off the stage had Kauser Baji not grabbed the sleeve of my cream sherwani.

"Stay put," she whispered loudly. "They'll come. It takes the girl's side some time to gather their group."

"Hurry up," I muttered, tapping my foot impatiently.

But the moment I saw her, time itself seemed to stop to capture that moment for infinity.

Clad in a traditional maroon and gold dress, a thin veil over the waves of brown tendrils cascading around her luminous face, she was absolute perfection. But it wasn't so much what she wore or how her makeup was done that had me under a spell. It was her infinite grace as she seemed to glide towards me, the sparkle in her eyes, and her plump lips molding into a breathtaking smile, all blending to give her a radiance that surpassed any spectacle I had ever witnessed in my life.

There was air around me, I knew, but somehow it had all escaped me in that moment. With my breath stuck in my throat, my heart wildly thudding in my chest, and before my sisters could stop me, I walked off the stage halfway down the aisle to meet her. To bring her closer to me quickly.

"You're not supposed to come all the way here. Wait near the stage like a normal groom. Everyone is laughing," her mother whispered harshly to me.

"Let him come," Sanam said, reaching out to clasp my hand.

I didn't hear the laughter that ensued, I just heard her delicate giggles that I breathed in, infusing my soul with their purity and joy. Maybe I had bucked tradition or should have waited by the stage and let her come to me, but nothing about this wedding was normal. Besides, I had already broken enough rules to get here.

"You look like a princess," I whispered to her.

Her hand clasped mine tighter. "And you, my handsome Prince Charming," she whispered back.

My cheeks burned. I grinned like a Cheshire cat. *She thought I was handsome.*

Glancing at her again as we walked down the aisle, I drank in her kohl-lined caramel brown eyes, the bronze-highlighted cheekbones, and the blush that accentuated her naturally pink complexion. She had always been the prettiest girl I had ever seen, but today, I could barely avert my eyes, when I should have been watching where I was going.

In the midst of me questioning how God's creation on earth could be so heavenly, I felt my foot hit something, and suddenly, instead of Sanam in my vision, there were carpeted steps and several hands reaching out to steady me as I stumbled forward.

"Kiddo, calm down." Kaukab Baji's mirthful laughter made me straighten up immediately.

"Don't worry, Sanam is used to it," Kauser Baji added, straightening out my sherwani. "He has a habit of falling hard around her."

My wife-to-be chuckled. "At least he didn't pull down all the lab apparatus this time."

Whispers of "So impatient" and "They're so cute" died down as she and I separated for the nikah ceremony, where we sat on chairs at opposite ends of the stage. The gathering fell silent, the weight of the moment heavy on all of us. None more than Sanam, who sat quietly, her head bowed, the humor of the last few minutes a distant memory.

The Imam asked her first.

"Do you accept Osman Tariq, son of Mustafa Tariq, as your husband?"

She looked up, her gaze landing on me, lips curving up slowly like she was savoring the moment.

"Qabool hai," she said in her honey-mellow voice, and I imagined the angels rejoicing at her words as much as I was in my heart. (I accept.)

The Imam asked me next.

"Do you accept Sanam Uzair, daughter of Zakariya Uzair, as your wife?"

The bitterness of the latter name was nothing compared to the sweetness of the former, and I didn't waste a second.

"Qabool hai." The words tumbled out before the mind could register them.

And just like that, it was done.

I heard voices congratulating me, felt hands patting me, but all I saw was my wife.

"Excuse me," I told whoever was speaking to me and walked over to her, drawn in by the way she took in a deep breath, her lips parting as her gaze shifted to me and held me captive.

The meters between us diminished, as did the years that passed. From eighth graders who first spoke over lollipops, to lab partners, to star-crossed lovers, and now husband and wife—our journey had been long, arduous, and so very painful.

But none of that mattered when I took her in my arms. The pain was worth it, the distance overcome and long forgotten.

Her body molded into mine so perfectly that it felt like we were two halves finally made whole.

"Don't ever leave me," she whispered, nuzzling her head into the crook of my neck and tightening her arms around my waist.

"Never. I promise," was all I said, and then everything stilled.

In silence, we had fallen in love, and in silence lay the beauty of our relationship. In silence, too, our hearts spoke to each other in a language only soulmates understood. In silence we stood now, reveling in the moment where our paths had finally become one.

How long I held her shuddering shoulders, or how long my tears dampened her veil, I had no idea. But eventually, she loosened her grip. I held on for a few seconds longer. Her soft hands wiped my tears, my rough ones wiped hers. She held my hand and led me to the main sofa at the center of the stage. I gripped hers tighter and followed her without hesitation.

From there on, we sat next to each other, mostly talking with others, sometimes with each other. There was a lot I needed to say to her yet, but this was not the place to say it nor think of it. For now, I simply took in the beauty of my surroundings, and that of my wife. My heart fluttered every time she squeezed my arm and introduced me to someone.

"This is Osman, my husband," she kept saying, each time with a radiant smile that washed our past into oblivion.

At first, I wondered at the redundancy of her statement: *who else could I be, sitting on the stage with her like this?* Then I realized that she, like me, still couldn't believe this wasn't a dream. And in verbal repetition lay reassurance that reality really was upon us.

A reality in which I was her husband, and she, my wife.

"Osman, look who's here," Kiran Api called out and I turned to see who she was pointing at.

"Mrs. Nazim!" I exclaimed and got up to hug her, like she was a long-lost aunt who had been a prime witness to our love story and not our biology teacher.

Then, I slid my hand into that of her former student and, with a smile that made my cheeks hurt, said, "This is Sanam, my wife."

KIRAN

This whole wedding might as well have been a comedy sitcom with an unrehearsed script and amateur actors. Much of it was due to the young couple on the stage, who obviously only had eyes for each other. From Sanam walking three feet ahead of the rest of her bridal entourage when they entered the wedding venue, to Osman rushing towards her the moment he saw her, him stumbling, and then their heartwarming embrace after the nikah, the two were in their own little world. And despite murmurings among the guests and displeasure shown by Sanam's mother, I decided to refrain from interfering.

After all, it was the young couple's moment, and they could do whatever they wanted. Who was I to insist on maintaining a protocol?

All in all, from where I stood alone in the corner, it was obvious to me that the event had gone as smoothly as possible. But before I could pat myself on the back, I heard a rustle of clothes beside me and the baritone voice that had always made my heartbeat skip.

"I know you had to dress up for your brother's wedding, lekin aap ko mere naazuk dil ka hi kuch khayaal rakh lena chahiye tha." (You should have thought about my fragile heart at least.)

Always so dramatic.

I stifled a laugh and gave him a side-eye. "If you have a heart problem, go see a doctor. Why are you standing here?"

He chuckled. "The doctor will tell me to avoid stress. But what to do when the person who gives me the most stress also brings me the most peace?" He turned to face me. "Quite the dilemma, isn't it?"

Shaking my head in amusement, I wondered how this man was able to regurgitate cheesy cinematic dialogues with such ease. Whereas, I hadn't even been able to gather the courage and words to say a simple "I accept your proposal" to him.

What's stopping you now? I knew my sisters would ask tomorrow.

But when I looked around at all those whose care had been entrusted to me—my sons who were chatting with Nael, my sisters who sat with their own families, and my brother who had never looked happier—I wondered, *what was stopping me right now?*

My duties were fulfilled, and he, looking dapper in his black sherwani, was standing inches away from me.

Say it now, my mind told my shy heart. For once, I didn't ignore it.

I took a deep breath and began, my voice almost a whisper. "Junaid, you asked me a question—"

"About the bouquets? Yes, I saw your message. You wanted white ones, not the peach ones," he replied.

Taken aback, I said, "Uh . . . no, not the bouquets."

"Oh, then about the catering order? Yes, Iftikhar told me, and I agree, chicken is better than fish."

"What? No, that's not it." I frowned.

Why couldn't he understand what I was saying? I might have kept staring at him in confusion if not for the way the corners of his lips turned up.

He thinks my discomfort is a joke. I huffed.

"You know what, forget about it." Scowling, I started to walk away.

Only a couple of feet later, he grabbed my wrist, pulling me back and making me swirl around until I almost collided with his chest. He let go quickly, and I stepped back, but not fast enough to miss the mirth in his deep brown eyes turn into a dangerous whirlpool of passion, pulling me under. Neither did it escape my notice the way his full lips moved as his voice dipped.

"You mean the question where I asked you to marry me because I am desperately in love with you?"

He's in love. That thought was overwhelming. Yet the magnetic pull he had on me refused to let me move or react. I could only stutter an incoherent reply.

"Yes . . . uh, yes. Th-that one."

His smile was back, but this time it was gentle and endearing. "What about it?"

"Nothing. You're so annoying," I replied, trying my best to sound irritated, but instead ending up giggling.

His smile widened, then disappeared altogether as he straightened, like he was a soldier standing at attention. "Permission to annoy you for the rest of your life as your husband, ma'am?"

"You're also a fool." I couldn't help shaking my head at his antics. But like always, neither could I stop myself from letting out that mirthful laugh in his presence or playing along with his theatrics. I straightened up myself, like I was his senior officer.

"Permission granted, Inspector." I smiled, probably the widest I had ever done in my life.

We stood in silence for a moment, letting our words sink in, and when he spoke again, I knew the exact reason I had always been drawn to him.

"My favorite sound in the world is your laughter, Kiran," he said softly. "I promise to keep making you laugh, even if it means repeatedly making a fool of myself."

The man had no ego when it came to me. And for that alone, I was willing to trust him with my heart, my soul, and the future of my family.

CHAPTER 64

Wedding Night

SANAM

When we reached our room that night, his arms wrapped around me, and I was back to letting myself drown in his comfort and warmth. I breathed in his addictive scent, and I felt every muscle in my body relax. If he hadn't been holding me, I might have collapsed from the sheer exhaustion of holding myself together, just for this moment—when I could let go of everything, because I had him to hold it instead.

"I've been meaning to say something to you," he whispered.

I pulled back. "Say it."

He guided me to the bed, and we sat together on its edge, his hands gently clasping mine. I might have worried about what he had to say, but the tenderness in his eyes and the earnestness in his voice had a way of soothing every unease.

He began softly. "There has never been a doubt in my mind that we were meant to be together, but I would be a fool not to recognize that you weren't entirely ready for marriage right now."

I shook my head anxiously. "Osman, our marriage is not a mistake."

His thumb caressed my cheek. "That's not what I am saying, Sanam. What I am saying is that we've been through hell and back, but now that we have this bond ordained by God Himself, nothing can keep us apart. So, we can slow down."

A gentle smile spread across his face. "You've barely had time to deal with your divorce and everything that led up to it. Whatever you need, whenever you need it, I will always be here for you. But we don't have to rush anything, if you don't want to."

I breathed out, the tension that had been weighing on me since we entered the room easing off my shoulders. *How could someone be this understanding and selfless?* I wondered, still gazing at him.

This was our wedding night, and for the past so many nights, I had stayed up, willing myself to be ready to give him what he deserved from his wife: all of me, even if the nightmares continued to haunt me. I had thought I could convince myself that I had moved on. But the wounds on my conscience were too deep, the scars left by my past not visible to anyone, yet felt by me in every moment.

"But you have rights over me," I blurted out, as if he might have forgotten that very line I had been taunted with in the past.

Instead, he smiled and moved closer, took me in his arms again, and whispered, "With rights come responsibilities, Sanam. And your comfort and consent will always be my responsibility."

A moment later, he got up from the bed and retrieved a gift bag from his closet. "By the way, I found the perfect wedding present for you," he said excitedly.

The bag held a pajama set—light pink in color, with heart-shaped red lollipops printed on it.

"You first spoke to me over a lollipop, and I thought this might remind you of how far we've come since that morning," he said quietly, blushing slightly.

"Gosh, Osman, this is the best gift I have ever gotten in my life—other than the clay heart, of course," I exclaimed. Wrapping my arms around his neck, I planted a kiss on his cheek, making him blush harder, and my heart fluttered at how adorable this man was.

"I don't care what you say. You. Are. Perfect," I declared.

That night, I lay in bed next to my husband, wearing a soft cotton pajama suit. In the silent comfort of the night's darkness, there was one thing I was absolutely sure of: as much as I loved and adored Osman, tonight I respected him even more. Maybe the difference between my past and present was him. His unconditional support, him understanding my unsaid needs, his mere presence in my life. He was the balm I needed for the wounds life had inflicted on me.

CHAPTER 65

Second Plaintiff

ZAIN

I had lost count of the number of cases that had been opened against my father. However, the one I was most interested in was Kauser's. From the call I had received a week ago, it seemed that another plaintiff was joining her case too—a woman who was seventeen when she accused my father of drugging her at a party she attended at our house. I could never have guessed who that woman was.

"Maham?" I called out in surprise when I entered Yusra's office.

Bile rose at the back of my throat. "What are you doing here?" I asked.

Yusra confirmed it. "Maham is the second plaintiff."

She narrated her side of the story, and I felt like throwing up. My ex-fiancée, the woman my father knew I was in love with, had been drugged by him, right in my own house.

I could kill that man with my bare hands right now.

"Zain, can you corroborate Maham's story?" Yusra asked.

Of course I could. I remembered that day like it had happened yesterday. I had told Maham that I loved her at the poolside, but my father called us inside a few minutes later and sent me away to check up on my mother.

I thought that was an odd request, as he had never really cared for his wife. But I was on a high after being told by my girlfriend that she loved me too. So I did as I was told, happily singing a tune in my head as I checked on my mother, who was fast asleep. When I came back, Maham, a cup of lemonade in hand, was about to follow my father into his study.

"Yes, I absolutely can. I remember everything."

"Good, then let's go over some questions that Asif's lawyer might ask," Yusra said and went to grab some papers.

I stayed still, unable to wrap my head around all the ways I had failed a woman I had claimed to have loved so deeply. "I was so fucking blind to my father," I muttered through clenched teeth.

Maham placed a hand on my shoulder. "He is a conniving man, Zain. Don't blame yourself for everything."

"Okay, let's start," Yusra interrupted, forcing me to put my rage aside for the moment.

The first few questions she asked weren't hard. I essentially repeated everything I remembered, including how Maham had been so sleepy by the time we had reached her grandparents' house, I'd had to help her up to her room. In retrospect, I should have realized how odd that sequence of events was. But call it stupidity on my part or plain innocence, I thought she'd had a really long day.

"You were her boyfriend, Zain. How can the court be sure that it wasn't you who drugged her with the intention of assaulting her?" Yusra asked.

"If that was my intention, why would I take her back to her grandparents' house?" I replied.

"So you're saying you've never purchased Rohypnol, also called roofies, or any other drug for the purpose of incapacitating someone else?"

That's when I paused. The guilt on my face must have been obvious, because Maham immediately asked, "Zain, what the hell did you do?"

"I . . . uh . . ." I couldn't even utter the words.

"Zain, if you can't answer that question, I can't put you on the witness stand," Yusra pointed out.

"But I remember everything about the night Maham was drugged, and I never did anything to her. I swear," I repeated.

"Except that you've bought Rohypnol before and used it on someone?"

"It was given to me by my father." I choked on my own words.

Visions of my father handing me a package with crushed pills in it and explaining how to use it flooded my memory. As did the moments I had dissolved it in fruit punch and handed it to my unsuspecting classmate, twice, at a party in Houston. The scandalous video made in the aftermath had proof of it all. And a copy of it was in my father's possession.

Suddenly, the disgust I was feeling towards him consumed my own soul too. The time that I had let anger dictate my actions had come back to haunt me. Just like my father had probably intended it to. Even when he was in jail, the man was using me as a pawn to get away with his crimes.

"I've only used it once, and it was in the US. My father wanted me to assault Sanam and force her to accept our marriage. But I couldn't go through with it," I tried to explain.

Yusra shook her head. "If we put you on the witness stand, your father's lawyer will use this to discredit you . . . or worse."

"What's worse?" I asked her, though I already knew the answer.

"They will ask you if you've ever used the drug yourself. If you say no and your father has evidence to the contrary, they'll show it, and you'll be in contempt of court, which is a crime. If you say yes, you'll be admitting to a crime too. Since you used it on Sanam in the US, perhaps you'll get away with it, because it's not under the jurisdiction of a Pakistani court. But it still compromises you as a witness."

I dared to glance at Maham. The revulsion on her face and the hatred in her eyes hurt more than it should have, yet it merely mirrored what I felt myself.

"Either way, I can't put you on the witness stand for this case," Yusra was saying when I made a decision.

For everyone else, that was the end of the conversation. But for me, it was only the beginning.

"Yes, you can. Put me on. Let me corroborate Maham's story, and then show the video of my father helping me drug Sanam, to show what he is capable of. I'll tell the truth, and I don't care what happens to me afterwards."

Maham was facing me now, but whatever she thought of me wasn't important. What mattered was that I made sure my father paid for each and every sin he had committed. I was done being his pawn.

CHAPTER 66

Say My Name

SANAM

Though it had only been a couple of days since our wedding, it already felt like I had been part of this family forever. Tonight, we had been invited to meet Junaid Bhai's family, now that he and Kiran Api were officially engaged.

Dinner was a success. The food was delicious, the company exquisite, the conversation hilarious. It was obvious that Kiran Api fit right into her new family, as if she had known them her whole life.

With that happy chaos behind us, I now stood alone in our bedroom window, enjoying the night sky. A vast palette of black that stretched until the earth met the sky, only interrupted by twinkling stars, so minute from where I stood, yet fiery balls of gas and mass in reality. Large enough to engulf you from nearby, they seemed harmless and beautiful from a distance.

Distance, both in time and space: perhaps that is what was needed to turn ugly memories into bearable ones. That, and losing myself in a man whose love was as vast as the night sky, and as intense as the starlight that touched me despite being galaxies away.

Soft footsteps walked up behind me.

"Absolutely breathtaking," I heard my husband say.

I smiled at him, snuggling in close. "It is, isn't it? I've always loved nights like these."

But instead of putting his arm around me, he turned me to face him and gently tucked my hair away. "I wasn't talking about the night," he whispered.

The tenderness in his gaze melted everything else around us. His fingers caressed my cheek, a feather-like touch, barely there—yet enough to ignite my skin in its wake when he leaned forward and his hushed voice grazed the shell of my ear.

"*You* are breathtaking, Sanam."

There it was again, my name.

Spoken like he alone possessed the right to say it. To breathe it. To embrace it. Like it consumed his soul the way he consumed mine.

"Phir se pukaro mera naam." The words escaped before I could even think about them. (Say my name again.)

It wasn't boldness that overtook me; it was a burning desire—a fire lit in the embers of my heart that I didn't want to suppress anymore.

I didn't have to. I could give in and allow myself to drown in him.

He paused, but then he understood, losing himself in the untold stories of my eyes, under the starlit sky.

His lips molded, breathing out my name again. "Sanam."

Serenity filled my heart; peace overtook my mind. I was where I was supposed to be.

Home.

I was home.

He was my home.

One more time, my heart begged, and my voice obliged.

"Phir se pukaro mera naam."

My arms wrapped around him, drawing him closer. His hands slid up my waist, and every muscle shuddered, but he held me tight. I held on tighter—my body flush against his.

His scent was the only air I could breathe, his warmth the only sensation I could feel.

"*Sanam.*"

It was barely a whisper against my lips this time, yet he said so much in that moment. From narrating the tale of aching desires and the painful years traversed, to silently asking permission to do what we both knew we yearned to do.

I closed the distance between us, letting the unbelievable smoothness of his lips and the incredible minty taste of his mouth silence my past.

Nothing mattered then, except me and him.

Our breaths tangling, our hearts beating in sync—only for each other.

His lips caressed mine, slowly and delicately at first, like he was savoring a dream, afraid it wasn't real. Then more deeply and intensely, his lips claimed mine, sucking out the air between us, leaving us breathless and our chests heaving in tandem.

It was unscripted, unrehearsed. But it was utter perfection. In its fervor lay the heat and passion of lovers who had long been denied their destiny, yet in its tenderness was the respect he gave to me, and I to him.

Our lips pulled apart, but we didn't. He held me close, and I let him, reveling in the safety of his arms and comfort of his chest, as I buried myself in him.

"I love you, Sanam," he whispered, his lips resting on my temple. "I love you so damn much, I wish I knew how to put it into words."

Glancing at him, I took in the depth of emotion his hazel eyes held. "You don't have to say it, Osman. I can feel it in every moment I spend with you."

That's when I decided to tell him everything about my past. I needed to let it out so it would cease devouring me from the inside. I had to tell him so I could feel whole again and love him freely, with all my heart and all my soul. Just the way he deserved to be loved.

"Remember when I said I trusted you with everything I had?"

"Of course."

"I think I have PTSD from everything that has happened to me over the last two years."

We were awake that whole night. I talked, and he listened, so attentively and without judgment, that I found myself unloading everything I had been holding in, from waking up in my dorm room, half-naked, dazed and confused, to the physical violence before Zain was arrested for DUI.

Never had I felt so light as I did by next morning, though I couldn't disagree with Osman when he gently suggested, "I think you should seek professional help."

When I finally went to sleep, I thought Osman had too.

OSMAN

Sleep was the furthest thing from my mind. Seething with anger, I waited until she was sound asleep before storming out of the apartment.

"Osman? Everything okay?" Phuppo asked when she opened her front door.

"No, it's not. Where is Zain?"

She pointed upstairs. Sprinting up, I flung open the bedroom doors until I found him, sleeping comfortably in his bed, while my wife tossed and turned with nightmares.

"Get up." I yanked the blanket off. "How dare you put your hands on her!" I yelled.

He immediately sat up. "Osman . . ." but couldn't finish his sentence. I wasn't a violent man, but in that instant, I couldn't hold back. Sanam's words echoed in my mind, fueling the punches landing on his face until he tumbled back.

Perhaps I should have been surprised that he never fought back or questioned why I was there, but I didn't care. Rage burned like an inferno, scorching my senses.

"For a moment, I thought you were worth the air you breathe," I spat in his face.

"I am not worth anything," he replied.

There was something in his voice that made me pause. His lip was busted, his shirt torn, but he sat still.

What was that? Regret? I refused to believe it. Scum like him never regretted assaulting a woman—like father, like son.

Yet, that is where I was wrong.

"Why'd you stop?" His voice cracked. "Finish me."

"I would, but like I've said before, I am not a monster like you." I glared at him.

"I am so sorry, Osman," he whispered, but that didn't stop me from placing a call.

"Junaid Bhai," I said as soon as he picked up. "Zain drugged Sanam and physically assaulted her when they were in Houston. I need you to open a police case against him."

There was a brief silence on the other end before my soon-to-be brother-in-law spoke. "Osman, this isn't within my jurisdiction. Sanam will have to file a complaint with the Houston police."

Last night, she had made it clear that she wanted to move forward, just as Kauser Baji had once resigned herself to do. And now, it seemed certain that my wife's abuser would walk away unpunished, just as my sister's had for so many years.

Yet, when I looked at Zain again—his bloodied face buried in his hands, his shoulders slumped, whispering apologies for everything—I wondered if he was truly getting off unscathed.

CHAPTER 67

Leverage

ZAIN

My face still throbbed with pain as a man in a police uniform gestured towards a small, dingy room in Karachi's central jail.

I wasn't here for myself; I had been beckoned by my father through his lawyer. For what, I had no idea. I was sure my father only saw me as his sworn enemy now. But a small part of me was curious enough that I had found myself answering his call.

The sound of footsteps made me look up. For a moment, I forgot I was in a prison, looking at a prisoner. My father's clothes looked pristine: black pants with a collared white shirt, minus his usual coat or tie, his hair neatly brushed and his chin cleanly shaven. A smug smile graced his face.

"You look . . . good?" I said, and it wasn't a question as much as a state-ment of confusion.

"And you look like shit."

He laughed and took a chair opposite me as the policeman who had brought him in closed the door behind him, leaving the two of us alone. "Did you think your betrayal would make me a guilty man forced to live like a measly pauper? Think again. I am nothing but a guest here."

"You are guilty of running a drug business, murder, theft, bribery and abduction."

"All lies. There is no evidence."

I looked at him, aghast. "What do you mean? I got you on tape admitting to everything."

He scoffed. "Where is that tape?"

"The prosecuting lawyer . . . has it?" I said slowly, starting to realize what my father was implying.

"The *government's* lawyer has it."

My heart sank as I realized the exact reason behind his calmness. He knew the people in the government, specifically the man who held the highest civil office in the land: Zaviyar Uzair.

"You have no relation to the prime minister anymore. I divorced his niece a long time ago, and she's married to Osman now. There is no way you can blackmail him."

He slowly shook his head. "You will always be stupid, Zain. Did you really think I would bank on my drunk, flaky son for leverage against the people in power? You have no idea who I am. I know things about Zak that would bring him to his knees, and with him, his brother's entire pious façade will collapse. Zavi has no choice but to drop his government's cases against me."

I gulped. My father was a shrewd and cruel man, and Zaviyar was never the angel he pretended to be. If my father said he had dirt on him and his brother, I knew he had enough to get himself exonerated by whatever trick he was going to play.

And I understood, too, why he had called me here.

There was *one* case that had not been brought against him by the government, but by his own niece and my former fiancée. Neither of whom he could control or who could ever be bought. And I was to be a witness in that case.

"I need you to say that you never saw me talking to Maham that night," he said.

I gritted my teeth, unable to hold in the anger boiling within. "And why would I do that when you were the devil that destroyed us? For all I care, you can go to hell."

The amusement on his face disappeared. He slammed his hand on the table and leaned towards me, until his face was mere inches from mine.

"You keep forgetting something, son. Those who feast on the fruits of others' labor are always tainted themselves as well."

"What does that mean?" I stared at my father.

"If you combine all the assets in your name, you'd be a multi-millionaire."

That didn't make sense. The only asset in my name was the apartment in Boston, and that was not even close to a million dollars.

"What assets?" I asked.

He gave a smug smile. "The apartment on Thames, the condo in Dubai, the chalet in Switzerland, to name a few. All bought with drug money and hidden so that the FIU will never find them—unless, of course, I ask my lawyer to release their information."

"You're lying."

"I am not. You signed a file full of papers when you were eighteen, accepting all those properties."

"You're fucking lying. I don't remember . . ."

And then I remembered. It was the night my father had forced me to email a rejection letter to Maham's university. He'd handed me a beer, a pen, and a file. With a despondent heart and a numb mind, I had done as told.

Stunned, all I could do now was watch in silence as his smile widened. "See how easy it is for a hero to turn back into a villain."

There it was. My father making the same mistake again of underestimating me. I had nothing to lose and everything to gain by seeing him behind bars forever. My own soul was already damned.

I leaned in too, wanting him to look me in the eyes and see exactly who I was when I spoke: a son, the exact opposite of his father.

"Release whatever the hell you want to. I would rather die in jail than spend my life being a coward like you."

Suddenly, the amusement vanished from his face. "You ungrateful brat! Is this the way to talk to your father who gave up everything for you?" he yelled.

"What the fuck have you given up?"

"My soul—so that you would have what was rightfully yours."

I didn't have to ask him to elaborate. He launched into a family history lesson right away.

"That vile grandfather of yours, Mr. Masood, took everything from me. I worked day and night to build Tariq Enterprise when it was nothing but a one-room office. Yet, I was never good enough for his daughter."

Turns out, my mother's decision to follow her heart instead of my grandfather's wishes had angered him so much that he had disowned me before I was even born.

My father's voice lowered, like he was about to make a confession. "*If* I colluded with Zak or rejoiced at the deaths of your grandfather and uncle, it was solely to give you the life you deserved, Zain." His hand came to rest over mine. "I am not the villain, son. The real villain of your life is your grandfather. And he got the ending he deserved."

That day, as I looked into my father's eyes—eyes that held not an ounce of regret—I realized that he truly believed his actions were justified. He wasn't a man who was delusional. He was a man whose conscience was dead, with no hope of revival.

"Nice story," I told him and rose from my chair. "But just because Dada was a vile man doesn't mean you're any less of a criminal. So, I *will* testify against you."

The man's jaw ticked. "You wouldn't dare."

Pausing near the door, I turned to face him. "Watch me—tomorrow in court."

I reported my conversation to Inspector Junaid. The US authorities, he told me, had found some evidence of fund misappropriation in ZakU's financial records, but my former father-in-law had hired a lawyer and was refusing to cooperate.

"Even if they find evidence of money laundering, it's going to take forever to prosecute Zakariya," the inspector had said. Besides, neither of us were convinced that was the "thing" my father had been referring to.

Though I wondered if someone else might know. I called her as soon as I left the police station, hoping I could convince her to gather her courage this time.

"Myla?"

"Zain!" Her cheerful voice came through the phone. "How are you?"

This was so typically her. All rainbows and unicorns, all the time. Which was exactly how I knew she was hiding a dark and painful past.

"Myla, listen to me carefully. I know your husband worked with my father to do some very bad things. And I am willing to bet my life that you know exactly what he did, but you're afraid of telling the truth."

There was no sound at all for a while, and then she simply said my name. "Zain . . ."

There it was. That small, scared voice that always came out when I brought up Zakariya Uzair.

"My father is using his past dealings with Zak as leverage against his brother, the prime minister, and he is going to get exonerated from all his crimes. If you know something, please, I am begging you, go and tell the Houston police."

She remained silent again but did not hang up, and so I stayed too.

Finally, a minute later, she spoke in that same small voice again. "I'm afraid, Zain. He said he wouldn't hurt me if I behaved. But if I tell someone, he'll trap me again."

My heart broke for her. "Then don't let him trap you, Myla. You have the keys to my apartment. Go hide there. I'll tell you how to change the security code."

"Okay," she said after a pause.

I thanked her and was about to hang up when I heard her say, "I wonder if Abu still remembers me."

"What?" I asked, but she had already hung up.

CHAPTER 68

Trial

KIRAN

"How are you feeling?" I asked Kauser on the morning of the trial as we walked up the courthouse steps.

"Strangely, quite okay. There is nothing that man's lawyer can do to me that he himself and his supporters haven't done already."

Iftikhar put his arm around her shoulders. "I am so proud of you."

Kauser broke out into a smile and leaned into him, her head resting against his shoulder. With her in safe hands, I glanced around for Junaid. He was standing with Yusra, but as I approached them, a vaguely familiar man rushed past me.

"Sir, any updates about my daughter?" he asked Junaid.

"Not any more than what I've already told you, Mr. Faisal. But don't lose hope. We are doing everything we can to find Nosheen," Junaid said, placing a hand on his shoulder.

With fiery eyes, the man gritted his teeth. "Inspector Junaid, all hope was lost the day my brother was born. Had I known the monster he would become, I would have killed him that day with my own two hands."

"Don't worry. Asif Ghazanfar will get the punishment he deserves."

I hadn't really been paying attention to the conversation until that point. Plenty of people had come up to Junaid, pleading for help when he was out in public. But that name, Asif Ghazanfar, caught my attention, just as I seemed to have caught the attention of the haggard man speaking to Junaid.

He walked over quickly. "Kiran, you might not remember me, but I apologize for everything my brother has done to your family. I wish I had never recommended him to your Dada. I pray now that he gets the worse punishment in this world and the hereafter."

With that, he was gone before I could register what he had said.

"Who was that?" I asked Junaid.

"Faisal Ghazanfar. Asif's brother. Faisal was the eldest among their five siblings and was employed by Masood Tariq. Apparently, your grandfather greatly respected him. And when Asif graduated from college and couldn't find a job, your grandfather hired Asif as a favor to his favorite employee. You can guess what happened to Faisal after your Phuppo eloped with Asif."

"He has a missing daughter?" I asked Junaid as we followed my family into the courthouse.

"Yes, she disappeared when she was sixteen, almost two decades ago. He accused Asif back then too, but no evidence was found, and the case was closed. After hearing Kauser's press conference, Faisal came to me requesting us to reopen it. We did. We're following up on some leads we got yesterday, but that's all I can say for now."

I hope he finds his daughter, I silently prayed for the distraught father.

This was yet another reminder: every time you think life is unfair to you, there is someone else who has it worse.

For me, in the next two hours, that fact hit a little too close to home.

Ordinarily, this would have been a closed court session, given the sensitive nature of what was about to be presented as evidence. Yet Kauser and

Maham had both insisted against it. To them, the shame of what had happened wasn't theirs, so why should they be the ones hiding from the public?

"All rise," the judicial assistant said, as the buzz of reporters quieted and Justice Hamad Niaz, the judge presiding over the session, walked in. I had heard good things about him and hoped that today we would see a show of his famed integrity as well.

I sat up front with my family, behind the table where Yusra sat with Kauser and Maham. To the right was the table where Asif Ghazanfar sat with his lawyer. I nodded to Phuppo and Zain, both of whom were seated nearby.

Yusra turned as soon as she saw me and quickly whispered, "Hey, Kiran, just a heads-up. There are more plaintiffs who wanted to join our case at the last minute."

"Really? Who?"

"I don't have time to explain. Wait and see," she said, and turned back towards the judge.

The judge addressed Yusra. "Would you like to call your first witness?"

"Yes, Your Honor," she replied, and Kauser took the witness stand.

She answered Yusra's questions, holding her head high, her gaze steady and full of confidence, with the occasional glance at her husband. That was the easy part. The next was where she would require every ounce of her strength and patience.

Asif's lawyer stood and walked over to the witness stand.

"Miss Kauser, you say my client came to your bedroom the night your mother died. How can we be sure that you were not hallucinating because of your grief?"

Yusra stood up. "Objection, Your Honor—calls for speculation."

"Sustained," the judge nodded.

But Asif's lawyer was undeterred and shifted closer to my sister. "Is it not true that there were others in that house as well at the time? In fact, your younger sister's room was adjacent to yours."

"That is correct." Kauser nodded.

"Then why didn't you try to scream? Or alert someone?"

"I was scared."

Asif's lawyer scoffed, dipping his head towards my sister. "Or did you like the attention you were getting from an older man? Especially at a time when everyone's attention was on your baby brother."

I wanted to throw something at him. How disgusting can a man get?

Yusra immediately jumped up from her seat again. "Objection, Your Honor—argumentative and prejudicial"

"Sustained. Counselor, please refrain from harassing the plaintiff." The judge frowned at the opposing lawyer, but that didn't stop him.

"How long ago did this event happen?"

"About twenty-three years ago."

"Do you remember what you had for dinner that night?"

"Uh, no."

"Or breakfast the next morning?"

"No."

Yusra was up for a third time. "Objection, Your Honor. He's badgering the witness."

Asif's lawyer smirked at those in the courtroom. "I am trying to show that she can't possibly remember anything from twenty-three years ago."

But to my pleasant surprise, the judge was on him again. "Sustained. Counselor, are you suggesting that sexual assault is the same as eating a meal?"

"No, sir," he mumbled, but the smirk on his face stayed.

We knew this was a frivolous lawsuit. Kauser had been prepared for stupid questions like these. But her hope had always been that she might inspire others to speak up. For her sake, I hoped that the newcomers who had joined her lawsuit had better luck than she did. Asif's shark-like lawyer was heartless, just like his client.

Fortunately, Maham's case was more recent, so Yusra had been able to find witnesses from that party who reported Asif Ghazanfar handling the teenaged Maham's drink before offering it to her, as well as how she suddenly seemed to lose her balance outside the party house when she stood next to Zain.

All that, I knew and had expected. But what caught me off guard was what happened next.

"I'd like to call Zain Ghazanfar as my next witness."

"Zain is going to testify against his father?" I asked Junaid. Though I suppose I shouldn't have been surprised after he had helped expose his father a few months ago.

"He's paying a price for it too," Junaid whispered with a solemn expression, confusing me.

My cousin, with a deep purple bruise on his cheek, and a swollen lower lip, narrated what he had seen and how his father had behaved when he had tried to take Maham away from him. That testimony should have perturbed Asif and his lawyer, but the smug looks on their faces told me they thought they knew something the rest of us didn't.

Their smiles disappeared when Yusra started asking Zain questions I had never expected her to ask.

"Mr. Zain Ghazanfar, in your statement you said that your father had been directly involved in drugging another young woman as well. Can you elaborate on that?"

His shoulders slumped when his gaze shifted towards Osman and Sanam. "My father told me to use Rohypnol on my ex-wife to force her to marry me—"

A sudden commotion from the defense table interrupted him. "He's a lying bastard. I had nothing to do with that!" Asif barked.

Yusra approached the judge's bench and handed him a USB. "Your Honor, this contains a video that Mr. Asif and his lawyer have already submitted to the court. It contains footage of Zain giving that drug to Ms. Sanam Uzair."

"Exactly. *Zain* gave the drug to Sanam," Asif scoffed.

Yusra ignored him and asked to have the video run on the large screen mounted on one of the courtroom walls. She skipped over most of the video to the last thirty seconds. Loud music blared in the background. There was a partial view of a woman with brown, wavy hair bending over, a plastic cup in her hand, and a man's hand on her back.

"I got it all on video," a familiar voice said.

A muffled response came from Zain, but the first voice was clear when it said, "This should knock her down for quite some time. Go do what I told you to do."

Yusra paused the video and zoomed it to focus on a mirrored wall. That's when a reflection became clear. Slick black gelled hair, dark, dangerous eyes, a clean shave, wearing a black Armani suit—the man smiled, without realizing that he himself was on camera too.

Scoffing at the opposing lawyer, she addressed Zain again. "What did your father ask you to do?"

Without lifting his gaze from the floor, he answered, "He told me to rape Sanam, but I couldn't do it."

The courtroom was in an uproar. Evidence of Asif Ghazanfar's consistent pattern of sexual crimes was now undeniable. Despite the judge's gavel pounding against the wood, demanding order, the murmurs only barely subsided.

I glanced at Sanam and Osman. She had her head tucked against his shoulder, her fingers gripping his tightly. He murmured something to her, his gaze burning with quiet fury as he shot daggers at Zain, then his father. If looks could kill, both men would have dropped dead on the spot.

When the room finally quieted, Asif's lawyer declined to question Zain, giving Yusra the opportunity to call her next, unexpected witness.

"Zarine Ghazanfar."

As the chatter in the room rose again, Asif jumped from his chair and started to yell, "Yeh do takke ki aurat . . ." when the judge's voice boomed across the courtroom. (This pathetic woman.)

"Mr. Asif Ghazanfar, if I ever hear you degrade women in my courtroom again, I will hold you in contempt and personally throw you in jail."

Asif glared at the judge, then grumbled and sank back into his chair.

Yusra began questioning my Phuppo, a frail woman with sunken eyes who looked nothing like the one I had come to despise in my twenties and thirties. And yet, as I realized in the next few minutes, I hadn't really known her at all.

"Ms. Zarine, could you please recall what happened the night you asked your nieces and nephew to leave the house?"

I glanced at my siblings; it was clear none of us knew what was going on. For the first time, Asif had a frown on his face. But he stayed quiet, and Phuppo kept her gaze averted from him.

"I overheard Asif talking on the phone," she began slowly.

"And what did you hear?" Yusra prompted.

"He was making a deal with someone. For my nieces, Kauser and Kaukab. He said he'd take five crores for the older one and three for the younger one."

I gasped, but it was hard to hear my own thoughts over the anger that boiled my blood. Neither did I have to glance at my brother and sisters to know exactly what was going on in their minds.

"What did you do then?" Yusra went on.

"I woke the girls up and told them to leave with their brother and never come back."

Phuppo looked towards me and then my sisters. Regret filled her eyes, but it was nothing compared to the guilt I felt at that moment.

"What happened when your husband found out about that?"

"He, umm . . ." She paused, but instead of fear in her eyes, there was determination. Sitting up straighter, she met Asif's unflinching gaze.

"He tried to find the girls, but he couldn't. He was furious when he came home, and he took it all out on me." Her voice quivered, but she recovered quickly.

"He violently raped me."

There was a pin-drop silence in the room.

"What happened after that?" Yusra went on.

"He left the house, and my helper, Bua, found me unconscious on the floor."

Another pause. I wasn't sure if that was the case in real life or not, but my brain seemed to have ceased working. My Phuppo had gone through so much because of us, and all along, I had blamed her for our miseries.

A hand squeezing mine unfroze my reality. "It'll be okay, Kiran," Junaid whispered.

I could only nod feebly, before shifting my attention back to the scene in front of me.

"Did you try to report him to the police?" Yusra was asking Phuppo.

She seemed like she was reliving every moment of her past. And it took everything in me to stop myself from running up to that witness stand and wrapping my arms around her. But I could also tell that she wasn't the meek, submissive woman Asif thought she was. Somewhere deep within her, there was strength and a passion for justice—for herself and her nieces. And that was enough to keep her going as dozens of eyes watched her, including the dark, terrifying ones of her husband.

"I did, but they said I couldn't file a case of rape against my husband. There is no law against marital rape in our country."

Even the judge heaved a sigh at that statement.

"You tried to file a report for domestic violence, though. What happened to that?"

I instantly knew the answer. She had dropped the charges in exchange for Asif staying away from Kauser and Kaukab. The more I thought about it, the worse I felt. Of course she would have protected us.

How could I have forgotten the times she had hugged me when I was a little child, or when she'd held my siblings and showered them with gifts and kisses? She had loved us when we were little.

And she had never stopped loving us.

"Those children were the only part of my brother that I had left, and I lived with a monster. I did what I had to do to keep them away from me. And him."

Her quiet, determined voice betrayed the years of hardship she'd had to endure, but it wasn't lost on any of us.

The opposing lawyer tried to intimidate Phuppo when he cross-examined her, telling her that she was a gold-digger for staying with her husband. But it was clear that he was failing miserably, especially when Phuppo recounted more harrowing tales of her trying to stand up to him, only to be beaten and abused in return.

"Women are strong, but there comes a point when we realize that our strength is what makes men insecure. And so, we hide that strength, hoping they don't see us as a threat, and we can get some semblance of peace."

Looking out at the courtroom defiantly, she said, "I am not going to apologize for what I had to do to survive with a man who would have sold me and my nieces in a heartbeat if he could. But I am sorry that it took Kauser going public with her story for me to gather the courage to sit here today and narrate mine."

It didn't help Asif's case that Bua was able to corroborate almost everything Phuppo had said. And the old woman was no less defiant than my Phuppo in the face of the opposing lawyer's attacks.

With their testimonies complete, leaving many eyes wet, I thought the proceedings would conclude. Instead, Yusra approached the judge's bench again.

"Your Honor, before we proceed to closing arguments, I request the court's attention for a brief procedural matter. In the past week, five more women have come to me with similar tales of abuse at the hands of Mr. Asif Ghazanfar. Their statements were submitted to the court as supporting evidence to establish pattern and intent." She held up a file full of papers.

"While we are not calling them as witnesses today, each woman has expressed a desire to identify herself publicly. Not as evidence, but to show that they are not afraid of the defendant."

Justice Hamad mulled over the request before nodding. "If they understand the nature of this moment and are not offering live testimony, the court will allow it. You may proceed."

Yusra turned toward the rest of the courtroom. "Ms. Bakhtavar Ali, who was an employee of GT Enterprise," she called out a name, and a young woman wearing a hijab stood up.

"Mrs. Shireen Mujahid, who worked at a retail shop located in a shopping mall owned by Mr. Asif." A woman, likely in her thirties, with brown hair in a tight bun stood up.

"Ms. Aarti Patel, who was standing at a bus stop when Mr. Asif's men forced her into a car." A woman with a plain white dupatta wrapped around her head stood up.

"Ms. Ayesha Jamal, who is the daughter of Mr. Asif's good friend." A young woman wearing cut-out jeans and a pink t-shirt stood up.

"Mrs. Michael Smith, a home health nurse who cared for Mr. Asif when he had a bad case of flu." A woman in a neatly pressed uniform stood up.

One look around the room made it evident that the only thing the women had in common was their courage—and a sexual predator. It proved yet again that sexual assault is caused by only one thing, and one thing alone: a man's lust for power over a woman.

Asif Ghazanfar was that man. He sat still with a blank expression on his face, staring ahead without blinking. With all the evidence piling up against him, the man's end was here, and he knew it.

After the closing arguments were made, the judge exited the room as police surrounded Asif to take him back to his jail cell, where I prayed he would stay forever.

I scrambled from my seat towards Phuppo, but was beaten by Kauser and Kaukab, who were already embracing the woman who had saved their lives at the expense of her own. When they finally left Phuppo, teary-eyed, but with a smile that spoke volumes about the relief she felt, I hugged her too.

"You should have told me," I told her.

"It wasn't your burden. After your parents, it was my job to protect you. I am sorry that I didn't see Asif's true colors until it was too late."

"I am sorry too, that I didn't reach out to you earlier."

"Don't apologize, Kiran." She cupped my face. "You did what you had to do to protect your family. I am glad you stayed away; otherwise, things would have gotten much harder for all of us."

In retrospect, I suppose I had to agree with her. But for now, guilt inundated me, and I vowed to be the niece a brave and selfl ess Phuppo like mine deserved. Besides, she was the only part of my father I had left as well.

ZAIN

"Investigators from the FIU want to see you," said the inspector with sympathetic eyes who came up to me while the rest of the people in that room seemed to be gravitating towards my mother. I glanced at the woman I had lived with most of my life and wondered how I had never realized the extent of her abuse.

I longed to be with her, to hug her and apologize for not noticing the signs when I should have. But then I saw her with my cousins. One by one, she embraced them, kissed their foreheads, and gently patted their cheeks. Her smile radiated pure pride and love—the kind only a mother could give.

She had never acted like this before. I had always thought she wasn't capable of showing motherly love. I realized then that she wasn't capable of showing it to *me*. To her, I would always be my father's son.

"I'm ready to meet them," I told the inspector, fully aware that this meeting would lead to my arrest on money laundering charges, just as my father had promised.

It wasn't as if my mother would notice my absence anyway—she had her brother's children with her now.

OSMAN

"Tell me how you're feeling," I asked Sanam later that night as we sat in bed, her arm curled around mine and her head resting against my shoulder.

She had clasped my hand the whole time we were in the courtroom. The witness accounts had been tough to hear, yet I was in awe of her courage to support the women who, much like her, had been victims of a man's lust for power.

"Safe," she replied quietly. "With you, I always feel safe."

But then she sat up and turned towards me. "Can I ask you something, Osman?"

"Always."

"Did you have anything to do with the bruise on Zain's face?"

For a moment, I wasn't sure what flickered in her eyes—disappointment, surprise, or maybe both. But something told me she already knew the answer.

"He deserved it," I said. "In fact, he deserves to rot in jail for hurting you. I wish you'd gone to the police back in Houston."

She must have sensed the storm building in me, because her hands found my face. Her thumbs brushed over my cheeks as she whispered, "If

I had, I wouldn't have had a reason to move to Boston. And maybe... we would've never found our way back to each other."

My heart clenched. How cruel—yet how strangely kind—fate could be. The same man who tore her from me had somehow led her back.

Sanam lay down, gently pulling me beside her and resting her head on my chest, her arm slipping around my waist.

"I don't need revenge," she murmured. "Zain will get what he deserves. I need this."

She held me tighter.

"Me. You. And peace."

I kissed the top of her head and told her, "I love you so much."

She told me she loved me just as much.

Peace was indeed a far more precious pursuit than revenge. Bathed in the dim light of the moon, she yawned and closed her eyes. As she slipped into sleep, I took in all her quiet perfection. Her eyelashes kissed the tops of her cheeks and fluttered until they stilled. She hung on to me tightly until her muscles relaxed. Lips that I could still taste turned up into a beautiful smile before they parted, and I heard her soft, slow breathing.

There was so much I wanted to experience with her, but it was clear to me that she was still healing from her past.

Besides, I was beginning to realize that while it felt incredible to be loved by her, there was no feeling in the world that could parallel that of being trusted, so wholly and utterly, the way Sanam trusted me. Enough to let herself be transported to her dreams and lose all her faculties while she lay in my arms.

Could I break that trust by asking her for something she wasn't ready to give? No. Never. The next step in our relationship was only hers to take.

Hugging her one more time, I let myself slip into slumber too.

But only a moment later, I jerked awake at the sound of my cellphone's text message alert going off. It turned out to be my siblings' group messages that were suddenly flooding my phone.

I assumed it was about Api's wedding planning, and was about to put my phone on silent when I noticed Sanam's name being mentioned repeatedly, which prompted me to read them more carefully.

Api's message was the first one.

Api: Junaid called. They found our father's killer.

Reading quickly through the initial frantic messages, I got to the shocked and unbelieving ones, and then the one with a name that made me lower my phone and look at the woman sleeping in my arms.

The wife who I could not imagine my life without.

The daughter of a man who had killed my father.

CHAPTER 69

Nexus

OSMAN

My arm was still tightly wrapped around my wife when another message made my phone buzz. This time, it was a direct message from Kiran Api.

Api: Awake? Come out if you can.

I wasn't going to be able to sleep after this anyway, so I carefully slid out of bed and walked into the living room where my sisters had gathered, along with Junaid Bhai, who sat in front of a laptop. They all looked up when I entered.

"You good?" Api immediately asked.

"Yes, but Sanam will not be when she finds out."

"I know," she sighed.

I took a seat next to the others. "How did we even come to know about Zakariya Uzair's involvement?"

"Myla, his current wife, went to the Houston police and told them everything," Kaukab Baji began to explain.

Junaid Bhai nodded. "Her name is not Myla—it's Nosheen. She is Asif Ghazanfar's niece, and your father found out what he had done to her."

As Junaid Bhai continued, I began to piece together where this was headed. With each word, a growing sense of panic settled over me—not for myself, but for Sanam. She had already endured so much because of her father. This could completely shatter her self-worth.

"Faisal Ghazanfar got a call from your father asking about his missing daughter the same day as Kauser told him about her own abuse," Junaid Bhai explained.

"So when Abu told me not to tell anyone, he must have had a plan to expose Asif," Kauser Baji said.

Junaid Bhai was convinced that this was exactly what had occurred. The envelope Shafiq retrieved from my father's car crash site had now been discovered by the Houston police at Zakariya Uzair's residence.

"It was addressed to Sikander Ahmad. I suspect your father had uncovered damning evidence and realized that the only way to counter the influence wielded by AWP's leader at the time was to expose it through the press."

"What was in the envelope?" I asked.

"More financial records," Junaid Bhai said.

"Of property sales?"

He shook his head solemnly. "Of human sales."

A chill went through me as I realized exactly what that meant. He confirmed my fears.

"Your father had just uncovered the tip of the iceberg. When the Houston police found that report, I knew that had to be the evidence Asif was using to blackmail his way out of the court cases. So we raided the one place we had overlooked the first time: the original office of GT Enterprise, a one-room office in a dilapidated building in old Karachi. That's where we found everything, from fake passports and compromising photos to phones with text messages, all indicating that young girls from various backgrounds had been abducted or conned into running away from their homes, only to end up in the hands of Asif Ghazanfar and Zakariya Uzair.

I am guessing that Asif supplied the drugs used to make the girls unconscious, and Zakariya provided the logistics of moving their human cargo."

He sighed deeply. "Nosheen, aka Myla, was meant to be trafficked. Except Zakariya took a special liking to her, so he kept her for himself. According to what she told the Houston police, she tried to run away many times but was always captured by Zakariya's men, drugged, and tortured. And when he took her to the US and essentially erased her identity, she simply gave up."

My heart sank with disgust and agony for a woman Sanam had spoken quite fondly of. Junaid Bhai reported that she was safe now and in touch with her father, and Zakariya Uzair had been arrested.

Api looked at her soon-to-be husband. "Evidence of human trafficking was not all you found, though, right?"

"No." His pensive gaze darted from my sisters to me as he shook his head again. "We also found correspondence with your ex-husband and a doctor. Zakariya gave orders to Shafiq to cut your father's brakes, which resulted in his car crash and death. And to the doctor, he gave orders to inject your grandfather with a lethal dose of potassium chloride. All for a hefty sum of money."

The end of that sentence merged with the sound of shattering glass from the hallway outside the living room. Soft footsteps quickly retreated from us.

SANAM

Thirst and the absence of a familiar warmth had woken me up. I tried to go back to sleep, but the muffled sounds coming from outside and a desire for cold water made me get out of bed and wander first into the kitchen and then the living room.

But the wedding planning that I had expected to be happening in that room wasn't what I saw or heard. Instead, there was Inspector Junaid uttering a truth that fundamentally changed who I was.

Not a woman who had given up her life for Osman's love, but the daughter of a man who had taken away the love Osman deserved from his father and grandfather.

The bedroom door opened, light from the hallway flooding the room and hitting the previously empty suitcase on the bed, now haphazardly filled with my clothes.

"I am so sorry, Osman. I promise I didn't know. I'll leave in the morning," I immediately said.

"What the heck are you talking about?"

"You won't have to look at me and be reminded of your father's and grandfather's killer anymore. I won't let that happen to you."

Guilt and foreboding filled me. A close-knit family like the Tariqs had been ripped apart because of my father. And I didn't need to guess that my uncle, and maybe even my mother, had known about it. How could this family ever look at me with the same love they had showered on me in the last few days?

Osman flipped on the switch so neither of our emotions could be kept hidden anymore. The distress in his hazels cut through me. So much pain, all because of me and my tainted bloodline—made up of murderers, cheats, and adulterers.

"I am so sorry . . ." I started to say, but his palm covered my lips, startling me.

"Stop saying sorry. None of this is your fault."

I stepped away from him. "I know it's not, but I also know that seeing me is killing you, Osman. You don't have to hide your agony."

He moved closer, his eyes frantically searching mine. "You think I'm in agony because of your father?"

"Then what else?"

"Take a wild guess, Sanam," he shot back, jerking his head towards my suitcase. "I walked into our bedroom and found you packing your clothes, saying you're leaving me. How exactly am I supposed to feel?"

"You'll hate me if I stay." I turned away from him.

He cupped my face, forcing me to look into his eyes again. "I couldn't hate you even when you left me that wretched message on my phone. Or when you were married to a man I detested. How could I ever hate you now?"

"But I'll always be my father's daughter . . ."

His lips crashed onto mine. He kissed me with a desperation that made my knees weak. In that instant, my past no longer mattered—only the present and the future, both consumed by unbridled passion and pure, unwavering love. My world began and ended with this man, who was mine beyond doubt, against all odds.

When he finally pulled away, his forehead rested against mine, his breaths warm and uneven.

"You will always be my *wife*."

Those words, spoken with such finality, settled deep in my heart, dissolving every trace of uncertainty. They should have left no room for questions. Yet, Osman wasn't the only one who had suffered.

"What about your family?" I reluctantly asked.

He stepped back and grasped my hand, smiling. "Let's go ask them."

If I had it my way, I would have holed myself up in this room from embarrassment. But something told me that a family who had raised my amazing husband couldn't be much different than him.

Kaukab Baji's arms were around me as soon as I stepped into the living room. "None of this is your fault. I hope you know that," she said.

"Let her sit, at least, Kaukab," Kiran Api told her.

"Come sit next to me." Kauser Baji patted the seat next to her.

Unbelieving, I gaped at them. "How are you all so willing to ignore my family background?"

Kiran Api smiled gently and glanced around at her sisters, her brother, and the inspector who was about to become so much more. "Look around the room, Sanam. We are your family now. And we always take care of our own, no matter what."

Without missing a beat, the conversation steered back to what Junaid Bhai had found.

"Were the papers that landed Basaam Fawad in jail a ruse?" Kaukab Baji asked.

Junaid Bhai nodded. "Your father did cancel Basaam's sale, but he wasn't the one who sent in the papers with all the financial details. We interrogated Asif Ghazanfar after raiding his old office, and he admitted that Basaam was becoming dead weight for the other two. He'd had too many run-ins with the authorities, and his business was dwindling. So they decided to hammer the last nail in his coffin and anonymously sent in the evidence against him."

Kiran Api sat back on the sofa. "It was the perfect plan. Basaam went away to jail for good, Abu was in a simple car accident, and if someone had suspected Abu's murder, the suspicion would have fallen on Basaam. Meanwhile, once things settled down, Asif reemerged to take over whatever was left of Basaam's drug cartel, and Zakariya continued to do what he had been doing before, until he was essentially put into exile by his brother. Though it seems like after Sanam's wedding to Zain, the two were starting to ramp up their business again."

My eyes widened. "Wait, did Zavi Chachoo know about this?"

Junaid Bhai shrugged. "I don't know for sure. But that would be the only explanation for how a relatively unknown and young politician like Zaviyar came to lead AWP. Someone must have known something to incriminate Zakariya, which made him unsuitable to lead his father's political party."

Osman noticed my frowning. "What are you thinking?" he whispered, but this wasn't my time to speak aloud.

The next morning, I tried to unwrap myself from his arms as the first of the day's sunrays peeked in through the curtains of our bedroom. Instead, he tightened them around me and pouted, whispering in my ear, "Don't leave me."

"I need to do something at Mama's house."

He opened his eyes partially. "Are you taking your suitcase with you?" he asked quietly, breaking my heart with his innocence.

"No, I am leaving that right here with my husband," I told him, placing a kiss on his forehead. He grinned like a child.

Soon, I was standing in front of a house, eyeing the unmarked car parked outside with men I recognized as my Chachoo's bodyguards. I shouldn't have been surprised that he was here on personal business. But I still felt a jolt when I saw the man I had held in such high regard all my life sitting on a sofa next to my mother, who was dressed in her nightgown.

"Having an affair and conspiring on how to dupe your respective spouses again, or still trying to hide my father's sins?" I asked, feeling the venom drip from my voice.

"Sanam." Zavi Chachoo quickly got up from his seat; my mother was less excited.

"What the hell, Sanam? Who said you could barge in here whenever you wanted?"

"I won't be long." I glared at her. "I just want answers."

Zavi Chachoo walked towards me, attempting to hug me like he always had. Unlike my mother, there was remorse in his eyes. But I didn't care.

"Don't touch me, Chachoo. I want nothing to do with cheats and liars."

"Sanam, listen, please. It's not what you think," he pleaded. "We were doing what we thought was best for you."

"You did this for me? What a joke." I scoffed.

He nodded fervently. "If the world had found out that you were the daughter of a human trafficker and a murderer, you would have had no life at all. That's why I told him to leave the country and never come back. I didn't know he would still keep his connection with Asif. When you and Zain got married, I even tried to warn him against starting his business again, but he never listened."

It amazed me how these two had managed to justify their actions, ignoring the damage they had done, even if they hadn't committed the heinous acts themselves.

"The way I see it, you only hid your brother's crimes so that AWP could still call itself the party of wholesome family values, and you could take over its chairmanship as soon your older brother left the country. And Mama hid it so she wouldn't get a bad reputation in her social circles or have to explain her connection to a man who preyed on young girls."

"Stop it, Sanam." Mama tried to speak, but I was seething.

"Stop what? Having affairs with one man after another? Like you do? First Chachoo, then my father, then Mr. Malik."

Her gaze hardened. "I never had an affair with Malik."

"Sanam," Chachoo intervened, standing up for my mother like he always had. "Those pictures you saw all over the media a few years ago were Shabnam handing over what she had found out about the girl Zak had captured. I couldn't be seen with her, given our . . . umm . . ." He hesitated. "Our history. So, I sent Malik instead. We never realized that Zak was having your mother followed."

"You could have saved that girl," I replied, tears springing to my eyes at the thought of what Myla must have gone through.

Chachoo shook his head solemnly. "There was nothing we could do. She was over eighteen by the time we found out, and married to Zak, who didn't let anyone meet her or see her."

Even if I believed that story, I still couldn't believe that they had gained actual evidence against my father all those years ago.

"Don't give me that BS argument." I snapped. "You could have still made an effort to save her. Instead, you buried the story and went on with your own self-absorbed lives."

My mother lived only for herself, but Chachoo had seemed different. He wasn't, and that hurt. Eyes filled with disappointment, I turned to look at him and lowered my voice. "You were supposed to be a decent man, Chachoo. What happened to you?"

His gaze lowered, but he remained quiet. My mother, as always, spoke instead.

"We did what we had to do to survive. It's a jungle out there. You either eat or you get eaten."

I twirled around to face her, tired of the nonsense she always spewed. "That is not true, Mama. And do you know how I know? My new family went through life a hundred times harder than yours. And they did it with integrity, and without destroying someone else's life. So don't you dare try to play the victim here."

She turned red in the face and yelled, "Shut your mouth!" But she was in for a surprise. The man who had stood by her all this time, accepting whatever she gave him, had finally made a choice. And it wasn't one that she had expected him to make.

"She's right, Shabnam. I've always had a soft spot for you. I would do anything to make you happy, even fight against my own conscience. But I am done fighting it now. I can't stand with you anymore."

"What are you saying?" Mama frowned at him.

"I am saying that if Zak gets extradited back to Pakistan, or the US authorities ask for assistance with gathering evidence against him, I will not stand in the way of justice or protect him and Asif in any way. No matter how that impacts us."

Mama scoffed. "Oh, yes, you will. If you speak the truth now, your past will become obvious. You will lose your position as the Prime Minister of Pakistan. Your political career will be dead."

He shook his head. With a stoic expression on his face, he looked squarely at my mother.

"Then I'll step down as the Prime Minister tonight. There are others within AWP who are far more capable and have more integrity than I do. It's time they lead this country, not a man who rose to this position because of nepotism, lying, and obstruction of justice."

Mama turned ashen. He also told her to get a lawyer.

"If someone asks me who I conspired with to cover up my brother's crimes, I will tell them the truth."

For the first time in my life, I saw my mother fearful. "But, Zavi, we didn't do anything." She reached out to touch his arm.

He pulled it away. "Exactly—we didn't do anything when we should have. And it's been killing me ever since."

I always used to see the world in black and white: the good and bad, evil and pious. But I was realizing now, as I stood in that eerily silent living room, that within all of us are gradations of gray, painted by our moral compass.

Sometimes that moral compass becomes faulty, and often it's love that's at fault.

For my ex-husband, it was the love he craved from his father. For my once beloved Chachoo, it was the love of a woman who never truly loved him back. Whatever it was, the past was done.

It was only the future that they could now be judged on.

CHAPTER 70

Second Chance

KIRAN

A couple of weeks after getting my brother married off, I was looking down at my own mehndi-painted hands, and the dull gold embroidered dress with intricate embellishments that draped over my body.

"Thank you for coming, Phuppo," I said to the woman who had become the parental figure I had long given up on.

"Of course, my child." She smiled and gave me a hug.

We had just reached the grand mosque of Karachi, located in the heart of the city, where we were met by the rest of my family and some of Junaid's.

Surrounded by them, I stepped inside, taking a moment to absorb the beauty around me—the intricate calligraphy adorning the walls, the soaring domed ceiling, and the brilliant chandeliers that bathed the space in a soft glow.

Then my gaze found a pair of familiar dark brown eyes. He stood near the Imam at the front of the mosque, waiting for me, his warm smile growing wider with every step I took towards him.

Like our boys, he wore a black sherwani, but on him, it looked regal. His hair was slicked back, his beard neatly trimmed, and he stood tall with a posture as straight as a soldier's. He had never looked more handsome—or perhaps I was simply seeing him through a different lens now, as we stood on the brink of a moment that would bind us as partners for life.

"Assalamu Alaikum," he whispered as we sat together, waiting for the Imam to get ready.

"Walaikum Assalam," I replied, keeping my gaze lowered as the weight of the moment bore down on me.

He leaned in, and I could feel a smirk on his face even without looking at him. "Dharkanon ko kuch toh qaabu mein kar aye dil. Abhi to palkein jhukayi hain; muskarana abhi baaki hai."

(Dear heart, control your beating. She has just lowered her eyelashes; she has yet to smile.)

I couldn't reply, my heart was fluttering too much, but I couldn't stop myself from grinning either. This man and his poetic dialogues were going to be the death of me.

Thankfully, I recovered enough to reply to the Imam, "Qabool hai," and looked up at a beaming Junaid when he said the same. With the formalities done, our lives now signed over to each other, I prayed for a future that was as full of joy and love as it was of romantic poems and witty humor. (I accept.)

"Umar qaid mubarak ho aap ko," I told him cheekily. (Congratulations on your life sentence.)

He let out a low chuckle.

"Ek umar toh kya, mein toh har jehan ka har pal aap ki qaid mein guzaarne ke liye tayar hun."

(What is one life? I am ready to be imprisoned by you in every moment of every life.)

If I hadn't noticed our sons approaching us from the corner of my eyes, I might have melted into a puddle right there. Instead, I forced a breath and pretended that my heart wasn't about to jump out of my chest.

Daniyal reached us and pushed his new stepbrother in front of me. "Mama, Nael has something to ask you."

"Uh, yes, yes." The boy blushed. "I was thinking maybe I could call you Mama too, like Daniyal and Danish. Because I used to call my first mother, Ami. Mama . . . would be, like . . . different."

"Absolutely, Nael. I would love to be your Mama, just like I am for Daniyal and Danish." I patted his cheek, and he grinned, so much like his father. Such a sweet boy.

A few feet away, Danish and Daniyal stepped up to Junaid, with one of them laying out a similar proposal. "Can we call you Abu? Since Nael calls you that too. We never really had a name for our other father."

"I mean, we just call him 'bloody criminal' now," the other added in all honesty.

"Then Abu it is," I heard Junaid say, before he embraced both of them, like a father embraces his sons, and my heart swelled with joy.

With the love the elders showered on me, and prayers they said for Junaid and me, my life felt almost surreal. I had gone from being an orphan who had buttressed the rest of my family for years, to this moment, where I had a life partner who could share my burdens, plus a whole family that made the pain of my parents' death a little less hurtful.

We all piled into the cars we had come in and headed to the Razzak residence, where a small wedding reception had been planned. Except the configuration of the passengers changed.

I got to sit with my husband.

"You're in a hurry," I chuckled as he drove off, gunning his Audi.

"Can you blame me? I've waited two years to run off with you." Slipping his hand into mine, he brought it up to his mouth and kissed the back of it, his warm lips on my flushed skin sending heat spiraling through me.

That morning, I had wondered how I would transition into being a wife when I had become so used to being on my own. But right there in the car, I knew the answer. We both filled a part of each other that only we were destined to fill. And each moment we had spent on this earth had all come together to this point, where we were finally husband and wife.

"Have I mentioned to you yet that I fell in love with you the morning we sat along the seaside, and you told me you would always have my back?"

He nearly slammed the brakes. "What?"

As soon as he stopped at a red light, I leaned over and placed my lips on his cheek. "I am in love with you, Inspector Junaid," I whispered, and gleefully looked on as his flustered face turned fifty shades of crimson.

Marrying him is going to be so much fun, I laughed internally.

OSMAN

"You look beyond beautiful tonight, Api," I told my eldest sister when I walked over to her at her wedding reception.

She chuckled and patted the seat next to her. "You know, normally I would be suspicious and ask why you were buttering me up." Then she looked over at my wife and smiled. "But it seems like you already have everything you've ever wanted."

"I do, and I have you to thank for all of it." I wrapped my arms around her in a side hug, trying not to get emotional. A hard act when the woman who has been everything to you, from your mother to sister, friend and confidant, is moving on to another life. I was happy for her, truly. But things would change from now on, and that part saddened me a bit.

"Are you crying?" She suddenly looked at me.

"No. There is something in my eye," I lied.

"Aww, come here." This time, she put her arms around me, like she had so many times before. And I put my head on her shoulder, like all the other times I had ever felt sad.

"You know what the first thing I thought of was when I held you in the NICU?" she asked softly.

"What?"

"This little boy and I will face this world together. And we did, Osman. Through the best and worst of it, we've been through it, holding each other's hands. Just because we are moving on doesn't mean that bond between us will change, ever."

When she let go of me, I looked around at the joyous gathering in front of us. It dawned on me then, this was the best of it. She and I had found the people we could face the world with. A world that was nowhere near as bleak as the day I was born and she'd held me for the first time in my life.

"We did good together, I think," I told her.

She nodded, a warm smile spreading across her face. "I think we did."

To the world, she might be strength and grace personified. But to me, she would always be the sister who never gave up on me when so many others would have. And to her, I would always be the baby brother our mother left behind in this world as a parting gift. Together, we were a sister and brother, like no other.

"I love you, Api." I squeezed her hand.

"I love you too, kiddo." She ruffled my hair.

KIRAN

I wasn't expecting Junaid to grab my hand at the reception, while some guests were still milling about, and lead me up to our room.

"Shouldn't we say goodbye at least?" I asked him. My own family had left, but I was afraid people from my new family would consider me to be rude.

He shook his head vehemently. "The invite said the reception was from 8 to 11 p.m., and it's 11:02. They can see themselves out. I have more important things to do."

"Like what?"

A redundant question, I know. But he actually did have something else in mind, other than what had been on my mind the whole day. And I sure felt stupid, temporarily.

"Like change out of this God-forsaken sherwani." He raised an eyebrow. "Why? Is there something else you want me to do?"

I blushed hard. Of course I wanted him to do something else.

"Of course not," I said instead.

He shrugged. "If you say so."

Though I am positive he also laughed under his breath while taking his sherwani coat off. But he didn't stop there. He started pulling off the shirt he wore underneath too, and I might have held my breath in anticipation. Unfortunately, he noticed that.

"You're welcome to gawk at me."

"I am not gawking. I am going to change too." I huffed and walked into the bathroom, annoyed at myself, and him.

It took forever to peel off my bridal dress and slip into what was supposed to be simple lingerie. The peach-colored silk nightie I wore was anything but that, now that I was looking at myself in a full-length mirror.

It ended well above my knees and the thin straps and deep neck left my shoulders exposed and cleavage visible. But it was either that or the cotton pajamas I usually wore, and a bold part of me wanted to do to Junaid what he always did to me—give the man a taste of his own cocky medicine.

So I did the unthinkable. I stepped out into the room without the silk gown that came with the nightie.

"Are you always this slow . . ." Junaid, now dressed in pajamas and a white half-sleeve shirt, began to say before his voice trailed off. To my utter amusement, the lips that had just been smirking slowly parted, and his eyes widened, wandering all over me.

"I am going to sleep, good night," I declared.

"What? Really?"

Somehow, I managed to keep a straight face and shrugged. "Why? What else is there to do?"

He stuttered something I didn't quite catch before running past me to one of the bedside tables. "I forgot . . ." Handing me a square box, he beamed. "To give you your wedding present."

It was a beautiful gold bangle, with an intricate carving on the outside and a row of tiny zircons along the edges.

"This is stunning, Junaid. Thank you so much. I love it!" I tried to slip it on, but he stopped me.

"Look on the inside."

There were more carvings there. But this time, it was a simple sentence in Urdu.

Meri har sahar ki pehli kiran—hamesha ke liye

(The first light of every sunrise in my life—forever.)

"Kiran" meant sunlight, and I couldn't believe the tender message he'd had transcribed with a clever play on that meaning. I glanced at him, uncertain how much to let myself interpret his words. But the moment his deep brown eyes—an enigmatic universe unto themselves—met mine, I knew.

His fingers gently teased the curled strands of hair framing my face as he leaned in, closing the space between us.

"Do you know why I would always meet you so early in the morning?" he asked, his voice so husky it made my skin tingle.

"I thought you exercised early in the morning," I replied naïvely.

He slowly shook his head, his eyes never leaving mine, making me desperate for the passion swirling in them. "Unless walking to the car and driving to wherever you were is called exercise, no, that was not the reason.

"It was because even a glimpse of you in the morning would make my day a thousand times better. And now I'll get to see you, my Kiran, first thing at dawn, without even getting out of bed."

He was so close, I could feel his warmth without him laying a finger on my skin. My façade dropped. I let my eyes fall shut and gave in to him, as his arm slid around my waist, drawing me near, and his lips grazed the side of my neck.

"But before dawn, there is so much I want to do to you," he rasped. "Unless you're too sleepy, of course."

I grabbed his shirt and breathed out, "Shut up and kiss me."

Who kissed whom first didn't matter. All that mattered were the voracious desires we had held back for so long, and even now tried to hide under humorous indifference. To feel each other, however we wanted, and take as much as we gave.

We weren't a couple that was naïve about the pleasures of intimacy. We had been there, done that. Yet to each other, we were new, and with that came some awkwardness, some shyness, and a whole lot of wow.

Like when his shirt came off for a second time, and his hard abs caught me by surprise, I blurted out, "I have stretch marks."

He chuckled, his hand dipping under the silk that barely covered me as his lips lit a trail of fire across my collarbone. "I bet they make you look even more gorgeous."

For two decades, I had closed my heart to love, accepted my lonely fate, and told myself I didn't need anyone to be happy. But what a tragedy it would have been had I not opened my heart again.

I hadn't been looking for love when I met Junaid. But later that night, as I lay in his arms, I knew that he was exactly who I needed.

"You're my second chance at happiness," I told him. "But this is it. I don't want any more chances after this."

"As if I would ever let you feel the need for another chance," he whispered, tenderly kissing my forehead. Then, of course, his alter ego took over. "Besides, you'll never find someone as handsome, honest, and humorous as me, even if you go looking for him."

The man wasn't wrong; he truly was a gem. And I loved every bit of him, even the self-assured, cocky part. Truth be told, that part of him was probably my favorite.

CHAPTER 71

Hope

ZAIN

A month had passed since I had been jailed without bail. True to his word, my father's lawyer had released the documents for international properties bought under my name as part of his money laundering scheme. The fact that I had no knowledge of them didn't sway the prosecutor who had been tasked with cleaning up the government's image after Zaviyar Uzair stepped down as the leader of AWP, the ruling party.

Yusra had taken up my case, much to my surprise. But even she had cautioned that the evidence against me was significant.

You deserve to be in jail, my conscience whispered, and I couldn't argue against it.

"Take this." A man in uniform shoved a tray of food through the small slit in the door of my jail cell. Though "food" was a term that could only be loosely applied to the yellow mush that lay on the steel plate in front of me. After days of eating the same tasteless "food," I had come up with a plan.

I'd shut my eyes and travel to places far away.

When all else fails, escapism is your friend, Dr. Tan had once said.

For a few minutes, I pretended that it wasn't the stale air of my prison cell that filled my lungs, but the fresh air at a resort in Skardu in the northern mountains of Pakistan. I could literally smell the rose-scented breeze on my face.

Wow, I told myself proudly, *at least I am good at something, even if it's mind games to escape my reality*. Deep breath in, deep breath out. I repeated the cycle, but that flowery scent never ceased.

Eventually, I opened my eyes—all good things in my life came to an end.

Unexpectedly, the rose scent continued to permeate the air around me when I came back to reality, but instead of the peeling walls and dim light from a single bulb that inundated the windowless room, there was a pair of gray eyes staring back at me. I nearly jumped out of my skin and stumbled backwards.

It was the crazy woman from Boston, her face just a few centimeters away from mine.

"What the hell, Ameerah? How did you get in here?"

"I am not Ameerah. I am her ghost." Gray eyes filled with mirth as the woman, or ghost, in front of me whispered hoarsely.

Hallucinations were a plausible explanation when I was just breathing in the air from Skardu, so I reached out and flicked her arm, *gently*. It was enough to set her off, squealing and cursing.

"Useless, idiot, stupid, dumbo," she scowled, rubbing her arm. Then she pinched me back, ten times harder, and boy, did that hurt.

She was definitelynotaghos St.

"Ouch! What is your problem, woman? I barely touched you."

She glared. "My problem? You went MIA, and *I'm* the problem?"

I stared back at her, quietly, taking a breath to calm myself. "In case you need glasses, I am not exactly in a position to return your stupid text messages."

"It was 20/20 last week."

"What?" I looked at her with confused indignation.

"My eyesight. I got it tested last week. I don't need glasses."

"Good." I gestured towards the door. "You can see your way out of here too."

"And why would I do that when I haven't even asked you what I came to ask?" She took out a paper napkin from her purse and dusted off a spot on the floor before sitting on it.

I moved back on the dingy mattress on the floor, crossed my legs, and closed my eyes. "I am busy, and I don't want you here."

She laughed. It was more like a scoff.

"Busy doing what exactly? In case you haven't noticed, you're in jail. You are in no position to say no to me, or to anyone else."

As much as I tried to deny it, I knew that no matter how far away I travelled in my imaginary world, the gray-eyed woman who knew no boundaries would just keep following me. I might not have been tortured like others in here by the police, but whoever let her into my cell was surely planning on torturing me psychologically.

With shoulders slumped, I yielded to her. "Fine. What did you want to ask?"

"Do you always meditate while you eat? Seems kind of cool. I should try it someday."

I slapped my forehead. "It is not *cool*. It is a coping mechanism, so I don't have to think about the disgusting food I have to swallow simply to stay alive."

"Ah, coping mechanism. Yes, that is a very good strategy."

"You asked your question—now leave."

"Oh, that was the primer. I have a whole other list." She pulled out two journals and a pack of pens.

"Ameerah, I don't know if you have a savior complex or whatever, but quit it. You shouldn't even be here in Pakistan, let alone in a bug-infested jail cell, talking to a fucking criminal," I growled.

"Watch your language, mister. I read about you in the news and know how you ended up in here. I even talked to your lawyer. And contrary to what you think, I am not stupid or naïve," she shot back, before something changed in her demeanor. The bright flame went out, leaving only burning embers. But even burning embers are enough to scald your skin and your soul.

"I know, Zain," her tone softened. "Most of it, anyway, and the rest I am pretty sure I can piece together. You should be proud of yourself."

Proud? I had no clue what was wrong with this woman.

"I drugged my classmate, then I forced her to marry me, before I did more unspeakable things to her. I am the son of a man on trial for selling drugs and humans—while I lived in comfort, enjoying the fruits of his evil. What part of that should I be proud of?"

"The part where you accepted your mistake and chose a path different from your father."

I stayed quiet; she didn't.

"There are people out there who care—" Ameerah was saying when I interrupted angrily, ignoring the moisture gathering in my eyes, threatening to show my innermost resentment.

"No one cares about me, Ameerah. Not even my own mother."

"She does—"

"No, she doesn't. I hate what my father did to her, I really do. But the whole time I was sitting there, listening to how she never reported him in order to save my cousins and to keep them away from the monster my father was, I kept thinking . . . why didn't she think of me? I lived with that monster too. Was I not worthy of saving? Why couldn't she have taken me and run, instead of accepting her fate and giving up on me? She could have fought for me too, you know, but she never did."

For once, Ameerah was quiet. In fact, she wasn't even looking at me. She was staring at the ground, making circles in the dust. I had never been good at reading people, a skill you fail to learn when everyone around you is two-faced and self-centered. But when she looked up at me, her gray eyes filled with melancholy, I couldn't look away from her. Like thick, dark fog, she was all I saw—whether I wanted to or not.

"Zain . . ." her quiet voice trailed off.

"My life is over, okay? I don't deserve your empathy or your sympathy. I don't even want it. Go away, please."

She simply shrugged. "What if your past was just the prologue of your life's real story? You can choose to close the book after that first chapter, or you could read on, and hope that it has a happy ending."

I wanted to believe her, but my book only had one ending: me being alone and miserable. A destiny, I was convinced, that had been written in my stars even before I was born. My grandfather's hatred of the unborn me had been the first plot point in that story.

Exasperated, I asked her for a final time, "What do you want from me?"

"The honest truth in answer to some questions." She paused to look at me in the eyes, like she was trying to decipher my soul.

"The first one is, why did you pull me behind you when your guard shot Osman?"

I didn't think she would have remembered that. I barely did. "You were innocent, and it was a reflex action. Didn't mean anything."

Nodding slowly, her gaze still trained on me, she replied, "It means something to me."

Her second question came quickly. "I know things are bad, but are they bad enough that you want to harm yourself or end it all?"

It took me a moment to realize what she was asking: had I thought about taking my own life?

Had it crossed my mind? Honestly, yes.

Had I entertained that idea any further? Honestly, no.

Part of me didn't want to answer her question at all. But the concern in her eyes was so deep, I couldn't bear to watch her agonize over someone like me.

I answered her question honestly. "I have no intent to harm myself."

"Good." She nodded, a look of relief flashing across her face. "Things may get worse, Zain. But please don't give up, and if you ever feel like you are about to, put down your thoughts here." She held up the journals and the pack of pens that lay next to her. "Whether you are angry or hopeless or lonely, let your feelings out."

"You want me to write down my feelings in these journals?"

"Yes, why? What is wrong with them?"

"For starters, they are *pink*." I balked, looking at the notebooks in her hand.

She frowned and made a face at me. "Oh, be quiet and take them, and stop being such a baby. Trust me, you'll be surprised at how helpful journaling can be."

Trust. What was that? Everyone I knew had either betrayed me or been betrayed by me. It was no surprise I didn't know how to trust, just as I didn't know how to love.

She got up from the floor and dusted herself off. "Oki doki. My work here is done for now. I'll be in touch. You make sure you stay alive."

And just like that she was gone, a dream evaporated in front of my eyes, taking with her the rose-scented breath of fresh air that had filled my lungs, leaving behind only the two pink journals and the cold, suffocating reality of my jail cell.

KIRAN

"How was he?" I asked Ameerah when she came and sat in my car, parked outside Karachi's central jail.

"He is coping," she replied solemnly. "Stuff he learnt in therapy."

I started driving, still with a heavy heart because of the realization that had hit me as I had waited for her. I had let my hatred of Phuppa and Phuppo affect my relationship with my baby cousin, who was only a couple of months younger than Osman.

Even if I forgot the part where I was his cousin, I had failed him as a teacher. I should have seen him for who he was: a child trying to find his way in this world. I didn't, and that was on me.

But as much as I regretted the past, there was nothing I could do about it.

"Don't worry, Ameerah. I'll check up on him as often as I can, and I'll make sure Phuppo comes by too."

"Thank you." Her voice cracked. "I know people think I'm stupid, but I understand what happens when someone loses hope—when they're shunned despite earnestly trying to atone for their mistakes. I've seen them wither away and die under the burden of their guilt in a society as unforgiving as ours. But you know what? Even God forgives His people. So why can't we?"

This girl and her heart had always amazed me. I'd had a front-row seat to the time in her life when she'd fallen for my brother, but then stepped back quietly when he didn't reciprocate. Yet, she never left his side when he needed her the most. It was like she had this primal need to save people from themselves, no matter how much it destroyed her.

She had done it for Osman, and now it seemed she was determined to do it for Zain. Perhaps it all had something to do with the person she had once known, who had lost all hope.

"I don't think you're stupid at all," I told her. "I think you're incredibly noble. But if you ever need to, you can talk to me about whatever and who-ever you want."

She kept looking out the window. "I know. I will. When I am ready."

CHAPTER 72

Love Story

SANAM

It had been a few weeks since we had returned to the US after our wedding. Osman had started his ER rotation, and I had applied to transfer my PhD credits to the university affiliated with the Children's Hospital of Boston.

Married life was good, but it was missing something.

Tonight, I returned early from the hospital, determined to change that.

Whether it was simply time, the therapy sessions I had attended, or my inner self feeling comfortable around a man who loved me so patiently—I knew I was ready for the kind of romance that consumed your imagination as much as it did your body.

Not that we hadn't been intimate. We had kissed plenty, from a peck on the cheek to more passionate kisses that took my breath away. But the desperation of his touch was always overshadowed by the humanity in his eyes. When I held back, he had understood without so much as a word from me.

But I didn't want to hold back anymore.

That evening, candlelight bathed my skin in a warm glow. A red dress clung to every curve, soft waves of brown hair cascaded past my bare shoulders, and my crimson lips completed the picture. Suffice, it to say, I looked like a woman waiting for her lover, whose every breath begged time to pass faster so she could be where her home truly was—in his arms.

A glance at the clock made me even more restless. There was still half an hour left till the end of his ER shift, and then another fifteen minutes' or so drive back home. I struggled to contain myself and keep my excitement at bay. To make matters worse, I could hear distant thunder and see the gray, rain-laden clouds obliterate the velvety night sky. It was going to pour soon, my phone's weather app predicted.

"This better not be a sign of the night to come," I said out loud, as if destiny would change at the mere whim of my words. But the universe was ready with an instant reply.

My phone pinged. It was Osman.

Husband: I'll be a little late. Have to pick something up on the way back.

You have got to be kidding me, my mind screamed as I frantically typed out a message.

Me: Please come home. You can pick it up tomorrow.

Husband: The shop won't be open tomorrow. I won't be long. I promise. See you soon.

Me: What shop? What are you picking up?

I didn't hear from him until he drove our new car up the driveway.

OSMAN

"Here is the chicken paneer and hot naans," the man said, handing me a heavy paper bag with a clay pot and warm bread, emitting the kind of heavenly aromas that was sure to put the smile I loved so much on my wife's face.

Life had been one hectic day after another since we'd gotten married.

But today, I had vowed, would be different.

Chicken paneer was Sanam's favorite dish. She loved to eat it straight out of the clay pot and get her hands dirty, something her mother would have forbidden her to do. Then there was the chocolate fudge cake, her favorite dessert, that had been banned in her home while growing up because dessert might as well have been declared haram as far as Shabnam Murad was concerned.

The sugar goes straight to your thighs, Sanam had been told.

But she was no longer just Shabnam's daughter—she was my wife, and in our home, she had every right to do whatever made her happy. The relentless downpour threatened to ruin my plans, but I braved the storm, managed to get everything, and finally pulled into our driveway, drenched but triumphant.

Unfortunately, I had counted my chickens too soon.

Turns out, when you have your backpack slung over a shoulder, a box of two-pound cake in one hand, and a hot clay pot in the other as you rush to get out of the rain, Mother Nature has no qualms about making a fool out of you.

A fact that I realized as soon as I stepped into a puddle and the worn-out soles of my work shoes lost their traction. I nearly stumbled, but managed to recover. The clay pot was not so lucky and went crashing to the ground.

"Ugh!" I exclaimed in frustration, debating whether I should try to salvage the naan or save the cake still in my other hand.

"Osman, are you okay?" Her panicked voice distracted me.

I looked up, and dropped the cake too.

All I saw was my wife in a little red dress.

SANAM

His lips parted, but words remained lacking. Instead, his heated gaze raked over me, saying everything I wanted to hear. He liked what he saw. Not that I was paying much attention to what he saw, because I loved what I saw too.

I had always thought he looked exceptionally cute in scrubs, but I wasn't prepared for what I saw now. His soaked clothes hugged his body, accentuating his well-built frame and tall stature. His hair was a tousled mess, with droplets clinging to his eyelashes.

Oh, please take me already, I desperately wanted to say out loud.

He grabbed my hand and started walking towards the house. "You're wet," he declared.

It's not just the rain. Even his rough hand clasping my smaller one sent waves of electricity through me.

Once inside, he let go of my hand but didn't move from my side. Which was good, because I might have jumped on him if he had.

"I am cold," I told him.

Swallowing hard, his gaze fixed on me, he asked, "Should I get some towels?"

My voice took on a sultry smoothness I didn't think I had in me. But then again, Osman had always brought out a part of me that was for him and him alone.

"Come on, Doctor." I batted my eyelashes, reveling in the way his gaze kept wandering to my exposed shoulders and the way his hands rested on my waist when I pulled him closer. "Surely you must know of other ways a husband can warm up his wife."

I could see it in his eyes. A fire burning that matched my own, clashing with the cautious part of him. His primal urges wrestled in a full-blown debate with a gentleman, and I knew exactly who I wanted to win that night.

"It's okay. I'm ready," I whispered, my cold hands already exploring his taut abdomen under his wet shirt.

"Sanam."

He breathed out my name through those full lips—lips I covered with my own—as his arms tightened around me and he kissed me back. Fiercely. Feverishly. With a passion that made me tremble in his arms.

With our lips locked, we stumbled to our room, where he paused, taking in the warm light of the candles and the shadows playing on the walls. He had once told me this had been the room where he'd dreamt of a life with me, unsure if it would ever come to fruition. Today, it would become the sanctuary where we broke down the final wall that had kept us apart.

"You planned all this?" he asked with a slight smile.

"I wanted our first time to be special," I admitted.

He sat on the bed, pulling me onto his lap until I straddled him, and he looked up at me.

"Sanam, listen to me . . ." he began, his palm resting against my face while his thumb gently stroked my cheek. The earnestness in his voice forced me to tame my desires for a moment.

"There is so much I want to do to you and experience with you, but my lust for you will never be more than my love and respect for you. So promise me that you'll tell me if you ever feel uncomfortable."

I thought it wasn't possible for me to love him more. But this side of him, the gentleman who could control his primal urges, was a side that set him poles apart from every man I had ever known. How could I not fall in love with him deeper than ever before?

"I promise," I whispered against his lips. "But if you keep saying my name like that, I am going to have to rip your clothes off."

An impish grin slowly spread across his face before he breathed out my name again.

"Sanam."

I yanked his shirt off.

In the moments that followed, time had no meaning, and neither did our past. All that mattered was us and now, opening ourselves, entrusting each other with the parts of us that we trusted no one else with.

Our union, and this moment, was a reward for our pursuit of perfection in an imperfect world that thought nothing of ripping apart those who loved for their own greed and lust. But this was a journey that would change us forever.

For is it even true love if it doesn't fundamentally alter the very core of your being?

The unwanted girl who had been nothing but an extra in everyone's life became a woman who would be the center of her husband's attention for the rest of her days.

The shy boy who had sat in the corner became a man with the strength to hold his wife and protect their love at the worst moments of their lives.

"I never want this to end," I told him as we lay, exhausted but exhilarated, in each other's arms.

He kissed my forehead and quietly replied, "Don't worry—ours is a love story that has no ending."

ABOUT ONE YEAR LATER

Epilogue One

KIRAN

"Have a proper breakfast before your exam." Junaid placed his lips on my temple and a plate of fried eggs and toast in front of me. I squeezed his arm, grateful for having him in my life.

A fl u rry of activity at the dining table pulled my attention from the notes I was poring over at the last minute. Our three sons were visiting from college, bringing their young adult drama with them. But today, they were all focused on me.

Danish fis t bumped me. "Don't worry, Mama, I know you will kick some a-s-s," he laughed, and so did his father.

"Watch your language," I warned him, and glared at his father.

Daniyal pushed his twin out of the way and hugged me. "Good luck, Mama."

"Thanks, but don't fight with your brother." I hugged him back.

Nael placed a pencil case in front of me. "Here you go, Mama. I put in a bunch of pens, pencils, sharpeners, and erasers. Everything you could possibly need for your entry test."

"Aww, thank you, Nael." I patted his cheek and he beamed.

Why was everyone doting on me today, you might ask.

Well, it was the day I would be taking the entrance test for law school. I might be the eldest student in my class, if I got in, but who could be a better lawyer than the woman who had successfully fought for justice against a system that preyed on the voiceless?

I was about to get up from the breakfast table when Junaid's phone pinged with a message. He silently nodded while reading it.

Sliding the phone towards me, he said, "I have a task for the boy when he gets out."

A message from Yusra was displayed on the phone's screen. I should have asked Junaid what kind of task he would offer the 'boy,' but first, I had to message my brother. He and his wife deserved to know about Yusra's success.

SANAM

The coffee machine whirred to life. Freshly ground coffee beans went into the filter, and soon a slim line of black coffee was pouring into a mug. As the rich, earthy aroma filled the air, I steamed the milk and poured it into the mug as well, creating a swirl of velvety goodness.

"That smells of perfection," a tantalizingly hoarse voice said in my ear before warm lips caressed my bare shoulder.

I turned, wrapped my arms around my husband, and gazed up at him. "You and me together—that's perfection. Lattes are just coffee and milk."

"Can't argue with that," he beamed.

He made us scrambled eggs for breakfast that morning, while I prepared another latte. In the comfort of our apartment, bathed in the soft glow of the morning sunlight, the two of us sat together and discussed our plans for the day.

Breakfast had become our sacred time together. It was the one part of the day when we could pause, reconnect, and savor each other's company before work and studies pulled us in opposite directions.

That day, I took the opportunity to ask him for something I had found myself yearning for, despite our busy lives, every time I passed by the park on the corner of our street.

"Osman, I want to be a mother."

A cautious smile spread across his face. "Are you sure?"

"One hundred percent. Why wouldn't I want to bring a child into this world when I love its father so much?"

Leaning across the table, he gently caressed my cheek. "I can't think of a single reason."

OSMAN

Me, a father?

I didn't remember the love of my father. Never even felt that of my mother. Yet, I'd known the day I married Sanam that the only thing that could surpass being her husband was being the father to her children.

"What's with the goofy smile?" Aimy asked after rounds that day.

"Nothing," I quickly replied.

"Come on. Tell me. I can keep a secret."

I nearly choked on my second cup of coffee. Telling Aimy was nothing short of announcing to the whole world. If aliens existed, she'd probably tell them too.

She glared at me. "You're a horrible friend."

"You're a horrible secret-keeper," I pointed out.

Her face contorted, and she stuck her tongue out. "At least your cousin stays silent and doesn't call me names."

I nearly choked on my coffee once again. "Which cousin? The one who is in prison for money laundering, drug use, and God only knows what else?"

"He has not been convicted of any of those crimes," she argued.

"Doesn't matter, Aimy. You know he is guilty of many things. Please don't tell me that you've been contacting him. He is not the project you need to make up for whatever happened in your past."

There was so much more to say, but she had that stubborn look on her face that I knew all too well. Nothing I said or did would have convinced her not to go down the path I feared she was already on.

"Zain is not a project, Osman. He is a human. And humans can make mistakes and still deserve a shot at redemption."

She stomped away, leaving me alone in the empty corridor. I took out my phone and read the message that Kiran Api had sent the night before. Sanam and I had nothing to do with Zain, and I was determined not to let him near my wife ever again.

But how was I to protect my friend from him?

During my lunch break, I called my sister.

"I can't believe Zain's going to be a free man. He's Asif's only son. How was he not involved in his illegal businesses?"

"All the evidence points towards his innocence," she replied. "We can't hold what his father did against him. That's not who we are, kiddo."

I could have argued with Kiran Api; she seemed a little too forgiving of a man who had done everything he could to destroy me. But I already knew what she'd say—our parents didn't teach us to seek revenge from those already repenting. And I had to admit, Zain did seem to genuinely regret his past.

"Any updates on GT Enterprise?" I changed the subject.

"Only that the FIU is liquidating most of the company's assets and will likely dissolve it altogether to pay off the fines and taxes Asif owed to the government. Whatever is left will be yours."

As the legitimate heir of Tariq Enterprise, I wasn't holding my breath for any large sum of money anyway. Still, there was one asset I had my eye on, for a very specific reason.

"What about the Tariq mansion?"

"Yusra thinks you'll be able to keep it. Though if I were you, I'd get rid of it. That house has brought us nothing but pain."

"No. I'll keep the house."

"Why?" she asked, surprised.

"I'll let you know when the time comes," I told her.

My sisters had been adamant about leaving the past behind. Our family had gotten the justice we sought. But what if the past could be used to build a future so vastly different, it brought comfort to the oppressed instead of wealth to the oppressor?

After all, the quest to bring hope was just as worthy as the quest for justice.

Epilogue Two

ZAIN

A year after his arrest, Zakariya Uzair was still on trial in the United States. But from what Yusra knew, he faced a potential life sentence under federal charges, including human trafficking, aggravated sexual abuse, and money laundering.

In Pakistan, however, the prosecution had moved unusually fast. Asif Ghazanfar's was a high-profile case, and the government—sans Zaviyar Uzair—was determined to make an example of him, partly to save face. Just a few months after his arrest, he had already been sentenced to rigorous life imprisonment, with all his jail perks taken away.

Most of the country had cheered. I tried too as well. But when it's your father—the man who used and broke you—no life sentence feels like enough justice. The anger doesn't go away. It festers. All I could do was will myself to not feel anything at all, lest that anger consumes me once again.

Besides, for people like me, who weren't in the spotlight, the judicial system still moved at a glacial pace. That reality was so widely accepted that no one questioned it when they learnt I had been in jail for a full year without being sentenced. For Yusra, though, it was a year spent in relentless pursuit of the truth.

Two weeks ago, she announced she would be filing a motion to dismiss the government's cases against me, considering the new evidence she had uncovered.

Turns out, the trip my father and I took across Europe before I started my A-Levels wasn't for father-son bonding. It was to convince sellers that they were transferring their property to a father on behalf of his minor son. Later, she persuaded Abu's associate, Azhar Saqlain, to record a statement admitting that he was present when my father gave me alcohol and forced me to sign the property papers soon after my eighteenth birthday—in exchange for becoming his defense lawyer for free.

Yet when she walked into my cell with Inspector Junaid and told me to gather my things, I tried to argue. "Why won't you let me stay in jail? It's not like I haven't done some really bad things."

Her gaze softened. "You have a lot to make up for, no doubt about that, but it won't be from inside this jail. Perhaps Junaid can help you lighten your conscience."

The inspector spoke from the corner of the room. "Interested in helping us expose the crimes of your friend Farhan and his politician father by going undercover?"

Undercover? Good guys went undercover, not a lowlife like me.

But then words scribbled in a letter hidden under my mattress echoed within me. *Sometimes, good and bad are not defined by one's actions, but by the choices one makes.*

Another sentence, from another letter I had memorized every word of, came to mind. *You can't undo your past, but you can change your future.*

"Zain? It may get dangerous—"

"I'll do it," I blurted out.

Redemption might never be possible for me, but someone kept writing that I needed to take a shot at it anyway. Besides, I knew enough about Farhan and his father to know that they deserved to rot in jail.

"Gather your things then," Yusra said with a smile.

A few minutes later, after being told to expect a call from Detective Fiza, I followed Yusra out, carrying a brown paper bag containing two dusty pink journals and a stack of letters—the only possessions I cared about in this world.

After months of being in a cold, dark cell, the mid-afternoon sunshine felt both like daggers piercing my pale skin and the warm embrace of a long-lost lover.

"Your ride's here," Yusra said.

I stopped dead in my tracks when I noticed a gray-eyed woman standing next to a car.

"What is she doing here?" I asked, trying not to panic.

"Ameerah is your ride home. I have other clients, too, you know," she replied, and waved goodbye before I could react.

"Get in the car, dummy," a shrill voice reached me.

I should have stood where I was. After all, I had vowed to stay away from her, hadn't I? Instead, I found myself walking closer, taking in a deep breath, filling my lungs with the smell of fragrant roses from the mountain tops of Skardu.

"I could have taken a taxi," I huffed, but got in the car when she scowled and held the door open.

"You have no money," she pointed out when she got in herself.

"I would have walked."

"You don't know where to go."

"Stop talking," I told her, afraid she would question why I was clutching my bag so tightly.

"Stop listening," she snapped back and started the car.

Though how could I stop listening when I had wondered for so many months how her voice might sound if she read aloud the words she wrote.

It was stupid, and she didn't need to know that, so I simply looked out the window.

Nothing much had changed over the last year, I noted. Just as before, I was still a villain—cleared of crimes I didn't commit but still bearing the burden of those I did, even if I couldn't be prosecuted for them on a technicality.

I was jolted out of my misery with a sharp pain in my forearm. "Ouch!" I swung around to face the woman next to me. "Why'd you pinch me?"

"Why didn't you ever write back? I sent you so many letters," she glared.

"I don't know what you're talking about." I averted my gaze, hoping it would be enough to stop her from figuring out my truth. Thankfully, she stayed quiet for a while after that, the noise of the city road filling the awkward void between us.

"Oh no," she suddenly exclaimed while looking at her phone, and pulled off the road.

"What happened?" I leaned towards the phone, but she shut the screen.

"I have this professor who is always after me. He reported to my division chief that I took vacation without permission, which is not true at all. I actually moved my scheduled vacation up by a few weeks." She seemed to be on the brink of tears. "Professor Mike hates me, Zain. What if he gets me kicked out of residency?"

How dare he make her cry, my jaw clenched.

Anger boiled within me, like it had plenty of times before because of that man. I could no longer hold back. "Hey, how come you're only capable of arguing with me? Why don't you ever stand up to that man, when you've been complaining about him for a full year—"

"*Ha*," she said loudly, startling me. Suddenly, the tears were gone. "You read my letters. All of them. Didn't you? That's why you know about Professor Mike." She waved her finger in my face. "Admit it, liar."

Of course I had read her letters. All fifty-two of them. How could I not have, when her words were the sunshine my soul craved during the anguish of my days, and I silently spoke to her in the darkness of my nights?

I had spent the last year in increments of seven days, reading and rereading her handwritten letters until a new one arrived, precisely every Monday. Still, I clutched my bag. She could never know my truth.

"Fine." I rolled my eyes. "Maybe I read a few of them when I was bored."

"Then why didn't you ever write back to me? I know that you were allowed to exchange letters. Inspector Junaid told me himself."

"I didn't write because I didn't want to," I muttered and looked out the window. "Just drive, Rah."

She was about to put the car in 'Drive' when she swung her head in my direction. *Crap*, I slapped myself.

"What did you just call me?" she asked. When I ignored her, she grabbed my chin and yanked my face towards her, like a freaking mafia don, forcing me to look into her inquisitive pools of gray that reflected my inner turmoil.

"You called me Rah," she answered her own question.

Rah. Another word for a path. Like she had been for me—leading me out of the darkness and self-loathing that would have consumed me until I was nothing but dust, with my soul free to meet its Maker. Yet here I was, alive and sitting in front of her —because of her.

The truth remained buried in the paper bag.

"Your handwriting is horrible. Have you ever tried to read your name? All I could make out was R-A-H. I can't help it if that's all I remember."

"It's a sweet nickname," she shrugged.

"It's stupid and corny," I insisted.

She hmphed. I clutched my bag more tightly.

Eventually, we reached a two-story house with a small front yard, in a part of town I had never really visited before.

"Why are we here?" I asked.

"This is home."

"Home?" I looked at her with confusion.

"Yes, where your mother lives. She moved out of your old house and bought this one with her own money," she replied with a smile. "Go on in. There is a whole welcome party for you."

Party? For me?

"I don't want a party."

"Okay then. What would you rather do?"

Sit out here.

"Nothing, I'll go inside," I said instead, and started to get out. When she didn't move, I stopped to ask, "Aren't you coming?"

"I'd love to, but I can't. I am flying back tonight and need to do some last-minute shopping."

"Suit yourself," I mumbled and got out quickly before my legs listened to the rest of me that didn't want to move from that seat at all. I was about to shut the door when she called out.

"I have one more year of residency left, and three more years of fellowship. That's four whole years before I'll be back in the country for good. Think you can rewrite your life's story by yourself? Or do you need me to continue the long-distance babysitting?"

"I am *not* a baby." I frowned. "Please go live your own life and stop bothering me."

Shutting the door quickly, I tried to walk away, but she was just as quick to roll down the window. "I mean it, Zain. You better not turn back into an imbecile. I'll be keeping an eye on you."

After staring at me silently for a few seconds, she muttered goodbye and drove away—out of my life, my present, and, I was convinced, my future.

The 'party' was more like a welcome brunch with my mother and cousins.

Ami had visited me a handful of times in jail. Sometimes she stayed; other times, she would bring some items, like more pens, and quickly leave. She wasn't curt, but she wasn't warm either. I suppose it's difficult to show emotions to a son who had followed in the footsteps of her tormentor.

It was only now that I realized she, like me, needed to heal from our shared past trauma. And time was the best healer. She had made a place for me in a house she called home. To me, that spoke volumes more than her absence in the past year.

"I am so happy to see you," she told me, hugging me tightly.

"Same here, Ami." I hugged her back.

After stuffing myself with scrumptious brunch and being doted on by the women of my family, Nosheen led us all up the stairs.

"Come on, let's show you your room," Kiran Api said with a smile.

"We tried to tell Phuppo that you're a grown adult, but she insisted on hanging some of your artwork from school," Kauser Baji laughed.

Ami kept my artwork from all those years ago? That was hard to believe. I thought she never paid attention to anything I did in school.

"He'll always be a kid for me," Ami defended herself with a chuckle.

"I chose the rest of the décor and bedsheets," Kaukab Baji smiled too.

With my paper bag in hand, I followed the women quietly, pausing when I entered my new room. It was only a fraction of the size of the room I'd grown up in, but it still looked like something straight out of a magazine— sleek shades of gray seamlessly blended with bold pops of color.

And here I was trying to forget a different set of grays—and a vibrant personality I had no choice but to surrender to.

"I don't even know what to say," I told them.

Ami came forward and hugged me again. "Beta, you don't have to say anything. It was our pleasure. But you must be tired now. Why don't you rest, and we'll see you in the evening."

While the others walked out, Nosheen came to sit on my bed beside me, and gazed at me like a big sister gazes at her little brother—with patience and understanding.

"How are you really doing?" she asked after a moment of silence.

"Could be better," I told her honestly.

She put her arm around my shoulders. "You could. But think about how far you've come. You're not the same man I posted bail for in America. You have a chance to restart your life now."

Restart, rewrite. There was a theme to the advice I kept getting. Perhaps it was time I heeded it too.

"How are you?" I asked Nosheen. "I wish I'd been here when you came home."

She shrugged, but her smile didn't diminish. "Could be better, but having a family is truly a blessing. As is a good therapist."

"Thank you for always being there for me," I told her, grateful from the bottom of my heart.

"Why wouldn't I be? You were the baby cousin who used to play in my lap." A faraway look flitted across her face. "I remembered you when you came to Houston, even if you didn't know who I was."

I was three years old when she was abducted. Too young to remember much at all. But in retrospect, it all made sense. The way she was always so protective of me. Hovering around when everyone else had all but abandoned me.

I had thought she was the sister I didn't know I needed. Turns out, she really was my sister—an older cousin kind of sister.

"It saddens me how much time we've lost. Our entire childhood gone because of the greed and lust of men," she said, and I thought about all the birthdays and weddings, dinners and brunches, that we could have spent together, but alas, the seeds of hatred between our families were sowed by design.

She patted my hand. "There is a lot we have to catch up on, but rest a bit first."

When Nosheen left too, I dared to take out my most prized possessions from the paper bag—a crazy woman's letters to me, and the letters I had written back to her.

I sat down on the polished wooden desk in my new room and read all of hers again: sighing at her words, laughing at her jokes, and clutching those papers tightly when it all became too much.

Then I opened the pink dusty journals. One of them was full of unsent letters. The other still had one page left. I found a pen and started to write.

One last letter to her.

Dear Rah,

I know now what selfless love is: letting go when you are unworthy of someone.

So goodbye.

I hope you find someone who knows how to love you the way you deserve to be loved.

Yours, Zain.

Acknowledgement

This book would not have been possible without the readers who read and appreciated it when it was just a messy first draft on Wattpad. I've said it before, and I'll say it again: readers make authors. And you all have been the best.

A huge shout-out to the professionals who helped me make this story the best it could be.

Sam Willow, I truly appreciate your encouragement and weekly emails. For a nervous first-time author, they were exactly the reassurance I needed.

Sejal Srinivasan, thank you for all your advice, the frequent text messages, for catching the plot holes, and for patiently listening to me rant about the book. It was an absolute pleasure working with you.

Ciara Hartford, you're an artistic genius. I'm in awe of how you managed to create such a gorgeous cover, rich with perfect symbolism.

Epica Book PR, I couldn't have done the marketing without you. Thank you for rounding up all my emotions and sleepless nights into a beautiful package of reels, posts, and so much more, and presenting it to the world.

Last, but most importantly, thank you to my family, who taught me the meaning of selfless love—whether as a daughter, a sister, a mother, or a wife. Love comes in all forms, and I've had the privilege of experiencing it in every one of them.

About the Author

Malika is a pediatrician by training. Born in Pakistan, she moved to the United States for her medical residency. The life of an immigrant physician—with a slight accent and a Brown identity—suspended between her birth country and her adopted one, has deeply influenced her writing.

As a published author of research papers and the occasional book chapter, venturing into contemporary fiction has pushed the boundaries of her comfort zone. But some stories insist on being told, and she considers herself lucky to have found people willing to listen.

When she's not treating patients or dreaming up new stories, she's probably chasing after her kids, watching crime dramas, or sipping real South Asian chai (not to be confused with the impostor known as a chai latte).

Find her on Instagram, Threads and Facebook @malikadauthor